Gentle
on my
Mind

D0288693

Also by Susan Fox

Body Heat

Caribou Crossing Romances

Caribou Crossing

Home on the Range

Gentle on My Mind

His, Unexpectedly

Love, Unexpectedly

Yours, Unexpectedly

Writing as Susan Lyons

Sex Drive

She's on Top

Touch Me

Hot in Here

Champagne Rules

Anthologies

The Naughty List

Some Like It Rough

Men on Fire

Unwrap Me

The Firefighter

Gentle
on my
Mind

SUSAN FOX

ZEBRA BOOKS
KENSINGTON PUBLISHING CORP.
http://www.kensingtonbooks.com

ZEBRA BOOKS are published by

Kensington Publishing Corp.
119 West 40th Street
New York, NY 10018

Copyright © 2013 by Susan Lyons

All Kensington titles, imprints, and distributed lines are available at special quantity discounts for bulk purchases for sales promotion, premiums, fund-raising, educational, or in-stitutional use.

Special book excerpts or customized printings can also be created to fit specific needs. For details, write or phone the office of the Kensington Special Sales Manager: Attn. Special Sales Department. Kensington Publishing Corp., 119 West 40th Street, New York, NY 10018. Phone: 1-800-221-2647.

Zebra and the Z logo Reg. U.S. Pat. & TM Off.

ISBN-13: 978-1-4201-3192-5
ISBN-10: 1-4201-3192-3
First Printing: September 2013

eISBN-13: 978-1-4201-3193-2
eISBN-10: 1-4201-3193-1
First Electronic Edition: September 2013

10 9 8 7 6 5 4 3 2 1

Printed in the United States of America

Chapter One

Brooke Kincaid hung up the phone and hugged herself. Beaming, she danced a few steps across the kitchen floor in time to Glen Campbell's "Wichita Lineman," the song playing on Caribou Crossing's country-and-western radio station. Her marmalade cat, Sunny, watched from a windowsill, tail twitching, golden eyes asking a question.

"A grandmother!" Brooke told him. "I'm going to be a grandmother."

Well, in fact she'd become a grandmother last fall when her son, Evan—newly returned to Caribou Crossing—married Jessica and became stepdad to her daughter, Robin, a wonderful ten-year-old. But now Jess was pregnant!

Oh Lord, Jess was pregnant. Brooke stopped dancing as all the fears rushed into her mind. Would Evan let her near the baby, given what a terrible mother she'd been to him? And would the baby be okay? What if Evan did have a predisposition for bipolar disorder even though the disease had never manifested itself in him, and he passed it on to the baby?

Sunny yowled, breaking Brooke's train of thought. He hopped down from the sill and came to wrap himself around her ankles.

The gesture calmed her, and so did bending to stroke his

sun-warmed fur. She'd acquired Sunny four years ago as a rescue cat, but the rescuing really worked the other way around.

"You're right," she told him. "I need to focus on the positive." Evan and Jess had made the decision to have a child, they knew about her own bipolar and alcoholism, and the decision was theirs to make. And yes, of course they would let her be involved. Her son had called her right away, the morning after Jess had shared the news with him and Robin. Brooke beamed again, remembering the joy in his voice.

As for her, at the age of forty-three she'd been granted a second chance, and she'd do things right this time.

She was fourteen when she got pregnant. Naively, she'd expected a pink-and-white girl doll, but what she'd received was a bellowing, demanding boy-child. She had messed up royally with Evan, and she blessed him for being generous enough to forgive her.

After ten years of estrangement, she had her son back, plus a wonderful daughter-in-law, a delightful granddaughter, and now a brand-new baby on the way. No clouds of worry were going to spoil this amazing day.

Johnny Cash's "I Walk the Line" came on the radio and she smiled. "So do I, my friend, so do I." She had stayed sober, gone to A.A. meetings, and taken her bipolar meds for almost five years. Now, she had even more motivation.

She ran her hand down her cat's golden coat and tugged gently on his tail. "It's all good, isn't it, Sunny?"

He pulled his tail from her grip and narrowed his eyes in mock annoyance, then began to purr.

Brooke laughed at his game. Until Evan had come back, she hadn't laughed—not this way, with genuine pleasure—in at least a dozen years. Now laughter came easily. "Life just couldn't be more perfect," she told the cat, reaching out to stroke him again.

But Sunny's ears twitched and he shook her hand off. His

hair rose, his eyes slitted, and he stared intently into space, at nothing visible to her.

Jake Brannon clung desperately to the handgrips of his Harley, fighting to stay conscious. He'd been losing blood for going on an hour now. Thank God for the fierce pain in his side; it helped him focus.

When he'd made his getaway he'd left his helmet behind, and now the wind made his eyes water and whipped strands of hair across his face. He squinted to see the road. It twisted away in front of him like a snake. A rough-skinned snake. Every time he hit a pothole the bike jerked and a fresh wave of pain radiated from the wound.

He hoped to hell the bullet wasn't still in there. If only he could stop to examine the injury and staunch the bleeding. But the man in the black truck was chasing him, and by now there were probably others.

His own fault. He'd been sloppy. Should have been in and out without anyone seeing him. Should be back in his motel room right now, sound asleep. Instead of riding the never-ending snake in the frail light of dawn toward, toward . . .

Damn, he was losing focus again. Where the hell was he? He'd avoided the highway in hopes of evading his pursuers, but the roads out here in the middle of British Columbia's Cariboo country were a maze. Would he ever find his way to the Gold Rush Trail Motel, to the sanctuary of that kitschy little room where sepia photos from gold rush days decorated the walls?

Jake narrowed his eyes against a pale rising sun. The sun was off to his right, which meant he was riding . . . north? He groaned. His brain was so damned fuzzy.

The bike's tires skittered over a spill of gravel and jounced into another hole. Pain slammed through him and he let loose with a string of curses. The wind whipped them away, and he imagined them streaming behind him in a series of little balloons like the speech in cartoons.

Focus, damn it. Best as he could figure, he needed to head northeast. The sun rose in the east, and the sun was hitting the corner of his aching right eye, so northeast had to be straight ahead. As the crow flies. If only the Harley were a crow . . .

Straight ahead. He tried to grasp that thought and hang on to it. But damn, his vision was as blurry as his mind. He blinked but the view got foggier, not sharper. There was something white . . . vertical white shapes marching in a row straight ahead of him. A fence? Oh Jesus, the road curved and he was heading straight for a fence!

He tried to yank the bike around the curve, but his sweaty hands had no strength. His world was turning gray and he was barely aware of the bike going down, spilling him free. Screaming pain roused him momentarily as his leg and hip scraped along the road. His head hit next and the gray turned charcoal. He heard his bike crash into something, and then the engine abruptly cut out.

His eyes closed and the blackness took him.

"Sunny, what's wrong?" Brooke asked, just as the peaceful country morning was shattered by a horrible screech of metal, then a crash. Not metal on metal but metal on . . . wood?

Wood? "My white picket fence!" She dashed to the front door, flung it open, and darted down the steps in her bathrobe and flip-flops.

A huge black motorbike was jammed partway through her fence amid a confetti of shattered white wood. Where was the rider?

Brooke rushed through the gate and found him sprawled on the gravel verge of the road, facedown, like a broken, abandoned toy. He was dressed in black—sneakers, jeans, and leather jacket. No helmet over that tumble of shoulder-length black hair.

Mo. He looked just like Mo. She flashed back to the age of fourteen, when she'd been utterly fascinated by the sexy nineteen-year-old bad boy. Back then, she'd had no idea how bad he'd turn out to be.

"Get a grip," she told herself. This man was *not* Mo, and he might be dying. She had to call 911. But what if he died while she was phoning?

Staring at the biker, she forced herself to take a deep breath. Although she'd taken a first-aid class, she couldn't remember a blessed thing. Another breath. She had to control the crippling panic.

Pulse. Yes, make sure he was breathing. If not, she'd have to start mouth-to-mouth and CPR.

Kneeling, she stroked his hair out of the way and slipped two trembling fingers around his neck to press against his throat. His pulse leaped strongly, so strongly that she jerked back in shock. Then she let out her breath in a low whistle of relief.

The man groaned and his body moved convulsively, turning so he lay on his back.

No, despite having bronzed skin, he didn't look like Mo, who'd been half Indo-American. He didn't look like a thuggish biker either. In fact, he was strikingly handsome, with strong, carved features. His mouth, framed by a dark beard, added contrast with full, sensual lips. If she'd had to administer the kiss of life . . .

Her cheeks burned. The thought of touching a man's lips with her own was shocking. It had been more than fifteen years since she'd shared any degree of physical intimacy with a man. Her ex-husband had soured her on men so thoroughly that she was positive she'd never be attracted to another one.

And yet there was something enticing about this particular face, this mouth.

She shook her head briskly, trying to recall the checklist the first-aid trainer had taught them. Immediate danger. Make sure he wasn't in immediate danger.

There was blood—he'd scraped himself up pretty badly— but no arterial spurts. He wasn't bleeding to death. He wasn't likely to be run over either, as he was well onto the gravel shoulder of the road. This end of Wellburn Road was quiet, down past the entrance to Bly Ranch. Her little patch of rented land was on Jessica's parents' ranch, and past her there was only Ray Barnes's place and a couple of other small spreads. Horses and riders often used this road, and people knew to drive cautiously.

So the motorcycle man was in no immediate danger. Now she needed to assess his injuries so she could tell the ambulance crew what to expect.

She studied his sprawled body. No broken limbs, as far as she could see. Head injuries? She rested her fingers gently on his skull and his eyes flickered open.

They were unfocused, dazed. An intriguing shade of gray with hints of blue and mauve. Wood smoke, she thought, on an October day. Gentle, dreamy eyes, belying the beard and black leather.

"Hello," she said. "Can you hear me?"

The muscles around his eyes twitched as his gaze sharpened. She read confusion, pain—then something that looked like fear. And then anger. Wood smoke turned to storm clouds.

When Jake's eyes first opened he figured he'd died and gone to heaven. Lord knows why a sinner like him would end up there, but a fair-haired angel was peering down at him. His vision was still blurry but he could see that her eyes sparkled blue-green like a tropical ocean. Rose-petal pink lips opened and she said something, but he was so entranced by her face that he didn't catch the words.

He wanted to reach out and touch a strand of that curly golden hair and see if it felt as silky as it looked. Or maybe she was a vision with no substance and his hand would slide right through her. The thought that he might never touch his angel almost made him cry.

No, damn it, that was pain that brought a rush of moisture to his eyes. Pain, shrieking through his body. He couldn't isolate it, couldn't assess his injuries; he was on fire in so many places. He wasn't dead—or if he was, this was hell, not heaven. What the fuck had happened? He must have been hit by a semi. No, he'd been riding his bike. . . . And it crashed. But he was a good rider. . . .

Ah, now he remembered. He crashed because he'd been shot. He'd messed up when he snuck into the grow op in the dark hours before dawn. Someone had heard him, come after him, shot him. He'd barely made it to his bike and escaped.

Hellfire and damnation! Drug traffickers were after him and if they found him they'd kill him. If he was right, one of them was the man who'd murdered Anika, the teen prostitute whose body had been tossed in a Dumpster down in Vancouver.

His body was in agony, a killer was after him, and his angel was either a hallucination or a real live woman he was somehow going to have to deal with. He had three choices: cry, scream, or cuss. For a man, that narrowed down to one. He let loose with a string of curses.

She froze like a terrified animal poised for flight.

He studied her more closely, realizing his vision had sharpened. Now he saw the fine lines around her eyes and mouth. The angelic face was older than he'd thought, and fear etched the lines even deeper. Damn it, she really was scared of him.

The black leather, the bike, some foul language . . . Did she think he was a member of a biker gang like Hell's Angels or Death Row?

Her eyes closed briefly, and when they opened their expression was calm. The tension in her muscles eased as she breathed deeply. But Jake sensed she hadn't truly relaxed; she was disciplining her body to hide her anxiety.

"I can see you're conscious and more or less lucid," she said evenly. "I'll go call for an ambulance."

An ambulance. Hospital, doctors, the Royal Canadian Mounted Police. He suspected the killer he sought was a prominent, supposedly respectable member of this community. Maybe even a member of the local RCMP detachment. Caribou Crossing was a small town; chances were, this woman knew the man. His angel might even be the devil's woman. Maybe that was why he made her so nervous.

Shifting her weight, she started to rise.

His hand shot out and grabbed her arm. "No!"

She tried to pull away. Under his firm grip, she was trembling.

He was sorry to hurt her, sorry to scare her, but he had no choice. He had to keep his presence in Caribou Crossing a secret or it'd blow the undercover operation. No police; no hospital; no drug-dealing murderers. No one could know that he—Corporal Jake Brannon, working U/C for the RCMP—was here.

Except that angel-face already did.

Suddenly she yanked hard, almost pulling her arm from his grasp.

The movement jarred his entire body, and pain made him gasp and bite his lip. She was strong for such a slender, gentle-looking woman.

She jerked again and agony weakened his grip. Exploiting his weakness, she wrenched herself free and scrambled backward.

He had to stop her from reaching the phone. There was only one way.

Struggling to stay conscious, Jake fumbled for the Beretta

in the shoulder holster under his jacket. He pointed it at her. "Stop, or I'll shoot you."

She froze, swaying on her feet.

Grimly he wondered which of them was going to pass out first. "Get back here."

After a long moment, too long for his sanity, she stumbled toward him.

He felt powerless lying there, his only weapons a firearm he would never use against her, and the force of his own personality. But he knew she was afraid of him and he had to play on her fear. "Kneel down." He needed her close, where he could read her face.

She obeyed, her movements jerky. "I was just going to call an ambulance." Her gaze flicked between his face and the Beretta.

"Don't call anyone."

"But you're hurt. You need help."

"I don't need doctors or cops."

She glanced at the firearm again, her eyes wide, and he could almost hear her brain working.

"Got it?" he said.

"You're an escaped criminal!" She spat out the words.

He'd miscalculated; somehow he'd tipped her past fear to anger. When he'd cussed and grabbed her arm she'd been scared, but now she was glaring at him like she'd love to get her hands on his firearm and shoot him between the eyes.

She might get her chance, because his vision was blurring again, his world once more fading to gray. He had to control her. Now. And fear was the key.

He shifted position and got a firmer grip on the Beretta. The movement hurt his side, but the bright edge of pain helped him focus. "If you call anyone, talk to anyone, you'll regret it." Trusting her was not an option. Even if it had been, he didn't have the time, the strength, to explain. He might pass out at any moment, and then she'd have the Beretta. He needed a threat that would bind her even if she got his firearm.

What did every person value the most? Their life.

"They can lock me up, but not forever," he hissed. "I'll get out and come after you."

"Then get it over with and shoot me now," she dared him, and he saw it had turned into a battle of wills. She was stronger than he'd expected. His beautiful, feminine angel was strong. It made her even more appealing.

God, his mind was drifting again. *Focus, man!* Her strength could endanger his mission. He had to find a threat that had meaning to her. "Your family. Everyone you love. If you betray me now, I'll kill your family. I won't be in jail forever. I'll come back."

She flinched as if he'd struck her, and her face went dead white.

Thank God. He'd found the right threat. She had family and she loved them. The threat was a complete lie, but she had no way of knowing that. To her, he was a violent criminal on the lam with a gun he had no qualms about using.

He was so exhausted he could barely think. Was there anyone else in her house? No, or they'd have run outside, too.

"I'm going to tell you what to do." He forced the words through gritted teeth. "And you will obey to the letter, or I promise you, I will kill your loved ones. If you call the police, if I go to jail, I'll come back as soon as I get out. If you leave town, I'll find you. You and all your family."

"I'll d-do it," she stammered, her whole body quivering. "Whatever you want."

"Get me into the house, then hide my bike. You have a garage or shed?"

She nodded.

His world was out of focus but he saw the movement of her head. "Patch up that fence. No one can know I'm here." He knew he was speaking, but the hollow rushing sound in his ears drowned out the words. "Cover up all traces of the accident. They can't find me. They'll kill me."

"The police won't—"

"No! Can't trust the police."

What was he saying? He didn't know anymore. Damn, he was losing it. Couldn't see. Couldn't think. Had to stop talking before he said too much. What else did she need to know? "Then see if you can . . ." He paused, fighting for breath, for the end of the thought. "Keep me alive. Got it?"

Chapter Two

"Got it," Brooke whispered.

Keep him alive? The man with the gun had to know it was in her best interests to let him die. Did he know, too, that she couldn't let even an injured bird die without trying to save it? Not that it was likely the biker would die from a few scrapes and maybe a concussion.

His arm dropped heavily. Had he lost consciousness again? Pray God, he had.

She grabbed the gun out of his lifeless grasp and leaped to her feet. She stepped a couple of paces away and trained his weapon on him. He didn't move.

After a few minutes she began to feel ridiculous. She darted forward, kicked his leg, then leaped back. There was no response. Clearly he was no threat to her now. She could run inside and call the RCMP.

She gnawed her lip. The police. She avoided them. It was a holdover from the days when she'd been a drunk. If she told them she was holding a criminal at gunpoint, they'd assume she'd leaped off the wagon and was on a bender.

She could persuade them otherwise. They'd lock this man up and solve her problem. But only her immediate problem. How long would he stay in prison? Long enough so he could be released to carry out those threats? She shuddered violently. If he hurt Evan! Or Jessica, Robin, the baby.

Surely his threat wasn't a serious one. But did she dare dismiss it and risk putting her loved ones' lives in danger?

She could call Evan. He was only a couple of miles away, up at the house he and Jess had built on her parents' ranch land.

No, she didn't want the biker anywhere near her family.

What she wouldn't do for a drink . . . Thank heavens she didn't keep alcohol in the house. Right now she'd have a mighty hard time resisting the temptation. She glared at the man. Why couldn't he have crashed into someone else's fence?

Can't trust the police, he'd said. *Trust* was an odd word for a criminal to use. No doubt he had reason aplenty to fear the RCMP because they'd jail him, but why would he say they couldn't be trusted?

They'll kill me.

Who? Not the RCMP, of course.

Maybe he wasn't an escaped criminal. Perhaps he was a gang member, and a rival gang was after him. Some biker gangs were involved in the drug trade and violence was a way of life for them.

She remembered the expression in those wood-smoke eyes when he first opened them. Dreamy. Gentle. Surely those eyes couldn't belong to a gang member.

She shook her head impatiently. The profanity that had issued from that mouth—the cusswords that reminded her so vividly of her abusive ex-husband—certainly did. As did the gun she clenched in her hand, and the threats he'd hissed at her.

If he belonged to a gang, how would his cohorts react if she had him arrested? They might carry out his threat and come after her and her family. For vengeance, or even as a sick, twisted matter of honor.

How could she decide what to do when she didn't have all the information? Lord, but she was an indecisive, gutless fool. When she'd thought him a criminal, when he'd threatened her life, she'd found the courage to stand up to him. But she'd crumbled the moment he turned the threat on her family.

If only she could lose herself in drink and forget all these worries. Except that was what she'd done for years, and look at how her behavior had hurt Evan.

She heard the far-off sound of an engine. What if a car came along? It would stop, and her ability to choose would be taken from her. The driver might even be Evan or Jess.

No, she realized the noise was coming from the sky, from a little plane flying low, a mile or so to the south, in the clear morning sky. Was it headed her way?

She couldn't do anything that might put her family at risk. Not again. When the man regained consciousness again, she'd deal with him. After all, she had the gun. For now, she would obey his commands to the letter, just as he'd said.

The decision gave her a sense of relief. Structure and rules were the tools she used to keep her life in balance. What threw her was the unexpected. Uncertainty meant danger, risk, the fear that she might tip back into the world she'd once known—where alcoholism and bipolar disorder controlled her, rather than the other way around.

She remembered one of the slogans her A.A. sponsor had taught her: God never dumps more on us than we can handle.

Life-and-death threats from a gun-wielding stranger were terrifying—but the biker had also given her a structure. Rules to follow, the means to cope. She could handle this situation, and keep her family safe.

First, get him into the house, out of sight.

She examined the gun, hoping the safety catch—if it had such a thing—was on. She tucked it in the pocket of her bathrobe. Then she studied the inert body. He had to weigh half again as much as she did. How on earth was she going to get him inside?

Brooke bent down and tugged experimentally at the collar of his jacket. His body shifted. She kicked off her loose flip-flops and set the soles of her feet firmly on the ground. Then she bent over, got a good grip with both hands, and began to pull, moving slowly backward and dragging him after her, inch by painful inch across the gravel.

Five years ago she wouldn't have been able to budge him. She was fitter now than she'd ever been in her life—from regular workouts, riding, and gardening—but even so they'd traveled only a foot when she had to stop. She straightened, gasping for breath as she stretched her fiercely aching back. Grimly she thought that her efforts might well kill him, but at the moment she wasn't sure she cared. And if she didn't care . . .

She did have the gun. The means to shoot him and ensure her family's safety. Could she make the police believe he'd attacked her and she shot him in self-defense?

Glancing down at the body that lay at her feet, Brooke let out a frustrated sigh. She could no more shoot him in cold blood than she could pick him up in a fireman's lift and cart him into her house.

A giggle escaped. The white picket fence she'd so proudly built last fall, when she'd moved into the rental house on Jess's parents' ranch property, had been split to kindling. A criminal's unconscious body sprawled on her front walk between the neat borders of impatiens, lobelias, and alyssum she'd planted on the weekend.

The giggles filled her throat and she pressed her fist against her mouth. She couldn't afford to indulge in hysterics. She had made her decision and she would stick to it. Besides, she had the gun. It gave her a power of her own—the ultimate power, if she could bring herself to pull the trigger.

She began dragging him again, feeling as if her arms were

pulling out of their sockets. After another foot, she gave up. "Look, mister, you're going to have to give me some help," she muttered, nudging him with her bare toes.

When he didn't stir, she let out a frustrated hiss and dashed inside the house to get a glass of cold water.

Kneeling beside him, she said, "Last chance to wake up." Receiving no response, she splashed the water onto his face.

Choking and spluttering, he came to, glaring at her. "What the hell? You're no damned angel!"

Oh great, now he was delirious.

"I'm no angel and I'm no weight lifter," she retorted. "I can't get you into the house unless you help."

"Fuck!"

"I'm not too thrilled myself."

They'd invented new swear words since Mo's time, she reflected as she helped the man stagger to his feet.

Grimacing, she put her arm around his waist and he wrapped his own arm around her shoulders, leaning so heavily she almost toppled. Together they lurched up the front walk. It reminded her of herself and Mo tottering home from The Gold Nugget Saloon. Home to Evan, whom they'd left alone. Evan, who would have done his homework and fixed his dinner, if they'd left any food in the house.

No, she was never going to drink again.

The worst part was getting the biker up the three steps to the porch. She was almost in tears from the ache in her shoulders. They had just made it through the front door when he began to fall. Her fingers scrabbled against the leather of his jacket, but she couldn't stop him as he crashed to the floor.

She squatted and, with trembling fingers, felt for his pulse. Still alive.

Her instinct was to tend to his injuries, but she remembered his instructions. She could even understand his logic. If "they" found him, they would kill him. The chance of him dying from his injuries was far slimmer.

Leaving him lying on the floor, she dashed outside, slipped her feet back into her flip-flops, and surveyed the mess. Her closest neighbor, Ray Barnes, a widower and retired pharmacist, often rode his horse the ten miles into town for breakfast.

She didn't have a lot of time to hide the signs of the accident.

Thank heavens the motorbike was partially propped up by her fence or Brooke never would have managed to get it upright. But, once she'd extricated it and had it rolling, it proved more tractable than the man. Soon it was locked in the garden shed.

Her hands were coated in dirt, oil, and blood and so was her robe. How could a couple of pavement scrapes generate so darn much blood? She ran inside, using the kitchen door and avoiding the man who might be bleeding to death in her front hall, and hurried upstairs to the bedroom.

Sunny, sitting on the windowsill, turned to watch as she ripped off the filthy robe. "Stay there," she told him. "Keep out of his way and be safe."

When she tossed her robe onto the floor, a clunking sound made her remember the gun. She pulled it gingerly from the pocket and scanned the room for a hiding place. In the end, she placed the ugly black weapon in her laundry basket and bundled the stained bathrobe on top of it.

She pulled on an old pair of jeans and a T-shirt, then ran outside again. The damage to her fence wasn't as bad as she'd first thought. Only three boards had shattered. She had a few leftover boards in the shed, and some white paint.

The man had lost so much blood, perhaps he really would die while she was fixing her fence. But he'd given her his list of orders, and concealing his presence ranked first.

Brooke kicked the gravel around to hide the bloodstains. Then she cleared up the shattered boards, nailed the new ones in place, and splashed on paint. Once it dried, it would be almost impossible to tell the new pickets from the old.

She'd just put the lid back on the paint can when she heard the steady beat of hooves on the dirt shoulder of the road. Hurriedly she shoved the can behind a fence post and stood in front of the freshly painted boards.

Ray Barnes slowed his chestnut gelding, Timony, from a trot to a walk, then pulled to a stop beside her and touched a hand to the brim of his Stetson. "Mornin', Brooke."

He was a touch deaf, so she spoke up. "Good morning, Ray. Hello, Timony." Normally, she'd have stroked the horse's neck, but she didn't want to step away from the fence. Hoping to divert her neighbor's attention, she gestured to the sky. "Another fine day." The small plane—or another like it—was back and headed in their direction.

He glanced up. "Yep, it is." Then he gazed into her yard, pushing his horn-rims up his nose. "Notice you put your bedding plants in on the weekend. Early for that, isn't it?"

She ground her teeth. Normally, she enjoyed chatting with him, but today she just wished he'd go away. "This place is pretty sheltered. I think they'll do all right."

"Maybe so." His voice told her he didn't agree but was too polite to come right out and say so. His eyes narrowed. "That's fresh paint on your fence. You repainting already?"

She sucked in a breath. Telling lies went against the grain of the new person she'd made herself into. Besides, if she said yes, she'd have to repaint the whole darn fence. "No, I, uh, there was a little accident and I had to make repairs."

He frowned. "Backed into your own fence?"

"I feel so stupid." And that was the truth: stupid for not handling this situation better. "Don't go telling folks, all right?" If he did, people would wonder if she was drinking again.

Ray scrutinized her face, eyes sharp behind his thick lenses. Looking for signs of a hangover? He grinned suddenly. "You didn't tell on me when I fell down my own back steps. Just brought me food until I got on my feet again. Guess I owe you one."

She smiled with relief. Back in January, when the snow had been so deep she'd had to shovel her driveway every morning before she unplugged her car from the block heater and drove out of the carport, she hadn't seen him either ride Timony or drive his truck down their plowed road in a couple of days. She'd gone to check on him. He'd been holed up, nursing a badly sprained ankle, low on food and barely able to hobble out to the barn to look after his horse. The elderly man hadn't wanted his children to know because they were after him to give up his house and move into an apartment in town. She'd helped him out and kept his secret, figuring he knew the lifestyle that was best for him.

"You need any help with that fence, just say the word," he said.

"Thanks, but I've got it finished."

The roar of a plane's engine made them both glance up. The small plane was right overhead now, flying low. Wondering if the pilot was someone they knew, Brooke waved. When Ray did the same, the plane dipped a wing and rose in the sky.

"Might be the Paluski boy," Ray commented. "Heard he took up flying."

After her neighbor rode away, Brooke glanced at her watch. Darn, it was nine-thirty. On a normal morning, she'd be finishing up her routine at the women's fitness center, all ready to have a shower and dress for work. The beauty salon opened at ten and Betty Anderson was coming in for highlights and a trim. But Brooke couldn't go to work with that man lying on her floor.

She went in the back door and tiptoed through to the front of the house, hoping a miracle had occurred and somehow he'd recovered and disappeared.

Unfortunately, he still lay there. She bent down again, her

whole body aching from the strain of the last hour's activities, and pressed her fingers against his throat. His pulse beat steadily. A strand of long black hair, damp from the water she'd splashed on his face, lay across his cheek and she smoothed it back.

Unconscious, it was hard to believe he was a serious threat to her family. But she remembered the "take no prisoners" glare in his eyes when he'd pulled his gun on her. She'd read enough mystery novels to know you didn't second-guess a criminal; you just obeyed, and hoped he'd let you escape unharmed.

She heaved a sigh and went into the kitchen to phone Kate Patterson, her boss and friend. Years ago, Jessica—the same Jess who had married Evan—had been the first person in Caribou Crossing to give Brooke a chance after she'd made her turnaround. Jess's aunt Kate had been the second. When Brooke finished her courses in Williams Lake, Kate hired her as a stylist at Beauty Is You.

How could she lie to Kate?

"Mornin'," Kate said when she heard Brooke's voice. "Mind picking up some donuts on your way? I've got a powerful craving for a jelly donut."

Brooke winced. She hated to disappoint anyone, and especially Kate. When she spoke, her voice sounded husky. It was strain, she knew, but it lent credibility to her words. "I can't come in today, Kate. I'm achy and I really don't feel well. I'm so sorry."

"No worries, hon. Just look after yourself. I can take a couple of your customers myself, and I'll postpone the rest. Give me a call later in the day and let me know how you're doing, then we'll decide what to do about tomorrow. But my guess is you're coming down with that summer flu that's been going around, and you'll be out a few days. Say, you need any groceries or flu medication? I could drop by after work."

Brooke shuddered at the thought of putting her friend in danger. "I'm all stocked up. Thanks for the thought, Kate. You're the best."

"Take care of yourself. Climb back into bed and have a real restful day."

Don't I wish, Brooke thought as she hung up. Right now double pneumonia had a certain appeal, compared to dealing with her escaped criminal or biker gang rebel or whatever he was.

Her body ached from exertion, her heart raced, and she craved a drink.

The radio was playing the Eli Young Band's "Crazy Girl." She flicked it off, squared her shoulders, and forced herself to walk into the front hall.

He hadn't moved from where she'd left him. She squatted down and noted the rise and fall of his chest. And the blood that pooled beside him.

Wearily she rose and went to the upstairs bathroom to gather medical supplies. She added some old washcloths and towels and went back down, pausing at the bottom of the steps. Yes, there was a long-haired, bearded man in leather and black denim lying on her hall floor in a pool of vivid blood. She hadn't been hallucinating. Her entrance hall looked like a scene from a B-grade movie.

And yet she felt an odd sense of familiarity. Uncomfortable familiarity. This man really did remind her of her ex-husband. The biker was striking, dangerous-looking, the same as Mo had been when she met him. Mohinder McKeen, the wild young man who'd dropped out of school. He'd worn a black leather jacket, ridden his motorbike without a helmet.

Mo had made her hot and uncomfortable and excited. Sexy. Later she'd learned about his selfishness, his immaturity. Still later—after he'd deserted from the Army—he'd become abusive. His drinking had turned into a way of life, one she'd adopted, too. There'd been physical abuse, but even Mo on his very worst day had never threatened to kill her or Evan.

Yes, this biker, with his smoky eyes and sensual mouth, was sexy-looking. But he was far more dangerous than Mo. She couldn't, for even a moment, let herself forget that.

Nor could she leave him on her floor indefinitely. Likely when she poured disinfectant on his scrapes he would wake up and together they'd be able to get him . . . where? Not upstairs, to her bed or the spare room that Robin used for sleepovers. Stairs would be impossible, plus she didn't want him in her bed or her granddaughter's. Bad enough he had invaded her life, her house. That left the living room couch. She ran out to the shed for a couple of the canvas drop cloths she used for painting.

Brooke layered the drop cloths on the couch, added old sheets, and went back to the hall. She couldn't put this off any longer. She had to find out the extent of his injuries. His jeans were shredded down one side, his jacket was scraped, and his clothes were stained with blood. But, as nasty as the scrapes might be, she doubted they'd have caused him to pass out.

He must have hit his head, and that frightened her. She could disinfect and bandage abrasions but a head injury might be serious. A concussion—and possibly worse.

She wanted so badly to call 911 and get this whole mess off her hands. But if she did, what assurance did she have that he wouldn't follow through on his threat and destroy her family? Whereas if she helped him and he decided she knew too much, he might try to kill her but he'd have no reason to hurt her loved ones.

Brooke wanted to live. It was ironic that now, when she had the most reason for living—after years when she'd often longed for death—now she might die. But better her life than that of Evan, Robin, Jess, and the unborn baby. That was something she knew absolutely.

She really needed a drink. Normally, when she felt this powerful a craving, she phoned Anne, her A.A. sponsor. But if she did, she'd have to explain why she was craving alcohol at 9:30 in the morning. No, she had to get through this by herself.

"I do not need a drink," she said under her breath. "I only want one, and I have control over my wants. More than a drink, much more, I want to be the woman I have become, not the one I used to be. I, Brooke Kincaid, am strong. I will not drink. This is a test. God wouldn't dump this on me if I wasn't strong enough to handle it."

In the early days of A.A. she had fought with her demons many times every day, but now she had her techniques perfected. She had her job and her workouts at the fitness club. She went to A.A. meetings regularly, attended church on Sunday, and also got together with Anne and with Tonia, the young alcoholic woman Brooke sponsored. Besides, there was always something to look forward to: seeing her family, going for a ride with Robin, working on the board of directors of Jess's new Riders Boot Camp— a charitable foundation Brooke had invested in, using the money Evan had sent her over the years. At home, in moments when she might feel lonely, there was Sunny, music, reading, cooking, gardening.

Rarely now did Brooke feel a serious craving. She walked the line and kept her life in a healthy balance. In control. She glared at the man on the floor. He might kill her but he would not make her drink.

And she'd do her best to make sure he didn't kill her. She had so many reasons to live—and she had a gun.

Brooke knelt down and wrestled the leather jacket off him, then gingerly unbuckled the shoulder holster. She sat back on her heels and studied him. Sunshine slanted through one of the side windows. Without the jacket, caressed by innocent sunlight, the man didn't look so frightening.

Feeling more confident, she carefully lifted his head. He wriggled and moaned. Gently she probed underneath the thick, springy hair and explored his skull. She found a sizable lump and even her softest touch made him groan.

He wrenched away from her, his eyes flying open. "What the hell?" Then his eyes narrowed and she knew he was remembering. Every muscle in his body tensed like an animal collecting itself, ready to spring. But was he predator or prey? Both, she guessed, and she also guessed this macho stranger hated being vulnerable.

"I haven't told anyone," she said quickly.

"Where's my gun?"

She let out air in an exasperated whoosh. "I've done what you told me. Your threat was quite effective. You don't have to hold me at gunpoint."

His mouth twisted. Did she amuse him or was he fighting pain?

"Tell me what you've done," he demanded.

"What I've . . . Oh, you mean . . ." She catalogued her activities, hoping she remembered everything on his list of orders.

"You didn't talk to anyone?" This man's steady gaze told her he'd know if she lied.

"I called work and said I was sick. And a neighbor rode by and saw the fresh paint on the fence. I told him I'd had a little accident and had to make repairs. He assumed I'd hit it with my car and I let him believe that." It still galled her.

His mouth twisted again. "Are you a bad driver?"

"No!" Not since she'd hit that stop sign, been diagnosed as bipolar, and started taking lithium. Not since she'd stopped drinking.

"Me neither." His voice was weak but she distinctly heard a note of humor.

He was beginning to seem more human, and something inside her softened in response. "You crashed your bike," she pointed out.

"Not my fault." The words grated and his eyelids twitched.

She realized he was fighting another wave of weakness. "Don't faint again!" She needed his help to get him to the couch.

"I won't." His eyes flew open and he glared at her.

Clearly she'd offended his male ego. It gave her a feeling of power that did wonders for her morale. "We've got to get you to the couch," she said firmly.

His eyes closed, and for a moment she thought she'd lost him again. Then they opened. "How far?"

"Not far. If you can just . . ."

He was already struggling to rise, his movements awkward and clearly painful. He made it to his feet and swayed. Like a drunk. A drunk who was just about to . . . She grabbed him around the waist before he toppled.

"Christ!" he yelped.

"I'm only trying to help."

"Get . . . me . . . to . . . the . . . couch." His jaw was clenched so tight the words barely came through.

Again stumbling like a pair of drunks, they made their way into the living room. She eased him to a sitting position on the couch and released him. Her hand—the hand that had circled his waist—was wet. With blood. So were her arm and her T-shirt. So much blood.

The man sat leaning forward, both hands on his thighs to brace himself.

Brooke focused on his tee, on the blood that had soaked through the dark fabric near his waist. This injury, unlike the bloody scrapes at his hip and thigh, didn't fit with his accident. How could he have hurt himself in that particular spot when the bike went down? Had he been stabbed by a fence post?

"I . . . need . . ." His words were so soft she could barely hear them.

"Yes?"

"A . . . drink."

Chapter Three

I need a drink. God how Brooke hated those words.

She was about to tell him there was no alcohol in the house when he said, on a sigh, "Water."

She leaped to her feet, ran to the kitchen, and came back with a glass of water.

When he raised his right hand to take it, he was shaking so badly that she cupped her hand around his and helped lift the glass to his lips. His hand was hot and dry, masculine and strong and disconcerting. Her own trembled too, and as soon as he'd finished the water, she pulled the glass away from him and stepped back.

When he spoke again, his voice was firmer. "Bandage me."

"I need to get your T-shirt off." And that required his help, to pull it over his head.

He squeezed his eyes shut. "Cut it off."

She found scissors and snipped the sleeves, the back, and the front. Sections of fabric fell away, revealing a lean, well-muscled torso. He was in fabulous shape—better than Mo had ever been, but then the most physical exertion Mo had expended was in lifting a bottle.

Dark, springy curls decorated his chest and the midline of his body, and she noted a couple of sizable scars. Had he crashed the motorbike before? Maybe he wasn't as good a driver as he'd proclaimed.

A piece of cloth stuck to his right side, where he was bleeding. Gingerly Brooke tried to ease it free.

"Oh, for Christ's sake," he grated out. "Pull!"

This man had invaded her peaceful life and threatened destruction. If he said pull, she'd darn well pull. Brooke yanked hard, the cloth ripped away, and the man's breath whistled through his teeth. She stared at the bloody mess that was his side. A gray veil slid across her vision and—

His hand grasped her wrist, his fingers biting into her. "Don't faint!" he commanded, just as she'd ordered him only minutes ago.

Blinking, she forced the grayness away. "I . . ." She swallowed hard against a surge of nausea. "I won't."

His fingers were a hot, hard bracelet around her wrist, imprisoning her, but when she pulled against them he released her immediately. He poked gingerly at his side. "Flesh wound. It just grazed me," he muttered, sounding relieved.

"What grazed you?"

"The bullet."

Bullet. She tried to get her mind around it. He'd crashed his bike into her fence and a bullet had gone through his side. The two pieces of information did *not* go together. Unless . . .

"You crashed because someone shot you?" Even as she said the words she realized how ridiculous they sounded. She couldn't imagine one of her neighbors taking potshots at a biker, even if he was an escaped criminal.

She studied his face, noting the pain and exhaustion but also an implacable control. He wasn't going to tell her what had happened. She should be relieved, because in this situation knowledge could be a dangerous thing.

Still, she had enough clues to piece together the story. He carried a gun. His body already bore scars. Likely he was a member of some drug-dealing biker gang. Perhaps he'd killed a rival biker and been shot in return. He'd managed to get away on his motorbike, but he'd lost blood, grown weak, finally crashed.

In all likelihood, both the police and the bad guys who wanted to kill him were combing the area for him. She'd already decided she wouldn't give him away, wouldn't risk her family. So the remaining risk was to her own life. If she knew too much, he might try to kill her rather than just sneak away in the night.

She'd always gotten a vicarious thrill from reading mysteries, but it wasn't any fun at all when she was smack-dab in the middle of her own thriller.

"I don't want to know what happened," she told him. "I'm not a threat to you."

The faintest shadow of a smile crossed his face as he murmured, "Good." He eased himself backward until he was lying on the couch. Hurriedly she wadded an old towel against his side.

"Just patch me up," he said. "Let me rest a bit, then I'll be out of your hair."

Patch him up. Just like when she'd first seen him, she thought of a broken toy. And that reminded her of Evan. From a headstrong baby he'd transformed himself into a model child, though by then she'd mostly been too out of it to care.

Brooke took a deep breath. Past sins. This man, because of his resemblance to Mo, was making her remember past sins. She knew she'd never free herself of the guilt but she also knew she couldn't change the past. Her focus now had to be on her new life, her new strength and integrity.

She put her hands on her hips. "Fine, I'll do my best with your injuries. If the b-bullet hole is just a flesh wound, then I can clean and bandage it, but I'm no nurse and I'm not going to try to stitch it." She'd pass out for sure if she attempted that.

Continuing the catalog of injuries, she said, "You have a lump on the back of your head. It's not bleeding but you may have a concussion, perhaps even a brain injury, and there's not a thing in the world I can do about that. Also, you have some pretty bad scrapes on your right hip and thigh. Your jeans are shredded and there's dirt and gravel embedded in the wounds. I'll need to clean them thoroughly and it's going to hurt plenty. First I'll need to get your jeans off. Shall I cut them off, too?"

He laughed. Her wounded criminal actually laughed. It was one quick burst, choked off—probably by pain—but it was a laugh. "What the hell," he murmured. "Guess I'm not going to be wearing them again."

To her astonishment his eyes were warm, friendly, glinting with humor. They transformed him into a different man and, without thinking, she responded to that man. "Isn't the ripped look back in style?"

He laughed again, then groaned. "Don't make me laugh. It hurts too much."

"So will what I'm going to do when I get the rest of your clothes off and take the antiseptic to your sorry hide."

"Be gentle, nurse."

And, irrationally, she wanted to. Their relationship had shifted, and for the moment she didn't see him as a criminal, just as a man. A man in trouble, who needed her.

His gray eyes narrowed, went a smoky purple, but this time it wasn't with pain or anger. It was desire. Pure, hot, animal desire.

And her body responded. Just like it had when Mo first looked at her that way, that summer in L.A. when she was fourteen. The ache between her thighs was a shock; she thought those sensations were long dead.

She sucked in a breath. What a fool! This man had pointed a gun at her.

Deliberately she looked away from his face. She kneeled on the floor beside the couch and tugged off his scuffed leather boots, then peeled off his socks. Head still down, she said,

"Jeans next. I think it'd be easier to slide them off rather than cut them." She made her tone as businesslike as possible, but the thought of seeing him near naked made her pulse dance crazily.

"Thought you'd never ask." His voice was teasing, sexy. It was hard to believe that a man in his condition could feel desire, but clearly he did, and it had revived him.

Furious at both of them, she glared at him. "Are you going to help?"

He raised an eyebrow. The dratted man knew he was getting to her, and he enjoyed it. He was making an amazingly speedy recovery.

If he was going to goad her, she'd darn well goad back. "Can't believe a big strong man like you is going to let something like a little bullet hole slow you down."

His jaw tightened momentarily, then relaxed, and his eyes gleamed. He'd seen through her ploy. "Can't believe a woman your age can't figure out how to get the pants off a man."

A woman her age? Ooh! She figured he was several years younger than she, but forty-three wasn't that old. She was going to get him for that remark!

Boldly she grabbed the button at his waist and forced it through the buttonhole. She grasped the tab of his zipper and yanked it down. The hiss of metal almost covered his surprised gasp, but Brooke heard him and pressed her lips together to hide her smile. She was embarrassed to be in such intimate contact with his body, but delighted in having called his bluff.

She gripped the waist of his jeans on both sides and began to pull. "Lift your hips."

He obeyed and the jeans slid down.

Her fingers snagged on soft cotton and she realized she'd caught the waistband of his underwear.

Before she could release it, his hands grasped hers, locking them in place.

She managed to free a hand and gave his a quick slap. "Let go. Believe me, I haven't the slightest interest in seeing your, uh, bare essentials."

It was an out-and-out lie. She was most definitely interested but she had no intention of indulging her curiosity. So what if it had been more than fifteen years since she'd seen a naked man? She could happily wait another fifteen, or longer.

She separated the worn denim from the black cotton and resumed her struggle with the jeans. She had to lean over him to get enough purchase, far too close to his body for her peace of mind.

The sickly, metallic scent of blood was in her nostrils, but underneath it was a far more earthy scent, musky and masculine. Tantalizing and arousing.

The body she was revealing inch by inch was, like his scent, utterly male. Lean, muscled abdomen, dark whorls of hair, firm thighs, bony knees, well-shaped calves. Not to mention the sizable bulges that pressed against clingy black boxer briefs. There'd been no way to avoid seeing those seductive shapes, what with her face only scant inches away, and now, even if she closed her eyes, the image was imprinted behind her lids.

Her cheeks burned. How could a man in so much pain experience arousal?

It was as unlikely as a woman who'd been threatened at gunpoint being aroused by the man who'd done it, but there was no doubting her reaction. Though she hadn't had sexual feelings in forever, she recognized the heat, the ache, the tingle. Now that her initial panic had worn off and she'd begun to interact with him, she'd started to believe he wasn't actually going to hurt anyone. And that made her an idiot. She'd read about Stockholm syndrome, where hostages begin to like their captors. Was it already starting?

Quickly she pulled the jeans off his feet and tossed them onto the coffee table. Determined not to reveal her feelings, she forced herself to meet his sultry gaze with a cool one of her own. In an effort to establish control, she asked, "What's your name?"

His eyes went from steamy purple heat to blue-gray ice in less than a second.

She realized her mistake. "Not your real name. And if there's ID in your pocket, I promise I won't—"

"There isn't."

"Good. But give me something I can call you other than 'hey, you.'"

"Call me . . . John."

"As in John Doe?"

"Like the unidentified corpses at the morgue? Yeah, call me John Doe. Except I'm not planning to turn into a corpse anytime soon." His expression cool and assessing, he cocked an eyebrow in an unspoken question.

"I won't turn you in to the police or anyone else. I don't want any harm to come to my family." She huffed out a sigh and said, a little grudgingly, "And I won't kill you or let you die. It's not in my nature, even though I hate the fact that you're here."

He watched her closely as she spoke, then nodded. "I hate it, too. Do what I say and I'll be gone soon and you'll be safe."

It was the second time he'd said that. Did he really intend to leave without harming her? He sounded sincere—or was that just wishful thinking on her part?

She reminded herself that she had his gun. "Good, then we've got the same goal. Want some aspirin? I'll have to run up to the bathroom."

He eyed her warily.

"Look, you trust me or you don't," she said.

He swallowed. "Aspirin would be good."

"Okay, then." She hurried upstairs, getting not only the pills but more bandages and rags. After she'd refilled the water glass, she helped him sit up enough to swallow the pills and drink the water, all too conscious of his naked heat under her arm.

"I'll get warm water to wash your wounds." She headed for the kitchen and placed a cooking pot under the tap.

"Hey!" he called.

She stuck her head through the door. "Yes?"

"What's your name, angel of mercy?"

She hadn't realized what a personal question it could be. How vulnerable it made her feel to give him her name. But she hated to lie, and he'd know if she did. Returning with the pot of water, she said, "My name's Brooke. As for being an angel of mercy, I bet you won't say that after I take the antiseptic to you."

She knelt beside him and, gritting her teeth, tackled the worst injury, anxious to get it over with. As she sponged blood from the bullet wound in his side, she realized his assessment had been right. The flesh was torn and ragged and he would have a new scar, but the injury wasn't serious and the bleeding had slowed to an ooze.

A liberal splash of antiseptic made him jerk and curse, but she kept going, taping on a bandage spread with antibiotic lotion. He'd have to watch out for infection, but a man with those scars on his body would already know that.

Turning her attention to the scrapes on his hip and thigh, she sterilized tweezers and extracted the grit. For a time she was too aware of his nakedness, and also of his winces and an occasional smothered curse, but then she lost herself in her work.

When she was done she sat back on her heels, her whole body one huge, exhausted ache. She glanced at his face for the first time since she'd begun to play nurse.

His gaze met hers steadily. "Thank you. I know that wasn't pleasant."

Her mouth dropped open. "Uh, no, it wasn't. You're . . .

welcome." She forced her weary body to its feet. "You should rest."

"You too, Brooke." His tone was gentle, his dark eyelashes fluttered, the lines carved into his face by pain relaxed, and his eyes stayed closed.

Absurdly, she wanted to reach out and stroke his cheek.

Instead she cleaned up the mess, cut up his ruined tee and jeans as rags and put them in the washer along with the bloody cloths she'd used to clean his wounds, then bundled his jacket into a garbage bag and hid it in the tool shed.

Finally, she sought the sanctuary of her sunny kitchen. She put the radio on low, sank into a chair, and rested her head in her hands. What was she going to do with John Doe?

A muted trill of birdsong made her lift her head. It was the clock Robin had given her for Christmas. Each hour, a different bird sang its song. The current one was a mockingbird, which meant it was twelve o'clock. The bird always reminded her of *To Kill a Mockingbird*, one of her favorite books. The theme, as she saw it, was that you shouldn't stereotype people, you should open your mind and find out who they really are.

What about John Doe? Who was the real man: the gun-wielding biker who had threatened her family, or the gentle man who had thanked her?

She leaned her head against the back of her chair. She would have liked nothing better than a nap but she couldn't imagine sleeping while that man was under her roof.

Sunny strolled in and leaped to her lap. He rubbed his head against hers and she scratched him. "Yes, it's safe to come out of hiding. What do you say? Feel like some tuna?"

She forked a bit of fish into his dish and made herself a salad with the rest, then went out on the back porch to eat, telling herself that she was much happier eating a healthy meal than drinking a few beers.

When she finished the salad, she lifted her feet to the railing—painted white to match the fence—and leaned back. The cat purred on her lap, while the soft twang of country music drifted out the open kitchen door and the sun's warmth caressed her gently and eased out the aches. It felt decadent in a way, being home at lunchtime on a weekday. Decadent, but unsettling. Routine was the key to her survival, and she would gladly have traded her sunny porch for the air-conditioned, chemical-scented world of Beauty Is You.

How was she going to get through the rest of this day? And how soon until John Doe recovered? Would he keep his promise and leave her unharmed?

Brooke tried to relax, to focus not on the dangerous man on her couch but on the warm weight of her cat, so peaceful on her knee. Sunny was her favorite stress-buster. At A.A. they'd advocated getting a plant, and later an animal. One goal was to learn responsibility, but there were also wonderful benefits like companionship.

She wove her fingers through Sunny's silky fur. He'd been such a tattered mess when she found him a couple of years ago, drenched and shivering at the back door of the tiny house she'd been renting in town. She'd let him in, figuring on taking him to the SPCA because she hadn't felt ready for the "get a pet" part of her recovery. After the disaster she'd made of raising Evan, she couldn't imagine assuming responsibility for another living creature.

But the storm that had brought him was a doozy, making the roads treacherous. By morning, when it was safe to drive, the cat had taught her what a fine thing it was to have a friend on a stormy night, and somehow he'd acquired the name Sunny. Once he had a name, she couldn't let him go.

They had adjusted to each other, taken care of each other, and it was he who'd given her the confidence to invite Robin for her first overnight visit after Brooke had moved into this house last fall.

She had resisted accepting Wade and Miriam Bly's offer of the rental cottage on their ranch land. It was like a dream come true—a nice house with its own sizable garden and no noisy, intrusive neighbors—but it had felt like charity. She'd given in when Jess's dad pointed out that the last tenants had run the place down and both the house and garden needed some hard work. Miriam, a kind and generous soul, had added, "We'd appreciate it if you'd give the poor place some TLC, Brooke."

Brooke had been so blessed in the past year.

Stroking Sunny, she reminded herself that she'd been thinking exactly that in the moments before John Doe crashed his Harley through her white picket fence. "We'll survive this," she murmured to the cat, "and life will return to normal."

"Supper?" The female voice drifted into Jake's consciousness and he struggled to open his eyes. Today it seemed all his body wanted to do was sleep—or pass out.

She'd roused him a few times, worried that he was concussed, asking him dumb questions like the name of the prime minister, and each time he'd fallen back to sleep immediately.

He gazed upward and squinted against the light. She was an angel again, the late afternoon sunlight behind her turning golden hair into a glowing halo. Brooke. She'd said her name was Brooke. A pretty name, but less dynamic than her golden hair, ocean eyes, pink-rose lips, and gutsy spirit.

He couldn't make out her features until she moved forward, out of the sun's dazzle. Nope, not an angel, not with that scowl. He would have grinned if it wouldn't have ruined his "I'm a hardened criminal" act. Suddenly he realized he was fully awake and not feeling entirely shitty. Best of all, he was alive and she clearly hadn't turned him in—or shot him. By the look on her face, she was pretty mad, though. He found he didn't like having Brooke mad at him.

He squeezed his eyes shut for a moment. Instinct told him to trust her, and he wanted to retract his threats. But he'd come to Caribou Crossing to hunt a killer, and that goal came first. Brooke might be involved with the killer, though it seemed unlikely.

"Supper?" she said impatiently, her brisk voice a contrast to the country ballad some sugary-voiced female singer was crooning in the background.

He realized Brooke was holding a tray, and something on it smelled just fine, like tomatoes and herbs. He shifted position, loosening the old blanket that was tangled around his waist, and bit down on a groan. "Help me sit up."

She gave an annoyed frown but set the tray on the coffee table, then gathered a cushion from a nearby chair and bent over the couch. "Lean forward."

He obeyed, wincing as pain lanced through his side. She crammed the cushion behind him and he gasped. His head felt like someone was riding a Harley around inside it.

"Push yourself up," she said.

If she'd been more gentle with him he might have complied, but her cavalier treatment annoyed him—even if he did deserve it. Besides, she was damned pretty and he wanted her to come closer. He had a vague recollection that she smelled of tropical flowers. Or had that been a dream? "Can't do it by myself," he said. "Maybe if you hooked your hands in my armpits and pulled me up?"

Her scowl grew even deadlier.

"Or you could just feed me," he suggested softly.

She gave a snort and muttered something that sounded

like, "Or you could starve to death." But she came closer and studied his position.

"If you got up on the couch, and kind of straddled me . . ." His body—naked but for boxer briefs—stirred at the idea. Even with that glare on her face, Brooke was one fine-looking woman.

She went behind the arm of the couch and leaned over the stacked pillows, grabbed him under both armpits, and gave a mighty heave.

He barely had a chance to appreciate the soft, exotically scented curls that tickled his face before pain nearly made him black out again. He bit down on the lip he'd mangled earlier, and managed to stay conscious, then gingerly shuffled his body into a semicomfortable position.

He lifted the light blanket that covered him and peered underneath. With cautious fingers he tested the dressings she'd applied.

"I checked an hour ago," she said. "I don't think there's any infection."

He imagined her examining his body while he slept, and the pulse of arousal quickened.

Her cheeks were pink and he saw a flutter at her throat, the quick lift of those fine little breasts. Damned if she wasn't aroused, too. He made a lazy visual inspection of her, admiring every soft curve. If he wasn't in so much pain he'd be tempted—

Christ, what was he thinking? He was holding this woman hostage until he got back on his feet, and right now he could barely sit up.

He had to figure out how to proceed with his investigation of Anika Janssen's murder. He had to work out a new cover story, get his handler Jamal's help in providing fake ID, and ask him to check out Brooke. Jamal was going to be pissed that he'd messed things up.

No, this was definitely not the time to be thinking about sex. Yet, with Brooke, it was hard to think about anything else. Jesus. Maybe he was concussed. His brain sure wasn't functioning. He had to pull himself together. First things first. "Have you got a husband coming home from work?"

She'd been standing absolutely still, as if his gaze had held her in a spell, but now she took a step backward. "No."

"Boyfriend? Kid? Anyone?"

"I live alone, except for Sunny." She waved a hand toward a chair by the fireplace and he saw a cat the color of liquid honey, curled in a ball.

Brooke bent to pick up the tray, then settled it on his lap and stepped quickly away. Soup, a grilled cheese sandwich, a glass of milk. A great lunch for a kid, he thought huffily. Still, the soup was obviously homemade, with chunks of tomato, onions, and mushrooms. Rosemary and garlic too, his nose told him. The bread was thickly cut, speckled with grain and maybe nuts, and didn't look like anything he'd ever seen in a grocery store.

Had she spent the afternoon cooking? For him? He didn't like it when women he was dating cooked for him. Made him think they were getting ideas. But right now, from his gunpoint hostess, he didn't mind it one bit.

She stood beside the couch, her body language wary, like a suspect poised to flee.

"Looks good," he said, and saw her face relax a degree. "Got a beer?"

She tensed immediately. "No. There's no alcohol in the house."

"Damn." It figured that the owner of a white picket fence would be a teetotaler. Could today's luck get any worse? He scowled at the glass of milk. Milk was okay, but after the events of this day he could really use a beer. Or three.

"Do you need anything else?" she asked.

Even though she'd earlier asked for a name to call him by, she never used the one he'd given her. "Not at the moment."

"Uh, what about the next couple of hours? I have to go out." She mumbled the words, almost swallowing the last of them.

"Out? You're not going anywhere!"

Chapter Four

A wave of exhaustion swamped Jake. Maybe he could control her tonight, but he had to stay in Caribou Crossing if he was going to find Anika's killer. When he set up a new cover, she'd have the power to blow it wide open. Fuck.

If only he could trust her with the truth. It seemed unlikely that this quiet woman with her cozy home, country music, and golden cat was mixed up with a murderer who sold drugs. But he already knew the criminal he sought wore a mask of respectability; how could he be sure Brooke's wholesomeness wasn't also a façade?

Besides, if she was innocent and he told her what he was up to, he might put her in danger. He was supposed to protect the innocent, not endanger them.

When he'd yelled, she had glanced down and retreated a couple of steps, but now she firmed her jaw and fixed him with a level gaze. "If I didn't turn you in today, I'm not going to do it tonight. Besides, I have to go." When she spoke the last words her voice quavered. "It's Tuesday night and I have a meeting to attend. I go every Tuesday. If I'm not there, people will call. Maybe even drop by."

He groaned. "Do what you did about your job. Call and say you're sick."

"I have to go." Her voice was shrill, almost desperate, her body so taut it almost vibrated.

"Why? What's so important about this meeting?"

"It's . . ." She swallowed, so hard he could hear her. "It's A.A."

She had managed to shock him. He'd never have taken Brooke for an alcoholic. She seemed so in control. But then, if she was a recovering alcoholic, she *was* in control. She was waging a constant battle for control over her cravings—and winning, one day at a time. No wonder she was so plucky when it came to dealing with him; she'd faced a tougher demon.

"I need to go," she said. "Today has been . . . hard."

Damn. He was sorry to put so much pressure on her, but at least she couldn't start drinking again if there wasn't any booze in the house. He shook his head, grimacing as the goose egg brushed the cushion. "You can't go. Sorry, but that's how it is."

"My family's the only thing in the world that's important to me!" Brooke's angry voice hurt his aching head. "I'm not going to endanger their lives, not for scum like you. I won't say a word about you being here. But I really need to go to my meeting." Across the room, her cat gave a yowl, leaped to the floor, and scurried away.

Jake glanced at the photographs on her mantel, which he'd studied earlier in a brief period of consciousness: the wedding picture with the attractive young couple, the girl on a horse, the same girl with Brooke. Who was Brooke to these people? The groom bore a resemblance to her, might be her younger brother.

He'd have taken the little girl to be her kid, but she lived alone. A niece?

Odd that there was no picture of Brooke with a man. She was pretty, sexy, obviously competent. But she was an alcoholic. And alcoholism was tough on relationships.

Still, it seemed she had her alcoholism under control.

She was an interesting woman. She could go head-to-head with a man she believed to be an escaped criminal. Despite her discomfort, she'd done a thorough job of caring for his injuries. She made tomato soup that smelled like an Italian kitchen. She put her family above all else—though that might be guilt over past behavior, from her drinking days.

Brooke was a recovering alcoholic. With no booze in the house, and hell-bent on attending her meeting. He respected people who could pull themselves out of the black hole of alcoholism, and he understood the constant battle they waged. He'd been through the whole mess with Jamal, his handler and friend. It was their secret that Jamal was a recovering alcoholic. If the department found out, he could be taken off undercover work.

Jake knew how important those A.A. meetings could be to alcoholics.

Besides, he realized, she was offering him an opportunity. If he could pull himself to his feet—which he was going to have to do soon anyhow, because he needed to take a piss and wasn't about to ask for her help—he could search her house and call Jamal for a background check. Then he'd be better able to judge if she was innocent. He'd also find his gun— unless she took it with her.

"Go to your damned meeting, Brooke," he growled. "Don't say a word about me, and come straight home after." Jesus, he must be brain damaged.

She swallowed again. "Thank you, John."

As Brooke pulled into her driveway after the meeting, the house was dark. She'd forgotten to turn on a light before she left.

John Doe was likely still there, her problems hadn't mag- ically been solved, yet she felt more at peace than she had since early that morning. She'd barely spoken a word to anyone at the meeting, making the excuse that she was a little under the weather, but she'd regained her equilibrium. Thank heavens her uninvited guest had let her go; she hadn't really expected that he would.

Inside the door she slipped off her shoes, then tiptoed into the living room. Not wanting to wake John Doe, she didn't switch on a light. It took her eyes a few moments to adjust to the darkness, but when they did she let out a gasp. Covers straggled off the couch but the man was gone.

Hurriedly she clicked the light switch and surveyed the room. The dinner tray, with empty dishes, rested on the coffee table. Sunny rose from one of the chairs, stretching. The other chair was empty. Brooke darted to the downstairs powder room but it, too, was deserted. She glanced toward the steps, then shook her head. If he'd felt well enough to go upstairs then he'd have chosen instead to leave—as he'd clearly done.

Realizing she'd been holding her breath, she let it out in a long sigh. She'd been granted her miracle and he was gone. She was safe, and so were her loved ones.

But how had he managed it, what with the bullet wound, the loss of blood, the bang to his head? None of the injuries was really serious, but darn the man, didn't he know he was too weak to ride a bike? He could crash again, do himself even more harm.

And why should she care, for even a moment?

Should she call the police, now that she was safe?

Automatically, she flicked on the radio. When she'd come to Caribou Crossing, she'd loved disco music and rock. Somehow, over the years, the sound of country and western had insinuated itself into her brain until it became comfort music.

As she sank into the chair across from Sunny's, Tammy Wynette was singing "Stand by Your Man," and Brooke almost chuckled at the irony. The cat hopped down and strolled across to rub her foot, then leaped onto her lap and let it be known that he wouldn't mind having his chin scratched. Brooke obliged.

"I should feel relieved," she murmured. "He's gone. My problems really have been solved." He was a criminal and he'd threatened her family. It was absurd to feel concerned about him. And yet, there had been something about him. . . .

She shook her head vigorously. He was handsome and virile and reminded her of Mo. He made her feel hot and edgy, just like Mo had, the summer they'd met. Yes, there'd been something about the mysterious John Doe, and it definitely hadn't been good for her peace of mind. She'd reflect overnight. In the morning, maybe she'd phone the police. Or maybe she'd wake up and find that this had all been a bad dream.

Sunny jumped down and stood in front of her chair, his tail arched. Brooke tugged gently on the furry tip. "Yes, kitty, it's time for bed." She took the tray into the kitchen, put the aspirin bottle on the counter, then rinsed the dishes and loaded them into the dishwasher. The cat shifted impatiently from one foot to the other, but Brooke wasn't about to leave dirty dishes lying around. She'd left that bad habit behind five years ago, when she cleaned up her act.

She clicked off the radio, folded the blanket, put the sheets and drop cloths in the washer, then gathered up her medical supplies and followed Sunny upstairs. The house was their own again, Brooke's life was her own again, yet she still felt unsettled.

When she entered her bedroom she froze in her tracks. John Doe, naked but for bandages and black boxer briefs, lay faceup on top of her bed. She darted forward to touch his throat, her fingers trembling so badly she could barely find his pulse. Yes, he was alive.

As she gaped at him, she felt an unsettling mix of relief and consternation. Why had he come upstairs? Had he sought a more comfortable bed, then, having exhausted his strength, collapsed on top rather than manage to get under the covers? Or had he been looking for his gun?

She dropped her medical supplies on the bed and darted into the walk-in closet to check the laundry basket. The gun was still there, along with the shoulder holster she'd hidden that afternoon. Relieved, she returned to the side of the bed. He hadn't pulled the curtains and the light from the moon and stars was sufficient so she could study him.

He really did have an amazing body. Male perfection, but for the old scars. Again she felt the unwelcome pulse of arousal, low in her belly. She wanted to lie on the bed beside him, touch that bronzed skin, feel the powerful muscles underneath, run her fingers through those crisp curls of hair.

Sunny leaped onto the bed and settled on the far pillow. Odd behavior for a cat who didn't trust easily.

As odd as Brooke's own ridiculous attraction to a criminal who had threatened everything she held dear.

What now? She'd sleep in Robin's room, with the door locked, and hope that in the morning John Doe had disappeared—for real.

She lifted the free side of the quilt he lay on, and covered him with it.

"What the . . . ?" He woke suddenly, jerked upright, cursed, and even in the dim light she could read his pain and disorientation.

"You're on my bed. You came upstairs. Why?"

"I . . ." He brushed his hand across his face, like he was clearing a spiderweb. "I don't remember. I, uh, wanted something. Oh yeah, aspirin."

"I left it on the tray. Didn't you see it?"

He shook his head, wincing. "I'll go down."

"No, stay here. The stairs are too dangerous for someone in your condition."

She hurried down to collect the aspirin bottle she'd left

on the kitchen counter. When she got back, her bed was empty except for the cat. "The amazing disappearing man," she muttered.

Then she heard the toilet flush in the bathroom across the hall, and water running in the sink. She smoothed back the bedspread and saw that it bore a large, dark stain. He'd bled on her prized quilt. She was furious, and worried. He couldn't afford to lose any more blood.

She gathered up her medical supplies and headed for the hallway. The bathroom door opened as she approached, startling her so much that she almost dropped everything. "You're bleeding—" she began, just as he said, "I had to—" They both broke off and stared at each other.

The bathroom light was bright and her unwanted visitor was all but naked. He didn't seem concerned and she was darned if she'd let him know it bothered her. Besides, there was a secret part of her that did enjoy the view, even if its effect on her body embarrassed her.

"You bled on my quilt. It's handmade, by a local woman. I love that quilt."

"I'm sorry." He swayed and gripped the door frame.

Quickly she rushed past him to deposit her burdens on the counter, then put an arm around his waist. He was so warm, so hard, so splendidly male. Her senses were on overload and her body responded as if this man were a lover, not an escaped criminal.

Surely she wouldn't have this reaction if he were clothed. Unfortunately, she didn't have any men's clothes in the house and she'd bet he didn't want her shopping for him in town. It dawned on her for the first time that he'd need clothes before he could make his escape.

"Let's get you sitting down," she said firmly. She guided him to the toilet and flipped the seat and lid down.

Grimly she studied the bloody bandage. She'd have to replace it. If he'd stayed downstairs, he wouldn't have started bleeding again. Bad enough he was a criminal; did he have to be a darn nuisance as well? Fortunately, once she unwrapped the bandage, she saw that the wound showed no signs of infection. She tended to it quickly, then doled out a couple of aspirin. "Go back to bed."

He rose, swayed, then staggered out of the bathroom. When she saw he was heading for the stairs she darted after him. "No!" If he fell down them, she simply didn't have the energy to tend to him. "You can use my bed."

She didn't want him in Robin's room. It would be a kind of profanity. She had to separate her granddaughter from this danger.

"I can't take your bed."

"You already did. Besides, you don't have the strength to go downstairs."

"I do."

His stubborn expression told her she'd again insulted his macho pride. Men could be such fools. She gave a growl of pure exasperation.

His face softened. "I'll do whatever you want. What do you want, Brooke?"

His gentle expression, his question, the way he said her name, all combined to weaken her defenses. For a moment she wanted to give in to the desire she kept trying to deny. She wanted to feel all of that hard maleness pressing against her own soft femininity. She wanted this man to hold her in his arms as if they were lovers.

She cleared her throat. "Get into my bed. It's easiest."

Without a word he turned and hobbled into her bedroom. He paused a moment by the bed. "Sorry about the quilt. Will it clean?"

She hadn't expected apologies from John Doe. "I think so. It's cotton. I'll soak it tonight." She pulled off the quilt and went to the hall closet for a blanket. When she returned, he was between the sheets.

As she spread the blanket over the top sheet, he said, "You came back alone. You didn't call the police."

"Your threat was effective."

"Sorry."

My gosh, another apology.

"I have no other choice," he said.

Perhaps it was true. How else could a seriously injured criminal keep her under control? But tonight he seemed far less the criminal and more just a tired, hurting man.

"How was your meeting?" he murmured.

"Good."

His arms rested on top of the blanket, and now he stretched one out and caught her hand. "You go every week?"

"Always on Tuesdays. Sometimes another time or two." She stared down at their linked hands, wondering why she didn't pull hers from his grip. His hand was hot, almost feverish, and hers trembled inside it.

"How long have you been sober?" He tugged gently and she eased down to perch nervously on the side of the bed.

"Four years, ten months."

His lips curled into a smile. "And how many days?"

She gave a choky laugh. "Twelve."

"Good for you. Won't be long until you have your five-year pin."

She nodded, feeling quiet pride.

"How long did you drink?"

"Since my teens. At some point it turned from social into a serious problem."

He squeezed her hand, then released it and, oddly, she felt bereft. But then he put his hand down again, this time resting it on her thigh.

She jumped. Male touch was a scary thing—with Mo she'd never known whether to expect a caress or a blow—yet now she couldn't bring herself to move away.

"Why did you drink, Brooke?" he asked gently.

She bowed her head. "I don't know. My dad drank a lot. Mo—my ex—drank heavily. But that's just an excuse. I picked up the bottle because there were lots of times when I hated my life, and hated myself, but I kept on drinking because I'm an alcoholic."

To a large extent her depression had been due to her bipolar disorder, but she hadn't known it then. Besides, that was another excuse. It amazed her that she was telling John Doe about her alcoholism; she certainly wasn't going to tell him about her other condition.

"Sometimes I was depressed," she said, "and booze—well, if it didn't make me feel better at least it dulled my awareness. Other times, when I was hungover and there was no alcohol around, I felt . . . awful." She shuddered. "I don't ever want to feel that way again."

He stroked her thigh. "Is that what keeps you from drinking again?"

"I've reached the point where I don't live in a constant state of craving. And when I do want a drink, it's not with the same intensity."

"What do you do when the craving hits?"

"I remind myself of who I was. How awful I was to everyone around me, and how miserable I felt. I think about how far I've come. I go to a meeting or call my sponsor. Or I talk to my family—not about the craving, just about what's happening in their lives. They ground me, they remind me my life is good now."

For some reason, it was easy to talk to him in the dark bedroom. Somehow, his hand on her leg had become a comfort, a reassurance, which was incredible if she stopped to think of who he really was.

"You're a strong woman."

Now she did dart a glance at his face, to see if he was making fun of her. His skin and hair were dark against the white pillow, and his expression, as best she could see it in the dimly lit room, seemed sincere. So did his voice.

"I lost my son," she said so softly it was almost a whisper. "I was a terrible mother. I drove him away. But he came back—just last year—and he forgave me. If I drink, I'll lose him again. Him and his family."

And she'd lose Evan and his family if John Doe harmed them. Her heartbeat quickened with fear.

It was as if he read her mind. He patted her thigh. "I won't hurt them. Help me for one more day, then don't tell a soul about me. That's all you have to do. The hard part is over, Brooke. I won't harm you or them, and I'll be gone tomorrow."

She wanted to believe him. "You're too badly injured."

"Flesh wounds. Headache, but no concussion. I'll be fine. Tomorrow."

He captured her hand again, and squeezed it in what felt like a promise. Then he set her hand down on the blanket and stroked it, his fingers caressing the back.

She watched, mesmerized, but then something made her look up.

Grooves of exhaustion and pain cut into his handsome features, yet his eyes flamed with desire. She couldn't look away.

He turned her hand over and stroked the tender skin of her palm, the inside of her wrist.

Sensation zinged straight to her center and she could feel her female flesh swell and ache.

"Brooke . . ."

She jerked away and leaped to her feet. "Good night."

Chapter Five

Jake woke to sunshine and birdsong. To pain and disorientation. To a warm presence curled against his side. He jerked upright, cursing at the pain, and the golden cat uncurled itself lazily and yawned. Brooke's cat. He was in Brooke's bed.

He lay back, remembering the last twenty-four hours.

In the black hours of the previous morning he had located the grouping of trailers he'd spotted doing aerial surveillance. A grow op could exist anywhere, such as an apartment or a house, but he and Jamal had speculated that out here in ranch country, the guy they were looking for would try to consolidate his operation well off the beaten track.

At first glance, Jake had taken the half dozen trailers and long shed for a small trailer park—then he'd realized the only access was a narrow dirt road, the buildings were almost hidden among trees, there was no landscaping or anything to pretty things up, and lights didn't show from the windows. The buildings were off all regular flight paths, and he didn't risk flying lower to see if the windows had been covered by blackout drapes.

Instead, he'd taken his readings from the air then come back on his Harley, to work his way through a maze of country roads. When he was close enough someone might hear the engine, he hid the bike in bushes alongside the rutted road, stripped off the motion-restricting leather jacket, and hiked the last mile.

He reconnoitered cautiously but saw no guards. If this was a grow op, these guys were overconfident.

There was only one vehicle on-site: a black Chrysler truck with big wheels, a canopy with tinted windows, and a mud-covered license plate. Unlocked. No registration papers. But, inside the back—bingo! Boxes containing bags of marijuana.

Hoping these guys were really stupid, he scraped mud from the plate and memorized the tag. A boggy patch supplied fresh mud to doctor the plate again.

The long rectangular building he'd seen from the air looked makeshift, its wooden walls blended in among the trees, and its windows, like the trailers', were dark. He guessed it housed workers, probably illegal immigrants.

He skirted the bunkhouse and eased open the door to one of the trailers. Inside, he found a thriving green crop. Lights, water, nutrients; marijuana wasn't hard to grow, and these folks knew what they were doing.

He'd have liked to go inside and search the trailer for clues to who ran this operation, but a radio was playing classic rock, suggesting that a guard or worker was on duty.

Perhaps he'd have better luck with the next trailer.

He slid the door shut carefully and slipped through the darkness to the neighboring trailer. But this time, when he turned the handle and pressed gently against the door, the damned thing squeaked loudly, and there was no music to mask the sound.

A male voice called, "Herb? That you? Jango?"

As Jake hightailed it out of there, the door crashed open behind him, and a voice yelled, "Hey!" A powerful beam lanced the darkness and caught him. Shots rang out. He knew he'd been hit but he didn't stop in his dash for the woods.

More shots sounded behind him but the trees provided cover and he got away.

He wanted to fire back, but that might've blown his chance of identifying the killer. He guessed the guy shooting at him was a minion who might not even know the identity of the top man. No, he and Jamal were handling this undercover, and he wasn't going to change the game plan now.

In a couple of minutes the truck roared to life and he froze behind a clump of bushes as the vehicle barreled down the road, its headlights acting like search beams. The driver must have been an idiot because he kept going, not stopping and listening to see if he heard another engine. Obviously he was certain the intruder had made his getaway by vehicle.

Jake regained the road and hurried toward the Harley, not stopping to deal with his wound, fearful the truck would return before he reached the bike. He made it safely, though, and pulled the Harley out of its hiding place. Shivering uncontrollably from shock, he managed to pull on his jacket, but forgot about his helmet. His side ached fiercely by then and he felt a little light-headed. He held tight to one thought: He had to get back to the motel before the driver of the black truck found him.

So he'd ridden hard, until finally his strength deserted him and he crashed. And ended up in Brooke's hands.

Small, shapely hands with unvarnished nails cut short. Capable hands that could be gentle when she wasn't scared or mad.

He turned his face into her pillow and inhaled an enticingly feminine scent. Almost, he wished he could have met Brooke in different circumstances. She had a few years on him—he'd learned her vital stats when he searched her files in her desk last night—but she was a strong, feisty woman, as well as a lovely, sexy one.

And, he was coming to think, she was an innocent one. When she'd been out at her meeting he'd called Jamal in

Vancouver. Not wanting to waste time in case Brooke
changed her mind and came back, he deferred giving a report
and just had his buddy run a quick computer check on her.
Aside from an impaired driving conviction from years back,
her record was clean.

Jake had then searched the house thoroughly and was just
going to see if he could log on to her computer when he felt
dizzy and barely made it to her bed before passing out.

He'd learned that she paid her bills immediately and kept
invoices and receipts filed methodically. Her employment
records were from a place called Beauty Is You, so he guessed
she was a hairdresser. Her son had sent her money over the
years they'd been estranged, and she'd saved every penny.
After he returned, she donated it to a charitable organization
called Riders Boot Camp, which her daughter-in-law started
up last fall. Brooke was an active member of the board of
directors.

As for hobbies, she had a collection of well-read books—
romances, mysteries, and biographies—and also made good
use of the library. She clipped recipes from magazines and,
from the stains and tattered corners, it seemed she actually
tried them out. She also had books on gardening.

Her house was a cozy nest of domesticity, in which she
clearly lived alone. But the girl Robin was a frequent visitor.
Brooke's granddaughter.

He was still stunned to think his angel could be a grandma.

He'd learned from his search that Evan, the son she'd
mentioned last night, was the man in the wedding picture.
Jessica was his bride and the driving force behind the no-frills
riding camp operation. Robin was Jessica's eleven-year-old
daughter. And Brooke was forty-three, several years older
than he'd guessed.

Jake would have thought that knowing she was a grandma
would make Brooke less attractive, yet when she'd come
home last night he'd had trouble keeping his hands off her.

In fact, he hadn't. He remembered the resilience of her thigh under thin cotton, the responsiveness of her hand as he caressed it. Just touching her hand had turned him on in a major way.

Oh Christ, what was he doing sprawling in bed musing about his sexy, reluctant hostess when there was a killer on his trail? When he was a step closer to solving Anika's murder, yet in desperate need of a new cover? He'd kept his time on the phone with Jamal to a minimum because he wanted to search Brooke's house, and now he really needed to talk to him and figure out a plan.

Jake had been traveling as Stan Browning, and had used that name to rent his room at the Gold Rush Trail Motel, as well as to charter the Cessna he'd taken up to scout for the grow op. The man he was chasing wasn't stupid. When he learned his operation had been infiltrated, he'd have checked with the small airports and probably the motels. Likely he knew by now that a long-haired dude named Stan Browning had paid cash at an airport fifty miles away to rent a small plane for a couple of days. That Browning had registered at the Gold Rush Trail Motel, and that he rode a motorbike. Jake's cover was blown. He dare not even go back to the motel to pick up the few clothes and toiletries he'd left there along with his fake ID. Nor—fuck it—could he use the Harley, even if it was functional after the crash.

Initially, when he and Jamal had constructed the cover identity of Stan Browning, he'd planned to appear as a shady, savvy drifter. A man who knew the drug scene and wanted to make some money off it. He'd hoped to infiltrate his quarry's operation in the same way he'd done with gangs when he worked undercover. But now the killer would be on his guard, so Jake had to think of a different approach.

Thank God he'd had his back turned when that beam spotlighted him. If he'd been facing the scumbag who shot him, it really would be game over.

He could call in the troops and shut down the grow op, but there was no guarantee that'd net them Anika's killer. If he was going to stick to the plan and do a U/C investigation of the upstanding citizens of Caribou Crossing, he needed a whole new cover. That meant he had to talk to Jamal. He glanced at the phone on the bedside table. No, it was too risky. Brooke was somewhere in the house, and might pick up a phone herself.

The cat head-butted him in the shoulder and he stroked it, feeling it throb before he heard a hearty purr. Yes, Jamal could help him work out a cover and get him the necessary ID, but before he called, it would help to know more about Caribou Crossing. Should he come in as a traveling salesman, a backpacker looking for some good hiking, or a dude who wanted to play cowboy?

He didn't want to drag Brooke any further into this, but she could be a useful source of information. She'd lived here for years, but, even more than that, she was a hairdresser. People talked to their hairdressers.

Could he get her chatting about the town? The idea seemed far-fetched, given what she believed him to be.

If only he were sure he could trust her. But even if he did, it could be dangerous for her if he took her into his confidence.

He gave the cat a final pat and eased himself gingerly toward the side of the bed. He ached fiercely but his mind was clear and his headache was ten times better than yesterday's.

As he headed for the bathroom across the hall, he noted a plaid robe lying on the foot of the bed. He'd have preferred jeans and a shirt, but his search last night had told him there were no men's clothes in Brooke's house. The robe would have to do, and at least it meant he could rinse out his briefs.

He did that, and hung them on the shower rail. She'd left him a toothbrush, still in its wrapper, and the aspirin bottle was a welcome sight. He probed his bandages warily and concluded she'd done a good job. No heat, no swelling, probably no infection. He'd have loved a shower, the opportunity to wash his hair, but settled for wiping himself down with a washcloth and dousing his head in the sink. He toweled his hair and ran his fingers through it.

Feeling far more human, he opened the bathroom door, planning to go back to the bedroom and put on the robe.

Naked, he stepped into the hall, then stopped abruptly.

"Oh!" Brooke gasped. She'd been about to enter the bedroom, and froze in the hallway, her gaze skimming his body, then settling on his package. Color flushed her cheeks and sexual awareness surged through him. She was utterly feminine in a pink blouse and slim-fitting beige pants that revealed her curvy hips and long legs. Utterly beautiful.

He remembered the softness of her skin under his fingers, and felt himself harden. He wanted her. And, much as she might hate him, she felt it, too. There was a heat that flared between them, like nothing he'd ever experienced before. If he stepped toward her . . .

Instead he strode past her and into the bedroom, grabbed up the robe, and held it in front of him.

She gripped the door frame as if anchoring herself to it. Staring over his left shoulder, she said, "You're up."

Behind the bathrobe, he definitely was.

"How are you feeling?" she asked.

Horny. Wasn't it obvious? He took a deep breath and the pain in his side brought him to his senses. "Much better."

"Good." She bit her lip, then finally focused on his face. "I guess you don't want me to go to work today?"

"Not today. But that'll be it. I'll be gone by tomorrow." He had to be. The longer he hid out at her place, the higher the risk of discovery and the greater the danger to her.

"Yesterday afternoon my boss called and we agreed I'd take another day, so I don't spread germs to our clients."

"What kind of work do you do anyhow?" He couldn't let her know he'd searched her house and already knew where she was employed.

"I'm a beauty consultant." She cleared her throat. "I'm going to make breakfast. Can you make it downstairs?"

"Thanks, that sounds great. Yes, I'll be down in a minute."

She frowned in puzzlement and he realized too late that he was behaving out of character, being too polite. He'd done it last night, too. His only hold over her was the threat that he'd harm her family, so he had to play a believable bad guy. He'd done it undercover, many times, yet with Brooke it was far too easy to break cover.

He scowled. "Bacon and eggs. The works. Coffee, too. Lots of it."

The grooves in her forehead deepened and he barked, "Now!"

She jerked, then darted away.

Jake frowned as he pulled on the robe. He hated bullying his sexy angel of mercy.

He tried to wrap the too small robe around his body, and scowled again. He'd screwed up at the grow op and now he didn't even have a pair of pants to call his own.

He thought briefly of abandoning the whole murder side of this investigation and foisting it back on the Vancouver Police Department. But the issue had become personal and he was determined to bring Anika's killer to justice—for homicide, not just for trafficking.

When he hobbled downstairs, the smell of frying bacon and fresh coffee brought a rush of saliva to his mouth, and his spirits rose. The sight of Brooke, leaning into the fridge to find something, was pure pleasure. A guy could get used to this—if the woman's motivation was something other than fear, or marriage.

He had a habit of moving quietly and he guessed she didn't hear him until he pulled a chair out from the table, because she took a sudden leap backward, away from the fridge. She shot him a quick glance—maybe to reassure herself he was decently covered—then said, "Bacon's on. Do you want your eggs scrambled or fried?"

"Scrambled."

She poured coffee into a mug and plunked it down on the kitchen table beside a pale blue milk jug and sugar bowl.

He sat down, wincing, and picked up the coffee mug. He blew on the coffee to cool it, then took a sip. She made a mean cup of coffee.

Almost subconsciously he noted the open back door, the fresh outdoor smell that underlay the stronger ones of coffee and bacon, the twitter of birds, the cat on a windowsill. The radio played softly, apparently permanently set on that country station. A newspaper lay on the table. The *Caribou Crossing Gazette*.

As he drank his first cup of coffee, he skimmed through the paper. This place could be the model for small towns everywhere. There were a few token stories about national and international news, but the prime focus was on tourism and local personalities and events: photos and scores from a Little Britches rodeo, the event schedule for Gold Rush Days Park, a farmers' market, a huge fish some tourist from Texas had caught, kids' sports, a church bake sale on Saturday, a Heritage Committee fund-raiser at the town square.

He tensed at the sound of a car engine in the distance, then relaxed when the car drove past. He turned his attention back to the article on the fund-raiser. His quarry was reputed to be a solid citizen, so he might be attending. Might even be the chair of the committee, a man named Dave Cousins, who also owned an inn called the Wild Rose.

What identity could Jake take on that would give him an entrée to the event?

Brooke put a plate of bacon, scrambled eggs, and hash browns in front of him. She added a couple of slices of the delicious bread she'd served the previous night, toasted golden brown. "Strawberry jam? Peach? And would you like orange juice? Milk?"

"Uh . . ." So much to choose from. "Strawberry jam. And orange juice." He clamped his lips shut before he said please and thank you. "I see this place has a Heritage Committee. Folks are really into restoring the old buildings?"

She gave him a glass of juice and put a jar of jam on the table. She sat down across from him, her own plate holding only a small serving of scrambled eggs and a slice of toast. "Caribou Crossing got its start as a gold-mining town back in the 1860s. A lot of gold rush towns became ghost towns when the gold wore out, like Barkerville, but that didn't happen here. Folks got into ranching, and for well over a hundred years Caribou Crossing's had cattle, cowboys, rodeos."

While she talked, he dug into the meal she'd prepared.

"So," she went on, "we're a historic site. One of our main sources of income is tourism, with both a gold rush focus and a cowboy one. Preserving and restoring our old buildings is a matter of good business as well as community pride."

"And this guy Dave Cousins is chair of the Heritage Committee?"

She frowned suspiciously. "Why are you asking about Dave?"

"No reason."

"He's a fine man." She spread a skim of jam on her toast and bit off a corner, giving the impression she wasn't saying anything more on the subject.

Right. Cousins was just the kind of man who might be leading a double life, selling drugs on the side. Heading down to Vancouver on the pretext of hotel business, doing drug deals, frequenting prostitutes. Killing a fifteen-year-old who got in his way.

"You planning on going to the fund-raiser they're holding?" he asked.

She glanced at him nervously. "I was. I volunteered to help prepare snacks. Dave is—" Suddenly she stopped and ran a hand through her hair, messing the soft curls. "Why are you asking these questions?"

"Just making conversation."

"Don't feel you have to be polite on my account," she snapped. "I'd far rather you told me when you're planning to leave."

He squeezed his eyes shut for a moment. He needed this information, yet could understand why she didn't want to gossip about her friends and neighbors with him.

He had a decision to make and it wasn't an easy one. It went against his nature and his training to trust anyone, but the evidence, not to mention his own instincts, told him Brooke was no criminal. But if she was innocent, trusting her with the truth could mean putting her in danger. He couldn't do that.

"You are planning on leaving today, aren't you?"

He glanced up, into anxious blue-green eyes. And for a moment he saw another woman's eyes—Mrs. Janssen's brown ones, swollen and wet as she talked about her daughter, Anika. Anika, a troubled teen who'd become a hooker and ended up discarded like trash in a Dumpster.

He was an undercover cop. He relied on sources all the time. This wasn't the time to get squeamish. If Brooke was his best chance of finding Anika's killer, he had to use her. And if he did, he had to protect her.

Her cat jumped onto his knee and he stroked it, feeling the purr throb against his hand.

"Sunny! Down!" At her firm tone, the cat leaped to the floor.

"All right, John Doe. What's going on? Isn't it time I knew? You look like a member of a biker gang, you order me around at gunpoint, and yet something doesn't ring true. If you've robbed a store or you're involved in a gang war— if, as you said yesterday, someone is trying to kill you—it doesn't make sense that you're sitting here eating bacon and eggs asking about heritage buildings in Caribou Crossing."

Her ocean eyes blazed at him. "Besides," she asserted, "Sunny is a good judge of character and he approves of you."

He let out a surprised snort of laughter. Damned if he didn't like this woman, as well as want to leap her bones. He kinked an eyebrow. "You trust your cat's judgment?"

"He was an abused stray when I found him. He's learned about human nature the hard way. If he says you're all right, I'm going to listen."

An abused stray. The cat had landed on her doorstep and she'd taken it in. Yesterday, she'd done the same with him. He didn't care for the analogy. He might be injured but he was tough, independent. Not abused, and certainly not a stray. He was a pro, on a job. "I'm RCMP."

She gave him an up-down look that took in his scruffy hair and beard, the skimpy bathrobe. "And I should believe that because . . . ?"

Damn but he liked her. "I don't have ID with me. I'm undercover, out of Vancouver. You can call there and confirm I'm a member."

"Or I can have our local detachment check you out."

"No. That's why I couldn't let you call anyone. One of your members may be dirty."

Her mouth fell open. Then she crossed her arms across her chest. "I don't think so!"

He got up carefully, trying not to jar his injuries, and re-filled his coffee mug. He brought the pot over to her. "More?"

She held out her mug wordlessly—she took it black too, he noted—and he filled it. When he glanced at her face he saw her eyes do a quick skim down his naked legs, up again, then quickly away. He remembered the way she'd stared at him when he was naked. His skin heated and his body responded, as it had then. He turned away to hide his reaction.

A half loaf of that homemade bread sat on the counter, tempting him. He cut a couple of slices. "More toast?"

She took a deep breath through opened lips. The air sighed in then out again. "One slice, please."

He put the bread in the toaster and, his body under control now, turned and leaned against the counter, watching her. "We have a lead that the guy we're looking for is viewed as a respected member of the community. That could mean a cop."

"Or a banker, businessman, lawyer, doctor. A schoolteacher, for heaven's sake."

"Yeah. But maybe a cop. So I'm not about to announce my presence to them. And that's not just me talking, that's my sergeant too, and he's running this op. If I'd let you call nine-one-one yesterday, the hospital would have had to report a gunshot wound."

She nodded slowly. In understanding, not necessarily agreement, and he remembered that she read mysteries.

Outside, he heard another car engine and turned toward the open kitchen door, waiting until the vehicle drove past. The toast popped and he carried the slices to the table, putting one on each of their plates. He forked up the last of his bacon and eggs, then applied liberal portions of butter and straw-berry jam to his toast. Everything tasted wonderful. "You make the jam yourself?"

Her mouth opened and closed. "Yes, I did." She put jam on her own toast, using twice as much as before.

He had her off balance; he could read the signs. He wasn't sure which was the bigger problem: the sexual pull between them or the story he was telling. Maybe he should just clear out now. She was a recovering alcoholic. How much stress could she stand? Besides, there was the prescription bottle he'd found in her bathroom last night. For something called Eskalith. What did a person take Eskalith for? He'd planned on looking it up on the Internet if he could get logged on to her computer, but he'd collapsed before he made it that far.

She reached out to shove the jam jar away from her and gave a little groan.

"What's wrong?"

"My neck and shoulders ache. From dealing with you and your bike yesterday."

Jake couldn't resist the excuse to get up close and personal with her unique blend of femininity and strength. He went to stand behind her and rested his hands on her shoulders.

Her body jerked.

"I'm not going to hurt you. Just massage some of the aches." He began to rub and knead gently, feeling how strained and knotted her muscles were. Tension, plus the unaccustomed labor yesterday morning.

He wanted to just enjoy the sensations of touching her, but his brain produced a mental checklist for him to run through. "You said you hid the bike in a shed? It's completely out of sight?"

"Yes. In my tool shed."

She'd told him she had fixed the fence. Last night he'd found his T-shirt and jeans—clean now—cut up in a rag basket in her laundry room. She'd even washed her own clothes, the ones he'd bled on. She'd really thought of everything;

clearly those mystery novels had trained her well. Except . . . "Where's my jacket?"

Her body tensed under his hands. "It's ruined."

"Yeah, I figured. And I liked that jacket." He dug his fingers deeper into knotted muscles, feeling them relax slowly, almost grudgingly. "What I mean is, where did you put it? You didn't throw it out in the garbage, did you?" Damn, he hadn't thought to check her garbage last night.

She shook her head, her curls a soft tickle against his fingers. "I didn't put anything in the garbage. Your jacket's in the tool shed in a garbage bag, your other clothes are cleaning rags now, and I washed all the bloody cloths I used. Even the bedspread you bled on is in the dryer. The stains did come out."

"That's good." His fingers stilled momentarily as he considered how much trouble he'd caused her. "Thanks." He began to massage again. "Thanks for everything, Brooke. If it hadn't been for you . . ."

Her shoulders moved up and down under his hands in a shrug. "I'm just relieved that your pursuer didn't turn up at my door. I couldn't have handled two guns in one day."

"I'd bet you could. You could handle almost anything if you set your mind to it." God but she felt good, her body so firm and warm under the thin fabric of her blouse. He wanted to lean down and bury his face in those golden curls.

"Don't overestimate me," she murmured, arching under his hands just like her cat did when he stroked it. "Yesterday I was right on the edge, just barely hanging on."

"But you did hang on. You didn't panic. You didn't drink. You decided you needed to go to a meeting and you made me let you go. Against my better judgment."

She turned her head to the side so she could see him. There was a mischievous gleam in her blue-green eyes. "Are you saying I got the better of you?"

He chuckled. "I guess I am at that. And you didn't even need a gun to do it."

He gazed into her smiling eyes and again felt the spark flare between them. He ran a finger along the line of her jaw, then drew it across her top lip, glad she didn't wear lipstick. Those pink lips parted, to let out a little sigh. Under the bathrobe, he was hard.

The world went still as they stared into each other's eyes.

A sound broke the quiet. This time Jake hadn't even noticed engine noise, but now he definitely heard the crunch of gravel. Someone had turned into Brooke's driveway.

Chapter Six

Jake leaped past her, ignoring the stabs of pain from his injuries, barely aware that his erection was rapidly wilting. He grabbed his plate, cutlery, and mug, the only things in the room that would give him away. Where could he hide? Outside, in the tool shed she'd mentioned? But did he dare risk sprinting out the back door, when someone might at any moment walk around the side of the house?

His firearm—the one he'd found concealed in her laundry basket—was upstairs. He'd left it in her hiding spot when he came downstairs, foolishly thinking more about Brooke than about danger.

She had sprung to her feet, and their gazes locked across the table.

"I'll be in your bedroom closet," he said. "Remember, you've never seen me."

He raced for the stairs, feeling ridiculous in bare feet and her plaid robe, carrying his breakfast dishes. Upstairs, he dashed into the walk-in closet, leaving the door open a crack, and retrieved his Beretta. Now everything was in Brooke's hands.

A firm knock sounded at the front door.

He held his breath. Could he trust her? If she believed his story, she'd know the threat to her family had been pure bluff.

He should have told her all of it. About Anika's death, her parents' remorse, and the hooker who called herself Sapphire who'd told him about the marijuana grower from Caribou Crossing who'd taken Anika on her last "date."

He heard Brooke say, "Sergeant Miller? What's going on?"

The RCMP. Miller, Jake knew from research he'd done before coming here, was the commander of the local detachment. Damn it! What reason had Jake given Brooke to trust him rather than the local cops?

He heard Miller ask if he could come in. Brooke barely paused before saying, "I've got coffee on. Would you like some?"

Brooke didn't like this man. Jake could tell that from her overly polite tone. Good. It was a point in his own favor because he knew that, despite her better judgment, she was beginning to like him.

"Thanks, Ms. Kincaid, but I don't have time for anything," Miller said. "Just wanted to ask you a couple of quick questions."

"Go ahead."

What did it mean that the RCMP commander was at Brooke's door? Was Miller the man Jake sought, and using his position to track down the person who'd infiltrated his grow op?

He tightened his grip on the gun. Brooke could already be in danger.

"Guess you're in a hurry to get to work," Miller said.

"Uh, actually I'm staying home today. I wasn't feeling well yesterday. I'm a lot better now but I don't want to pass bugs on to my clients."

Jake noted that nothing she'd said was an out-and-out lie.

"So you were home all day yesterday?"

"Yes, until evening. I didn't want to miss my A.A. meeting."

Jake would bet it galled her to mention the meeting. But

in a small town her alcoholism wasn't likely to be a secret, especially from the police. Perhaps that was why she didn't like Sergeant Miller. Maybe she'd had run-ins with him in her drinking days.

"Did you hear or see anything unusual yesterday?"

"Unusual? Such as?"

Jake breathed a quiet sigh of relief. She was on his side. God knows why, but she'd decided not to turn him in.

"Didn't see any strangers passing by on the road?"

Jake tensed. Was Miller hunting for him? If so, didn't that have to mean he was dirty, involved with the grow op, maybe even the killer himself?

"I didn't notice any strangers on the road."

Despite his anxiety, Jake had to grin at that. Technically, he'd been on the shoulder, not the road itself. He'd gotten the sense yesterday that Brooke didn't like to lie, and her behavior this morning confirmed it.

"Ray Barnes rode by on his way to breakfast," she said, "and we spoke for a few minutes. We noticed a small plane flying over. Ray thought it might be the eldest Paluski boy."

A small plane? Looking for him? Had the pilot seen him, seen Brooke helping him into the house, moving the Harley? Was that why Miller was here? No, if that was the case, surely he'd have been here yesterday.

"After that I was either inside or sitting on my back porch," Brooke went on. "Why are you asking these things? What's happened?"

Jake, too, sure as hell wanted to know why Miller was there.

"There was a break-in at Patel's store. Happened early Tuesday morning."

"Oh, my. What was taken?"

"Not much. Broke a display case and got some jewelry. May have been scared off before he could get anything else."

A break-in that occurred the same night Jake was shot?

A coincidence, or was it staged? By Miller, if he was the bad guy, to give him an excuse to hunt Jake?

"He?"

"That's the most likely scenario. Couple folks said they heard a motorbike riding down the back roads near here, just around dawn. Going fast."

"Hmm. I'm not sure I'd recognize a motorcycle engine as opposed to a car. I don't recall much traffic on the road, though."

"Okay then, Ms. Kincaid, guess that'll be it. Oh, by the way, Ray Barnes said you had a little accident with your car? This'd be Monday night, same night as the break-in?"

"Oh!" For the first time she sounded flustered. "That's right. Yes, Monday, but it was early evening. I, uh, backed into my own fence and took out a couple of boards."

A lie. Her first out-and-out lie.

"How'd that happen?"

"Well now, it was so silly. I was heading to Bly Ranch for a meeting of the board for Riders Boot Camp. Anyhow, I realized I'd forgotten the pie I'd baked. I should have just parked the car on the road and walked back, but instead I decided to turn around. I misjudged the distance and clipped the fence."

"Didn't hurt yourself?"

"Oh no, I'm fine."

"Didn't notice any damage to your Toyota. Hope you don't mind, but I strolled into your carport and took a look."

He could almost hear Brooke grinding her teeth in an effort to stay polite. "No, it was just the fence that suffered."

"Saw the repair job you did on the fence. Did that yourself yesterday? When you were home sick?"

Damn, Jake thought, the man wasn't bad at all.

"I don't like leaving things undone."

But Brooke was good too. Alcoholics had experience telling lies and half-truths. He knew she hadn't lied about the board meeting, because he'd seen the agenda and her notes on her desk. Good thing, because he'd bet Miller would check that story.

"You tell your family and the rest of the board members about your little accident?"

"No. I was embarrassed and I didn't want them to worry."

"Hmm. Well, if you remember anything else, you give me a call."

"Of course. But I'd likely remember if I'd seen a man speeding by on a motorcycle."

Jake crammed his fist against his mouth to stifle a snort of laughter, then listened as they said polite good-byes. When he heard the front door close, he slipped to the bedroom window, stood to the side, and watched as the police car drove away. He stayed there for a few minutes, to make sure the sergeant didn't come back.

Boards creaked and he swung around, Beretta still clenched in his hand, as Brooke stepped into the bedroom.

Her eyes widened.

He stuffed the firearm into the pocket of her robe. "Thanks. I, uh, found my gun."

She thought about that for a moment. "Last night. That's why you were upstairs."

He nodded.

"All right, Mr. John Doe, come back downstairs and tell me the whole story. Starting with your real name."

Brooke trailed her uninvited guest as he painstakingly made his way down the stairs. She'd heard his running steps as he pounded up those stairs ten minutes ago, and guessed he was now suffering the aftereffects. She didn't know whether to feel sorry for him. She still didn't know for sure if she believed his story—or if he was simply a common criminal who had broken into Vijay Patel's gift shop and somehow gotten shot in the process. She had checked his jacket pockets when she'd hidden it in her shed; there was no loot, no ID, no nothing.

And thinking of pockets, she didn't like it that he had the gun stashed in her bathrobe pocket.

Nor did she like it that the garment looked so skimpy on him, baring expanses of virile chest and legs, reminding her of everything that lay beneath the thin flannel. He should have looked absurd in the robe, together with his beard and the hair that curled to his shoulders. Instead, he looked sexy and dangerous.

She didn't like how good his hands had felt, massaging her shoulders, touching her lip like a kiss. Nor did she like the way he could, with just one glance, make her burn for him. Nor the way her mind kept returning to the image of him as he'd emerged, naked, from the bathroom. Nor how his body, under her scrutiny, had begun to harden.

She was a grandmother, for Pete's sake. She shouldn't be having these thoughts. What was this—a second adolescence? If so, she should really worry. Just look where the first one had landed her.

Brooke grabbed the coffeepot, refilled their mugs—her third cup, and normally she only allowed herself one—and plopped down in a kitchen chair. Grimly she said, "Talk."

He sat across from her. "My name is Jake Brannon."

"Jake Brannon," she repeated, thinking that the name suited him.

"Corporal Brannon. You can call headquarters in Vancouver and ask for Sergeant Jamal Estevez—"

"Jamal Estevez?" she broke in. That name was as unusual as Mohinder McKeen, her ex's, and she guessed that it, too, had a mixed-race origin.

"Yeah, he's coordinating this op. He'll confirm my identity."

"This 'op.' The operation that has you working undercover

in Caribou Crossing hunting some man who's known as a pillar of the community. Because?"

"Because he killed a fifteen-year-old girl in Vancouver."

"Oh!" The words sent a chill through her. Could it be possible? Was one of Caribou Crossing's respected citizens a murderer? Maybe even Sergeant Henry Miller?

She'd never liked Miller—not since he'd been so snarky and suggestive to her back in her drinking days—but she couldn't imagine him murdering a girl. But then she couldn't imagine anyone in Caribou Crossing committing such a horrible act.

"Who was this girl? How would someone from Caribou Crossing be involved with a Vancouver teenager?"

"Anika, the victim, had parents who were very religious, old-fashioned, strict. She rebelled. That's normal, right? Well she got into drugs, sex, partying hard. One night she didn't come home. When she finally showed up, her parents said that if she did it again, she shouldn't bother ever coming home because she wouldn't be welcome."

Brooke thought about her own teen years. She'd been a pampered princess until she got pregnant. Her parents hadn't thrown her out then; they'd tried to fix things. "That's harsh," she said slowly, "but I guess they just wanted her to shape up."

"Yeah, well, you don't make a teenager shape up by insulting them and threatening them." Jake sounded annoyed, and Brooke wondered if it was at her or at Anika's parents.

"Anika stayed out again?" she asked.

"She ran away. To the street. She wanted to be independent, to live her own life. I can relate. Can't you?"

Sure. She'd craved excitement, asserted her independence, fallen in love with a sexy bad boy. "I suppose. But how did she survive?"

"She started out with casual jobs, waitressing and so on.

But she got pretty heavily into drugs. It was inevitable she'd end up in the sex trade, to pay for her habit."

An addict and a sex trade worker, at age fifteen. At the same age, Brooke had been married with a baby. Bad enough, stupid enough, but nothing like what had happened to Anika. Her own parents had, in their fashion, stood by her. They'd made her and Mo get married, and then they'd taken the two of them into their own home. Mo got along with her dad better than with his own; the two of them had shared more than a few beers.

Shoving away the memories, she said, "Her parents didn't report her to the police as a runaway?"

"Yeah, but the police get so many of those reports. She didn't get arrested, so she didn't come to their attention. Anyhow, she dyed her hair red, got a pimp, used the street name Foxy. Young girls are popular." He drained his coffee mug and put it down.

This sounded so far removed from the peaceful world of Caribou Crossing. Brooke had grown up in the city—in L.A., a very big city—and when she and Mo left, she'd pined for years, missing the bustle and excitement. Yet when she cleaned up her act and took charge of her life, she'd opted to stay in Caribou Crossing rather than return to city life. She had traded excitement for serenity; with her health issues, that was a necessity. Besides, she'd wanted to prove herself here, with everyone watching. In the anonymous city, it might be too easy to slip. Now, when she thought of Robin and the new grandchild growing up, she was grateful they all lived in the country.

Although, if Jake Brannon was telling the truth, Caribou Crossing wasn't the safe place she had believed it to be. She took a gulp of coffee, then realized she was getting anxious, and caffeine wouldn't help. She put her mug down and shoved it out of reach. "Go on."

"Anika's body was found in a Dumpster in Blood Alley."

She shivered. "Blood Alley?"

"It's in Gastown. Businesspeople, tourists, addicts, they all frequent it. Anika's isn't the first body to be found there. She'd been knifed savagely and either had been raped or had had rough sex before she died."

Brooke wrapped her arms around herself. "And you're investigating her death?"

"Uh, sort of. See, the police system doesn't work the same way in Vancouver as it does up here. You have your RCMP detachment and they handle everything. Vancouver has its own police force. The munis—the VPD—handle most cases, like homicide."

She nodded. "Yes, I know that from books and TV."

"Okay. So, the RCMP investigates drug crimes, illegal smuggling of aliens, national and international crime. In Vancouver we sometimes work with the munis, but off the top there wasn't any reason for us to be brought in on Anika's case. It appeared to be a straightforward murder of hooker by john."

Straightforward. Oh yes, she was glad she didn't live in the city, where such crimes were considered straightforward. "How did you get involved, then?"

"To start, I was the guy who found her."

"Oh!" She envisioned the shock of discovering a girl's body, partially clad, bloodstained, tossed in a Dumpster like rotten garbage.

"I had a meeting with a CI—a confidential informant—in Blood Alley. We finished up and I walked down the alley, heard a noise in a Dumpster, and found her."

"A noise? She was alive?"

He shook his head. "No. It was, uh, an animal."

A rat? She shuddered and wrapped her arms tighter around her body.

"Soon as I ascertained she was dead I called the munis. My part in it should've been over then. But I got drawn back in." His own coffee mug empty, he hooked Brooke's, raised it, and took a long swallow.

"How?"

"Her parents got in touch with me. They wanted to talk to the man who'd found their daughter. They felt guilty, wanted to understand what had happened."

Jake twisted the mug back and forth between his hands. "I couldn't tell them anything useful. And . . . they got to me. They'd been too strict but at least they did it because they loved their kid. They were scared by the things she was doing, the company she was keeping, and they didn't know what to do. They did the wrong thing, but at least they tried."

He swallowed hard. "When they identified her body, they barely recognized her. She'd lost twenty pounds, her hair was chopped off and dyed red with purple streaks, she had a couple tattoos and a dozen piercings. Track marks, of course. Some of the track marks and piercings were infected." He swallowed again. "Poor kid was HIV positive, but that information wasn't disclosed to her parents."

"They'll never forgive themselves," Brooke said, knowing it for a certainty. The damage she'd done Evan was different, but never would she forgive the woman she'd once been. Guilt. It never died. You just learned how to move past it, if you were lucky.

"They made their mistakes because they loved her," Jake said again, "and some bastard sliced her up and threw her away like last night's garbage. It isn't right that he get away with it."

"No, it's not." She studied his troubled face. "You must have seen a number of murders. What's different about this one?"

"I found her body, and she was so young, and her parents are so . . . tormented."

This man might superficially remind her of Mo, but in fact he was very different.

As if to reinforce her perception, Sunny jumped down from the windowsill, strolled across the floor, and leaped casually into Jake's lap. Jake scratched him under the chin. The cat slitted his eyes and began to purr.

Jake Brannon had Mo's striking good looks and his sexual magnetism, yet he seemed like a decent man. As his long fingers caressed the cat's fur, she thought of them on her shoulders, imagined them on her breasts.

No, it was impossible. There might be chemistry between them but that's all it would ever be. He was younger than she, plus he was a cop with a high-risk job in Vancouver. And she, for heaven's sake, was a grandmother. And an alcoholic with bipolar disorder. She needed stability, not some crazy fling with a—

His voice interrupted her train of thought. "So I started asking around, just casually, while I was working other cases. Turned out one of my CIs, a hooker not much older than Anika, knew her pretty well."

"You've got an informant who's a teenage hooker?"

"I'd seen her on the street. Then she got pulled in when she went after some drunk who attacked another hooker, stopped the guy from beating her up. She's a good kid. Lots of street smarts. Smokes a little weed but stays away from the hard stuff. Anyhow, Jamal and I had a talk with her, and she's worked with us for over a year. She's come up with some good tips."

"Isn't it dangerous having a prostitute who knows your identity? I mean, if you're working undercover? She could, uh, blow your cover."

"Jamal and I don't do much U/C in Vancouver. Mostly, we get sent other places."

She tried for a moment to imagine his life, but it was impossible.

"Anyhow," he was saying, "Sapphire's reliable."

"That's an unusual name."

"Street name. Won't tell us her real name, where she's from. Little idiot. She's got so much going for her, she could make it in school, get decent work."

She could hear in his voice how much he'd like to get Sapphire off the street. "What about the files on runaway children? You might find Sapphire there."

"Tried that. No luck. There are just so damned many runaways. Lots don't even get reported. They leave foster homes, group homes, parents who abuse them or don't give a damn. What Sapphire's running from is probably as bad or worse than what she's found. Besides, like I said, she's one of the smart ones. She's saving money rather than spending it on drugs. She's savvy about screening johns, insists on condoms, won't go near a needle."

She nodded sadly. "What did she tell you about Anika?"

"The night before Anika died, her pimp sent her on a date with a john who wanted a young girl for the whole night. The next day, Anika was badly bruised, but she played tough. Told Sapphire it was no big deal, the guy had paid well, he had some great dope, and he wanted to see her again that night. That was the night she died. I'm betting that john killed her."

"It sounds like it."

"Anyhow, the guy had given Anika some primo BC Bud and—"

"BC Bud?" Brooke broke in. "Marijuana?"

"Yeah. Anyhow, on Saturday afternoon she and Sapphire smoked some of the stuff. Anika more than Sapphire because Sapphire says too much makes her mind fuzzy and she doesn't like that. It makes her careless. Well, it made Anika talkative and she said some things about the john. She knew he was a grower right off 'cause he was boasting about 'his weed' being better than anyone else's."

Brooke tried for a moment to imagine Anika's world, then decided she didn't want to.

"Some other guy came to his hotel room," Jake continued. "Anika never said which hotel, by the way. She got shoved into the bathroom. She didn't really care—she had a joint to keep her company—but she did overhear some bits of conversation. Enough to realize the two guys were arguing. She figured her john normally sold to the other guy but he—her guy—was trying to get out of their deal. Said he'd do better selling directly into the States himself. Boasted about how he'd done it before. The other guy said they've really cracked down at the border and there've been a lot of busts, but Anika's john just laughed and said he'd have no problem."

"If he was wearing an RCMP uniform, driving an RCMP vehicle, he wouldn't. Is that what you're thinking?"

"It's a possibility. Or if he was a businessman or professional with a legitimate business reason for crossing the border. They've busted trucks purportedly carrying pure water, beer, recycled paper, so there are no guarantees, but if he had a NEXUS card, drove a regular car, and had a briefcase full of professional papers, chances are he could smuggle a trunkload at a time."

"All right, so the john was a drug dealer. Why kill Anika?"

"Maybe he figured she'd heard too much. Or he's just one sick dude who gets his kicks that way."

Brooke shuddered yet again. After a moment she said, "What made you think the man came from Caribou Crossing?"

"He was drinking some fancy rye called Caribou Crossing and offered Anika a drink. She tasted it and said it was too strong for her. He said, 'Don't dump on my hometown drink.'"

"He didn't seem worried about her finding out where he came from."

"He'd been drinking, smoking dope with her. Maybe it just slipped out, and he realized later and decided to kill her."

"So you're looking for a man from Caribou Crossing who drinks rye by the same name, and travels to the States on business."

"And is a pillar of the community. Anika overheard some joke about that. Along the lines of 'What would the folks back home think if they knew the truth?' "

"Didn't Sapphire report all this to the Vancouver police?"

"No. They've picked her up for soliciting. She doesn't trust them."

Brooke could identify with not wanting to talk to the police. But it was interesting that the girl, knowing Jake was RCMP, had trusted him. So did Sunny.

Brooke wanted to trust him too, but she wasn't that naïve. Before she phoned to check him out, there was one other thing she was curious about. "You didn't pass Sapphire's information along to the police?"

"I did. Without naming her, or I'd lose her as a CI. I talked to Jamal first, and then we went to the officer in charge of Anika's case and told him there appeared to be a drug connection. So, we're working together on this. The munis are handling the investigation in Vancouver, and Jamal and I are dealing with the Caribou Crossing end. We figured the best way to start was for one guy—me—to come in U/C. Normally we'd work with the local RCMP, but obviously that's not an option. In fact, if I get any hard evidence that Miller or one of the other members is crooked, Jamal'll probably have to hand it over to Internal Affairs and they'll take it from there."

"But you'd rather handle it yourself."

"Don't want to damage anyone's reputation unless I'm sure. And . . . yeah, I'd like to nail Anika's killer myself. Internal investigations can go on forever."

Brooke nodded, then walked over to the phone that sat on

the kitchen counter. "Your sergeant in Vancouver is Jamal Estevez?"

"Yeah. And the number is—"

"No, thanks. I'll get it from directory assistance."

He nodded, seeming to approve of her caution. As she dialed she watched his hands. Would he go for the gun and stop her?

Chapter Seven

No, Jake just continued to stroke her cat.

Sergeant Jamal Estevez had a deep, reassuring voice, and everything he said confirmed Jake's story.

"I need to talk to him," Jake told her.

She handed the phone over.

It was true. He was RCMP. Which meant her family was safe. He'd only threatened them as a means of controlling her, until he knew whether he could trust her. Anger sparked first, but then relief washed through her, weakening her knees. She sank into a chair.

"Yeah, I found the op," Jake was saying to Jamal Estevez. "Rented a Cessna and scouted around at dusk and dawn, found a bunch of trailers that looked suspicious." He glanced at Brooke, and she had the feeling he was talking to her as much as to the sergeant.

She listened as he concisely related how he'd located the grow op, snuck in, then had the bad luck to run into a squeaky door and a man with a gun. Now she knew where the bullet wound had come from.

"Nah, I'm fine," he said into the phone. "Brooke's a good nurse." His eyes widened momentarily; then he quickly said, "Oh, I didn't tell you. I missed a turn on my bike and ended up in her yard. She's my safe house. This morning I decided to tell her the story. Seems like a trustworthy lady."

His face muscles were taut and Brooke had a revelation. Not only had he found the gun last night, he'd reported in to Jamal and asked him to check her out. When he looked at her again, she scowled.

Jake raised his eyebrows in a question, and she turned her back on him and began to tidy the kitchen. He kept talking to Jamal—or, rather, listening. She heard him say "Uh-huh" a couple of times and guessed Jamal was telling him her life story, or at least as much of it as the RCMP could access. Feeling annoyed and vulnerable, she turned on the tap and started to rinse dishes and load the dishwasher.

When she finished, Jake was saying, "Well damn, a stolen license plate, eh? Okay, here's something else to check. Brooke got a visit from the local commander, Sergeant Miller. He had some cock-and-bull story about a break-in at a local store and the perp escaping on motorbike. So either Miller's been fed a line of bull or he's spun the tale himself. Don't like to think that, but it's suspicious that he'd be doing the ground-level investigation himself rather than sending a constable."

He paused. "Yeah, let me know if the store was really broken into. Oh, and someone was flying around in a little plane yesterday morning. Might have been looking for me. Should check flight plans at the airports."

The little plane. It had never occurred to her. . . . She turned back to Jake and touched his arm to get his attention. "The plane was around for quite a while. When I was mending the fence it was circling down south—too far away to see me. Then when I was talking to my neighbor—the one who rode by?—it was overhead."

Jake repeated the information to Jamal, listened for a moment, then said to Brooke, "What's the store that was allegedly broken into?"

"Vijay Patel's gift shop. It's called Gifts of the Caribou."

He repeated the information to Jamal, listened, then turned to Brooke again. "We need to know who owns the land where they're running the grow op. I was on a road called Pike, about an hour southwest of here, and turned off onto a dirt road that didn't have a name marker. It twisted through some woods, up through some hills. I followed it about five miles before I hit the grow op. Any idea who might own that land?"

"I've never even heard of Pike Road."

"She doesn't know," he said into the phone, then gave the coordinates of the grow op.

She thought again about the story, the parts he'd told her and the parts she was piecing together from his phone conversation with Jamal. "Can't you just—" She was thinking out loud, but broke off when Jake turned to her and asked, "What?"

She shrugged apologetically. "Raid the grow op? Shut it down?"

"Not good enough. The man we want probably isn't there. The workers would just be his flunkies."

"But they'd know who he is."

"Not necessarily. He's probably got illegal immigrants hidden up there, working the op. They may never have seen him or heard his name. Even if they know him, and are willing to cop a deal and identify him, we'd only get him for drugs. I want him for murder."

He was right, and she felt naïve.

Then he said to her, "The names Herb and Jango ring any bells?"

"Jango. There was an aging hippie by that name who used to live out in the hills and grow his own marijuana. Just for personal use, I'm pretty sure. He'd come into town every week or so to get supplies, and he reeked of dope. But not a bad guy. He belonged to the Marijuana Party and believed marijuana should be legalized. He had a pal, another guy like him, whose name might have been Herb."

"What happened to them?"

"I don't know. They haven't been around for a year or two."

Jake related the information to Jamal. "Our perp may have set these old boys up with a fancy operation in the hills, kept them happy with BC Bud, brought supplies out to them. Told them to stay away from town."

He listened for a moment. "Next thing we need to do is work out a new cover for me."

"Ditch the beard and long hair," she muttered.

"Just a sec," Jake said into the phone. Then, to her, "What?"

Oops, she should probably keep her mouth shut. "Nothing."

"Tell me what you said." He sounded exasperated.

"If you want to mingle with pillars of the community, go for clean-shaven and short-haired. Besides, if whoever shot at you got any kind of look, they'll be expecting long hair."

"Let me call you back," Jake said to Jamal, and hung up the phone.

He leaned back in his chair and studied Brooke. "They saw me from the back. Hair, not face. So, do you cut men's hair or just women's?"

"Of course I cut men's hair. I can transform you. Add . . . oh, a conservative suit and tie, maybe a pair of wire-rimmed glasses." She studied him—the animal vitality that was so distinct even when he wore a woman's bathrobe. "You should carry yourself differently, though. Try not to look so . . . masculine."

He flashed a grin that stole her breath. "What are you making me into?"

"Well, let's think about it. What would make you seem the most harmless?"

She studied him, wondering if harmless was possible. Then she had a brilliant idea. "You need an introduction from someone in town who vouches for you. So you're not really a stranger." This was actually kind of exciting. Again she was in a mystery novel, but now that the danger had passed she was having fun.

"True. But the only person I know is you, and I'm not putting you on the line."

She was relieved and insulted all at once. Insult won out. "Ever since I met you, you've been ordering me around. Where do you get off, making decisions for me?"

"This one's for your own protection."

To protect her, he'd take more risk upon himself. She should let him. It was his job, after all. The last thing she was was a risk taker. Yet she knew Caribou Crossing and he didn't. Without her, the danger to him would be greater.

This was about more than playing mystery novel; she actually cared about this man's safety. Enough to risk her own.

Or maybe she was doing it for the poor dead girl and her parents. Was this some kind of atonement for her own flaws as a mother?

Oh well, whatever her motives, she felt a strong sense of purpose. "We need a story that will let you carry out your investigation without casting suspicion on either of us."

"I won't let you do it."

She ground her teeth together. Why would she want to help such an obnoxious man? "Let's brainstorm then," she proposed, "and see what we come up with."

"You know Caribou Crossing," he admitted. "I'd appreciate your insight."

Accepting that minor concession, she leaned her elbows on the table. "You're limping and wincing so do we need to build some kind of accident into the story?"

He shook his head firmly. "By tomorrow no one will be able to tell I'm injured. Not when I'm dressed, anyhow." He gave her a wicked, slanting look.

She tried very hard to imagine him dressed, from buttoned-up collar down to socks and shoes. The standard advice for when you were nervous around other people was to imagine them in their underwear. With Jake, it was much better for her peace of mind if she imagined him dressed.

The phone rang. She raised an eyebrow and Jake said, "Answer it. But be careful."

It was Evan, who'd heard through the grapevine that she was under the weather. How amazing this was, having a son who was concerned about her health. "I'm feeling much better," she reassured him. "I'm staying home today, just to be safe."

"Need anything? I'd be happy to pop by."

"No, but thanks. And I'll be back to work tomorrow."

"In that case, how about coming over for dinner tomorrow, to celebrate the upcoming addition to the family?"

"Dinner tomorrow?" Brooke glanced at Jake, who raised his eyebrows questioningly. Thinking that this could be an opportunity to try out whatever cover story they designed, she said to her son, "Can I wait and see how I feel in the morning? With Jessica pregnant, I don't want to bring any bugs into your house."

"Sure. And if you feel up to it, come early and have a short ride with Rob. She loves going out with you."

"I love it, too." Despite living in ranch country, Brooke had never been on a horse until last fall, when Jess's daughter had wheedled her into trying it. Now, one of her favorite things was going for a ride with her granddaughter. "I'll call in the morning."

"My son," she told Jake after hanging up. Her new closeness with Evan still felt like an unexpected and undeserved gift.

Returning to business, she planted both elbows on the table and stared at Jake. "All right, let's give it our best shot. What's a healthy guy your age doing showing up in Caribou Crossing right now? A tourist? An unemployed person looking for work? Maybe a lawyer wanting to set up a small-town practice?" She nodded. "I like that. It would give you a reason to talk to lots of people in town."

"Yeah, but a lawyer might be too threatening to the man I'm hunting."

"Right. We want inoffensive. Innocuous. An accountant?" Then she shook her head. "No, you probably don't have any experience with accounting. You're more of an action guy, right?"

"Yeah, I like the action part of the job. The danger, the risk. But I've got a knack for figures. Sometimes I get stuck on that kind of U/C job. White-collar stuff," he added with a touch of disdain.

"And instead you'd rather be . . . hmm, let me see . . . undercover as a drug-dealing member of a biker gang?"

"Well, yeah." He gave a shrug remarkably similar to Robin's "well, duh" one.

Brooke promptly decided to turn him into an accountant. "You know, the accountant cover could really work. We've only had three accountants, and one of them, Ellen Christiansen, just folded her practice and retired to Victoria with her husband."

"How did I hear about the job possibility? Did she advertise her practice for sale?"

"No. The only way you'd have heard is through a contact. We're back to you knowing someone, which means me."

"I could say I know Ellen."

She shook her head. "Her daughter lives in town and she talks to Ellen regularly. What about this? You're my cousin. We used to play together as kids." She shook her head again. "No, you're too young. How old are you anyhow?"

"Thirty-five."

Eight years younger. Young, handsome, sexy, addicted to danger. She shouldn't be attracted to him. "I used to baby-sit you," she said grimly.

"Mmm, every boy needs a sexy baby-sitter." He sent her another of the heated gazes that made her body tingle.

She tried to ignore the distraction. "Look, I had this cousin about your age back in L.A. My dad's brother's son. His father was killed in a car accident and his mom had a job. I baby-sat him and his sister after school and sometimes on weekends. Then his mom remarried and the family moved away. So, let's say you're him. We'll say your mother's new husband was Canadian, and your family moved to Vancouver. You grew up, studied accounting . . ."

She snapped her fingers. "Try this. You work for a big firm, but recently you've been thinking you'd like to get out of the rat race, be your own boss. When Ellen left last month, I thought of you and gave you a call."

"A cousin whom you've never mentioned to your son?" he asked skeptically.

"We haven't seen each other in ages, and just keep in touch with Christmas cards each year," she said triumphantly. "Last Christmas, you mentioned that you were thinking of making a change, so when Ellen left I let you know there was work here for an accountant. You decided to come up and check things out. To see if you'd like to live here." She was on a roll and could feel the energy flowing through her veins.

It was kind of like the manic cycles of her bipolar.

The thought was like a slap in the face.

"You're good at this. It could work," he said grudgingly. "I'd have more credibility with you to vouch for me, but I'm not happy about letting you do it." He studied her closely. "And you're nervous, too. You've gone pale."

"I . . ." She pressed her hands to her cheeks and rubbed color into them. The lithium worked, she reminded herself. Natural energy was a different thing from mania. "I'm fine. Too much caffeine."

"No such thing." He got up to refill his mug again, frowning when the carafe yielded only a couple of spoonfuls of brew. After drinking them thirstily, he thrust the mug under the water tap and filled it up. He came over to rest a hand on her shoulder. "I can't let you do it."

She, not he, was in control of her life and made her decisions. She scowled up at him. "Do you want to catch Anika's killer?"

His hand dropped, his jaw tightened, and he nodded.

"Well, so do I." And she'd enjoyed the last few minutes, planning and working with him as if they were partners.

Jake studied her face again and must have seen her determination because he gave a resigned nod. "So be it. But we'll be very, very careful."

As he had read her face, she read his voice. He hated the idea of having to be careful, of needing to look after her. Well, he'd just have to live with it, because he needed her.

"Jamal will build me a solid cover story," he said, "in case anyone checks me out."

She tilted her head to one side. "He's your boss?"

Jake winced slightly. "Sort of. We've known each other since we both signed on more than ten years ago. Had the same goal—to fast-track through the grind and get into U/C work. We worked together more than a few times. Make a good team."

"He was your partner before he was promoted?" She wondered why Jamal, not Jake, had been given a higher rank.

"U/Cs don't have partners, but yeah, sometimes we'd be part of the same team. Still works that way, except now he's the guy who coordinates the operation. He's good. Damned good."

She could well imagine the strong bond that could develop between people who risked their lives together. Undercover, in enemy territory with no one to trust but the other members of their team.

Jake reached for her hand. "You asked me my name but you've never used it. Say my name, Brooke."

Her hand jerked under his but she didn't withdraw it. "Jake." She said it softly and it tasted fine on her lips.

He squeezed her hand. "I'll keep you safe. I promise you that." His smoky eyes peered intently into hers and she read his sincerity.

"I believe you, Jake."

"We'll work on the cover story together, until we're both letter perfect."

She nodded.

"And I won't leave you alone. It's logical that you'd invite your cousin to stay with you, right?"

"You want to stay here?"

"To keep you safe."

Safe. How could she feel safe with all that virile masculinity sharing her home?

Standing in front of Brooke's full-length mirror, Jake assessed her handiwork.

He was clean-shaven and his wavy hair was trimmed so short it didn't curl. The gray suit added to the image of respectability, along with the pale yellow shirt and the tie striped in charcoal and yellow. So did the prissy gold-wire glasses. Yeah, he could pass for an accountant. As long as he left the Beretta behind.

Brooke, disguised in her oldest clothes with a cap covering her blond hair, had gone shopping in Williams Lake, a fair-sized city an hour and a half away. She assured him she'd seen no one she knew as she purchased men's clothing, accessories, and toiletries.

While she'd been gone he had spent the time resting, on the phone with Jamal, or doing research on Brooke's computer.

One portion of that research still haunted him. Eskalith, Brooke's prescription drug, was lithium. Commonly used for treating bipolar disorder, also called manic-depressive illness.

Not only was Brooke a recovering alcoholic, she had a mental illness.

In his Internet search, he had found that many victims of the disease responded very well to medication. His eyes had widened as he'd scanned a list of famous people who were bipolar. Yeah, some people functioned extremely well. His gaze had caught on the name Patty Duke. He'd seen a book coauthored by her on Brooke's shelf.

While she was still out shopping, he'd skimmed through the book, whose other coauthor was a medical writer. It was enlightening, but he had trouble relating some of what he read—particularly Patty Duke's descriptions of mania—with what he knew of Brooke.

When Jake had heard a car engine and looked out the window to see Brooke's Toyota, he had hurriedly returned the book to the shelf. The disease was her secret and he wouldn't confront her. But he shouldn't involve her in his investigation. She was too fragile.

It had been difficult, though, to reconcile his image of fragility with the vibrant woman who'd unloaded her packages on the living room table as she'd chattered about her shopping expedition, and tossed out new ideas she'd come up with for his cover.

And he'd realized something. Illnesses weren't the same thing as weaknesses, and the way she coped with her alcoholism and bipolar disorder was a testament to her strength. So he'd gone along with her and let her transform him. Now he was Arnold Pitt.

He assumed that when Pitt had been a kid his nickname would have been Armpit. When he'd said that to Brooke, he'd won himself a laugh. The first laugh he'd heard from her. It made him want more.

It made him want to know this woman in different circumstances. As his body healed, it got harder and harder to resist his attraction to her. Grandmother she might be, victim of two serious diseases, but she was also a dynamite woman with her bouncy hair, slim curves, and iron will.

She'd bought him a razor, a comb, deodorant. She hadn't bought condoms. He knew, from searching her house, that she wasn't on the pill and didn't have any other contraceptive devices. Just as well. His life was complicated enough without sleeping with Brooke, even if she'd let him.

She entered the bedroom and he turned to her. "Will I pass?"

She patted him on the shoulder approvingly. "You look just fine, Arnold. You've stopped looking like Rambo."

"Look like a wimp," he grumbled.

"That's what we're aiming for, right? The opposite of your previous look."

Look? Only a woman would call an undercover disguise a "look." "Well, it beats the bathrobe." He winked at her, knowing her cheeks would color. He'd grown kind of attached to that old bathrobe, particularly when he noticed how she couldn't seem to look away from the bits of naked flesh it revealed.

Maybe she *would* let him sleep with her.

Not that he was going to try. Well, probably not.

"Can I get out of these clothes now?" He hooked a finger into the knot of the tie and pulled it loose.

"Of course. That's why I bought casual clothes for Arnold."

He took off the suit jacket and began to unbutton the neck of his shirt. Her gaze followed his fingers. He liked the way she watched him; he liked the fizz of awareness in the air between them. He shouldn't wish that one of these days he'd get to see her take off her clothes. Or, better still, do it for her.

He was down to the fourth button when the phone rang. They both jumped.

She scurried across the bedroom and grabbed the handset

from the bedside table. "Oh, Jess, I'm glad you called." She sank down on the side of the bed, sitting on the freshly cleaned quilt. "I was going to give you folks a call this evening." Her gaze met his and he nodded to let her know he realized she was talking to her daughter-in-law. The "cousin" story was about to get its first test.

He kept unbuttoning his shirt, then pulled it out of his pants, noting that Brooke was still watching. Awkwardly he peeled the shirt off without hurting his side too badly. He hung the garment neatly on the back of the chair and put the annoying glasses on the bureau.

Jess had obviously asked Brooke how she was feeling; she replied that she'd definitely kicked the bug. In turn, she asked about Jess's health, then listened, making "uh-huh" sounds.

Time to have some real fun with Brooke. To gauge the likelihood she'd let him sleep with her. Just in the interests of science. He whipped his belt through the loops and watched her eyes widen.

Chapter Eight

Brooke was saying to Jessica, "I have a surprise. Did I ever mention my cousin Arnold?"

He unbuttoned his pants.

Her gaze slid away then, under lowered eyelashes, returned. "Oh, I didn't? Well, when I was a girl in L.A. I used to baby-sit him."

She stuck her tongue out at Jake and he gave a surprised grin. Now she made no bones about watching as he slid his zipper down. He liked this bold, playful mood of hers.

"He was a sweet little boy. An egghead. Wimpy little kid."

He barely suppressed his laugh. He toed off the leather loafers she'd bought and slid his pants down, removed them and his socks at the same time.

"Anyhow," Brooke said, "he's an accountant in Vancouver and we exchange Christmas cards. He said he was thinking of making a change, starting his own practice in a small town, and I thought of—"

She broke off, apparently interrupted by Jessica—or, he'd like to think, struck dumb by the sight of him in his boxer briefs. Black ones she'd bought, the same brand he normally wore.

"Yes, that was exactly my thought. I've heard a number of

people say how much they miss Ellen. So I mentioned it to him and he's driving up tomorrow. He's going to stay a few days and check out the town, see if it's a place he might want to live."

He had to get back at her for that "wimpy" crack. He stretched his shoulders, then craned to check the dressing on his side, twisting his hips in her direction.

"Hmm?" she said distractedly, her gaze following his every movement. He hadn't proved whether she'd go to bed with him, but he knew she liked his body.

He slid down the right side of his briefs and checked the bandage on his hip. When he looked back at Brooke, her cheeks were even rosier.

"Oh, he'll stay with me. It'll give us a chance to catch up on old times." She ran her tongue around the outside of her lips. Not nervously but deliberately. "And get to know each other again." She'd turned the game back on him.

He didn't know if she was just messing with him, or sending an invitation, but his body responded and his underwear began to feel too tight. He should turn away but he didn't. He wanted her to know the effect she had on him. And he wanted to see if she'd look away.

She raised a hand and toyed with a curl of hair, twisting it around her finger as she held the phone to her other ear. But she kept her eyes on him. "Dinner tomorrow would be lovely. Arnold would love to meet all of you."

Under her gaze, he was growing harder and harder.

She covered the receiver with her hand and swallowed, a loud, gulping sound, but she didn't look away. "No," she said distractedly into the phone, "no riding this time. But soon." A soft chuckle. "Oh, I don't think Arnold's the horsy sort."

Jessica said something that made Brooke laugh. "Yes, you did convert Evan, so anything's possible."

He had to touch her. He strolled toward the bed. Her eyes

grew rounder as he approached, but she didn't move. He stopped a foot away from where she sat.

Her gaze focused on his groin, then lifted to his face. Hurriedly she said, "Fine then, we'll be over about five-thirty. See you then." She put the phone down, her hand shaking. "Jake?" The word was a breathy sigh.

"Brooke." He gripped her shoulders, pulled her up to stand in front of him.

"I . . . I'm a grandmother," she blurted out.

He gaped, then threw back his head and laughed. "What's that got to do with anything?"

"How can you be . . . turned on by a grandmother? I'm older than you."

"Do I look like I care?"

"I . . ." Her forehead creased. "Do you have a thing for older women?"

He laughed again. "I have a thing for you, Brooke Kincaid. This thing." And he pulled her flush against his body, letting her feel the full strength of his desire.

She gasped, her body tensed, and then she began to melt against him.

He loosened his grip on her shoulders so he could wrap his arms around her.

She tensed again and leaped away. "No!" In a flash she disappeared out the door.

Jake let out a groan of pure frustration. "Down, boy," he muttered. She was right, though. Mixing pleasure with business wasn't the smartest move.

He hung up his discarded clothing in Brooke's closet. She had insisted on giving him her own bedroom, pointing out that the bed in the other room—her granddaughter's room—was too short and narrow for him.

Brooke would sleep there herself. Just across the hall. And they'd share a bathroom. How would he—how would they—survive the proximity?

He tried to turn his mind to business and review the plan they'd developed. Jamal was arranging for a car with plates registered to Arnold Pitt and a wallet full of fake ID. He'd drive up to deliver it, so the two of them could confer in person. Tomorrow at lunch, Brooke would sneak Jake out to meet Jamal at an isolated spot called Zephyr Lake. An hour or two later, Arnold would officially arrive in town, at the beauty salon where she worked. She'd give him her spare key and directions to find her house. They would have dinner with her son and his family.

They had their work cut out for themselves tonight, as he boned up on Arnold's family history and the news he and Brooke might have exchanged over the years.

He surveyed the clothes she'd bought, and chose neatly pressed khakis and a crocodiled golf shirt. Gag. He wanted well-washed jeans and a T-shirt, but she hadn't bought that kind of clothing for Arnold. Even in his leisure hours, Arnold was a neat-freak.

He was tempted to leave the glasses lying on her bureau, but he should get in the habit of wearing them. If they left his nose, someone might pick them up and realize they weren't prescription lenses.

Pleased at how quickly his body was healing, he sauntered downstairs. There was something to be said for rest. Normally, when he was injured, he was back on the job immediately and it took him longer to recover. He began to whistle now, some made-up melody.

A delicious smell drew him to the kitchen, where Brooke turned from stirring something in a pan on the stove. "Jake—"

He didn't want to rehash being rejected. Quickly he said, "Arnold. How do I look?"

"Very Arnoldy." She managed a smile. "But are you sure Arnold whistles?" Good, she wasn't going to mention the scene upstairs.

"It's his one vice. A guy can't be serious all the time."

"I suppose not."

"Something smells great. Chicken?"

"Yes, it's chicken paprikash. It has paprika and cayenne. I hope it's not too adventurous for you, Arnold."

"I hate that name. You know that, don't you?"

She laughed—a genuine one—and his heart jumped. "I know you do. That's what's so great about it. It's so unlike the real you. Unlike Jake."

He liked the way she said Jake. He'd like it a lot if she'd say something like, "Why don't we go to bed now, Jake?"

Instead she said, "Sit down. You're still an invalid."

"I'm fine."

"Then you can make salad." She pointed to a basket on the counter. "There's early lettuce, radishes, and herbs from the garden, and tomatoes and cucumbers in the fridge."

The lettuce was dark green and leafy, and the radishes were pink and white with dirt clinging to their roots. He washed the vegetables, then began to rip lettuce into a ceramic bowl Brooke had placed on the counter.

The kitchen table was set for two, the cat dozed on a braided rug in the corner, and Brooke had just put a pot of water on to boil. Now, she was assembling oil, vinegar, and herbs on the counter, to mix her own salad dressing, he figured.

He'd had more domesticity since he met this woman than he could remember in years. "You like gardening?" he asked.

"It's satisfying. Orderly, productive, and economical." She handed him a couple of tomatoes, half a cucumber, and a wicked-looking knife.

"And you make jam."

"And I can fruit and freeze vegetables. I make tomato sauce, chutney, sweet corn relish."

"All that domestic stuff." He guessed this stuff was new since her drinking days.

"Yes. It probably seems trivial to you, but I enjoy it. It keeps me busy; it's good exercise. I eat well and I make nice things to share with my family." She sounded a touch defensive.

"I'm not putting you down, Brooke. It's good to find the things we enjoy."

She dropped dried noodles into the now-boiling water. "How about you? What do you enjoy? What are your hobbies?"

"Work takes up most of my time. But I like it."

"Bringing criminals to justice." Now she was stirring flour into a measuring cup with sour cream in it. She clearly wasn't, like so many women, obsessive about calories. Another thing to like about her.

He tossed tomato and radish slices into the salad bowl, and began to cut cucumber. "Yeah. But I also like the excitement, the danger. It gets my adrenaline flowing."

She tilted her head and studied him from where she stood by the stove, stirring the sour cream blend into the pan of chicken. "The people who care about you must worry."

"There's no one. My life doesn't allow for that kind of relationship."

"Your life or your job?"

"One and the same."

"Hmm. So there's no special woman?"

He gave a quick laugh. "I'm not into relationships. Just casual, short-term stuff. I'm up front about it." Maybe that was why Brooke had run away, up in the bedroom. It was pretty obvious what kind of guy he was. Just as obvious as her white picket fence and domesticity.

"What about your parents?" she asked. "Siblings?"

"No siblings and I haven't seen my parents in a long time. They hate what I'm doing." He was tired of having Brooke probe into his life. It wasn't that he didn't like the spark of interest, the hint of concern in her eyes, but he knew he'd only disappoint her. She wanted him to be some noble crusader, and in fact he was just a loser kid who'd been lucky enough to be set on the right course and find a job where he could do some good yet still indulge the daredevil inside him.

"What about you?" he asked, watching as she shook the oil and vinegar dressing and drizzled it over the salad.

"Parents and one sister. We're barely in touch." She put the salad bowl on the table, then drained the noodles. "I guess you'll have to know some of the family background," she said reluctantly. She dumped the noodles in the middle of a platter, then topped them with pieces of chicken coated in a pale orange sauce thick with chunks of onion.

He took the platter to the table, sniffing appreciatively as his stomach growled.

Brooke put her hand on the fridge door. "Would you like a beer?"

"Beer? Thought you didn't keep alcohol in the house."

"I bought some today."

Was this some kind of test? "I don't need to drink."

"Well, that's good news," she said dryly. "But I don't mind if you do. I'm not so weak willed I'm going to grab a beer bottle out of your hand."

"Are you sure?"

She huffed out a sigh. "I wouldn't have offered if I wasn't sure."

He figured it'd be an insult if he didn't take her at her word. "Thanks, I'd love a beer."

She opened the fridge, took out a bottle, and handed it to him. "Glass?"

"Nope."

"Of course not. But when you're being Arnold, I'd advise you to drink from a glass."

She poured mineral water from a bottle into a glass, dropped in a slice of lime, and gestured him over to the table. "Let's dig in. And I'll tell you about my family."

They sat across from each other and served themselves.

When he tasted the chicken, he almost moaned. "This is great. You're sure a good cook. Did you learn from your mom?"

She gave a rueful grin. "What a subtle way of easing me into the story. No, I only got into cooking in the last few years. Once I was sober."

He nodded in acknowledgment of what he'd suspected.

She sighed. "All right, my family. My parents were traditional. Dad worked, came home, drank pretty heavily, watched sports on TV. He might have been an alcoholic, but if so he was a quiet one. Mom was a housewife and she was pretty low key. In these days, we'd probably say she suffered from depression."

His afternoon's reading had told him that bipolar disorder could run in families, and was often associated with alcohol or drug abuse. The deck might have been stacked against Brooke from the beginning—in terms of both genetics and environment. And then she'd gotten pregnant in her teens and married a guy who drank. What a life she'd had.

"But on the whole, I was lucky." Her words were such a contrast to his thoughts. "My parents loved me, Erin wasn't too bad for a kid sister, I had pretty clothes, lots of friends, enough pocket money to buy lip gloss and go to the movies. Cousins to hang out with—and that's where you come in."

"Arnold was your dad's brother's kid, and he had a sister?"

She swallowed a bite of chicken. "Good memory. I guess that's crucial in your job. Yes, Arnold was the youngest child of my father's brother, Mark. His wife was Becky. Uncle Mark died, leaving Aunt Becky with three kids to look after, Arnold being the baby. There was an athletic older brother, about my age but too jockish and boring to interest me, then a cute, outgoing sister a couple of years older than you. You were the quiet, well-behaved one."

He snorted. "Oh yeah, that sounds like me."

"It sounds like Arnold."

"Fair enough."

"Anyhow, when Arnold was nine or so, Aunt Becky married Peter Pitt and they moved away. Our families didn't stay in touch."

"Okay." He reflected. "We'll go through the names, ages, other details later. So, Cousin Brooke baby-sat Arnold and his sister?" He sipped his beer, which went perfectly with the spicy chicken.

"Yes, to make money to buy clothes, music, magazines, make-up. I liked Arnold." She gave him a teasing grin. "You were a funny little kid, but kind of cute."

He made a face at her, and she laughed.

"What did you talk about when you were baby-sitting us?" he asked. "Boys?"

"One special boy," she said, no longer smiling. "Mo. Mohinder McKeen. Evan's father."

"Unusual name."

"His mom was Indo-American and his dad was white. Mo was hot, and he fascinated me. I was fourteen; he was nineteen, a dropout. He belonged to a gang, or maybe that was just macho talk. He made the boys at school seem like children." One corner of her mouth tipped up in a wry expression. "He had long hair, rode a motorbike, wore a black leather jacket."

"Uh-oh. Definitely trouble."

"I'd been raised like a princess in a protected castle, and that life seemed so tame once Mo started to pay attention to me. I realized I had a wild side, just waiting to break free."

"He took you for a ride on his bike and got you all hot and bothered?"

"Hot and bothered," she said wryly, "then pregnant. At fourteen."

"Ouch. What did you do?"

"Our parents were conventional. We got railroaded into marriage. Mo wasn't thrilled, but he went along, probably figured nothing much had to change. Mo didn't have a job—he never held a job for long—so he moved in with my family.

For the first few weeks it was fun. Great sex, in a bed. Going out with 'my husband.' Knowing I'd nabbed the sexiest guy in the neighborhood. The girls were green with envy."

Jake had almost cleaned his plate but Brooke was toying with her food. "Eat your dinner," he said. "You can tell me this later."

She stared at her chicken, then ate a bite. "I won't let Mo ruin my appetite. Not at this late date." She dragged some noodles into the sauce and twirled them around her fork.

"I was so young it seemed like a game. I had this gorgeous husband and I was going to have a sweet little baby girl. The baby was always a girl, in my mind, and looked like a doll I'd once had."

"Blond and blue-eyed?"

"Of course. Though why I thought that, with Mo being so dark, is beyond me. Anyhow, I started to get fat, as Mo termed it. He spent more time at the bar with his friends. Guy friends, and girls as well. He came home stinking of beer and perfume. He admitted he'd been screwing around on me, but said it was my fault. He was a normal guy with normal needs, and he sure wasn't going to have sex with a blimp like me."

"Asshole." Jake wondered what had happened to McKeen. Hopefully, only bad things.

She nodded. "He hit me a couple of times when he came home drunk. My father gave him a talking-to. Dad might've been a drinker but he never hit Mom or us girls. Anyhow, he told Mo he couldn't behave that way while he was living under our roof. Mo's answer was to enlist in the Army."

"The Army? A bad-boy gang member?" Jake snapped his fingers. "Sanctioned violence?"

"Yes. An excuse to be a bully; I'm sure that's what he thought. Access to weapons."

Her ex sounded like a real prize. What had Brooke been thinking? But of course, at fourteen, who thought with anything but their hormones?

"Anyhow," she went on, "after he left, I had a baby boy. Kind of a cross between Mo and me. Tawny hair, skin that looked permanently tanned, blue-green eyes. Cute, but an absolute handful. Restless, curious, noisy. Evan drove me crazy. I was really unhappy for a while. Postpartum depression, I guess."

Or the beginning of her bipolar disorder, he wondered.

"Anyway," she said, "Evan was like a new lease on life for my mom. She adored him and she was so patient. She gave me an excuse to avoid responsibility, to be a kid again. I started feeling better, went back to school, hung around with my friends, didn't act maternal at all. Sometimes I almost forgot I had a baby."

Selfish, yes, but she'd been a child herself. Everyone was self-centered at that age. Besides, where was the baby's father? "Did Mo stay in the Army?"

"Deserted." The word fell flatly between them.

Jake let out a whistle. "Couldn't hack the structure, discipline, hard work?"

"I'm sure he had problems taking orders and I gather he kept getting in trouble, but he did make it through basic training. Then it got personal between him and some lieutenant. Mo said the guy was an asshole, always provoking him. More likely it was the other way around."

She let out a long, resigned sigh. "One night a group was drinking at a bar, and I guess Mo was drunk—maybe he and the lieutenant both were—and he attacked the lieutenant with a broken beer bottle. He ran away before they could arrest him."

"And kept running? You said he deserted."

"Yes, he kept running, picking up Evan and me along the way. He sweet-talked a lady with some peace activism group. Made her think he was one of them, had seen the error of his ways, and that's why he'd deserted. She and her contacts got us into Canada with fake ID. He went from being Mohinder to plain-old Mo, and we became Kincaids. Someone got him a job as a mechanic in Saskatchewan."

"Why did you go with him?"

She gave a small, sad smile. "Because we were married. Strangely enough, it meant something to both of us. I wish I hadn't."

Jake drained the last of his beer.

"Another?" she asked.

If this was another test, he didn't know the right answer. "Thanks. I'll get it."

"Be Arnold," she said, as he scraped the chair back from the table.

He squared the chair up neatly and, taking small, almost mincing steps, walked to the fridge. "If there's no sherry," he said in a fussy voice, "I suppose I must settle for beer."

"Why, Arnold," she said sweetly, "I should have thought of it myself. Tomorrow I'll be sure to buy a bottle of sherry for you."

"Do it and you're dead, doll," he growled in his best biker-gang voice.

Her laugh was beautiful—an unreserved, melodic sound.

He resumed his Arnold character, opening the beer carefully and pouring it slowly into a glass. "May I bring you anything while I'm up, Cousin Brooke?"

At her head shake, he resumed his seat. "If it wouldn't be too impolite to ask, cousin dear, how did you and your husband come to part ways?"

"I think I liked you better as Jake."

"God, I hope so!"

She rested her chin on a hand. "We moved around Canada, changing places at least once a year. Mo would lose his job, get in a fight or some other kind of trouble. He couldn't afford to get arrested because his prints were on record, but that didn't keep him out of trouble; it just kept us on the move."

She raised her shoulders and lowered them. "He was

drinking a lot. Me too. Sometimes we partied, and drinking was part of that. But a lot of the time I was so unhappy, and I basically drank to drown my sorrows. I lost my family, and so did Mo."

"Lost them because . . . ?"

"If we stayed in touch with them, the Army might have traced Mo that way. Besides, I was so embarrassed by what a mess we'd made of things."

"That must have been hard."

"Not so much for Mo—he and his parents didn't get along—but yes, for me. It was just the two of us. And Evan."

Brooke sighed, and her eyes were sad. "The worst thing was, I didn't know how to look after a child. I was a spoiled kid and, uh, moody. Evan would have been better off if I'd left him with my mom."

She shook her head. "Sometimes I'd be supermom. I'd buy Evan new clothes, play with him all the time. But then something would happen. I'd go out drinking with Mo and forget about Evan, or I'd get depressed and neglect him. He became so well-behaved—probably trying to win our attention, our love—but it had the opposite effect. We were relieved he was self-sufficient, and left him alone."

He hated seeing the sad, guilty expression in her pretty eyes.

"I honestly did love him to bits," she said quietly, "but sometimes I hated the fact that he existed. If I hadn't gotten pregnant I could have been a happy, normal girl, back in L.A. Having fun, dating, finding a nice man to marry."

That might be true. He'd read that people who had the genetic predisposition for bipolar disorder didn't always end up getting the disease. Environmental influences like stress could precipitate its onset. He wondered when Brooke was first diagnosed. And whether she'd ever tell him about her illness.

"One thing I've learned as a cop," he said, "is how a single action can have huge, life-altering repercussions." He thought of Anika's parents telling her that if she didn't obey their rules she wasn't welcome in their house. They'd take that back in an instant if they could go back in time.

Brooke nodded quickly. "Sleeping with Mo, not insisting he use a condom. Stupid."

"If you'd only known, right? That's what people always say."

"The worst part is how it affected Evan." She fidgeted with her fork. "It was so wrong of me to blame him, but I wasn't a well-balanced person. I was erratic, irresponsible, sometimes so desperately unhappy that I thought about killing myself." She shoved her plate away, her meal only half finished.

"Anyhow, we came to Caribou Crossing. Mo got worse. Year by year the drinking, the violence, escalated."

She sucked in a noisy breath and let it out slowly. "He hit Evan. And I didn't stop him. I didn't usually see it happen and I told myself Evan was just clumsy. And he was. Clumsy, not athletic, but super smart. Yet on some level I knew what was happening. I didn't know what to do and took the easy way out, pretending everything was okay. There's no excuse for my behavior." The pain in her eyes reflected a level of sorrow he'd never experienced.

"You were an alcoholic." And alcoholics were experts at denial.

"I was. And I should have realized it," she said firmly, "and sought help. I had other problems, too, that medication would have helped, but I was such a mess that it never occurred to me to ask for help. Evan survived thanks to the kindness of Jessica Bly's parents."

"Jessica? The woman he married?"

"They were best friends from the day he started school here. They lost touch after high school and only found each other last year, when Evan came back."

"Came back?"

"He left town right after twelfth grade. Got a scholarship

to Cornell, then a job as an investment counselor in New York City, and then he built his own company. He'd always believed he didn't belong here, and he worked so hard to get out. But then he came back to check out an investment for a client, met Jessica again, and they fell in love. He decided to stay."

"That's quite a difference, Manhattan to Caribou Crossing."

"He fits here, now that he's willing to give the place a chance." She smiled a little. "And, thanks to Jessica's intervention, he's also given me another chance. Before last summer, I hadn't seen or spoken to him in ten years."

Ten years. She really must have been a dreadful mother, to drive her son away like that. It was so hard to believe, as he looked at her now. "The mother he came back to must have been pretty different from the one he'd left behind."

"Lord, I hope so."

"What happened to Mo?"

"When Evan was ten, the Blys figured out that he was being beaten, and notified the authorities. The RCMP came to question Mo. I was out shopping and when I came back, he was packing. He didn't tell me about the cops—I only found out this past winter what the Blys had done—he just said we had to move again."

"But you didn't go with him?"

Her elbows rested on the table and she dropped her head into her hands as if it were too heavy to hold upright. "I said Evan needed to stay in one school, be with Jessica, make some other friends. I'd told Mo that before—it's why we'd been in Caribou Crossing longer than anywhere else—and I guess he knew I wouldn't change my mind. But he wasn't about to stay and straighten out."

Brooke hadn't been completely insensitive to her son's needs. But nor had she straightened herself out once Mo was gone. She'd said she'd been sober for less than five years.

Her face pale, strained, almost tortured, she stared into his eyes. "I hate telling you this. It's harder, much harder, than doing it at A.A. There, they understand. They know what it's like; they've been there themselves."

"I've got some idea, Brooke. I'm not judging. But why are you telling me?"

"Because Caribou Crossing knows. They saw me when I was like that. If you're going to be my cousin—and more importantly, if you're going to trust me to help you—you have to know who I am."

Looking at her face, he could for the first time believe she was old enough to be a grandmother. And yet he wasn't put off by that, nor by her confession. Instead, he felt an overwhelming urge to protect her. "That's not who you are, Brooke. It's who you were."

Her throat muscles rippled as she swallowed. Her eyes glistened, and when she spoke her strained voice revealed her battle with tears. "Who I was is part of who I am. The people of Caribou Crossing have been generous about allowing me a second chance, but there's no forgetting who I was. Like, with the fence. I told Mr. Barnes and Sergeant Miller I backed into it, and so, automatically, they wondered if I was drinking again."

"Why did you stay here? Wouldn't it have been easier to move when you got yourself turned around?"

"Yes and no. On the surface, it would have been easier. But don't you see, Jake? Staying here, the entire town is my conscience. If I ever slipped, everyone would know."

"You're not going to slip." He said it with certainty.

Her mouth tilted up at one corner but there was no warmth behind the smile. "Thanks. But I'll never be sure. I live every day with the knowledge of how easy it would be to slip. Thank heaven for Evan and Jess and Robin. They're my true motivation."

He frowned, again thinking about the timeline of her story. "You said Evan didn't move back until last year. But by then you'd been sober roughly four years. He and his family weren't your motivation to stop drinking."

Her brow began to wrinkle and he reached across the table and grasped her hand. "Why did you stop, Brooke?"

Her hand twitched under his and he squeezed it gently. "Tell me." He needed to know—not because of their cover story but because he had a powerful desire to understand what had turned this special woman's life around.

She glanced down at his hand, then back up, and he realized something else about Brooke. She was one of those rare people who wouldn't lie to make herself look good.

"I'd been at the pub, drinking too much, partying way too hard. As usual. I drove home. As usual. I'd had one DUI but so far—heaven knows how—I'd managed to avoid having an accident. But that night I was really flying and I crashed the car into a stop sign. It was the luckiest night of my life, in two ways. I didn't hurt anyone else, and I did hurt myself. I wasn't wearing a seat belt and I cracked my head. They kept me in the hospital for several days."

"It forced you to dry out."

"Which hurt even worse than my head. But the really amazing thing was—" She broke off and her eyes widened anxiously.

She'd been going to tell him she'd been diagnosed with bipolar disorder. He'd bet his Harley on it.

She slid her hand out from under his and jumped to her feet. "I'm going to make tea. Do you want some? Or coffee? There's apple crisp for dessert. Would you like ice cream with it?"

Why was she so scared? How did she think he'd react? He gave her the respite she sought. "Coffee sounds great. And definitely ice cream. Everything tastes better with ice cream."

When he got up to help, she said, "Let's have dessert in the living room. You go put your feet up. I'm sure you're worn out by now."

Yes, though the beer helped, he felt every single bruise and scrape, not to mention the bullet wound. He limped into Brooke's cozy living room and sprawled gratefully on the couch. Sunny followed him and jumped up to settle beside him. It was peaceful. Damned peaceful.

But Jake couldn't relax. How was he going to persuade Brooke to open up? And why did it mean so much to him—to Jake the man, not Jake the cop—that she do so?

Chapter Nine

Being alone in her kitchen brought Brooke little relief from anxiety. She clicked on the radio, to hear Merle Haggard singing "I Think I'll Just Stay Here and Drink." How many times had she drunk beer in The Gold Nugget Saloon, listening to good old Merle sing drinking songs?

She turned the radio off again and got to work preparing coffee and tea and dishing out apple crisp. Jake knew about her drinking. Should she tell him about her bipolar disorder?

She was embarrassed to admit to it, and particularly to him. Not just because she was attracted to his sexy good looks but because he was the kind of man she respected. A man like Evan and like Dave Cousins, Jessica's ex-husband. A person with a quiet strength, a soul-deep integrity, the conviction to follow through on what he believed in. She wanted him to think well of her.

Brooke gave a snort. Keeping an important secret was just as bad as telling a lie. If she didn't tell him, *she* wouldn't think well of herself.

She took the bowls of apple crisp from the microwave, spooned ice cream on top of Jake's, then put the lid back on the container of ice cream. She watched the ice cream melt at the edges of the dessert, trickling into the cinnamon-scented apples. Then she yanked the top off the ice cream again and served herself a spoonful. This was not a time to worry about her healthy diet.

She loaded up a tray, marched into the living room, and dumped it down on the coffee table.

Jake, lounging on her couch like he belonged there, tilted an eyebrow at the clatter. Sunny, who'd been dozing beside him, shot her a quizzical gaze.

Brooke grabbed her bowl of apple crisp, took a deliberate bite, chewed and swallowed, then announced, "I have bipolar disorder."

Jake swung awkwardly to a sitting position, favoring his injured side, and reached for his own bowl. "I know."

"You—" She gaped at him, then slumped down in a chair.

"Your Eskalith. I checked it out."

"How dare you!"

"I'm sorry, but I had to know everything about you. To know if I could trust you."

She squeezed her eyes shut, then opened them again when he said, "When you were at your meeting last night I called Jamal and got him to do a background check on you."

"I know. And you searched my house and found the gun."

"Oh." He gave a snort of laughter. "You know my secrets and I know yours."

She shook her head, knowing it wasn't the even match he'd suggested. She barely knew anything about the man.

He scooped up some dessert, then paused with the spoon halfway to his mouth. "Eat it before all the ice cream melts. It's better that way."

Automatically she took another spoonful, trying to enjoy the taste while she thought about what he'd said. Not only did he know how much she spent on hydro, what kind of underwear she wore, and what brand of tampons she bought, he knew about her condition. Amazingly, she wasn't as offended as she might have expected to be. Perhaps it was because she understood the need that had motivated him.

He'd known she was bipolar when he'd pressed his hard, aroused body against her. Not only did he know she was a grandmother, but he knew she was an alcoholic and bipolar, and he still wanted her. He wanted her physically, and he trusted her to help him with his cover.

She smiled down at her apple crisp and took another spoonful. It really was delicious.

"Brooke? You're smiling." He sounded surprised. "What are you thinking?"

"Wouldn't you like to know?" How could she feel so comfortable teasing him? He was a powerful man, skilled and familiar with the use of force. Not a man to be trifled with.

Mo had been a smaller, less powerful guy, but he'd been big enough to brutalize her and Evan. Somehow she knew Jake would never use his strength against her.

"Brooke?"

"Wh—" The phone interrupted and she hurried to the kitchen with Jake limping behind.

It was Dave Cousins, Jess's ex, the owner of the Wild Rose. "Hey, Brooke, rumor has it you're under the weather."

"Where on earth did you hear that?"

"Went to get my hair trimmed today and my favorite barber was home sick."

"I'm sorry, Dave. I'm fine now, going back to work tomorrow. And don't worry about the fund-raiser. I've made most of the appetizers and they're in my freezer." She'd done some on the weekend, and more yesterday, while Jake lay on her couch dozing.

"I wasn't worrying about the food. Just wanted to make sure you're okay."

Why was it so hard to let herself believe that people like Dave and Kate could care about her? For decades she'd distanced herself from the people around her, and now it was difficult to relax the barriers.

"Thanks, Dave," she said softly. Seeing Jake's gaze on her, she took a deep breath and went on. "I'm bringing a guest on Friday. My cousin, Arnold Pitt, from Vancouver, is coming to town tomorrow. He's an accountant and might be interested in setting up practice here."

"Well now, wouldn't that be great."

"Yes. He is my favorite cousin."

Jake lounged close by, a hip propped against the kitchen counter, looking very male and very Jake.

"What's he like?" Dave asked.

"I haven't seen him since he was nine or ten. As a kid he was sweet, and a complete nerd."

"Got a wife and kids?"

"No, he's single. In his midthirties. Might well be gay." She winked at Jake.

"If he's used to the gay scene in Vancouver, he'll find Caribou Crossing pretty dull."

"That's why he's coming up. I mean, not to check out the gay scene specifically." She paused, her lips twitching as Jake's shoulders shook with silent laughter. "He wants to see the town, meet some people, check with the RCMP about the crime rate, talk to the bank about financing. Get together with some of the folks in the town council and chamber of commerce. I thought the fund-raiser would be a good place to start."

"Sure would. See you both then. And I'm real glad you're feeling better, Brooke."

"Good night, Dave, and thanks." She hung up, warmed by his concern.

Then, briskly, she turned to Jake. "That reminds me, I still have mini-quiches to prepare for the fund-raiser. I'll do them before I go to work in the morning." It looked like she wasn't going to fit in a single trip to the fitness center this week.

"We'd better get on with your briefing. I don't want to get to bed too late."

As soon as the words slipped out of her mouth she wanted to take them back. Bed was not a subject she wanted hanging in the air between them. How was she going to sleep, with him across the hall in her bed? Naked. She was so sure he slept in the raw that she hadn't bothered to buy pajamas, though she had purchased a bathrobe.

She turned on her heel and strode into the living room. "All right, I was telling you about my bipolar. My psychiatrist thinks there's a genetic component, then environmental trauma made it manifest itself. Having a baby at fifteen, then losing my family, friends, everything I'd known and loved, being dependent on Mo in a relationship that was so dysfunctional."

"Yeah, that'd be a hell of a lot for any young girl to handle."

"I'd never been depressed in my life until after I had Evan. Once I started cycling, I still tended more toward depression than mania, but I did have manias, too. Then I'd get jobs and be superproductive, I'd be the life of the party, but I'd also drink too much and do crazy things. I was manic when I had the accident, and for the first day or so in the hospital. Really manic. Couldn't lie still, I was talking so fast no one could keep up with me, I'd invented a cure for cancer." She broke off, realizing she was talking almost as fast as she had when she was manic. He must really think she was crazy.

"I skimmed through that Patty Duke book this afternoon." He nodded in the direction of her bookcase. "I've got an idea what it's like."

"Oh." He knew what it was like and still he hadn't rejected her. She swallowed hard. The worst part was over. "Anyhow, a doctor at the hospital diagnosed me. I saw a psychiatrist, got started on lithium and it's been amazing. My condition is under control."

She picked up her mug of cinnamon-apple tea and curled up in her favorite chair while Jake again made himself comfortable on the couch. "It was an eye-opener. I'd had a lot of reasons for drinking but the main ones were Mo and my own depression. Well, Mo was gone and I realized that at least some of my depression was due to a chemical imbalance in my brain. My stay in the hospital dried me out, and the night they released me, I went to my first A.A. meeting."

There. It was all out, on the table, the whole truth about Brooke Kincaid. She felt exhausted, drained, but also lighter and freer.

"You haven't had a drink since the night of the accident?"

She had relaxed too soon. Darn him for asking that particular question. Of course, she could just nod and let it go. . . .

His smoky eyes were steady on her. How did he manage to be so nonjudgmental?

"I faltered a couple of times in the first few months. But I hated the way I felt. So I finally stuck at it."

"Four years, ten months, and thirteen days." His smile was far too warm.

Sexual heat, and now genuine warmth. She didn't know how to deal with this.

She put down her mug, determined to get back to safe ground. "All right, we need to go over the family tree and some more family history. Then I guess you'll want a rundown on some of the people in town? The RCMP officers, mayor and council, chamber of commerce, and so on?"

"Let's stick with the family stuff tonight. I know you're tired. It's been a stressful couple of days. I'll get up when you do in the morning and we can talk while you're making appetizers. Maybe I'll even help."

"Do you know how to make mini-quiches?" she asked mischievously.

"Hey, I learned to take the stew out of the can before I nuke it. I'm trainable."

There'd been times she'd eaten tinned stew for dinner, cold, straight out of the can. When she'd bothered to eat at all. Did Jake really feed himself from cans? Maybe when he was undercover and didn't have some pretty woman in his life to share his meals.

Yesterday, with his scruffy beard and leather jacket, with his motorbike and his gun, it had been easier to believe he was familiar with danger. Tonight, in his Arnold Pitt getup, it was far more difficult. And that, of course, was the point of the disguise. She mustn't fall for it herself. She must never forget who this man really was, and how poles apart their lives were. He risked his life on a daily basis; she sought to maintain stability and balance one day at a time.

"As for the respectable citizens of Caribou Crossing," he said, "I'll raise the subject tomorrow at your son's place. It's a natural topic for Arnold to be interested in."

"All right then, let's talk about the family. Do you want a pad of paper and a pen?"

"I'll remember."

And, as she recited details she'd all but forgotten herself and responded to his occasional query, she did get the sense that his brain was filing each piece of information methodically. His body must be aching but he gave no sign of it.

For her, talking about her family was stressful. She'd been close to her parents and sister, then had drifted so far away, letting her abusive husband be the anchor that held her down. After Mo left, it was her drinking and her depression, her misery and embarrassment at what a mess she'd made of her life, that kept her out of touch.

As part of her A.A. twelve steps, she'd contacted her parents and sister to confess her alcoholism and bipolar disorder. Since then, she'd sent birthday cards and an occasional e-mail and they did the same, but they had their own lives. They didn't need her.

As she talked to Jake, it struck her that she wanted to try

harder. Perhaps she would even fly down for a visit. Or invite them up, when Jess delivered the new baby. Her parents hadn't seen their grandson since he was an infant, and now they were missing their great-grandchildren, too. All because of her. And then there was her sister, Erin. They'd shared a room, been so close. . . .

Brooke realized Jake had risen from the couch and was standing in front of her calling her name. "You're exhausted. Asleep in your chair."

"Not asleep. Just reflecting. Making some new resolutions."

"Oh? Want to talk about it?"

She smiled up at him. The man sounded sincere. And she did find herself wanting to tell him. But not tonight. His face was drawn with pain and fatigue. "Some other time. We've both had enough for tonight."

He sank down to squat in front of her, which must have been sheer misery for his wounded body, and gripped her hands where they lay folded in her lap. "Are you sure you're all right with this? We can still find another way, without involving you."

Her hands felt warm and safe, enfolded in his. She shook her head. "Count me in. Unless you're having second thoughts. I don't have professional training, but—"

"You were perfect with Sergeant Miller. I'm not worried about your competence; I'm worried about you. This is a lot to ask you to take on."

The stress, he meant, not just her safety. She was a bit worried herself. After all, she was the woman who lived her life by structure and routine. And yet . . .

"You know," she said with a sense of discovery, "I'm actually excited. In a good way, I think. Not manic, just energized. Like I said, I had a wild side as a girl, a side that craved excitement and adventure. I'm getting in touch with that part of myself again. It's like living in a mystery novel. It's almost fun to have a legitimate—even honorable—excuse to lie, to play a role. Besides, I'm not in it alone, am I? I've got you."

"Partners," he said warmly.

"Partners," she repeated, trying to keep her voice steady as she prayed she'd be able to live up to his expectations.

"And now," he said, "I bet you'd like a nice relaxing bath."

That would be the second thing on her wish list. First was to tug on his hands, pull him closer, taste that sensual mouth . . .

No, she was getting carried away by the unaccustomed thrill of letting a little excitement into her life.

"I'd love a bath," she murmured. "You take the bathroom first, then you can get to sleep."

"If you think I'll be able to sleep while you're splashing around naked in the bath . . ."

As a general rule, Brooke found baths to be very relaxing. But tonight, even though she was exhausted, the knowledge that Jake was just across the hall kept every nerve in her body alert. It would take nothing for him to walk the few steps and open the door.

She knew he was thinking about it. Just as she was.

It would take nothing for her to get out of the bath and walk those same few steps.

She rotated her head on achy shoulders and sloshed warm water—water scented with dried lavender and rose petals from a homemade bath bomb—across her breasts. She glanced down at her naked body. Yes, since she'd been diagnosed she'd exercised and dieted herself into decent shape, but the fact remained she was a forty-three-year-old grandmother.

It was still difficult to believe that Jake found her attractive, but his body's response was undeniable. Maybe he'd been undercover and hadn't had sex in months, and he was just horny. But there was a personal kind of sparkle in his eyes. Something that said he really was looking at her, Brooke Kincaid, not just at a body with breasts and hips.

As for her being attracted to him—well, any woman would be. He was a stunning man, whether sporting the gypsyish long hair and beard or the trim haircut she'd given him. Utterly stunning. Sexy. In perfect shape. Perfect, virile shape. Not to mention that he was strong, brave, and smart, yet could also be gentle, understanding, and nonjudgmental.

He was really pretty darn amazing.

What would it hurt to have sex with him?

She squeezed her thighs together against the ache between them.

They both wanted it.

She hadn't wanted a man forever, which made her body's unabashed reaction to Jake an utter surprise. Why not give in to it? They could have a fling. A wanton fling with absolutely no consequences.

She squeezed shower gel onto a bath sponge and sat up to soap her neck and shoulders. The sponge had the same rough texture as Sunny's tongue. Her flesh stirred and prickled at its caress. Sex . . .

She and Mo had had some hot sex in their day, but gradually sex had become a tension-fraught act. Rarely did they join out of affection and pleasure. It was make-up sex after a fight, or sex to distract him from getting angry and hitting her. Could she ever enjoy sex unreservedly?

Did she even still remember how to have sex? She'd had only one lover. How many had Jake had? Dozens? He'd be good, very good.

She lay back against the bath pillow and considered that notion. Maybe not. He was a man who lived for excitement and danger. He might be quick and greedy. But somehow she didn't think so.

He'd find her boring, inadequate. Middle-aged. She shuddered. It couldn't happen.

What was she thinking? Even if lust overcame her common sense, she knew for sure it couldn't happen. She hadn't bought condoms and she certainly wasn't going to risk pregnancy!

She took a deep breath and let it out slowly. There, the question was answered and she could relax. Gradually the tension slipped from her body and, in its absence, exhaustion seeped into her bones. Bed was going to feel so good tonight. If she ever managed to summon the energy to pull herself out of the tub.

Jake sure as hell wasn't asleep. He lay in the darkness sporting a boner and wondering how long Brooke was going to linger in the bath. If she fell asleep, he'd have to go rescue her.

The phone shrilled and he jerked upright, cursing as pain lanced through his injured body. The phone sat on the bedside table. She'd forgotten to take it away, and the only other handset was down in the kitchen. Who was calling, and what would they do if she didn't answer?

He heard splashing and thumping from the bathroom; then she darted into the bedroom, a dripping vision wrapped in a fluffy rose-colored towel. His hard-on went on full alert.

Her legs, which he'd always seen in pants, were long and lean. Her arms, too, were well-shaped. Above the towel, her shoulders were strong and the top curve of her breasts was pure femininity. She'd washed her hair; it was damp, piled haphazardly atop her head, a few unruly tendrils clinging to her forehead and neck. Her skin was flushed almost as rosy as the towel, and the air filled with the scent of roses.

"No, you didn't wake me," she said breathlessly into the phone. She covered it with her hand and whispered, "It's all right; it's my neighbor. He's a night owl."

He nodded and leaned back against the pillows.

Brooke's gaze traced his naked torso, then dropped lower,

to where only a sheet draped his lower body. A sheet that was tented by his erection.

She moistened her bottom lip and glanced away.

Into the phone she said, "Yes, Sergeant Miller dropped by here, too. He was looking for some man who robbed Vijay's store. I hadn't seen or heard anything strange myself. How about you? Were you able to give him any help?"

As she listened, her free hand kept a death grip on the top of the towel.

He could reach out and with one hand yank that towel away.

Perhaps she read his intention. She took another step away from the bed and turned her back on him.

He admired the curve of her spine, the roundness of her backside under the towel, the firmness of her calves.

"Yes, he asked me about that," she said. "Though I can't see what it's got to do with the thief he's looking for." She listened again, then said, "It's all right."

Another pause, and then, softly, "Ray, just so you know, I wasn't drinking."

After he replied, she said, "Thanks. I really appreciate that. Good night."

Brooke stood for a moment, still with her back to Jake, then turned around. "Ray apologized for telling the police about my accident. He was flustered by having Sergeant Miller on his doorstep. He also said he didn't figure I'd been drinking."

She looked solemn, relieved. Beautiful. Without seeming to be aware of it, she stepped closer to him and put the phone back on the nightstand.

He couldn't resist any longer. He reached out, grabbed the hem of her towel, and gave a little tug. It wasn't strong enough to pull the towel from her grip, just enough to urge her toward him.

She didn't move.

If she resisted they might end up in a tug-of-war. He had a sudden vision of both of them stark naked, the towel stretched between them as each yanked their own end.

"Sergeant Miller asked him if he heard a motorbike," she said, her voice breathless again. "He didn't. He's a little deaf."

Jake should care, but at the moment all that mattered was Brooke. He tugged again, gently.

She let him pull her toward the bed, then down to sit on the edge. "Jake—"

"You're beautiful, Brooke. God, you're so beautiful." His fingers, still gripping the hem of the towel, rested on her thigh. If he moved his fingers a few inches . . . But he didn't. He didn't want to scare her away.

That flowery scent filled his nostrils and he breathed in greedily. Tonight she was a garden. Simple scents like rose and lavender, but underneath hovered that exotic tropical aroma he'd noticed before. "What's that scent in your shampoo?"

"My shampoo?"

"Some kind of tropical flower. It makes me think of Polynesian women with grass skirts and blossoms tucked behind their ears." And bare breasts.

"It's called plumeria," she murmured. "You're right, it's tropical."

He reached out to take a curl between his finger and thumb.

A pulse jumped at her throat. "I have to go."

"No, you don't. Why fight it? You're attracted, too. Aren't you?"

A pause, then she said, "Yes."

He took his hand from her hair and nodded. "You don't like to lie."

She stared down at his other hand, where it rested half on the towel and half on her naked thigh. "No. Once, lies were such a habit, I couldn't tell them from the truth. Now it means a lot to me to know the difference, and choose honesty."

He felt a surge of regret. "And I'm making you lie." He released the towel.

She could leave now, but she didn't.

"I think we should call this cousin thing off," he said. "You shouldn't have to lie for me. I'll work out some other story."

She shook her head assertively. "No, we've been through this before. I won't feel guilty about lying this time. Like I said, it's kind of exciting. Besides, it's the safest way. It gives you the best cover."

He reached for her hand and intertwined his fingers with hers. "It's not the safest way for you. It's safer if you don't even know me."

She stared fiercely into his eyes. "No! You're my cousin, Arnold Pitt."

"Why, Brooke?"

"Because of Anika and her parents. Because of me; I want to do this. And because . . ." Her glance drifted down to touch their linked hands. "I care what happens to you."

Her and her honesty. It made him want to be honest, too. "And I care what happens to you. I don't want to put you in danger and I don't want to make you lie."

"You're not making me do anything. This is my choice. And I've made it. So would you please shut up about it?" Her ocean-colored eyes glittered, and the energy flowing between them was so strong he couldn't resist it.

"Hey, Brooke?"

Warily she tilted her head. "What?"

"If you've got a craving for excitement, maybe we could start out with something that's exciting but not too dangerous."

Her cheeks grew pinker. "What did you have in mind?"

"How about a kiss?"

Her face stilled; then her lips curved into an impish grin. "You don't think that's dangerous?"

The only danger was that he'd combust spontaneously, he was so on fire for her. "Just a kiss. Or maybe two."

She glanced down at the tented sheet and gave a little shiver. "That's not all you want."

"I don't have any condoms. So, unless you have something . . ."

She shook her head.

"I'm clean," he said. "I swear. But we can't risk pregnancy."

"We certainly can't!"

"Then it can't get too dangerous." He released her hand and fingered the top of the towel where it wrapped across the front of her body.

Her own hand still held one corner firmly.

He ran his fingers up to hers, cupped her hand, and tugged her closer.

Chapter Ten

Brooke held tight to the towel, though her hand was trembling. So were her knees. This was the most exciting thing that had happened to her in decades.

One lover, that was all she'd ever had. She'd never been attracted to anyone but Mo. Not until now. Now she was seriously attracted. So attracted her body coiled tight with desire and anticipation.

What was the harm in just, for once, abandoning caution and going for it? Although she'd known Jake only a short time, she was positive he wouldn't hurt her. Not physically. And he couldn't hurt her emotionally because she knew this was just sex, and he'd leave when his job was done.

But sex with him wouldn't be a cold, emotionless act either. She cared for him and he cared for her, and that was something to celebrate.

She had two choices: keep their relationship platonic and suffer the might-have-beens, or make the sexy most of their time together.

He wasn't into serious relationships, which was perfect. She couldn't let herself contemplate anything serious because she wasn't capable of that kind of responsibility. Much less handling the stress of being with a man who on a daily basis faced danger. But Jake was offering something very different—something her lustful body told her she was more than capable of.

"Brooke?" His fingers stroked her chest above the towel, making her quiver. It felt so good to be touched, to be touched sensually, to be wanted sexually, by this man. "Just lie down with me," he urged.

Oh, how she wanted to. She wanted to turn out the light and slip under the covers and press her soft body against his hard, virile one. She couldn't remember ever wanting anything more. Not even a drink.

"You blow hot and cold," he murmured. "Why is that?"

It was true. That afternoon, when she'd been on the phone with Jess and he'd been undressing, she had been flirting. Somehow she'd felt safe, with the phone in her hand. She'd been fine, playing her sexy role, until she hung up. Until he took her in his arms. And then she'd panicked. "I don't mean to be a tease."

"I know. But what are you scared of?"

It was a darn good question. Was she scared he'd find her ugly? Not really. He'd seen the wrinkles on her face; a couple of stretch marks across her belly weren't likely to put him off. She wasn't a centerfold but she wasn't soft and saggy either.

She wasn't married; he wasn't married; they were consenting adults. Besides, they weren't even going to have sex tonight. Not real sex.

She shivered at the thought of what they might do. If they'd had condoms, the outcome would be easily foreseen. Actually, when she thought about it, it was more tantalizing this way. People could do a lot in bed besides have intercourse. She remembered. . . . And with the memories came the certainty that she could please this man.

Suddenly she found herself grinning down at him.

He looked so surprised that she smiled even harder, until he grinned back.

"What am I afraid of?" she said. "That I might like it too much." Laughter bubbled up in her and she let it flow out.

"I sure hope so," he said, his smoky eyes gleaming a sultry mauve.

No strings. Just fun. One night—maybe more—of feeling utterly alive as a woman. Sexy memories to bring a secret smile to her lips in the years of grandmotherhood.

Yes, Jake Brannon was exactly what she wanted right now.

She took a step back so his hand fell away from her towel, and then she leaned forward and tapped him on his sheet-covered hip. "Shove over, John Doe, Arnold, Jake, whatever the heck your name is."

He gave a hoot of laughter and obeyed as she reached to flick off the bedside light.

"Hey!" he protested, but she dropped her towel and hurled herself into bed beside him, and that shut him up.

Brooke caught her breath as her body came up against Jake's. For a few moments she reveled in pure sensation, feeling the sleek hard press, the crispness of hair, inhaling the musk of aroused male. She buried her nose in his chest and breathed deeply, then sneezed as a few curls of chest hair tickled her.

They lay on their sides facing each other, and gradually their bodies adjusted and intertwined. Jake's arms came around her and she hugged him back, wrapping her arm high on his rib cage, avoiding the bandage at his waist.

His face was in her still-damp hair and he dropped tiny kisses on the top of her head. "Ah, Brooke, you feel wonderful." His hand swept slowly down her back, dipping into the curve at her waist, stretching out to cup a buttock. Urging her body even closer so his erection was pressed tight between them.

She wriggled upward a couple of inches, seeking the intimate contact her body yearned for. Between her legs she felt the moisture of desire, a sensation she'd forgotten until Jake entered her life. She pressed that dampness against the base of his shaft and he thrust convulsively, stroking against her swollen lips, the aching bud of her clitoris.

She whimpered with pleasure, with need, amazed at how quickly arousal had built. Was this the effect of so many years of celibacy, or was it Jake? Who cared? All she knew was, if he kept doing what he was doing, she'd explode in seconds.

He groaned, thrust again, then grabbed her hips and shoved her away. "Too fast," he gasped, "too much, too fast." He took a couple of noisy breaths. "It'll be over before I've even kissed you."

How exciting to know he was as aroused as she was. "Oh," she whispered, "you wanted kisses, too?"

He chuckled. "I want everything, I want to taste you from head to toe, and especially in between. I want my hands to know every inch of your body. And I wouldn't mind too much if you explored mine."

Here in bed, with the lights out, she wasn't a sedate, recovering alcoholic, a grandmother; she was just a woman. A sexy woman. "I'm not averse to exploring," she murmured throatily. "Hmm, where should I start?"

Too hot now, she tossed off the sheet, then boldly wrapped her hands around his penis. "Would this be a good place?"

Oh my, he felt amazing, filling her hands with his pulsing heat. Like the rest of his body, this part of him, too, was bigger than Mo had been. She could imagine him inside her and the thought made her squeeze her thighs together. She wanted to stroke up and down his shaft but guessed that, if she did, he'd climax in two seconds flat.

But who said one orgasm meant the end? She had a feeling Jake would recover quickly. And while he did, maybe he'd follow through on that promise about tasting her. So why not, for once, let go caution and fly where impulse took her?

She curled her fingers around him and began to slide them up, then down. Slowly. She circled the velvety head with a fingertip, found drops of moisture, and spread them. He groaned, muttered a protest, but she kept moving. And as she stroked him she imagined he was thrusting inside her.

Jake's hips pumped convulsively and she knew there was no stopping now. She just wished . . .

And then his fingers were on her, between her legs, stroking too, and pressure built inside her. She whimpered and writhed against his hand, and then his fingers found her swollen bud.

So many sensations. And contrasts. The throbbing, thrusting organ in her hand, his finger circling, squeezing gently, driving her body into a frenzy of need. Any moment now . . .

Oh, yes! The climax erupted in waves of exquisite sensation, rocking her body, arching her into the hand he'd cupped tight around her.

She rode delicious waves of sensation. How had she lived without this feeling?

When her breathing slowed, she realized her hand still circled him. She'd become so focused on the pleasure he was bringing her, she'd forgotten to keep stroking him.

He was still hard—achingly hard, she guessed—and when she tightened her grip he groaned, "Yes, Brooke."

He'd brought her such ecstasy that she wanted more intimate contact. She released her grip and shifted position, kneeling beside him, leaning over. She circled the tip of him with her tongue, tasting him, amazed at how smooth and satiny his skin was. She circled faster and his hips began to pump again. Then she opened her mouth and took him inside.

He shuddered and gasped, "Brooke, I . . ."

She slid her lips up and down, ran her tongue along his shaft, and he groaned again, then exploded. Wanting all of him, she swallowed as he pumped again, and again, emptying himself into her.

Finally, when he was done, she lifted her head.

He grabbed her roughly by the shoulders and hauled her

up and across his body. "And now we kiss," he muttered just before his mouth fastened on hers.

This was no lazy, satisfied, after-sex caress; this was a hungry, demanding kiss, almost an assault on her mouth. It told her, in no uncertain terms, that Jake Brannon wasn't finished with her.

She kissed him back with equal hunger. Since she first saw him she had wanted to kiss those sensual lips, had wanted—if she was honest—to be naked with this man. And now she had it all, and she was going to enjoy it.

Jake woke to see sunlight filtering through the gauzy curtains at the window. Pale peach-colored curtains. Not the grungy miniblinds in his Vancouver apartment. Brooke's curtains.

Her body wasn't touching his but he felt her warmth, heard soft breath whisper against her pillow. He grinned to himself, then rolled over—Christ, did he hurt, from the major ache of the bullet wound to the minor one of the lip he'd gnawed—and gazed at her. She was curled on her side, facing him, still asleep. Silky brown lashes dusted the upper curve of her cheekbones; tangled blond curls hid her ear. Her lips were curved in a smile.

His grin widened. Dynamite. They both had plenty of reasons to smile. Last night had been dynamite. She was dynamite. He couldn't remember having sex that good with another woman. Was that because of, or despite, the fact they'd never actually had intercourse? Today he'd buy condoms and tonight they'd find out.

The morning sun was gentle but still revealed the delicate lines etched near her eyes and mouth. He'd been messing around with a grandmother.

The sexiest grandmother on the whole damned planet.

Hell, she was Brooke. She wasn't a bunch of labels like

"grandmother" and "recovering alcoholic"—she was Brooke. And she was dynamite.

He had the hard-on to prove it. He'd have thought that, after the number of orgasms he'd experienced last night, his cock would've been in shock and resting, but that sure wasn't the case. He wondered what imaginative things Brooke might find to do with this particular boner. . . .

Then he remembered that she'd intended to get up early and bake mini-quiches. Probably she normally set an alarm or maybe woke with the morning light, but last night had obviously worn her out.

He grinned again. He'd found one or two imaginative ways to make her come, too.

She deserved to sleep, but he knew she'd be annoyed with herself if she didn't make those appetizers. If it'd been him, he'd have just gone to the store and bought something, but he figured that wasn't her way.

He leaned over her, wincing at his assorted aches and pains. Funny how he hadn't noticed them last night. He touched his lips to her cheek, then pulled back.

She wrinkled her nose, scowled. A hand drifted up, brushed at a curl of hair, then fell back again.

He kissed her nose and retreated.

Her eyes squinted tighter shut and then her lips curved. She remembered whom she was with. And, thank God, she was glad.

"Hey, faker, I know you're awake," he murmured, kissing her ear.

She didn't open her eyes but her smile widened.

He put on a used-car-salesman voice. "Have I got a boner for you."

She gave a splutter of laughter but kept her eyes closed.

"Or you could teach me to make mini-quiches."

"Oh!" She darted upright, her eyes wide with horror. "I forgot. How late is it?"

The covers pooled at her waist and, for the first time, he saw her naked body. Half of it, anyhow. And it was as lovely as he'd imagined when he'd explored it in the darkness. But half wasn't enough. He flicked the covers back and studied her. He'd seen women with bigger breasts, flatter tummies, but he'd never seen a naked female body that aroused him the way Brooke's did. He reached out to trace a silvery stretch mark.

"Jake!" She reached for the covers.

He gave another flick and they fell to the floor. Now he, too, was revealed in all his naked—and appreciative—glory.

"Oh!" She gaped at his erection. Then she shook her head, as if to clear it. "We really did . . . I mean, last night we . . ."

"We sure did."

She transferred her gaze to his face. "Oh, my gosh."

"To put it mildly."

He leaned forward to touch his lips to hers.

Her hands came up and she held his face between them, gazing into his eyes. "Oh, Jake."

He kissed her again and her mouth opened under his. Despite his arousal he made it a tender, gentle kiss and she responded in kind.

"Good morning, Brooke. And thank you for an incredible night."

"You, too." She ducked her head. "Incredible is the right word."

He lifted her chin. "No regrets. Please?"

"No. No! How could I regret it? I'm just feeling . . . shy." She gave an unladylike snort. "Boy, is that silly. After the things we did to each other."

"We're lovers now. No shyness, no regrets. Deal?"

"Lovers. I like that. All right, Jake, it's a deal. And now I need to shower and head down to the kitchen." She scrambled out of bed, giving him a fantastic view of her slender back, curvy butt, and shapely legs.

"I'll come with you."

She tossed a seductive look over her shoulder. "To the shower?"

He clambered out of bed. Took a look at his erection. "If you make it a cold one."

She stood waiting as he walked over to her. Then she wrapped her fingers around his cock and he gasped at how good it felt.

"Or not," she murmured.

Brooke backed her car down the driveway and into the road. She glanced at her house, saw Jake standing at the living room window, and waved. He waved back.

Her lover. She had the contented ache between her legs to prove it, and her mouth couldn't stop smiling.

She forced herself to concentrate on the road, to negotiate traffic when she hit the highway, to make a donut stop as private penance for deceiving her boss.

Kate greeted her with a hug. "Golly, the rest did you good. You look great."

Sex would do that, Brooke thought. Especially sex with a considerate, imaginative, utterly sexy man like Jake. She thrust out the bag of donuts. "Jelly and double chocolate."

"Yummy." Kate reached into the bag and pulled out a sugar-coated treat. "Jelly first, and chocolate for dessert. How about you?"

"Maybe later. I spent the last couple of hours making mini-quiches for the Heritage Committee fund-raiser and I can't face food at the moment." It had been fun working in the kitchen with Jake. Flirting, touching. Surprisingly, the quiches had turned out fine.

"Isn't it great news about Jessica's pregnancy?" Kate said.

"It sure is. I can't wait to see her. Speaking of which, don't book me too late tonight. I'm going over for dinner. And, by the way, I have good news of my own."

"Is that why you're looking so sparkly?"

"I guess. Well, combined with having a grandchild on the way. Anyhow, I've got a cousin coming to town for a few days. He should arrive this afternoon."

"A cousin? Well, won't that be fun for you."

Brooke tried not to blush. "His name is Arnold Pitt. He's an accountant in Vancouver and has been thinking about moving to a smaller town and setting up his own practice."

"What perfect timing, with Ellen leaving town." Kate brushed sugar off her fingers with a napkin, then reached into the donut bag again.

"That's why I mentioned it to him."

Waving a chocolate donut, Kate said, "Wouldn't that be great having your cousin living in town? I can't wait to meet him."

"You'll get your chance. He's driving up and I told him to come into town and find me here."

"You'll want to leave early and take him over to your house."

"No need. I'll give him directions; then he can head over and settle in." Brooke opened the appointment book. "Who's booked for today?" She tapped a finger between two appointments. "Is it all right if I take lunch here? I need to run a couple of errands." Like pick Jake up and drive him to Zephyr Lake, where he'd get his car and identity papers from Jamal Estevez.

"That works fine."

Kate poured herself a cup of coffee to go with her second donut, and Brooke donned her Beauty Is You smock and slotted the tools of the trade into the appropriate pockets. The bell at the door tinkled and she went to greet her first client. "Morning, Maria. Come on in. Want a cup of tea or coffee?"

As she went through the familiar routine, Brooke had a

growing sense of unease. She felt like two people. Kate and Maria were interacting with her the way they always did, and she was behaving normally too. But she didn't feel normal. She wasn't normal.

When Maria left, Brooke hurried into the washroom and stared at her face in the mirror. Same old face, yet a different person stared out of the eyes. Overnight, she'd become a woman who was involved in a murder investigation, a woman who was lying to her friends. A woman who was having hot sex with a younger man.

She felt jumpy and excited, and it scared her. Could she be cycling toward a manic spell despite the lithium? She was tempted to take an extra pill but she'd promised her psychiatrist she wouldn't self-medicate. Perhaps she should call and ask him if the dose should be increased temporarily. Panic surged through her. She couldn't cope with this. What on earth was she thinking?

The shop bell tinkled and she guessed it was Chester Morton, who was scheduled for a trim. Hurriedly she splashed cold water on her cheeks, then went to greet him.

Chester was a quiet man and she was thankful for that as she worked on his graying hair and tried to suppress her panic. Maybe she should call Anne, her A.A. sponsor. Except she wasn't craving a drink; she was just edgy.

After Chester came Mrs. Battison, one of the dear old ladies who got her hair cut and permed every few months. She was a widow who lived alone, and this was a social outing for her. She'd been a barrel racer many decades ago, and Brooke always enjoyed hearing her reminisce about her days on the rodeo circuit, before she won the event at the Williams Lake Stampede and also captured the heart of one of the judges. Bill Battison had persuaded her to hang up her saddle in Caribou Crossing. Today, Brooke was too jittery to concentrate, and settled for making periodic "mmm-hmm" sounds that she hoped she timed appropriately.

When she'd rolled Mrs. Battison's white hair onto curlers and applied perm solution, Brooke went into the tiny office and called her psychiatrist, Dr. Allenby. Fortunately, he wasn't with a patient. His wife, who managed his office, put Brooke through to him.

"I'm feeling a little . . ." She paused, not wanting to use the word *manic*. It wasn't exactly right. "On edge. Excited, wound up. I'm afraid I may be cycling."

"You're taking your lithium regularly?"

"Of course."

"You haven't been manic in four years. We checked your lithium level last week and it was fine."

"I know."

"So, you're feeling excited and wound up. Anything special happening in your life?"

She gave a nervous laugh. What would he say if she told him the truth? "Jessica's pregnant, which is a thrill. As well as a worry, of course." When Jess and Evan had talked about having children, the whole family had sat down with Dr. Allenby to discuss the chance of the baby having bipolar disorder.

"Babies never come with guarantees," the doctor said now. "Concentrate on being happy, rather than on worrying."

"I'm trying. Also, I have a cousin—I haven't seen him in years—coming to town this afternoon for a visit."

"And that's exciting too. You're looking forward to seeing him, but nervous. Brooke, it's all right to have feelings. You don't want to be emotionally dead."

No, but she'd been careful not to involve herself in emotional situations. Until Evan returned to town, the most emotion she'd experienced was pleasure that a bride's hairstyle turned out perfectly, or enjoyment at having Sunny's company on a cold, snowy night.

"We've talked about this," Dr. Allenby said. "Normal people have highs and lows, and so will you, even on lithium. Like when your son returned to town, and when he and Jess got hitched."

True, but then her primary emotion had been delight. Although it was also true that she'd been on edge about attending the wedding when the whole town knew her and Evan's history.

"Seems to me this might just be a stressful, exciting time in your life," the doctor was saying.

She chuckled. "It definitely is. So, you think it's normal, what I'm feeling?"

"When my wife and I heard that our first grandchild was on the way, you'd have sworn we were manic. We rushed off to Williams Lake and maxed our charge cards buying clothes and games and toys."

It was difficult to imagine the mellow Dr. Allenby dashing around like a besotted granddad, but he was an honest man so she believed him. As usual, he'd made her feel better.

"Want to come in and talk some more?" he asked. "I'll test your lithium level again, if you want, but I really think it's just excitement."

"I think you're right. You've helped, by normalizing what I'm feeling. You're my reality check, Dr. Allenby."

"Call me anytime. Or make an appointment and we'll have a nice long talk."

When she returned to check Mrs. Battison's perm, Brooke smiled at the elderly lady. "Guess what? My daughter-in-law's pregnant! Isn't that the most exciting news?"

"Oh my, dear, that's wonderful. You must be thrilled."

Thrilled. Yes, she was. By Jess's pregnancy and also by having spent a wild and wicked night with Jake. She was entitled to be thrilled. Dr. Allenby had given her permission. No, more importantly, she'd given herself permission.

After they'd talked about the baby, she told Mrs. Battison about Cousin Arnold. As she did, she realized something ironic. A policeman was using her, Brooke Kincaid, to create a cover story of respectability. How far she'd come in the last five years!

Chapter Eleven

When Brooke called to say she'd pick him up in fifteen minutes, Jake changed into the gray suit. He couldn't bring himself to button the shirt at the neck. Reluctantly, he folded a tie and stuffed it into his jacket pocket. He figured Arnold for a guy who'd choose formal when making a first impression.

Hungry, he made a couple of peanut butter and jam sandwiches and ate them standing up. Then he made one for Brooke and wrapped it in waxed paper. She needed regular meals; he'd learned that fact from his research on bipolar disorder.

When he put the ingredients back in the fridge, his eyes lit on last night's apple crisp and he couldn't resist. He hauled out the casserole dish, whipped off the lid, and dug a spoon into the contents. The stuff tasted just as good cold, without ice cream, as it had last night. He took another spoonful.

A car crunched down the driveway and he hurried into the living room to make sure it was Brooke. She slid out from behind the steering wheel and walked toward the house, her legs long and bare and shapely under a casual skirt. She climbed the front steps and he opened the door.

"Great legs," he commented.

"As I recall, yours aren't so bad either."

He slammed the door shut, then caught her in his arms and kissed her with a morning worth's pent-up horniness.

She pressed her body against his and responded wholeheartedly.

Man, she was something. Once she'd finally overcome whatever scruples were holding her back, she was the sexiest, most generous lover imaginable.

She pulled out of his arms, giving a shaky laugh. "Hold that thought, Jake."

He grabbed her hand and pressed it against his fly. "I'd rather you held it."

Her blue-green eyes sparkled up at him. "Later. I promise. You have to meet Jamal, and I have a client at one-thirty."

He groaned resignedly. "Oh, before we go, I made you a sandwich."

"You did?"

"Thought you might not have time to get lunch."

"That's very thoughtful of you. Thank you, Jake." She headed for the kitchen and he followed. She saw the apple crisp casserole on the counter, and lifted the spoon out of it. She raised an eyebrow in his direction.

Realizing what he had done, he said apologetically, "I should've dished it out into a bowl."

"That would be the civilized way," she agreed. She held the dish out to him. "Another bite before we go?"

After he ate a bit more he scooped up a small mouthful and held the spoon to her lips.

She paused only a moment before accepting. "Dessert before first course. You're a bad influence." She picked up the wrapped sandwich. "This is mine?"

"Peanut butter and jam. Nothing special. Hope it's okay." Now he almost wished he hadn't done it. She was such a good cook, she probably never ate plain stuff like that.

But she was smiling. "Sounds great. Oh, and there are a

couple of donuts in the car. If you aren't full from the apple crisp."

When they reached the front door, he checked to ensure the coast was clear. They hurried to her Corolla, where he hopped into the back and lay down on the seat so it would look like she was alone in the car. Thank God he didn't get motion sickness. Bad enough that his healing wounds were throbbing.

She tossed the donut bag back to him and he bit into a jelly donut as she started down the road.

"I hope Sergeant Estevez can find Zephyr Lake," she said. "It's out of the way."

"That's the idea. Don't want anyone seeing us. And don't worry about him; the car will have GPS."

"Teenagers hang out there at night in the summer, but during the day—especially this early in the year—there shouldn't be anyone there." Sounding nervous, she'd been repeating information they'd already gone over, but now she added a new bit. "Evan proposed to Jessica there."

He finished the donut. "Yeah?" Taking another donut from the bag, he said, "Want a bite?"

She glanced back. "Chocolate? I shouldn't. I'll get fat."

"Not going to happen. Besides, if you do, I'll just have to exercise it off you."

If he twisted just right, he could peek between the two seats and see her arm, her denim-covered thigh, her bare knee. He watched her knee move up and down as she worked the gas pedal. "I'm going to stop somewhere and buy condoms," he said.

Her shoulders shook. "Now there's a plan. But don't do it in Caribou Crossing or you'll really have people wondering about Arnold."

"I'll drive down the highway to the next town and find a drugstore there. Got a favorite brand?"

She spluttered with laughter. "You think I know the brands

of condoms? Pick whatever you like best and I'm sure they'll be just fine with me." And then she gave a shiver, a big one that moved from her shoulders down through her whole body.

He knew exactly what she was thinking. "Tonight I'll be inside you, Brooke." And he was, yet again, hard.

After a few moments of silence she said, "Jake? I feel kind of . . . unbalanced with you. I told you the most intimate details of my life. It's different from sex. Sex is intimate but it's—well, for us, it's about fun, right?"

"For sure."

"And it's mutual. But with the talking, it's all been about me. I feel like we're on an uneven footing. I'd like to know more about you. Not Arnold, but Jake."

"What's to know? I'm thirty-five, single, a U/C cop. My life's pretty much about work, but that's okay 'cause I love my job. There's never—well, hardly ever—a dull moment."

"You said you don't have much time for relationships, other than casual ones."

"Job keeps me busy."

"You said your parents don't like your job?"

"No. I haven't seen them in a long time. They were disappointed with how I turned out."

Her head swung toward him. "Disappointed?" She huffed. "I should think they'd be proud."

He liked how she stuck up for him. "What does Evan do?" She'd already told him, but he had a point to make.

"He's an investment counselor."

"And Jessica has this riding camp she's started?"

"Yes, and she's wonderful at it."

"How would you like it if one of them was an undercover cop? Investigating drug trafficking, gang wars? Or if that's the career your grandkid chose?"

"I'd worry myself sick," she said promptly. "But I wouldn't be disappointed in them." She braked and stopped, and the sound of traffic told him it was an intersection.

"Well, good for you. But my parents had other plans for me." He gave a quick, humorless laugh. "Hell, even accounting wouldn't have satisfied them. They wanted medicine or law."

"What do they do?" She put the car in motion again.

He wished he could sit up and get his bearings. "Mom does charities. Cultural ones. Dad's a lawyer. Corporate commercial. He makes a lot of money."

"And that's what they wanted for you?"

"Pretty much."

"But you're not that kind of man. I don't imagine you were that kind of boy?"

"Nah. But they kept trying to make me into one. Respectable, boring. They didn't see me. Didn't want to see me. Didn't care what I wanted."

"I suspect that made you rebel."

"Yup. I was hell-bent on getting away from them and being as different as I could possibly be."

She nodded, and when she spoke her voice was sad. "Evan was like that, but for different reasons. His father and I were such losers. He knew he wanted a different life, and he had to get away to do it. He was driven. And he made it. Top of his class, a scholarship to Cornell."

"As a Canadian?"

"Actually, he has dual citizenship. Even though I'm uncomfortable around the police, I went to them after Mo left and I told them everything. I guess they could have charged me for helping him conceal his identity, but they didn't. And I did get back my own identity papers, and Evan's. Proof that he was an American citizen."

"You stayed Kincaid, though, rather than go back to McKeen or your maiden name?"

She shrugged. "It was easier. This way, only the police knew about Mo, not the whole town." She made a turn and the car's tires left pavement and hit a rougher surface. "This is the road to Zephyr Lake."

He risked lifting his head, saw a narrow road with barely room for two cars to pass, meandering between two fenced acreages with cattle grazing.

Playing it safe, he ducked down again. "Why Cornell?"

"They had a program that interested him and it was close to New York City, where he wanted to end up. He said Manhattan was the hub of the world." She gave a soft laugh. "Mo and Brooke's son at Cornell. It's just amazing. But that's Evan. He can do anything if he sets his mind to it."

She pulled to a stop. "Sergeant Estevez isn't here yet. No one is, so you can come out."

He extracted himself slowly and painfully from the backseat and stretched, making a careful survey of his surroundings. It was a pretty spot. A deep blue lake sparkled in the May sunshine. Scattered trees and rock formations lined it. He could imagine teenagers coming out here to talk, swim, drink some beer, smoke a little weed, make out.

Brooke opened the driver's door to the fresh air, unwrapped her sandwich, and took a bite.

"Jamal will be here soon," Jake said. "If you need to get back to work, just leave me here."

She glanced at her watch. "No rush yet."

He climbed into the passenger seat, figuring he could scrunch down out of sight if anyone else came along.

Brooke turned to study his face. "You and Evan and Anika all have something in common. You felt you had to escape your parents. Is that why you care so much about kids like Anika and Sapphire?"

He hadn't thought of it that way. Musingly, he said, "I did leave home early. I was sick of my folks pushing me to be something I wasn't." He glanced at her pretty, concerned face and admitted, "I was a lot like Mo. A thrill seeker. Drove too fast, drank too much, did some drugs, hung out with a bad crowd. Lived on the edge. Worked at this and that."

She frowned. "An odd path to lead to the RCMP."

"Yeah, but I was lucky. Worked a construction job where the boss was engaged in human trafficking. The RCMP got a tip and investigated. I got talking to a couple of members about undercover work and decided to join up."

"They took you? I mean, after the drugs and so on?"

"Not right away. These two guys kind of took me on, as a cause. Guess they saw some potential. You bet they made me clean up my act. Luckily, I'd never been busted so I didn't have a criminal record. I went to Simon Fraser University, took the criminology program, did lots of volunteer work with high-risk kids, hooked my RCMP buddies up with a few informants."

Brooke touched his arm. "You really did turn yourself around. Congratulations, Jake."

"Ah hell, don't give me too much credit. It was a kick, just a different kind."

"Mmm. Once they'd accepted you, didn't you say you and Jamal fast-tracked to get to undercover work?"

"You start out on general duty, but my U/C pals gave me some tips on how to move through the system."

"How?" Her eyes were bright with interest, and he remembered those mystery novels on her shelves.

"Go to the U/C guys and volunteer your off-duty time. We helped with surveillance and drug busts, flipped a few sources. Kept working with high-risk kids; volunteered with the community policing centers. We proved we had what they wanted. Got references, commendations, wrote the undercover exam at five years."

"Stayed away from drugs."

"Hell, yeah."

"Watched your drinking?"

"Uh-huh."

"You're not an alcoholic."

He shook his head.

"But you know a lot about A.A. Like how we count sobriety in days, and about the five-year pin."

He tried not to squirm. "You pick up a lot on the streets."

She tilted her head and held his gaze. "It sounded like personal knowledge. Like someone close to you was an alcoholic. One of your parents?"

"No way."

"Then . . ."

"It's not for me to say. You know that."

"Of course." She studied his face some more. "Jamal."

"Shit, Brooke." How in hell had she picked up on that?

"He's the only person you talk about. It's obvious you're close." She frowned slightly. "He is sober now, isn't he?"

"Two years. But look, you can't tell anyone."

"I won't. Alcoholics don't; you know that."

He had trusted her with so many things already. He reached out and grasped her shoulder, feeling its firm strength. "Here's the deal, Brooke. No one in the RCMP knows."

She nodded slowly. "There'd be consequences, wouldn't there?"

"They'd be wary about trusting him, especially with U/C work. There's a lot of alcohol and drugs around when you work U/C."

"Lots of temptation." Her brow furrowed. "But it's not fair. He's sober."

"That's why I keep his secret. He's not endangering anyone's lives anymore." Damn, his mouth kept running off when he was with this woman.

Of course she pounced on his words. "Anymore?"

He sighed. "We were working a long assignment together. I was undercover; he was my handler. I'd been on the street more than a year. That's when I figured out he had a real problem. He wasn't reliable anymore."

The furrow deepened. "Your job is dangerous. You need someone you can trust absolutely. You didn't report him?"

He shook his head vigorously. "We'd been together a long time. I said we don't work with partners, but Jamal and I are close to that."

"But . . . what did you do? Nothing?"

"Nah. Nothing's not something I'm good at."

A quick smile flashed. "I can believe that. So?"

"Soon as the assignment ended and we got a few weeks' leave, I took him out of town and dragged him into A.A. meetings."

"You can't make an addict give up their addiction. They've got to want to."

"He was sick of me bitching at him. He got off the booze so I'd get off his back."

She shook her head. "I bet he realized that he'd let you down but you'd been there for him. That someone cared enough about him to try to help. I'd think that would be a good incentive."

He shrugged, then studied her. "You didn't have anyone, did you?"

She shook her head. "Lucky Jamal," she murmured, "to have you as a friend."

"Anyone would have done it."

"Sure." She slanted him a smile. "Whatever you say, Jake." She'd stopped eating while they were talking, but now lifted the second half of her sandwich and took a bite. "This is good. Thanks."

"Welcome." He sat back, keeping an ear open for the sound of an approaching vehicle and enjoying watching her. Noticing a ragged white scar on her right arm, he ran a finger down it. "What happened here?"

She glanced at it. "Sunny. When I first brought him inside. I probably should have gotten stitches but there was a bad storm and I was wary about driving to the hospital."

"I'm surprised you didn't toss the cat back out into the storm."

"Like you tossed Jamal away when he let you down?" She shook her head. "I told you Sunny was abused. He was hurting, he was scared, and so he struck out. I can't blame him."

"You're generous. And patient." As he well knew.

"Well, I've had some experience." She gazed down at the steering wheel. "Being damaged myself. I hurt people, let them down. Mostly I hurt Evan, but there were others. I was in so much pain myself that I didn't care, didn't even notice, if I hurt others."

She turned to him, her expression serious. "You can't imagine the relief of knowing that you actually have an illness. It doesn't take the guilt away or make anything right, but at least you understand that you're not really a horrible person."

"I can't imagine anyone ever thinking that you were."

"You didn't know me then," she said flatly. "I was awful."

He circled her wrist with his hand. "I know you now. You're a fine person." He was leaning over to kiss her when his keen hearing picked up the sound of an engine.

Jake was good for her ego, Brooke thought as he ducked below the dash. She watched a car park across the dirt lot, and squinted to see the make. "It's a silver Lexus," she told Jake.

A man climbed out and stood by the car. "Tall, maybe an inch or two taller than you, and bigger through the body. Muscular, not fat. Dark skin, good-looking." She squinted again, to sharpen her vision. "His facial features look like a mix of black and Hispanic."

Jake eased his head up and verified, "Yeah, that's Jamal. You think he's good-looking?"

She chuckled. "Almost as good-looking as you. But wow, he's distinctive. That guy goes undercover?"

Reaching for the door handle, he said, "He's versatile, good at disguises. We have to be, to do our kind of work."

They both climbed out of the car, and Jamal strode over to them. He was a formidable man, she decided, but for the twinkle in his eyes when he stopped dead and studied Jake.

"Arnold Pitt," he said softly, "as I live and breathe." Then he gave a rich chuckle and said, "Too, too funny, man," and whacked Jake on the back.

Jake whacked him too, with somewhat more force.

Jamal turned to Brooke. "Ms. Kincaid, I'm Jamal."

"Brooke." She held out her hand and he shook it. His grip was firm and she found herself liking him. She could envision him blending into a biker gang, but right now his eyes were smiling, his short curly hair was neat, and his jeans and black T-shirt were clean.

"You're the one transformed my man?" he asked.

"I am. What do you think?"

"Think you should be workin' for us. Did so fine a job I'd hardly know him." He chuckled again. "Wouldn't wanna know him."

Jake whacked him again. "Gimme a break. I don't want to know me either."

Partners. Friends. Their closeness was obvious to her, yet she suspected they'd never spoken of it to each other. Spenser and Hawk, she thought, remembering Robert B. Parker's novels. So who did that make her? Susan Silverman, Spenser's "main squeeze"?

But Susan and Spenser's relationship—unconventional as it was—had been founded on a deep love and it lasted for years. Her and Jake's was based on lust and liking and would be over in a few days. The thought brought both sadness and relief. Already she knew she'd miss him, but she needed a safe, structured life. Caring for Jake would be anything but safe.

And, speaking of structure, she informed them, "I have to

get back to work." She pulled a key from her pocket. "Jamal, this opens my shed. Slip it under my back door when you're ready to go."

Yesterday, Jake had determined that his Harley was operable. It was a liability, though. They couldn't afford to have anyone snoop around and find it. Jake and Jamal would drive to her place, where Jamal would collect the bike and ride it back to Vancouver. Then Jake would drive into Caribou Crossing and show up at Beauty Is You.

After he'd made a side trip to buy condoms. Hopefully, he would do that after, not before, parting ways with Jamal. Trying not to blush, she nodded to Jamal. "Good luck."

"And you, Brooke. Our boy'll take care of you."

She gave him a saccharine smile. "And I'll do my best to get him back to you in one piece. Without any more bullet holes."

Jamal slapped his thigh and laughed. "I like you, girl."

Girl. A forty-three-year-old grandmother. It was almost flattering.

Chapter Twelve

Brooke decided that, rather than moon over Jake, she would help out with the investigation. That afternoon, she subtly steered conversations with her clients.

Silvia Campinelli was first, with a picture of Angelina Jolie from *People*, and a request for the same hairstyle. Brooke learned that the woman and her young lawyer husband were living way beyond their means. She suspected, though, that their behavior had nothing to do with crime and everything to do with inexperience. They'd have their comeuppance when they missed a mortgage payment.

Her next client, Melody Sampson, was a loan manager at one of the banks. A single woman, she was career focused. In the past she'd mentioned that she hoped to transfer to a bigger branch in a larger town like Williams Lake, then ultimately to Vancouver. As Brooke stacked foils for highlights and lowlights, she asked Melody how work was going.

"Good, good," the young woman responded briskly. "Next week I'm going to Vancouver for a training session on client development. It's quite prestigious to be chosen."

"Congratulations. Who chose you? Was it Mr. Cray?" Howard Cray was manager of the bank where Melody worked.

Brooke had never liked him; he was a cold man and always seemed to be looking down his beaky nose at her. She was quite happy banking with the credit union.

"Yes, he attended the course himself, and thought it would be useful for me."

"Oh? Does Mr. Cray go to many courses?"

"A couple of times a year. And there are financial-planning sessions, management meetings, and so on. He's down in Vancouver quite a bit. Lucky man!"

Hmm. A respectable man who made lots of business trips. "I imagine Margaret and their son enjoy those trips," she probed.

"Oh, they don't usually go. Margaret's caught up in her own career. I think they—" She broke off, then beckoned Brooke closer, to whisper, "They're not very close. They lead quite separate lives. Both very career focused." She added more loudly, "Not that there's anything wrong with that."

"Not at all." Brooke separated a few strands of hair, spread them on a piece of foil, and brushed on color.

"I just think it's not fair to get married and have kids if you're going to be obsessed with your work."

"I agree. But the Crays' son is a teenager, right? He probably doesn't want his parents interfering in his life anyhow. Besides, I get the impression they're pretty generous with him." The boy always had the latest clothes and electronic gadgets, and his parents had given him an expensive car when he turned sixteen.

"You can say that again. And I suppose you're right, that they're not being bad parents. Margaret didn't get her real estate license until Anthony was in elementary school. Before that, she was home with him."

"They live in a really nice house, don't they? I guess she found it for them?"

"Yes, a few years ago. It's utterly fabulous. It could be in

Architectural Digest. The Crays have the staff over every Christmas."

"Generous."

She sniffed. "Snobby. They only want to show off the house, furniture, art. Plus, I think it's bank policy that the managers do some socializing with staff, so Howard makes Margaret arrange a catered party."

"Must be nice to be rich," Brooke murmured.

"One day I'll have a really nice place of my own," Melody stated confidently. "But it won't be any house in the country."

"No?"

"A penthouse in the city. That's what I've got my heart set on. No more stench of cow and horse shit, no more roosters crowing before dawn. No shoveling snow or swatting mosquitoes."

Brooke grinned. "You sound like my son did when he was a teenager."

"But he ended up coming back. You won't see me doing that."

The bell at the door tinkled and they both turned their heads.

It was Jake. Rather, it was Arnold Pitt, with his tie perfectly knotted and the light glinting off his glasses.

Brooke wiped her hands on a towel and stepped toward him but Kate got there first. She was saying, "May I help you?" when Brooke broke in with, "Arnold? Is that you?"

He turned toward her. "Brooke? Cousin Brooke?" Then he caught her hands in his. "I'd recognize you anywhere. Same curly blond hair."

She squeezed his hands, and then they both let go. She touched her hair self-consciously. "It gets a little help these days."

"You work in the right place for that."

Kate cleared her throat and he turned to her. She stuck her

hand out. "I'm Kate Patterson, Brooke's friend and coworker. She's been so excited about you coming for a visit, Arnold."

He shook her hand. "I've been quite excited myself. Brooke was my favorite relative when I was a child."

"She says you're an accountant in Vancouver?"

Brooke couldn't leave Melody with half her foils done, so she stepped away, letting Jake field Kate's questions.

"Who's that?" Melody hissed.

"A cousin of mine. He lives in Vancouver but is thinking of moving here."

"He's crazy."

Brooke saw Melody watching Jake in the mirror. "He hasn't decided for sure," she told her client. "It would be a big change."

"He's big-city cute, isn't he? I can just see him walking down Georgia Street with his briefcase and smartphone. On his way to a power lunch with a big client."

"I suppose. But Evan was like that when he was in Manhattan, and look how well he's adjusted to Caribou Crossing. He's more at home in a cowboy hat than wearing a tie."

She finished the foils and patted Melody's shoulder. "I'm setting the timer for fifteen minutes; then I'll check you. Would you like another magazine? A cup of coffee or tea?"

"I'd love a coffee, thanks. Black."

Brooke brought it to her, then rejoined Kate and Jake. "Sorry, but I was in the middle of a color job. Melody's an up-and-comer at one of our local banks."

Jake cocked his head. "Image is important. That's really what you help people with, isn't it? It's more than just haircuts and color; it's a look. One they choose to express their personality. Or to hide their true personality, I suppose."

Brooke almost chuckled. As an undercover cop, he knew as much about creating an image as she did.

"Exactly," Kate agreed. "For example, I can tell from

looking at you that you're not from Caribou Crossing. That hairstyle is terrific, but it's urban. If you do decide to move, you'll have to get Brooke to restyle your hair to something a little more casual. Otherwise people might be hesitant to approach you."

"Except Melody," Brooke said dryly. "She's already decided you're big-city cute, and that's exactly what appeals to her."

"Good heavens, cousin, are you match-making me?"

The two women laughed and Brooke marveled at how Jake managed to convey a completely different character than his own. He wasn't overly prissy, just more formal and less macho than his real self, and it made a huge difference.

"Arnold, I sketched out a map to show you how to get to my house." She dipped into a pocket of her smock and pulled out a folded piece of paper. "Take a look and see if it's clear."

She'd been tempted to write him a silly, sexy note, but had realized that curious Kate might want to take a look at the map, as she was now craning to do.

"It's excellent," he said, "though you didn't need to. My car has GPS, and so does my smartphone. Accountants don't believe in getting lost."

Both women chuckled, and then Brooke handed him her spare key. "Make yourself at home."

"Thank you," Jake said. "Now I should get out of your hair, if you'll forgive the expression." He gazed at Brooke, and for a second she saw the real Jake behind Arnold's glasses. He wanted to touch her. She knew it. But he didn't think it would be in character for Arnold.

She flashed him a sudden smile and leaned forward to grip his shoulders and plant a kiss on his cheek. "It's so good to have you here, Arnold."

"Oh! Well, thank you, Brooke. It's good to be here. Good to see you again." He managed to look both pleased and flustered—a perfect Arnold reaction.

When he had gone, Kate said, "What a nice man. Has he changed much since he was a boy?"

"He was a geeky kid, and now he has more poise and polish. The glasses are new, but I guess number crunching all day is hard on the eyes. As for personality, it's hard to tell yet. He was a sweet boy, so I hope he's turned into a nice man."

"He's staying through the weekend?"

"That's the plan. Unless we scare him off."

Jake didn't really expect that they'd have sex when Brooke got home from work, so he tried not to be disappointed when she dashed in saying, "Sorry, I'm running late. Give me five minutes and I'll be ready."

He had a feeling this wasn't the time to join her in the shower. Still, he was awfully tempted when the water came on.

She was almost true to her word. It was no more than ten minutes until she was back downstairs, dressed in figure-hugging jeans and a greenish blue top that made her striking eyes even more intense. When she stretched up to drop a quick kiss on his lips, he smelled minty toothpaste. He couldn't resist drawing her to him for one long, full-body hug.

"Did you get the condoms?" she whispered, her breath tickling his ear seductively.

"I've got my priorities straight." It had now been almost twelve hours since he'd last seen her naked and he didn't know how he was going to make it through the evening.

She hurried to the kitchen to retrieve the chocolate-mint layer cake she'd taken from the freezer that morning.

He followed. "How far is Evan and Jessica's place?"

"Only five minutes' drive."

"Let's compare notes before we go. Do we have time?"

She checked the bird clock on the kitchen wall. "Ten minutes. I don't like being late. But I am curious. Did Jamal have any new information? I like him, by the way."

"He likes you too. Let's see. That store, Gifts of the Caribou, really was burglarized."

"Yes, Kate told me."

"If someone was looking for a reason to ask questions about a guy on a motorbike, faking a crime would give him one. Jamal couldn't find anything against the owner of the store, Patel. What do you know about him?"

"His family came from India, he grew up around here, and he's married to a woman he met in India when he was visiting relatives. I think it was an arranged marriage, but it seems to have worked well. They've got three kids. Vijay has always struck me as a nice guy, polite but a little pushy. A typical salesman. His store is nice; his family is nice. I can't see him being a criminal."

"Any trips out of town, like to shop for inventory?"

She shook her head. "The family goes to India every couple of years to visit relatives. And Vijay has a brother who's a doctor in Vancouver, who they visit once or twice a year. I can't imagine him sneaking out on them and visiting a hooker, doing drug deals." She sighed. "But that's the point, isn't it? The killer isn't going to be the most likely person."

Then she said, "Your informant, Sapphire, didn't say anything about the bad guy's race?"

"Anika didn't give her any physical description. If you had to name the most likely man, who'd you say?"

"Hmm. Sergeant Miller is a self-important sexist bully. I'm almost sure Randy Sorokin, the chair of the chamber of commerce, abuses his wife. After living with Mo, I recognize the signs. But even if he's an abuser and Miller's a sexist pig, that's a long stretch from prostitutes and drugs." She paused.

"Yes?" he prompted.

"There's Howard Cray, the manager at National Bank. His eyes spook me. He smiles, but his eyes never warm." She told him about the conversation she'd had with Melody, one of Cray's employees.

"Trips to Vancouver," Jake said thoughtfully, "mainly alone. Throws money around. The manager of a Caribou Crossing bank doesn't make the kind of money to buy an *Architectural Digest* type of home. And you say he and his wife and son all have BMWs?"

She nodded. "His wife sells real estate and maybe she does really well, but the economy's been depressed for the last few years and property values are down."

"One of them could have inherited money," he mused "I'll get Jamal to see what he can find out. Cray's a good lead, Brooke. It's logical for Arnold to chat with a bank manager if he's thinking about setting up a business. What about Miller and Sorokin? Any trips out of town?"

"I don't know."

"Living beyond their means?"

"No. The Sorokins seem . . . normal, from the outside." Her voice gave a tiny quaver.

Jake's hands tensed, wanting to make fists. He hated men who hit women, and he especially hated the idea that someone had done that to Brooke.

"Miller's a redneck," she went on. "Spends a lot of time in the bar watching sports, drinking, shooting pool, hanging out with the guys. He has a rancher-style house, a wife who doesn't work outside the home, a son about twelve, and a daughter a few years younger. The son is big for his age, good at sports, but a bully like his father. The daughter is a little princess. Pretty clothes, dancing lessons."

"Nothing very suspicious there."

"I guess not," she said reluctantly. "But I really don't like the man."

Jake suppressed a grin. If the RCMP were to act on female intuition, Miller was obviously their man. If only it were that easy. "What's his drink?"

"I've seen him with beer. Hard liquor too, but I don't know

what kind." She gestured toward the clock and picked up the cake. "Let's take your car."

Once in the Lexus, she balanced the cake platter on her lap. Too bad. He'd have liked to put his hand there. High up on the inside of her thigh.

He turned the car in the direction she indicated. "You said they live close by?"

"We all live on Bly Ranch."

"Oh yeah? That seems a little close for comfort."

"It works surprisingly well. Wade, Jessica's dad, had a stroke a while back. Jessica and Robin moved in to help with things, and Wade and Miriam added Jess to the title for the ranch. When she married Evan, they added him too, and he's handling the finances. Now they've all allocated part of the ranch land for Jess and Evan's house and her Riders Boot Camp. Evan cashed in some investments so they got the house built last fall."

"And your house is on the Blys' ranch too?"

"I was in a run-down rental in town, and the Blys' rental cottage was sitting vacant. They made me the offer, and persuaded me it wasn't charity, so I moved in. I love being out here in the country. It's so peaceful and quiet." She gave a snort of laughter. "Or it was, until the guy on the Harley came along. But anyhow, I love being close to the family. Robin taught me to ride and we go out a couple of times a week. And also, I'm a partner in Jess's new business."

"A partner in a new business? That sounds a little risky." And Brooke had told him she was risk averse. "Is that the Riders Boot Camp you mentioned?"

"Yes. And the money I invested is money Evan sent me over the years."

"Why didn't you spend it?"

"I couldn't. It didn't seem right. So I saved it, with the idea—which seemed crazy at the time—that maybe one day he'd need my help. As it turned out, Jess had this dream of opening a no-frills riding boot camp, and she needed investors—or donors, actually, because it's set up as a charitable foundation. It seemed like a perfect use for the money."

"It does." The more he knew of Brooke, the better he liked and respected her. "A charitable foundation? How does that work?"

"Basically, those who can afford it pay to attend. People who are disadvantaged and would really benefit from the experience but couldn't possibly afford it get scholarships. Donor investments fund the core operation and the donors get tax deductions and camp privileges. Evan worked out all the details. He's a whiz at things like that."

"Says his proud mom." He was curious to meet her family. It still seemed hard to believe Brooke had a grown-up son who had his own wife, kid, and baby on the way.

She chuckled. "I surely am. You can't believe how good it feels to have him in my life, and just down the road. Speaking of which—" She gestured toward two wooden signs marking a road on the right.

One sign, weathered and comfortable, said "Bly Ranch." The other, its carving fresh, said, "Riders Boot Camp" and featured a logo of two tooled cowboy boots leaning against each other.

"The logo was Robin's idea," Brooke said proudly. Then, with concern in her voice, she went on, "They're really good people. I hate to deceive them. Particularly Evan, because I lied to him so much when he was a kid. Can't we tell them the truth?"

"I'm sorry. It's not a matter of trust, Brooke; it's for their own protection. It's easy to let something slip. Bad enough you're taking the risk, but I'll look after you. We can't endanger them as well."

"No, of course not," she said quickly.

The narrow road was lined by split-rail fences. Cattle,

including a number of calves, grazed on both sides of the road. Buildings came into view ahead. An old-fashioned farmhouse with flowers in the garden, a barn, outbuildings, all old but in good shape. Another "Bly Ranch" sign, this one new.

"Keep on the main road," she directed, excitement lighting her voice. "The boot camp's up here. Everything's new since last summer. It's amazing how quickly it all went up, but Jessica wanted to start operations this year."

Now Jake saw horses rather than cattle, then another Riders Boot Camp sign. Brooke pointed out the various buildings: a barn and a wooden-fenced ring, a rustic lodge, a handful of small log cabins for couples and families, and a bunkhouse for groups of kids and single adults. "It's no-frills," she reminded him, "not a resort. It's all about the horses and riding."

Like the signs, everything looked fresh and a little raw, but he admired the way the buildings had been laid out among the trees. "A nice setup," he commented.

She nodded in agreement and directed him a little farther. Pointing, she said, "There. That's Evan and Jess's house."

This house, too, looked brand new, though he could see how attractive and homey it would be when the wood aged. Landscaping was minimal, and he'd bet Brooke itched to get her hands on the garden.

"Oh, my gosh," she said breathlessly, "it just really hit me, what we're doing."

He parked in front of the house and turned to her. Her forehead was wrinkled with anxiety. He'd have kissed the lines away if he wasn't afraid someone might glance out one of the large front windows. Instead he touched her hand briefly. "It'll be okay. Remember, I'm Arnold. Neither of us can forget that. But you and I are family, so we don't have to be too formal with each other."

When she reached for the door handle he said, "Wait for me. I'm a gentleman."

He slid out of the car and paused a moment to adjust his tie and smooth his jacket. Then he walked around the car, careful to move like an uninjured man, and opened the passenger door. He took the cake from Brooke, balanced the platter on one hand, and extended his arm to assist her.

"I'm your cousin, not your ancient grandmother," she hissed.

He choked back a laugh. "You're a lady."

She swung out of the car so quickly and nimbly he had to step back. Then she grabbed the cake from him and marched to the front door. "Knock lightly a couple of times," she instructed him. "Then open the door. It'll be unlocked."

He complied, then stood back to let her enter first.

She called "Hello" as he glanced around at a pleasantly, if somewhat sparsely, furnished living room. Hardwood floors with rugs scattered about, paintings and photos of horses on the walls, a wooden staircase leading up to the second floor. This room told such a different story from Brooke's own main room. She was a homebody who'd built herself a cozy nest; her son's family was too busy to care much about their surroundings.

"Gramma!" a young voice shrieked from upstairs. A girl scampered down the stairs, apparently prepared to launch herself straight at Brooke.

Jake rescued the cake in the nick of time, trying not to wince as the sudden motion wrenched his healing wounds.

"Robin." Brooke hugged the girl close.

Yes, she really was a grandmother. As the two separated, Jake got his first good look at Robin. Brooke had said she was eleven, but he'd have taken her for a year or two older. Brooke was about five feet six, and the girl, slim and fit, came up to her shoulders. She'd end up taller than her grandmother, he'd be willing to bet.

And likely a beauty too. She was already showing the

signs, with her even features, glossy chestnut hair in a ponytail, and expression of lively interest.

"You must be Mr. Pitt," she said.

"Call me Arnold." He put the cake down on a sideboard by the door and held out a hand.

She put hers into it and shook firmly.

"And you're Robin."

"And we're some kind of relations, but Mom and Evan and I couldn't figure out exactly what to call it."

"Well, I'm your grandmother's cousin. Her father's brother's son. So why don't we make it easy and just say we're cousins too? Cousins by marriage, I suppose."

"That's right, because Evan's my stepdad."

"Did I hear my name?" a male voice asked, and Jake turned to see a man enter the living room.

Brooke's son. A real grown-up man, roughly his own height and build. Evan gazed at him with a friendly, curious expression, but before greeting him, Evan hugged Brooke. "Hi, Mom. Glad you're feeling better."

Her eyes lit, telling Jake she didn't take hugs from her son for granted.

She hugged him back, almost fiercely. "The father to be. Oh, Evan, I'm so thrilled for you." She released him and turned to Robin. "For all of us. Gosh, Robin, you're going to have a baby brother or sister."

"Yeah, it'll be so much fun!"

"And a big responsibility too," Brooke said, shooting a quick, apologetic look in Evan's direction, an acknowledgment of her own shortcomings.

He responded with a rueful expression and a shrug that seemed to say, *What's done is done. Let's move on.* Perhaps sensing she needed reassurance, he said, "Glad you feel that way, Mom, because we're counting on you to baby-sit."

Brooke swallowed hard. "Any time. Absolutely any time."

Watching the two of them, Jake thought how much they'd

been through, and were still going through. Years during which she'd been ill and not known it, and had abused Evan—emotionally, if not physically. Their eventual reconciliation. The integration of Brooke into Evan's new family.

And now, a cycle starting again. A baby. Jake would have bet his Harley that Brooke would be the most perfect, most trustworthy grandmother any baby could hope for. He was pretty sure Evan knew that too. But how the poor guy must wish that his mother had been there for him, the way she would be there for his kids.

Evan held out his hand. "I'm Evan Kincaid. Welcome to our home."

"I appreciate your hospitality. I'm Arnold Pitt." Damn, Brooke's unwillingness to lie was contagious. He found himself hating to deceive this man.

"Where's Jessica?" Brooke asked. "And how's she feeling?"

"She's in seventh heaven. No morning sickness yet and—"

He broke off as a door opened somewhere in the house, then slammed again. "She had to dash down to Boots to check on a new gelding."

Boots, Jake gathered, was short for Riders Boot Camp.

"It's the new one the horse whisperer sent," Robin said eagerly. "He's a beaut."

"Horse whisperer?" Jake asked.

"A man named Ty Ronan," Brooke said. "He's down in the Fraser Valley and he heals rescue horses that have been physically and emotionally abused. Jessica takes some of them to train for use at Riders Boot Camp."

So the camp was a charity not only for disadvantaged humans but for damaged horses as well. Damn, but he liked these people.

A young woman in jeans and cowboy boots dashed into the room. "Sorry I'm late."

She was Robin, in adult form. Add a few curves, a mature beauty. But it was the same ponytail, same smile.

She hugged Brooke. "Gramma for the second time. Can you believe it?"

Well, no one around here was letting him forget that Brooke was older than he, and had a whole tangle of family bonds. Thank God their relationship was a temporary one, or he might be having reservations.

What was he thinking? Of course he'd be having reservations, and her age and family would be the least of them. The phrase "long-term relationship" wasn't in his vocabulary.

He did, however, seriously want to squeeze Brooke's cute little butt. She was showering hugs on everyone but him, and he felt left out.

Jessica welcomed him with a warm handshake. "This is exciting, Arnold. You're the first of Brooke's family that we've met. You're going to have to tell us everything about her when she was a girl."

He laughed. "I do have some stories."

Brooke gave him a punch on the arm. "I have more stories about you."

"That sounds like a threat, cousin. You were always good at threats. Did they teach you that in baby-sitter school?"

After they'd all shared a chuckle, Jessica said, "Arnold, I'm afraid we're not exactly gourmet chefs around here. We have steaks marinating to throw on the grill. You eat meat, don't you?"

"That sounds good, thank you."

"We'll eat out on the back patio." She flashed a grin. "The air here's the best you've ever smelled, and the mosquitoes mostly don't come out until after dusk."

"Liar," Evan teased.

He led them through a large, well-appointed kitchen and onto a patio with a slatted-wood dining table and chairs with cushioned seats. "Now, what can I get you to drink, Arnold?"

Jake hesitated. What was the socially correct thing to do, given Brooke's alcoholism? Perhaps Evan recognized his quandary, because he said, "I'm having a glass of wine myself. It's a gamay nór from Grey Monk in the Okanagan."

"Thank you. I'd like that." Wine wasn't his drink, but he figured it would be in character for Arnold.

Evan poured wine for the two of them and fruit juice with club soda for the three females. Robin reported that the baked potatoes in the oven had another ten minutes to go, Evan lit the barbecue, and Jess brought a bowl with marinated steaks from the kitchen.

When Jess sat down, Evan stood behind her, his hands resting on her shoulders. "So, Arnold, Mom says you're thinking about leaving the city. Did she tell you I've recently done that myself?"

"Yes, after you'd worked in New York for many years. It must have been a big change."

"But definitely worth it." He bent to drop a kiss on the top of Jessica's head.

"Brooke said you've set up your own investment-counseling business here. Has it been hard or was the town receptive?"

"It's a friendly town. Conservative, but in a good way. The slower pace of life took some getting used to but it's great. It's much, much healthier."

"I can believe that. And down in Vancouver, the crime rate is troubling, as is the case in most big cities."

"Caribou Crossing's not exactly crime free." Brooke picked up his lead neatly. "But our crimes tend to be minor ones. Like vandalism by young people who are bored and unhappy." She glanced up at Evan. "Did you hear Gifts of the Caribou was broken into?"

"Yeah. Not much was taken, apparently. Vijay had an alarm system, so when the thief jimmied the door it went off. The guy smashed a display case, snatched a few pieces of jewelry, and made his escape before the police got there."

"One of those bored teenagers?" Jake asked.

"Probably so."

"What about drugs? That's a big problem in Vancouver."

"Not here," Jessica said. "It's a very clean community."

"Oh, puh-leese," Robin contributed, and all heads swung her way.

Chapter Thirteen

The girl rolled her eyes above the rim of her glass. "People use drugs here. Even at my school. We're not all that goody-goody."

"What in holy blue blazes are you talking about?" her mother asked, her voice high pitched.

Evan, too, gaped at the girl. "Some of the kids at your school use drugs?"

She shrugged and put the glass down. "Well, duh. They're, you know, that kind of kid."

"What kind of kid?" her mother asked.

"You know," Robin repeated. "Like Gramma said, bored and unhappy. Their older brothers and sisters use drugs and they think it's cool."

"Cool?" Evan sounded appalled.

The girl shrugged again. "Not me, I don't think that. It's like smoking, right? It's just stupid, they're killing themselves, but they don't see it that way. Or they don't care." She turned to Arnold. "Oops. You don't smoke, do you?"

"You think I'd confess to it now if I did?" he teased.

He hadn't figured that the drug expert in the crowd would be the eleven-year-old, but now that he had her on the subject he figured he might as well probe a bit further. "Where do the kids get their drugs?"

"Like they'd tell me? I figure the kids in elementary school probably get them from their brothers and sisters, or their friends' brothers and sisters."

"So there aren't drug dealers hanging out at the schools?" Jessica asked anxiously.

"I don't know. No one's tried to sell me drugs."

"Does the RCMP do anything about the kids who use drugs?" Jake asked.

"They have a no-tolerance policy," Jess said.

Robin gave a very adult snort. "The cops are so dumb. Once or twice a year some of the Williams Lake RCMP come into the school with dogs. Drug-sniffing dogs."

"That doesn't sound dumb," Jessica said.

"The druggies always know ahead of time. The cops hardly ever catch anyone, and if they do it's some moron who tried the stuff for the first time, not one of the real druggies."

Jessica bounced to her feet. "On that note, I'm going to finish off the salad, and, Evan, you'd better get those steaks on. Before Robin scares Arnold off moving to Caribou Crossing."

Obediently, Evan transferred the marinated steaks to the barbecue. To Jake, he said, "Meals are a bit thrown together because we're all so busy, but we figure the important thing is that we have an opportunity to sit down together and talk."

Jake remembered "family dinners" with his parents, where they grilled him about how he'd done in school but didn't want to hear anything else from him. Nothing about his interests, his dreams. He was sure dinners at the Kincaid household were very different.

He took a sip of wine and tried to imagine himself in Evan's shoes. Coming home from work, putting dinner together with his wife and daughter, then sitting down to eat and talk about their days. He choked back a snort. What would he say? "Only saw two dozen addicts shooting up today. Interviewed the girlfriend of a gang member who got beat up one too many times by her man and she'd like to talk but she's terrified he'll kill her."

He turned to Robin. "Cousin Brooke says you taught her to ride."

The girl's face lit up. She had big brown eyes, just like her mother's. Evan's eyes, he had noticed, were blue-green, like Brooke's. Idly he wondered whose eyes Evan's and Jess's baby would get.

And then the thought hit him. Bipolar disorder was believed to have a genetic component. Evan didn't have it, but might he carry the gene? He and Jessica were having a baby. Had they considered the risk it might have bipolar? As he tried to concentrate on what Robin was saying, he found himself hoping that everything came out right for this family.

Soon the simple dinner was on the table and they all dove in. The food was plentiful and delicious.

As they ate, Jake heard the story of how Evan and Jessica, childhood friends, had rediscovered each other the previous year when Evan stayed at the Crazy Horse resort ranch, where Jessica had been working as head wrangler.

He also learned about Jessica's parents and Robin's father, who turned out to be Dave Cousins, the upstanding citizen who owned the Wild Rose Inn and chaired the Heritage Committee.

The subject turned to Jessica's Riders Boot Camp, where horse lovers would not only get lessons in Western riding, but in how to care for and communicate with horses. As Jessica spoke, it was obvious that her passion for horses was deep and abiding.

"Brooke told me about the charitable aspect," Jake said. "That's admirable."

Eyes bright, Jess said, "There are so many underprivileged people who could easily head down the wrong path. We'll help them develop confidence, physical competence, and a sense of responsibility. And learning how to care for and relate to a horse will also help them with human relationships."

If teens like Anika and Sapphire—hell, a teen like himself—had gone to a place like that, it might have changed their lives. "I'm impressed," he told her.

"We could always use a good accountant who's willing to work pro bono," she promptly said, and everyone laughed.

"Seriously," she added, "I'd love to give you a tour of Boots, if you have time one day."

"And I'll take you riding!" Robin said. "If you don't know how, Gramma and I will teach you."

"Hmm," he said dubiously. "That's a nice offer, but horses are a little out of my league."

"It's hard to live in Caribou Crossing and avoid horses," Evan said wryly.

After Brooke's chocolate-mint layer cake had been consumed with relish, Robin said, "I have to go do homework. Nice to meet you, Arnold. Sure hope you decide to move here."

"Thank you, Robin. It was a pleasure to meet you too."

"What's your homework tonight?" Brooke asked.

"I have to finish this story I've been writing. The only thing is, I'm not sure if it should have a happy ending. Maybe that's just, you know, too easy?" She tilted her head. "What do you think, Gramma? Do you believe in happy endings?"

Brooke tilted her head in an identical way. "Yes, but I don't think they should come too easily. A happy ending means more if the person has to work for it." She gave the girl a quick hug. "You're my happy ending, Robin. You and Evan and your mom, and the new baby."

Robin grinned. "Thanks. Oh, and don't forget Cousin Arnold. If he moves here, that would be another happy ending, wouldn't it?"

Brooke glanced at him. "Yes, I suppose it would."

"Homework means homework," Evan said. "Get to it, young lady. And no e-mail or texting until you're done."

"Oh, Evan, you're so mean to me." But she said it in a teasing way and wrinkled her nose afterward.

Her stepfather reached up to squeeze her shoulder as she went past his chair and she planted a kiss on top of his head. The two grinned at each other and Jake thought, *She's got her father's smile*, before he remembered that Dave Cousins, not Evan, was the girl's biological father.

"It's cooling off," Evan said. "Arnold, why don't we go into the living room and you can ask me some questions. I know there must be a lot of things you want to check out if you're contemplating opening a business here. I've just been through the process, so I can give you a lot of information."

"Trying to get out of doing the dishes," Jess grumbled in a joking way.

"Who, me?" Evan asked with pretend innocence.

"I think it's a good idea," Brooke said. "Jessica and I will deal with the dishes and tidy up. You men go ahead and talk."

Jake nodded thankfully. Evan had given him the opportunity he'd been hoping for, and he intended to take full advantage. Besides, much as he enjoyed Brooke, he'd be glad to get away from her for a while. Seeing her with her family was driving him crazy. He knew she belonged to them; he was glad for her happiness with them. But in some small way, for a very short time, he wanted her to belong to him too. He didn't want their relationship to be a secret. He wanted to touch her, claim her, have her smile that special way she only smiled with him.

That sexy, cocky way that was pure woman.

As Brooke walked to the car with Jake, she found she'd almost come to think of him as Arnold. She could understand why he was so successful with his undercover.

They waved their good-byes to Evan and Jessica, who stood in the lighted doorway, then Jake backed out of the driveway. After he headed the car down the road she touched his arm tentatively. "Jake? Are you still in there?"

He chuckled. Jake's chuckle. With one hand he loosened the knot of Arnold's tie, and then he reached over and put his hand on her thigh. High on her thigh. "Fooled you?"

"You're very good."

"Wait 'til we get home, babe, and I'll show you how good I can be."

Babe? Maybe she should be offended but she kind of liked it. After a night of being Gramma and Mom, it felt just fine to have her sexy young lover call her babe.

"I'll hold you to that," she said, and her voice came out in a sultry purr. "Or should I just hold you?" She unbuckled her seat belt and leaned over to run a finger across the fly of his suit pants. They were passing Wade and Miriam Bly's house, and she thought how shocked Jessica's parents would be to see her now.

Jake caught the hand and pressed it to him as he grew under her touch. In the distance she saw headlights from a car on the highway.

He pulled his Lexus onto the narrow shoulder of the road and clicked off the ignition and lights. Unbuckling his seat belt, he asked, "Is anyone likely to be driving this road?"

She had started to shake her head when he pulled her into his arms for a kiss. A kiss that stole her breath and seemed to go on forever. She kept her hand on his erection, and his own hand snuck between her legs and pressed hard.

When they both came up for air, he said, "Bed or parking?"

"Parking?" The word burst out as if she'd never heard it before.

"Was that a yes or a question?"

"I've never gone parking in my life. When I was a girl in L.A., Mo had a bike, not a car and—"

"Brooke, it's not that I don't care about your life story, but this isn't the time."

"Oh, right. Uh, what about condoms?"

"In my wallet. I'm never going to be caught unprepared again."

Parking. Like horny teenagers. "I choose parking. We could go to the lake or—"

"Here. Right here. No one can see us."

She glanced ahead, to the occasional distant lights on the highway, then back in the direction of Wade and Miriam's home and ranch buildings. It was possible that someone from Riders Boot Camp might go into town, or be returning, but Jessica pretty much wore the guests out with her vigorous riding program.

Parking . . . It sounded more exciting, less serious, than sex in a bed. And, after all, that was what she wanted from this man, wasn't it? Fun and excitement.

Jake had stripped off his jacket and hurled it into the backseat, and was now yanking off his tie. He toed off his shoes and she bent to remove hers. He reached across her, found the lever that reclined the passenger seat, and suddenly she was falling backward.

"I'm coming around," he said. "Can't climb over the console." He slipped out the driver's door.

They would never fit in the passenger seat. The back might be a better bet. But Jake seemed to know what he was doing. He flung open the passenger door. "Scrunch over."

She scrunched, sliding onto her right hip and feeling the console press into her backside.

He slid in beside her and somehow managed to close the door behind him.

The car light went off and she wriggled, trying in the darkness to fit her body to his, wondering how they'd ever remove sufficient clothing to complete the act. When he'd suggested parking it had sounded like fun, but now she had second thoughts. "This will never work."

"Oh yes it will." He did some wriggling of his own and let out a small hiss of pain.

"Jake! I forgot all about your injuries. You can't do this."

"Believe me, babe, the pain in my side is nothing compared to the ache in my—" He broke off and pulled her blouse out of the waistband of her jeans. His hand snuck inside, his palm warm on her back. He flicked the hook on her bra, and then his hand found its way to her breast and she sucked in a breath.

"God, Brooke, you feel good." He squeezed her nipple gently between his fingers and ran his thumb over the tip.

"That feels wonderful." His fingers worked magic on her breast, magic that arrowed straight down her body and ended up between her legs.

She and Jake managed to pull her blouse over her head and free her from her bra. Then she attacked the buttons on his tailored business shirt. Finally she was able to run her fingers through his curly chest hair and press her bare breasts against him. "Above the waist," she murmured. "What's that called, necking or petting?"

"Don't worry about it because we're not stopping there." He unbuttoned her pants, slid down the zipper, and squeezed his hand inside, fanning it out over the front of her panties. Pink silk bikini briefs. Not that he'd know about the color, but her own knowledge made her feel more feminine. She'd always loved sexy lingerie but had given it up for many long years. Recently, she'd begun to indulge herself every now and then.

She'd never thought a man would see her lacy self-indulgences.

His fingers were close, so tantalizingly close, to where she wanted them to be, but her pants were too tight to allow him proper access. Shamelessly she lifted her hips, wriggling her pants and panties down her legs until she could toe them off her feet.

Completely naked now she reveled in the sensations, even the mildly uncomfortable ones like the hard edge of the console digging into her. The slide of Jake's hand down the curve of her hip more than made up for any discomfort.

"You are an angel," he murmured.

She looked down to see her body, pale and gleaming. Her eyes had adjusted to the dim light; it wasn't really so dark. She glanced out the window. "Starlight." The stars were so clear here, but when she'd come to Caribou Crossing, she'd never even noticed them. She'd been so mad at Mo; she'd missed L.A. and her family so badly. Now she'd never look at the stars again without thinking about this time with Jake.

Hungry for him, she fumbled with the buttons at his waist. It took the two of them to rid him of his pants and underwear. He retrieved his wallet and pulled out a condom, which he put on the dashboard.

"You're sure you're okay?" she asked.

"No, I'm dying of sexual frustration."

She giggled. "Tell me again why kids go through all this?"

"Because they don't have access to a bed."

"Hmm. And we do."

He captured her breast again. "Hey, this was your idea."

"Liar." She reached down and gripped his erection.

"Okay, I confess. Brooke, I'd have sex anywhere with you."

"Anywhere?"

"You're taking that as a challenge, aren't you?"

She stroked up and down and he caught his breath. She wanted to lean down, to circle him with her tongue, but there was no possible way she could bend her body that way. "All right," she said, "I know how the pieces are supposed to fit together. I just can't quite figure out how to make it happen in a car seat."

"When the time comes, I'll show you."

"The time hasn't come?"

"Nowhere near. That pretty pink mouth of yours is still talking. I want you moaning and whimpering and sighing."

"You've been watching too many dirty movies."

"Uh-uh. I was listening to you, Brooke Kincaid. In bed last night."

"Oh! Did I . . . make sounds? I didn't realize."

"You made music, babe."

"It was a duet," she said softly.

"That it was. Your part was just a little prettier. I probably sounded like a caveman."

"Pretty much."

He put his hand on hers, which was still stroking him, and stilled its action. "Stop, I'm getting ahead of you. And sex is one place where the guy should never go ahead of the lady."

One of his arms was under her, cradling her in a manner that certainly wasn't comfortable for her and couldn't be for him either. But there was no other place for it to go. His other hand, though, drifted down her body, caressing here, tickling gently there, making her forget the discomfort. "Ladies first?" she murmured, shivering as his hand moved lower. "Such a gentleman."

"Not me. You talking about Arnold?"

"It's not Arnold I want." His hand found the spot she'd been waiting for it to find, and she sighed instead.

"Can I touch you again?" she asked.

"Above the waist."

"Such a prude."

She found one of his nipples and rolled it between her fingers, but most of her attention was focused on his hand. She eased her legs farther apart.

"Tell me what feels good," he murmured.

"That. All of it. Everything you do." She whimpered and twisted, trapping his hand between her thighs, wondering how he could know her body so well. When she relaxed her thighs again, he slipped a finger inside her and she clenched, wet and needy.

Her hand again found his erection.

He jerked and gasped. "Hey, that's below the belt."

"Your belt's long gone. Besides, I've caught up with you. How about a little action?"

"Can you reach that condom?"

She stretched to retrieve it from the dashboard, ripped open the packet, and rolled the latex onto him.

"You'd better take top," he said, "or I'll crush you."

"How do I—"

But he was already grasping her hips, moving her and holding her up as he slid beneath her. A few minor contortions, a stifled moan of pain from him, and he was laying back in the seat with her straddling his thighs. "Thank God they're only flesh wounds," he muttered.

"It's not too late to quit."

"Oh yes it is."

His erection was a hard, hot column rising irresistibly in front of her and she was reaching for it when he said, "Look outside."

"What? Why?"

"Make sure there are no cops with flashlights."

She threw back her head and laughed, and she was still laughing when he grasped her hips and brought her farther up his body to press firmly against him. She eased up just slightly and slid against his penis, caressing him with her moist heat, finding just the right angle, knowing that if she kept it up much longer they'd both come. Just like last night.

But tonight they had another option. She lifted her body, balancing awkwardly with one knee on the seat and the other between the seat and the door. She caught him in her hand, held him tight, then gently eased herself down, beginning to take him inside her.

His body arched and he groaned. She knew he was holding

back, wanting to thrust hard and deep, but letting her control the pace. But now she, too, wanted him hard and deep, and so she jerked forward, encompassing him in one quick move.

He grabbed her hips again and held her tight against him, neither of them moving, for several very long seconds. Then he loosened his grip and she began to slide up and down, sometimes fast, sometimes painfully slowly. But then need overcame her and she thrust her body against his, twisting, grinding, gasping for breath.

He plunged up to meet her, his body arching off the seat and taking her with him. She gripped his hips, using his body for leverage as they pulled apart then plunged together.

And then he made that sound in his throat, the one that meant he was close, couldn't hold back, and her own excitement level ratcheted up another notch.

She knew how it felt when he came in her hand, and in her mouth. Now she held still, waiting for him, knowing that when he took those fast final strokes he would carry her with him.

And he did. And she couldn't remember ever feeling such pure physical bliss.

When the powerful waves of orgasm finally subsided, she collapsed onto Jake as he sank back into the seat with a stifled groan.

"Are you all right?" she asked. "I keep forgetting you're injured."

His teeth flashed white in the dim light. "I'm a macho dude. A little bullet hole isn't going to stop me."

"I guess it was some other guy who fainted the other day."

"I didn't faint. I passed out from loss of blood. That's a different thing."

"That's your story and you're sticking to it?" She kissed his shoulder.

His arms tightened around her and he kissed the top of her

head. "Damn right. And if you value your life you won't be telling anyone otherwise."

"Ooh, I'm so scared. Gonna come after me with your gun?"

"Nope. The other thing in my pocket."

Laughter shook her body. "Oh, Jake, I do like you."

"And I like you, Brooke. A whole lot."

"So, you figure we ought to take this act home to bed?"

"That's the joy of being grown-ups. We've got a bed. Might as well make use of it." He stroked her back in a long caress that swept from the top of her head to her buttocks and made her shiver. "Besides, you need a good sleep. I didn't let you get much rest last night."

"I'm fine."

"You might not be if you don't get enough rest."

She realized what he was talking about, and groaned. "Those darn books on bipolar. You know far too much about me."

"Sleep, regular meals, exercise. Jess and Evan fed you, we just took care of the exercise part, and now it's time for sleep."

She wondered what it meant that he was so concerned about her. Was it just part of being a cop? "So, short of feeding me sleeping pills, how are you going to ensure that I get a good night's sleep?"

"Wear you out, babe."

An hour and a half later, Jake smugly thought that he'd kept his promise, though he'd worn himself out in the process. As he lay in the darkness with Brooke cuddled up beside him, he ached from head to toe. And he felt wonderful. Since they'd come home they had used another two condoms.

"Mmm," she purred, "I'm definitely going to sleep well tonight. You're just what the doctor ordered."

He smiled and stroked her bare shoulder. "The meds you take—the lithium—it really works for you?"

"Yes, I'm lucky."

"You'll be on it for the rest of your life."

"Until they find something even better, or cure the condition."

"Side effects?"

"Very few."

"That's great." He thought about Evan and Jess's baby, and wondered about its future. "But not everyone's so lucky. The meds don't always work. Some people hate the side effects. Some refuse to take the drugs."

"You absorbed a lot of information."

"I'm used to reading for information. It's a kind of focused skimming."

"And you remember without taking notes."

"Yeah, well."

"Honestly, Jake, I'm fine. The lithium really works for me."

"Uh . . . I was wondering about Evan. And the new baby."

"Oh. Now I see where you're heading."

"Yeah. But if you don't want to talk about it . . ."

"It's okay. Yes, there may be a genetic component to bipolar disorder. For me, through my mom and probably her mother too. Well, Evan's fine so far, and he's almost thirty. Onset usually occurs by early adulthood, especially if there's lots of stress, as there certainly was when he was young. I really don't think he's going to turn out to be bipolar. Or an alcoholic."

"Hard for him, not knowing for sure, though. Hard for Jessica too, I'd think."

She nodded against his chest. "Jess and Evan came to me after she accepted his proposal. She loved him very much and had no qualms about marrying him, but they both wanted to know exactly what might happen. We've had some frank discussions about bipolar and alcoholism."

"And now they're having a baby."

She sighed, her breath warm against his skin. "They talked

to their doctor, my doctor, and my psychiatrist, and decided to take the risk. The odds are their baby will be fine."

He heard the concern in her voice and guessed that if Jess and Evan's baby had bipolar disorder she'd blame herself. But he reminded himself of all the things she'd survived, and knew that she was strong enough to cope with whatever hand of cards the fates dealt her.

"The kid couldn't have better parents or a better grandma. Or sister, in Robin."

"Thanks, Jake. At least if there's a problem, we know the symptoms to look for, and the treatments. As my psychiatrist says, no baby comes with a guarantee."

"I guess not. I've never really thought about having kids."

"Haven't you?"

"My relationship with my parents is fucked up, and my job's my life. No, I can't imagine ever marrying or having kids." Though, he had to admit, being with Brooke's family had given him a twinge or two of envy.

"You're not exactly the domestic type." He heard a smile in her voice.

"How about you? Would you have another kid?"

She shook her head, silky hair caressing him. "No. Partly because of the chance it would inherit my illness, but also, I don't know how I'd do with the stresses of raising a child. I'm good as long as I live an orderly life. Grandchildren are all the excitement I'm ready to handle."

Chapter Fourteen

Brooke woke to a series of pleasant sensations. The warmth of sunshine on her cheek. A purring ball of cat curled against her stomach. And, best of all, Jake's naked body spooning her backside.

Jake's aroused naked body.

"Yum." She reached an arm back and touched his hip, his buttock. She squirmed backward, wriggling even closer against him and breaking contact with the cat.

Sunny turned to give her his "we are not amused" look, then rose slowly, stretched languorously, and strolled to the edge of the bed. He glanced over his shoulder but Brooke didn't say "stay," and he leaped to the floor.

"He's had me to himself for a long time," she said as Jake parted her legs from behind and slipped his erection between them.

Her body was swollen and achy from last night's lovemaking, yet she felt a quick surge of arousal. "Sore," she murmured even as she shifted position to give him better access.

"Don't want to hurt you." He pulled away.

"No, don't go."

He gripped her hip, urging her to lie flat on her back.

Then he straddled her and kissed her softly, just a quick touch on her lips. Then light little kisses on her shoulders, her breasts, her stomach. He eased her legs apart and kneeled between them, backing his way down the bed. He ran his hands under her and lifted her lower body, raising her to his face. And then, using his lips and tongue, he fed the flame of her desire.

She was helpless in his hands; she couldn't even touch him. All she could do was respond. Finally, hot and slippery and nearing climax, she said, "I want you in me, Jake. Now."

He glanced up, his face flushed. "Sure?"

"Positive."

He eased her down and she rolled quickly, her hand scrabbling on the bedside table, finding a condom.

In seconds he was inside her and in only another few seconds she was coming apart around him.

He thrust hard and deep, so she felt every wonderful inch of him. Then his body shuddered and he groaned her name.

After he'd collapsed beside her, when they were again curled close together, she said, "If you were here longer, I'd go on birth control. I'd love to really feel you come inside me."

"I'd like that too."

She smiled against his chest. "Would you settle for pancakes?"

"Huh?"

"For breakfast. I have a craving for banana pancakes with maple syrup." She also loved having someone to cook for.

"Sounds great. Is there a place in town we can go for breakfast? So you could introduce me to a few townspeople."

Instantly, she sobered. Jake wasn't here for her personal enjoyment; he was a man on a mission. "Yes, of course."

After they'd both showered, Jake took his time shaving so he could watch Brooke get ready.

Clad in a blue robe, she toweled her hair, combed it, then scrunched it between her fingers. No hair dryer, no curling iron. No fuss. One kind of lotion around her eyes, another on the rest of her face, and yet another on her body. She added a little make-up around her eyes, the mascara brown, not the harsh black most women wore. And that was it. Those rosy lips needed no enhancement, nor did her glowing cheeks.

She grinned at him. "I know Arnold's a neat-freak, but I don't think you could shave any closer."

Realizing he'd shaved the same patch at least ten times now, he put down the razor and went to pick out clothes. Figuring he'd set up meetings with people like Sergeant Miller and the banker Cray, he decided on Arnold's navy suit with a white shirt and a navy tie that had a thin burgundy stripe.

He was pulling on his pants when Brooke came into the bedroom, slipped off her robe, and put on a bra and panties. The fabric was peachy colored, barely darker than her skin, and so filmy he could see her nipples and pubic hair. A tiny band of lace edged the top of each garment. The panties were cut high on the side, making her long legs look even longer.

She tossed him a grin. "My, what big eyes you have, Mr. Pitt."

"I was on my way to grandmother's house and look what I stumbled upon. How'm I going to wait until tonight?"

"Hmm, let me see. Willpower? Better yet, Arnold power. Just be Arnold."

He zipped his fly over a growing erection. "Poor Arnold. He never gets to have any fun."

Brooke donned a mint green blouse and a khaki skirt. "Hurry up, slowpoke."

Man, was he slipping. He was taking longer to get ready than a woman. Of course, he was a little distracted.

They took his car into town, a scenic ten-mile drive of ranch land, patches of forest, and rolling hills.

When they reached the outskirts of town, he gestured

toward the "Caribou Crossing" road sign, like a pedestrian crossing one but with the silhouette of a caribou instead. "There aren't really caribou around here, right?"

"Not for a long time. It's a tourism thing. That symbol has become the unofficial town logo."

He nodded, then asked, "Where d'you want to eat?"

"The Wild Rose Inn."

"Dave Cousins's place," he said.

She nodded. "It's a popular spot for breakfast, not only with tourists but with a number of the locals."

He'd made a quick but thorough scan of the town of Caribou Crossing yesterday afternoon, so he drove straight to the picturesque hotel.

"Parking's off the back alley," Brooke said.

"It's a nice building," he commented. "Heritage?"

"It dates back to the eighteen sixties. It was a gold rush hotel and saloon, but of course it's been renovated a lot over the years."

In the parking lot, he was surprised to see a couple of hitching rails with three horses tied up. "People ride into town?"

"People ride everywhere." She went to stroke a chestnut horse with a white blaze down its face. "This is Timony. He belongs to my neighbor, Ray Barnes. Ray will definitely want to meet my cousin." She grinned. "You can touch the horse, Arnold. If you're thinking of moving here, you'll have to get used to horses."

"I don't hate horses," he said, putting on Arnold's voice and a doubtful tone.

She chuckled, glanced around, then said in a low voice, "You do this so well. Well enough that I'm not even attracted to Arnold. You're nice enough, personable enough, but the spark that makes you Jake goes into hiding."

"You get the easier job, then."

"How do you mean?"

"When we're out in public, you aren't attracted to me because I'm Arnold. But you're still Brooke and it makes me crazy to know I can't touch you, wink at you, even make real Jake-to-Brooke eye contact."

She gave a very female, smug smile. "I'm glad it makes you crazy."

The back door of the hotel opened and a young couple with a little girl came out. The child wore a souvenir T-shirt with the same logo as on the road sign. "Oh, look!" the girl said excitedly. "Horses! Can I touch them?"

"Not without the owners around," the mother cautioned. "They might bite."

"Words of wisdom," Jake commented in his Arnold voice.

He and Brooke went in the door the tourists had come out, and he studied the lobby of the Wild Rose Inn. The place had a "home on the range" feel, including sepia photos of miners and cowboys, furniture that was more rustic than antique, and twangy country music playing at low volume, yet there was also a subtle elegance.

The theme carried through to the restaurant, which was almost full on this Friday morning, the babble of conversation almost drowning out the music.

As they threaded their way to an empty table, a hand waved and an elderly gent with horn-rims and a head of thick silver hair said, "Brooke. Don't often see you here."

"Good morning, Ray. No, I usually have breakfast at home, but my cousin came to visit. He's thinking of moving here to start up an accounting business and I want to give him a taste of the town. Ray Barnes, my neighbor, meet Arnold Pitt, my cousin from Vancouver."

The two men shook hands. The old guy had a strong grip and shrewd gray eyes behind those thick lenses. "Why don't you two join me?" he offered.

Brooke glanced at Jake, who decided it wasn't a bad idea. "That's kind of you, Mr. Barnes," he said.

"Ray, please. We country folk don't stand on formality."

When they were all settled at the table, Jake noted that Brooke didn't go for pancakes, instead choosing a blend of fruit, yogurt, and granola. Trying to balance his own hearty appetite with Arnold's city sensibilities, Jake stuck with bacon, eggs, and toast though he'd rather have had the rancher's special—steak, eggs, and hash browns—like Ray.

Sitting with Ray Barnes proved to be a good decision, as it turned out the man was a retired pharmacist who knew all the townspeople. Jake could only imagine the secrets he'd learned over the years, but the man didn't let any slip, not even by the slightest shift of his expression when he greeted the liquor store manager, then a woman who owned a clothing store, a couple of doctors who were in practice together, and several others.

Brooke quietly ate her breakfast and let Ray Barnes take over, introducing Jake as Arnold and telling people, "Let's make this young fellow understand what a wonderful town we have here."

Unfortunately, people followed Ray's instructions, gushing about business opportunities and the healthy environment, when what Jake really wanted to hear about was the seedier side of Caribou Crossing. Still, it was a starting point. He was making lots of contacts.

Brooke left to go to work, and Jake sat on for a while with Ray. "This Wild Rose Inn seems like an impressive business," he said to the older man. "I understand it's owned by a man named Dave Cousins. Is he around?"

"Haven't seen him this morning," Ray said. "He'll be at the big fund-raiser later today. You should get Brooke to bring you."

Jake nodded. "We're planning on it. How about you? Are you coming?"

He shook his head. "Already gave Dave my check, but I'm a morning person, not much for going out in the evening.

Like to stay at home with a good book. It reminds me of all the years my wife and I would sit down together after supper, out on the porch in summer or by the fire in winter." His gray eyes held a wistful expression.

"I'm sorry you lost her," Jake said. "It must be tough."

"Yeah, but a person carries on. We had a lot of good years, and I have a store of memories to keep me company." His gaze sharpened. "Fellow your age, you should be looking for a nice girl to share your life. Caribou Crossing's a good place to settle down and raise a family."

The way Evan Kincaid had. Yes, if he'd really been Arnold, there'd have been something appealing about that. "You're probably right. It's hard meeting nice women in Vancouver. They're so busy with their jobs, their friends."

"Mark my words, Arnold Pitt, you move to Caribou Crossing and I'll be dancing at your wedding before the year is out."

At the end of the afternoon, Jake drove Brooke into town again for the fund-raiser. They slipped into a loading zone by the town square where several teens helped them unload the appetizers she'd made, then drove away to find parking on a side street.

When they strolled back to the square, Jake realized their steps were keeping time to the music that filled the air. He didn't recognize the song, but—inevitably—it had the unmistakable twang of country and western.

When they arrived and purchased admission tickets, he saw that the square—a park with lawns, flower beds, benches, a bandstand, a gazebo, and several decorative wire-framed caribou—had been fancied up with Heritage Committee banners and posters featuring its restoration projects. Tables along the side held food, drinks, and silent auction items, and young people in white straw Stetsons and Heritage Committee T-shirts circulated with platters of food.

"There'll be everything from chuck wagon stew to sushi," Brooke commented. "Everyone brings their specialty."

The crowd was diverse too, with seniors in wheelchairs, babies in strollers, and everything in between. Clothing ranged from business suits like the gray one he wore to shorts and flip-flops, but there was a preponderance of Western shirts, Stetsons, and cowboy boots. Two uniformed RCMP officers, one female and one male, mingled; both were younger than Sergeant Miller, who was nowhere to be seen.

The scene was colorful and cheery, the scent of food made his stomach growl, and though he'd never been a country music fan he was getting used to the twang. Though he wasn't thrilled about playing Arnold, it was pleasant doing U/C work in a place like this rather than a seedy biker bar.

He had spent a moderately productive day. Sergeant Miller had been out when he had dropped by the detachment, but Jake had spoken to a couple of bank managers and a number of businesspeople. He'd even had lunch with Howard Cray, the bank manager Brooke had been so negative about. He had to agree; superficially, the guy said the right things, but underneath, he wasn't one bit likable.

Now here Cray was again, working the crowd with a plastic highball glass in his hand. He saw Jake and headed over. "Pitt, we meet again."

"Cray. Yes, my cousin was kind enough to bring me along."

"Ms. Kincaid." The man acknowledged her with a dip of his head but there was no warmth in his voice.

"Mr. Cray," she returned in the same tone, then, "Excuse me, gentlemen."

Brooke looked terrific in a simply cut sleeveless blue dress that gently molded her curves. Curves that Jake's fingers itched to touch. He tried not to watch her swaying butt as she hurried away from them, and restrained himself from fisting his hands when he caught Cray ogling her.

"It's an impressive turnout," he said to Cray, discipline

keeping his tone civil. "Are you on the Heritage Committee yourself?"

"No, though I did tell you I'm a member of the chamber of commerce, didn't I?"

Only four times. "You did. You people are, in a very real sense, the town leaders. I'd certainly like to meet some of the other members."

Cray puffed out his chest. "Let's get you a drink, then I'll introduce you to Randy Sorokin, the president of the chamber."

Jake crossed the square in Cray's wake.

Brooke stood near a flowering bush, in animated conversation with a good-looking man roughly Jake's own age. They appeared far too friendly. There were times he wished she really did look like a grandmother.

As he and Cray stood in the short line at the bar, he asked the man, "What are you drinking?"

"Caribou Crossing Single Barrel rye."

Jake waited to see if he'd add the same words Anika's john had spoken, about it being the hometown drink. When he didn't, Jake asked, already knowing the answer from his research, "That's made around here?"

"No, but it is Canadian. Since its release a few years ago, it's become the hometown drink for whisky connoisseurs."

His pulse jerked but he kept his face expressionless. "I guess that was inevitable, given the name."

"You want to fit in here, you should have a glass."

Jake liked rye. He wasn't so sure about Arnold, but figured the accountant would try it—to fit in, as Cray had said. "Sounds good to me." Jake placed his order, then tasted the drink.

"What do you think?" Cray asked.

He nodded approvingly. "Smooth. A little wood, a little spice. I like it."

"Thought you would." Cray glanced past Jake's shoulder,

then waved a hand and called out. "Randy, just the man I wanted to see. Come over here a minute."

Sorokin was a stocky man in Western wear, with a blunt, friendly face. He greeted Jake warmly, then, as Jake lifted his glass again, said, "What's your poison? Has Howard got you drinking our hometown drink?"

Damn. It seemed everyone referred to the rye that way. "He has," Jake confirmed. "When in Rome, as they say."

Sorokin gave a hearty laugh. "You're about as far away from Rome as you can come, my friend. But it's a fine town, Caribou Crossing."

It turned out that he owned the largest construction company in town, and Jake sized him up as the kind of man who had no problem rolling up his sleeves and getting his hands dirty alongside his crew. He was bluff and hearty and had a lot of insights to offer about the town's economy and his fellow businesspeople. Arnold had little in common with him, and Jake wasn't about to trust the man. Brooke's instincts told her Sorokin abused his wife.

Over the next couple of hours, Sorokin, Cray, and Brooke introduced Jake to others, and he also talked to people he'd met at breakfast and during the day. He moved from group to group around the square, sipping the excellent rye, enjoying the treats served by the young people in their Heritage Committee T-shirts, asking as pointed questions as he could manage without arousing suspicion.

There was no sign of Miller, but the two RCMP officers kept a close eye on the crowd. With quiet efficiency, they shut down a couple of teenage boys who were getting rowdy, helped a young mother who'd temporarily lost her little boy, and collared a loose dog and returned it to its owner to be leashed. They also mingled and socialized, and he was looking for an opportunity to talk to one or both of them when he saw Brooke talking to the female officer.

He debated going to join them, but figured he'd get

Brooke's input first. When the two had gone their separate ways, he drifted casually in Brooke's direction.

She said brightly, "Having fun, Arnold?"

"People are being very kind to me," he said in Arnold-speak.

"I know you mentioned that one of your concerns is finding a community with a low crime rate." Her voice was loud enough to carry over the twangy music, and he noticed a couple of people tuning in to their conversation. Fine. If someone got nervous that might tell him something.

"I've spoken to the mayor and the president of the chamber of commerce. They've been very reassuring."

"You should talk to Corporal MacLean. She was just telling me how her boss, Sergeant Miller, keeps right up with the latest developments in crime prevention and detection." She tugged his arm gently and he let himself be led across the park as she continued to talk.

He admired her tactics. If she whispered, she'd arouse people's curiosity. "That's admirable," he said, equally loudly.

"Yes, Karen says he attends seminars and visits police departments, crime labs, and so on, all over the country and in the States as well. He's always bringing back material to share with his officers."

"Well now, isn't that interesting." He gave a nod of appreciation.

She led him to the attractive uniformed brunette. "Corporal Karen MacLean, this is my cousin, Arnold Pitt. I'm sure you can allay some of his concerns about crime in Caribou Crossing."

"Thanks." He held out his hand and got a firm shake in return. "I was actually hoping to talk to the sergeant too. Miller, is it? Is he around tonight?"

The corporal shook her head. "He's away on personal business this weekend."

"Oh? Out of town?"

She narrowed her eyes slightly. "I believe so. He'll be in on Monday. In the meantime, you can talk to me."

"I appreciate that. Thanks for taking the time."

Brooke said, "I'll leave you two to chat. Evan and Jessica have just arrived, and I want to say hi."

"Say hi from me too." He glanced over as she walked across the square.

"Jessica looks well," MacLean said. "I hear she's expecting."

He refocused on her face. "I guess word travels quickly in a small town."

"Bet on it." Her dark eyes studied him appraisingly. "It's hard to have secrets here."

She was just being a cop, he told himself, curious about any stranger, and particularly one who was considering moving here. "That would take some getting used to," he said with a reserved smile. "Vancouver is so anonymous. You tend not to even know your neighbors. I admit that the idea of community is appealing, though."

He glanced over to Evan and Jessica again, noticing that they were receiving congratulations from a number of townspeople. Tonight, Evan wore good pants with a shirt, tailored jacket, and tie. Jessica wore tan jeans, a Western-style shirt, and fancy red cowboy boots. Her glossy hair—which tonight lay loose on her shoulders—was damp. He guessed she'd come in from the horses and had a quick shower. He guessed also that she wasn't much of a woman for feminine clothing. Still, she was very attractive. When she reached Brooke's age, she'd probably be lovely. Like Brooke.

When he glanced at MacLean again, he caught her studying the happy couple too. Her sharp brown eyes had softened with a wistful expression.

"I imagine this is a good place to raise a family," he said.

"It can be, as long as you keep them occupied with healthy activities."

"Do you have a family yourself?" He was curious about this woman, who worked under a sergeant who rubbed Brooke the wrong way and might even be a criminal.

She shook her head slowly. "I don't think marriage and kids are in the cards for me."

The woman looked to be thirtyish. She was tall, fit, and striking, with the kind of high-cheekboned face that belonged on a model. "Er, pardon me if I'm being too personal, but why not?"

She wrinkled her nose, for a moment looking more cute than striking. "That's okay. I raised the subject. And the answer is, my job. I love it. It's what I've always wanted to do. But most men find a woman cop a little intimidating."

Should Arnold find her intimidating? No, the guy might be a bit prim and proper, but he wasn't lacking in self-confidence. "Insecure men. You wouldn't want someone like that anyhow."

"True," she said, "but it seems there aren't a great many secure men in Caribou Crossing. Those that are, are married to women like Jess. Or were." She tipped her head in the direction of the good-looking guy Brooke had been so friendly with earlier.

"Excuse me?"

"Oh, haven't you met Dave Cousins?"

"No, not yet." Jessica's ex-husband; Robin's father. Brooke had mentioned that Dave was very much a part of the family, that the divorce had been amicable, and that Robin spent half her time with Dave and half with her mother and Evan. She hadn't said why Dave and Jessica had broken up.

He turned back to Corporal MacLean. "So there you are. Dave is available and likes strong women."

She was scanning the crowd, no doubt checking for anything that needed her attention. "No, he's not available. The poor guy." Her gaze returned to Jake's face. "The love of his life, Anita, died of brain cancer and it's like his heart died with her. He's still efficient, friendly, active in the community but it's like the real Dave just isn't home."

"That's sad."

"Isn't it? I mean, imagine loving someone that much and then losing them."

He couldn't even imagine loving someone. Or wanting to. Love, in his book, was a dirty word. When his parents had ordered him to do this or not do that, they'd always said it was for his own good, and because they loved him. Women talked about love when they were pushing for marriage. In his experience, people used the word *love* when they wanted something from you, not because they genuinely cared for you.

Of course, what he'd seen last night at Evan and Jessica's was a whole different thing. And then there'd been the way Ray Barnes had spoken about his deceased wife, and the memories that still kept him company. . . .

Chapter Fifteen

"You're thinking of moving to Caribou Crossing?" MacLean's voice broke into Jake's thoughts.

He realized she was eyeing him with an interest that was personal as well as professional. He liked the corporal and doubted she was involved with the grow op. He'd probably enjoy working with her. But she did nothing for his libido.

"I'm considering leaving Vancouver. One reason is the amount of crime. The gang murders, drive-by shootings, police chases, drug-related deaths."

"Yes, that's the negative side to a big city."

She broke off as a teenage girl offered a platter with sushi and Brooke's mini-quiches. Taking a piece of sushi, she said, "We have a great Japanese restaurant in town."

He popped a piece of sushi in his mouth and took a quiche as well. "And Cousin Brooke made these, so you know they're good."

MacLean smiled and helped herself to one. When the teen moved on, she took another quick scan of the crowd, then picked up the conversation. "I've worked in Vancouver, and it's not what I'd choose. Here, our crime tends toward minor B&Es, the occasional stolen car, vandalism, domestic violence, and spousal abuse. It's nasty, but not in the same league." She bit into the quiche and made an "mmm" sound.

"I was quite shocked when Robin talked about drug use by students."

"She did?" Karen's dark eyebrows arched. "At Sir Matthew Baillie Begbie Elementary?"

"I didn't hear the name. But she said some kids at her school use drugs. She thinks they may get the stuff from older siblings."

Karen shook her head slowly as she chewed another bite of quiche. "I think she's been seeing too many TV shows. We have zero tolerance for drugs in Caribou Crossing. It's one of Sergeant Miller's policies. He handles most of the drug cases personally; he's that invested in it." Though her words were positive, her tone when referring to her superior officer was neutral.

Jake wondered if the man was more invested than Karen MacLean knew or was saying. Was he protecting his own business by handling the cases himself? Was this pretty, seemingly straightforward brunette involved, or did she suspect? "Oh? Robin said something about bringing in dogs to check the schools?"

"Yes, he does it a couple of times a year," she said, looking a little troubled, "with dogs trained to sniff out drugs."

"It seems the serious druggies know the dates ahead of time."

"What?" Her sharp eyes raked him and he thought her surprise was genuine.

He was about to probe further when a male voice said, "Karen, are you going to introduce me to the new guy in town?" It was Dave Cousins.

MacLean, still frowning slightly, made the introductions and Jake shook hands with Jessica's ex-husband. Dave's handshake was strong, his gaze assessing but friendly. Soon the three of them were engaged in an animated discussion about the virtues and flaws of Caribou Crossing.

Jake had trouble believing either was involved in anything criminal, but it was too early to rule anyone out.

Cousins glanced at his watch. "Have to go. It's speech time."

"And I should patrol the perimeter," MacLean said.

The band onstage finished its number and Dave Cousins took the microphone, first thanking the musicians, then thanking everyone else for being there. He talked briefly and enthusiastically about the work done by the Heritage Committee and its plans for the next couple of years. Then he introduced the mayor, who raved about how the committee's work had benefited the town. Dave then thanked everyone for offering their support by buying admission tickets, and reminded them that envelopes for additional donations and pledges could be obtained from any of the people in Heritage Committee T-shirts.

Next, the woman who had organized the silent auction announced the winners, and then the guests returned to their schmoozing.

As the evening progressed, Jake met most of the people who were there, plus renewed his acquaintance with Evan and Jessica. He ate a number of tasty snacks and downed a second glass of rye, then switched to soda. Along the way, he gained a wealth of information, much of which would have been useful to Arnold, but unfortunately, little of it seemed relevant to Anika's death.

By ten o'clock, most of the crowd had dissipated. His body ached and he wanted to be alone with Brooke. He wandered over to her. She'd put on a cream-colored sweater that looked soft and touchable. He struggled to keep his hands to himself as he murmured, "Feel like leaving?"

"I'm ready if you are, Arnold."

They made their way among the remaining guests, saying

polite good-byes here and there. Dave stopped Brooke and they hugged. "A success," she said.

"Thanks for your help."

"Anytime."

As they walked away, Jake said, "He seems like a nice guy."

"I honestly think he's the nicest man in town."

"Karen MacLean mentioned that the woman he loved had died. But you said he's Jessica's ex-husband. I'm confused."

"Jess and Dave married right after high school. She was pregnant with Robin." She paused, lifted her face to the night air, and took a deep breath.

Jake did the same, enjoying the purity, the scent of a flower he couldn't name, and the slight chill edge that cut the left-over heat of the day. The band was still playing, but softly now, a female singer crooning another country song he didn't know, but it was obviously a love ballad.

"They had a happy marriage," she went on as they left the groomed grass of the park and stepped onto the sidewalk. "They loved each other—still do—but it was, oh, a quiet kind of love. Not the same kind of thing as Evan and Jessica have. Or Dave and Anita did."

All this talk of love. It was such a foreign concept to him. Her body was tantalizingly close as they strolled to where they'd left the car, but there were a few people on the streets so he didn't let himself touch her. Soon, he promised himself. Very soon. "So, Dave and Jessica got divorced, and then he met Anita?" he asked.

"No," Brooke said. "Anita was a high school teacher from Toronto. She was looking for a quieter life—just like in our Arnold story—and she got a job here. She was fascinated by the town's history, joined the Heritage Committee, and she and Dave . . . Well, I guess it was love at first sight. But he was married. They tried to do the honorable thing and resist the attraction."

A couple walked toward them on the sidewalk and Brooke went quiet, then carried on when they were out of earshot. "Jess realized Dave was upset about something. She finally got him to talk about it."

"She must have been pretty upset herself." In his experience, women could be possessive and jealous, even when you made it damned clear the relationship was purely casual.

"Yes, but she understood. Jessica is a very generous woman. She said they should get divorced so Dave could be with Anita, because that kind of love is something rare."

"Huh. Can't imagine many women reacting that way."

"No, but Jess knew something about that kind of love. She and Evan were friends from the moment they met, in grade two, and somewhere along the way they fell in love. But Evan's driving goal was to escape Caribou Crossing, and Jess knew it. They didn't acknowledge their love, not even to themselves. Jess did love Dave, and he was a wonderful husband and father, but it was a different kind of love. When Dave talked about how he felt about Anita, she realized that was how she'd loved Evan, and maybe still did."

Jake guessed he could see there were different kinds of love, and some were better than others. Some were generous, not selfish. "So she gave Dave a divorce, and then Evan came back to town and they got back together?"

Brooke nodded.

"A happy ending." It was clear how much Evan and Jessica loved each other.

"For everyone but poor Dave. He was shattered when Anita died of brain cancer."

"That's what Karen said. But he seemed okay to me."

"He's a very controlled man. He doesn't want to inflict his pain on the rest of us, but it's there. If you knew him before, you'd see the difference. He . . . aged. How old did you take him for?"

"My age, I guess."

"He's not even thirty."

They'd reached the car, and stopped walking. "Poor guy. Guess it's a whole lot safer never to fall in love."

She turned to him, flashing a quick smile. "That's the truth. If I hadn't fallen for Mo—" Then she broke off and looked thoughtful. "Well, who can say? I wouldn't have Evan. And he and his family are the joy in my life."

As Jake held the passenger door and watched her slide in, he thought about that comment. The joy in her life. Did he have joy in his? His work, he supposed. It was great, always challenging and exciting. But you could hardly call it joyful.

He thought of Corporal Karen MacLean talking about how much she loved her job, yet the wistful way she'd watched Evan and Jessica told him she yearned for more.

But that was her. Not him.

He went around and climbed into the driver's seat. "Let's blow this pop stand, babe. I want to take you to bed and screw your brains out."

Brooke laughed. "Well, you're definitely Jake again."

"It drove me crazy being Arnold. I wanted to give you a squeeze." He reached over to shove her dress up and put his hand on her bare thigh, and suit action to words. "I kept noticing who you were talking to, what you were doing."

"You sound almost—" She broke off and fussed with her seat belt, trying to get it done up without dislodging his hand.

His mind supplied the word she'd avoided. Jealous.

Huh? That couldn't be it. He didn't get jealous. That was something women did. He tried to explain. "For the time I'm here, you're my woman. I want to be able to touch you."

"Your woman?"

Crap. Now he sounded possessive. Quickly, he corrected himself. "Sorry, I don't mean, like, ownership. I mean that we're together, and I wish we could act that way in public."

"I'm a little surprised," she said slowly. "I mean, I'm

hardly some gorgeous young thing you'd want to show off on your arm."

He gaped at her. "You were the most attractive woman there tonight."

She batted his hand off her leg. "Oh, garbage. Flattery is very nice, but make it believable. Jessica was there, not to mention Karen, whose company you seemed to be quite enjoying, and Silvia Campinelli, and—"

"I stand by what I said." He gripped the wheel tightly. She thought he was a guy who'd use cheap flattery? He gave her the straight goods. "Karen MacLean is striking, Silvia could be pretty if she didn't wear so much make-up, and Jessica will be lovely when she's your age and has a few character lines. But you were the one, Brooke. Hands down." He paused. "I never flatter women. If a guy lies to a woman, it'll only cause him trouble in the end."

She was quiet for a bit. He'd been utterly sincere and he hoped she realized it. Yeah, he knew she was older. He wasn't denying that. It just didn't matter. She had a pretty face, a sexy body, and most of all, she had the kind of beauty that came from inside. The better he got to know Brooke, the more beautiful he found her. "Can we go home now?" he asked.

"Yes, please."

As he pulled away from the curb, she said, "Jessica passed along a message from her daughter. Robin wants us to come over tomorrow afternoon. She has her heart set on teaching you to ride."

"I don't think that's high on Arnold's priority list. Nor mine. I'm trying to catch a killer."

"What's your next step?"

"The only suspect we've identified whom I haven't met yet is Sergeant Miller, but he's away this weekend. In the meantime, there's a lot of research to do on the people I've met."

"Can Jamal help?"

Actually, Jamal could do it more easily from Vancouver,

given all the resources they had there, compared to Brooke's old computer and slow Internet connection. "Yeah, I guess," he admitted.

"Horses are part of the way of life here. It'll give the Arnold story more credibility if you say you've gone riding. Have you ever been on a horse?"

He shook his head. "After you've ridden a Harley, who'd want to ride a horse?"

"It's surprisingly fun. Kate already told me I could get off early tomorrow. We're slow on Saturday afternoons." Her tone was more neutral than wheedling, but he'd come to realize that Brooke rarely put her own wishes first. It was almost as if she didn't believe she deserved to get what she wanted—or even as if she was scared to want things too much.

"You'd like to go riding," he said.

She shrugged. "I enjoy it. And of course I love being with Robin. Besides, it would give you the perfect excuse to buy a pair of jeans."

"Oh well, in that case, sure, let's go."

"Oh yes! Thanks, Jake. It'll be fun. You'll see."

"Maybe." He reached for her thigh again. "But I do know something that will definitely be fun. I'm taking you home, babe."

Saturday morning flew by for Brooke, as she and Kate prepared a bride and three bridesmaids for an afternoon wedding and looked after a handful of other customers. They barely had enough of a break to devour Greek salads from the deli. Usually, Brooke packed her own lunch, but Jake had thrown off her routine. That would be a troubling thought if she let herself dwell on it, but she felt happy and healthy. She reminded herself of what Dr. Allenby had said: It was normal to feel excited when good things were happening in her life.

When it was time to leave the salon, Brooke said, "Are you sure you don't mind, Kate? You've been on your feet all day. I feel bad about leaving you alone."

"There are only a couple more clients. I'll be fine. 'Sides, how many times have you filled in for me when I took personal time? Just go, enjoy. And take pictures. Your cousin seems like a sweet guy, but I can't quite picture him on top of a horse in a Stetson."

"If anyone can loosen him up, it's Robin."

Humming, Brooke drove home.

When Jake came onto the porch to greet her, she smiled to see his long legs encased in denim. Fortunately, the neatly trimmed hair, golf shirt, and glasses made him look far different from the leather-jacketed biker.

They went into the house together, where he gave her a long, toe-curling kiss.

Reluctantly, she pushed herself out of his arms. "Robin will be waiting. I'll just run up and change."

"Can I watch?"

"No way. You don't have enough willpower." She loved it that this gorgeous, sexy, experienced guy found her so attractive.

Laughing at his exaggerated groan, she hurried up the stairs. Quickly, she changed into well-worn jeans, a Western shirt with blue trim, and the tooled cowboy boots she always cleaned and polished after each ride. She clapped a tan Resistol—the brand of cowboy hat favored by Jessica and Robin—on her head, took her camera from a drawer, and clattered down the stairs again.

Jake, who'd been sitting at the computer on her desk, turned at the sound, and gaped. "Man, look at you. You make one hell of a sexy cowgirl."

She flushed at the compliment while he shut down the computer.

As they climbed into Jake's car, she had a sudden concern. "How are you feeling? Are you healed enough to be doing this?"

"I'm fine. It's just sitting on a horse, right? How strenuous can it be?"

"Seriously? You've never seen a rodeo?"

"Not really."

"Don't underestimate cowboys. And cowgirls. You ought to see Jessica and Robin. But I'm sure Rob will take it easy on you. She helps her mom with the boot camp students, and she's used to soft city slickers."

"Hey, watch it, lady," he returned, and they both laughed.

"Did you connect with Jamal this morning?" she asked, curious whether there was anything new with the investigation. Last night, she and Jake had been caught up in love-making, then fallen asleep. She'd even slept through the alarm and had to rush to get to work on time.

"Yeah, we talked for an hour or so."

"Any leads at his end?"

"He tracked down the location of the grow op, did a title search. The land is owned by an old guy with Alzheimer's who lives at a care facility in Williams Lake. Name of Bob Baxter?" He glanced over at Brooke.

She shook her head. "Doesn't ring any bells. But if he has Alzheimer's, he's sure not your mastermind. Does he have any relatives around here?"

"No, his only relative—and likely the person who'll inherit the land—is a nephew who lives in Toronto. He's a doctor. Visits Williams Lake once a year to see his uncle. Gideon Baxter?"

"A distinctive name. I don't know him."

"He checks out clean," Jake went on. "We figure the grow op is squatting on the land without the Baxters knowing.

There's a large stream running through the property, so they'll be getting their water from it. No power bills are going to that address; they've circumvented the power meter or have one of their people working at BC Hydro. Jamal has employee names and will start checking them out."

"You said they're using trailers?"

"Yeah. So in theory—if they look after them—they could move the whole op to some other remote spot if they wanted. Like if the uncle dies and the nephew sells the land, or if they suspect someone's on to them."

"If the nephew's an upstanding guy, he'd hate to hear how the land is being used."

"I know. But once we've nailed Anika's killer, we'll bust the grow op and everyone associated with it."

"The sooner the better," she said firmly. Although that would mean Jake leaving town. . . .

"Agreed. By the way, I told Corporal MacLean what Robin said about drugs in the schools. She seemed genuinely surprised. Said Miller's got zero tolerance, but she also said he handles the drug cases himself. Could be he's covering for his own operation."

Much as she disliked the sergeant, the idea that he'd do something like that still shocked her. "How would you find out?"

"Not sure. At least not how to do it legally and find evidence that's admissible in court. Got to hate it when the criminals have more rights than the victims," he grumbled.

"I guess it does make it hard for you to stop the bad guys."

"Sure as hell does. I'd like to just break into the guy's house, and maybe the RCMP detachment."

"But the rules are there for a good reason," she protested, even though a part of her agreed with him. If someone was selling drugs to innocent children like Robin, they had to be stopped.

"Here's another question for you," he said. "Any of these

names mean anything to you?" He listed off three names from memory.

"Mr. Yarrow is a retired lawyer and I think Julia Reddick is a flight instructor. What was the other one again?"

"Richard Snyder."

She shook her head. "Doesn't ring a bell. What's the significance of these names?"

"They took small planes up on Tuesday morning." He turned onto the Bly Ranch road. "Jamal's checking them out and looking for any connections with Miller, Cray, or anyone else we've identified as a possible suspect."

They passed the spot where they'd gone parking, and her body heated at the memory. "We're meeting Robin at Boots. That's where they keep their own horses as well as the ones for students."

He drove past Jessica's parents' house and their ranch headquarters, then turned into the driveway for the boot camp and parked in the lot. Three saddled horses were tied to a hitching rail, but not a soul was in sight.

"On Saturday," Brooke said, "Jess usually takes the guests for a long ride with a picnic lunch in the middle."

Robin burst out of the barn door, dressed in jeans, T-shirt, and boots. Her hair was pulled back in a ponytail and her hat hung down her back, secured by a cord around her neck.

As she ran to meet them, Brooke swung out of the car. She greeted Robin with a warm hug. "Hi, sweetheart."

"Hi, Gramma," the girl responded excitedly. She turned to Jake, who had come to join them. "Hi, Cousin Arnold. This is going to be so cool. Trust me, there's nothing to be afraid of."

Brooke saw the glint of humor in his eyes as he responded in Arnold's voice, "I hope you're right."

The girl glanced down at his feet, clad in polished loafers. "Come into the barn. We've got some spare boots."

Brooke hooked her arm through his as they all started for

the barn. "If you get addicted, like I did, you'll have to buy your own."

"And a Stetson, I suppose," he said dryly.

"Resistol," Brooke and Robin said in a duet, then both laughed.

"Uh-huh," he said in a tone that indicated it was never going to happen.

"Mom says Evan was the same in the beginning," Robin said to Brooke.

"I bet he was," she agreed, still mildly astonished that her city slicker son who'd been hooked on Manhattan had settled down so happily in Caribou Crossing. He'd undergone an amazing transformation, mostly thanks to Jessica and their love for each other.

Brooke and her companions stepped from the sunny yard into the dark barn, pausing for their eyes to adjust. She inhaled happily, savoring the sweet, fresh scent of hay and apples. It dawned on her that her own transformation had been even more dramatic than Evan's. She'd gone from being the town drunk and a dreadful mother to a wholesome woman who got her highs from things like blooming flowers, the scent of hay, and mostly the company of her family.

"Take off your shoes," Robin told Jake.

When he obeyed, she sized up his sock-clad feet, then selected a pair of Western boots from the half dozen on a rack. "Try these."

He slid his feet into them. "Huh. They're not bad."

She nodded. "I'm good at judging. Now you just need a hat." She picked up a black Resistol. "Are you a black kind of guy?"

Chapter Sixteen

"Dark and dangerous?" Jake said. "Not hardly."

Brooke smothered a giggle. "Give Cousin Arnold the black one, Rob. It'll help him find his spirit of adventure."

Behind the wire-framed glasses, Jake rolled his eyes at both of them. He took the hat and perched it at a silly angle on his head.

Robin, who grew taller every day, went up on her tiptoes and adjusted it.

"You'll never win with her," Brooke warned him. "You might as well surrender now."

"Why do I have the feeling that's how it is with all the women in the family?" he asked.

He'd been teasing, but Robin took the question seriously. "Because we're strong. Mom says we're all strong. Her and me, Gramma Brooke, and Gran Miriam."

"I can see that," he said in a serious tone. "And that's a very good thing to be."

They headed out to the yard again, where Brooke stroked the pinto mare she normally rode. "Hi there, Beanie." The horse's name was Full o' Beans, but everyone abbreviated it. Enjoying the smell of horse and the feel of rough, warm skin under her palm, Brooke watched Robin introduce Jake to a buckskin gelding called Sage. As Jake tentatively let the horse smell his hand, then patted the animal, Brooke wondered how much of his caution was an act. Was it possible that Jake, the man who hunted the toughest criminals, was nervous around horses?

With Robin instructing him on how to mount, he put his left foot in the stirrup, reached up to grasp the saddle, then paused, as if the task was beyond him.

Robin touched his upper arm, just below the sleeve of his golf shirt. "You have muscles," she said firmly. "Use them."

With a surprised laugh, Jake tugged himself up, swung his leg over, and landed in the saddle.

Brooke mounted easily and Robin vaulted onto the back of her bay mare, Concha. They started off across the barnyard at a walk, Robin riding beside Jake, issuing instructions. Brooke trailed behind, smiling. Last summer, she'd been the one learning from this talented girl.

Robin took them along a dirt service road first, then moved ahead of Jake to lead the way onto a well-used trail.

Brooke watched Jake's back. When he played Arnold, he slumped a little, which disguised his size, muscularity, and strength. Now, on the back of a horse, his body fell naturally into Western riding posture, which, she'd learned, was more relaxed than the straight-backed style of English riders. She could see him getting the feel of his mount, starting to move as if they were one being.

When the path widened, she moved up beside him and asked softly, so Robin couldn't overhear, "How does it compare to being on a motorcycle?"

"Slow," he responded with a grin. "But there are some similarities. Have to say, I like the hat better than a helmet."

"Wait until you race across a field with the wind in your hair."

His eyes brightened. "You do that? Brooke, the cautious one?"

"Well, I don't race as fast as Robin, but yes. It's such a free feeling."

He studied her, and she sensed that he understood. In her structure-ruled life, there were few things that felt as free and liberating as letting Beanie run with the wind.

"Ready to try trotting?" Robin called back.

"Sure," Jake called. "I'm feeling brave."

"Trotting can really jolt you around," Brooke warned, worrying about his bullet wound as she held her horse back to fall in behind him again.

"Not if you sit it properly," Robin said. She stopped Concha, waiting for Jake to catch up so she could ride beside him. "You need to really feel Sage's movements and kind of absorb them. Don't tense up and fight it, but don't sag either. Let your lower body follow the movement, so your back and tummy move forward and back just a little. Keep your upper body and hands calm and steady."

"That's a lot to keep in mind," he said doubtfully.

"It's like learning any other physical activity," the girl said. "At first you concentrate, almost too hard, then it just kind of clicks and you start feeling it rather than thinking about it."

"I'll give it a try."

They started out at a slow trot and Brooke took pride in automatically doing all the things Robin had listed, feeling her body move comfortably along with Beanie's. She grinned to herself, remembering the ache in her butt and thighs after her first few rides.

Jake did his share of flopping around and moaning, while Robin laughed, teased, and coached him, to no avail. The girl slowed them all to a walk. "Okay, Cousin Arnold, let's figure this out. What kind of exercise do you usually do?"

"What makes you think I do any?"

"Like I said, you have muscles. You don't spend your whole life sitting at a computer crunching numbers."

"Smart girl," he said, his tone admiring and, to Brooke's sensitive ears, also holding a touch of ruefulness at being caught out by a child. "You're right. Desk work's hard on the body, so I try to get to the fitness club before work every day. I do the typical routine: treadmill, machines."

"Huh." Robin's one syllable made it clear she thought a fitness club was a poor substitute for riding and ranch work. "When you run on the treadmill, you don't just use your legs, right? It's a whole-body thing. Core strength, balance, keeping all the parts working in harmony?"

Jake studied her with surprise as he agreed, but Brooke wasn't the least bit startled by the girl's knowledge and the way she applied it. She'd had a good teacher in her mom, and was an integral part of Riders Boot Camp.

Robin coached Jake some more; then they tried a trot again and this time he did better—or allowed Arnold to do better. "You're a good teacher," he breathlessly complimented Robin.

When the trail came out by a small lake, Brooke made Jake pose for a few photos and he said, "I'll have to get copies from you. My mother and siblings will never believe it."

"You could get an office in town," Robin said, "and a house that's a few miles away, like near where we live, and then you can get a horse and ride to work."

"You've got it all worked out, haven't you?" Jake teased her.

Brooke knew the girl's plan would never come true, yet Robin's words sent a twinge through her. Having Jake nearby sounded appealing. Imagining him as part of her life . . . But no, that was ridiculous. It wasn't what she wanted, and it certainly wasn't how he saw his life going.

She forced a smile. "Rob, do you think Arnold's ready to learn how to lope?"

"Lope?" Jake asked. "Is that another word for gallop?"

Robin promptly launched into an explanation of the two gaits and the differences from the English-riding canter, and Brooke thought how well the two of them got along. Even when Jake was playing Arnold, his own qualities like respect for others, curiosity, and sharp intellect came through.

They rode on, with Robin instructing Jake and telling him about some of the flora and fauna, and Brooke let herself relax and enjoy herself. Half an hour later, Jake held Sage back to ride beside Beanie. "Having a good time?" he asked.

"I love doing this. When I cleaned up my act I learned meditation as a way to de-stress, but riding in the country is even better. I lose track of time, live in the moment. Jessica and Evan talk about stopping to smell the roses, and it's amazingly healing."

His polite but rather baffled expression told her he didn't get it. She wouldn't have expected an undercover cop to understand.

"You can cover a lot of country too," he said reflectively.

Guessing his train of thought, she said, "Yes. And you see riders all over the place. No one thinks anything of seeing a horse and rider following some country road or trail." If he wanted to visit the grow op, doing it on horseback would be less obtrusive than using a vehicle. Still, she wished he wouldn't. She didn't want another bullet hole in his sexy hide.

"You can stay for dinner, right?" Robin called back to them. "Dad's coming, and Gran and Gramps."

A rueful smile tugged at Brooke's lips. When she'd first been drawn into these big family dinners she'd felt so uncomfortable. Now she knew everyone accepted her and she loved nothing better than a family get-together. Tonight, though, she'd have preferred to be alone with Jake. Putting selfish thoughts aside, she said to him, "As well as being wonderful people, Jessica's parents have lived in Caribou Crossing forever, and Dave's one of the community leaders. You couldn't find better people to talk to."

"Sounds great," he said enthusiastically. "If they don't mind me smelling of horse. I didn't bring fresh clothes to change into."

Robin hooted. "We *love* the smell of horse, Cousin Arnold!"

When Jake rode into the barnyard with Brooke and Robin, the girl said, "Mom's group is back."

The yard didn't look any different, but he noted a few people on the porches of the cabins and bunkhouse, many with a beer or soda in their hand. Robin waved at them and they waved back, and Jake thought that he could sure go for a beer.

He swung with Arnoldy clumsiness from Sage's back, his body aching. It wasn't just the bullet wound; riding a horse used a different set of muscles than riding a Harley. He experienced another unusual feeling too. Despite the nagging pain, he was relaxed and almost . . . content.

Normally, he was either caught up intensely in his work, exhausted after a demanding job, or restless and wanting to get to work again. Yeah, occasionally he and Jamal relaxed over pizza and a game on TV, but contentment hadn't been a word in Jake's vocabulary. This must be what Brooke meant about de-stressing and stopping to smell the roses.

"You did great," Robin told him, her eyes sparkling as she took Sage's reins from him. "Don't you love it?"

"It wasn't bad at all. I'm not sure I see myself riding to and from work, but I'd do this again." And he would, happily, as Jake, though likely he'd never get the chance. At the beginning of the week, the investigation would heat up again, with Sergeant Miller and other prominent townspeople available to be interviewed by Arnold. Jake hoped to wrap up the case within the week, and at that point his subterfuge would be exposed. He felt a pang at deceiving nice people, but that was what the job demanded. Brooke would explain it to her family and friends and they'd understand why it had been necessary.

Seeing that Brooke was taking off her horse's saddle, he asked Robin, "What do I do next?"

She coached him through removing Sage's saddle and exchanging the bridle for a halter, then brushing the horse, demonstrating with her own horse. He noted that Brooke was quietly and competently managing on her own.

As Robin turned the horses out into a grassy paddock, Jake went into the barn. In the spirit of being Arnold, he returned his Resistol to a hook on the wall and changed back into loafers, wishing for either sneakers or sandals. And a beer. He really wanted an ice-cold beer.

Robin took him and Brooke up the road past the boot camp buildings to her home, where Evan, looking tanned and healthy in a T-shirt, cargo shorts, and sandals, greeted them. "Feel like a beer?" he asked Jake.

Would Arnold drink beer? Hell, yeah—at least to be polite. "That sounds good."

"I'll get the drinks," Robin offered, and bustled into the house.

She returned in seconds with two beer bottles, which she handed to Jake and Evan, and two bottles of a carbonated fruit drink, one for Brooke and the other for herself.

Everyone opened the drinks and took long swallows; then Jessica came from the house, wiping her hands on well-worn jeans.

They'd barely settled in chairs on the wide wraparound porch when Jessica's parents arrived on foot. Miriam Bly was trim in casual pants and a pretty shirt, her sandy hair and freckles giving her a youthful appearance. Her husband Wade's hair and beard were mostly silver, and he walked with a hint of a limp, but there were muscles on his rangy frame and his handshake was firm. His eyes, the same deep brown as Jessica's and Robin's, were as friendly as his wife's gray ones.

The introductions had barely been made when Dave Cousins arrived. Also on foot, in jeans and boots, he said, "I rode over. Malibu is down at Boots."

As the group got set up with drinks and began to chat, Jake watched for signs of strain between Jessica's husband and her ex, but there were none. The men acted like brothers, joking and slapping each other's back.

Brooke had a pretty amazing family. And, he found out over the next half hour, every one of them was determined to make him welcome and sell him on the idea of moving to Caribou Crossing.

Jake and Brooke managed, on one pretext or another, to insinuate the name of everyone he was investigating into the conversation. None of the family did business at Cray's bank, and no one liked him. As for Sergeant Miller, Wade Bly said, "He's a hands-on guy. Gets involved in things himself, takes things personally."

"Too much so, maybe," Dave Cousins commented.

"What do you mean?" Brooke asked.

"Remember that constable, Mac Jones?" Dave said. "He came into the Wild Rose a lot, and we got to be friends."

"He left Caribou Crossing a year ago," Wade said. "Got transferred, right?"

"He requested the transfer. Didn't get along with Miller. He said the man didn't let him do his job, and kept taking work away from him."

Jake filed that information away.

At the next lull in the conversation, he said, "Someone at the fund-raiser mentioned a place that might be coming up for sale. I think the owner's name is Baxter."

"That'll be Bob Baxter," Wade said. "He's in his late eighties, has Alzheimer's. He's living in a care facility and likely won't last much longer. Pity. He was a good man, loved this place.

Has a nephew, name of, let me see"—he ran his hand over his short silver beard—"Gideon, that's it. Lives back east somewhere. Has a family, seems happy there. I imagine he'll sell the place when his uncle passes on."

"I don't think it'd be right for Arnold, though," Miriam said. "Bob sold his house back when he moved into the facility. The property Gideon will inherit is undeveloped land out in the middle of nowhere."

"Arnold has to be in riding distance of town," Robin put in. "He's going to get a horse."

"Right," Jake said dryly. "You just keep thinking that."

They all laughed, then moved around to the back patio and settled in for a dinner of barbecued chicken and ribs, potatoes baked in foil, and corn on the cob. The topic of conversation moved to a discussion of Riders Boot Camp and Jake listened, impressed by how involved and committed they all were. Though it was Jessica's dream, they'd made its fulfillment a family project. Wouldn't it be nice if all families were like this one.

Miriam and Jessica went to the kitchen, to return with two peach pies and a tub of vanilla ice cream. He tasted the pie, which Miriam had made, and moaned. Brooke's eyes, across the table, danced with amusement.

This was, bullet wound aside, the sweetest assignment he'd ever drawn.

Adroitly he steered the conversation to drop a few more names, but learned nothing new.

The evening wound up early. Evan walked Jake and Brooke to the car. "We're on a different clock here," he said. "Go to bed early and get up at or before the crack of dawn. Takes some getting used to. But it's a healthy way of life."

Jake held the passenger door for Brooke. "I guess it is. Thanks for a most enjoyable evening, Evan."

He climbed in and pulled away from the house. "You have a nice family."

"I know. Did you learn anything useful?"

"Snippets, but not a lot. Either your family doesn't know any real dirt on our suspects," Jake said, "or they aren't going to gossip with a stranger. We'll see if Jamal digs up anything more, like on the trips Cray, Miller, and Vijay Patel take."

"You talked to Vijay at the fund-raiser, didn't you?"

"Yeah. He said all the right things about the break-in at his store, for what that's worth."

"What else can I do to help?"

He smiled warmly at her. "You're doing great. Just keep asking friendly little questions of your clients. But don't push. I'd rather not solve this murder than have you in danger."

"Honestly? That's . . . reassuring." Her tone was serious, not joking.

"Hell, Brooke." He broke off and shrugged, not sure what he wanted to say to her.

She was a strong woman. But she hadn't always been. The murder victim, Anika, hadn't been strong, but maybe she could have been if she'd been given the right chance. And then there was Sapphire, his informant, who believed she was so in control but lived such a dangerous life. Was there any way he could get her to quit the streets?

He reached over to rest a hand on Brooke's jean-clad thigh. "What made you turn your life around? Was it really the bipolar diagnosis?"

She gaped at him, obviously surprised by the change of topic. After a moment of reflection she said, "Yes, because I realized it wasn't all my fault. I had an illness, and it was treatable. Then I was able to admit what I'd never acknowledged before: that I was an alcoholic. But that can be handled too. It was like a new lease on life. I could never undo the wrongs I'd committed, but I could start living a decent life rather than always feeling like a failure, feeling depressed and guilty."

He took that in, the only sound for the moment the low

hum of the car's engine. "If you knew someone who was in a bad place in their life, what would you say to help them turn it around?"

Though he was watching the dark highway and sparse traffic, he felt her gaze on him. "Depends on the person, their situation, my relationship with them. Like you with Jamal. I'd want them to know they had options. When you're really down you can't see any way out, so I'd try to show them a way. And let them know someone cared." She paused, then asked, "Who are you thinking of?"

"Sapphire. Anika's friend."

"You want to get her off the street."

"Yeah. Dumb, eh? She's just another hooker; there are hundreds like her."

"Oh, Jake, you can't save them all."

He pulled into her driveway and turned off the engine. "Probably can't save any of them," he said gruffly.

She rested her hand on top of his and squeezed. "It won't stop you from trying to help Sapphire."

"I guess not."

"You saved Jamal."

"Ah hell, Brooke, he saved himself."

"With a little help from a friend. You showed him a way out, and let him know someone cared if he took it. Maybe you can do the same for Sapphire. I can see why you want to try."

They climbed out of the car and walked toward the house, up the steps, and onto the porch. Brooke didn't open the door and go in. Instead she sat on a slatted-wood couch with green-and-white-striped cushions. She patted the seat beside her.

He sat, putting an arm around her shoulders and drawing her close.

"Jake, tell me honestly what you want out of our relationship."

Where had that question come from? "Your company. For as long as I'm in town." He thought he'd been clear about what kind of man he was, but now he worried. "You weren't thinking—"

"No!" Her head shook vigorously against his shoulder. "No, that's exactly what I want too. It's the only way I could do this. I don't want a permanent relationship with a man; it terrifies me to think of that kind of commitment." The words flew out; then she paused, ran a hand through her hair, and went on more reflectively. "Well, maybe years down the road. If the lithium still works and I'm ten or more years sober. It might be nice to have a companion as I get older. A man who likes a quiet life, values family, enjoys gardening and quiet evenings by the fire."

"A white-picket-fence kind of guy." He gestured past her neat garden to where the row of white pickets gleamed dimly under the starlight.

"Exactly. I guess, basically, the opposite of you."

It was true. The last thing he wanted was a sedate, boring life. So why did her words feel like jabs, poking under his skin and right into his heart?

He thought about what she'd said, tried to build the picture in his head, and some of it definitely came into focus. He could imagine Brooke and some silver-haired guy gardening together, going riding with the grandkids, enjoying dinners with the rest of the family. But what about in the bedroom? This was one hell of a sexy lady. Would the picket-fence guy satisfy her in bed? And what about the side of her that liked the excitement of living inside a mystery novel, as she'd put it?

Her voice broke into his thoughts. "What do you see for your future, Jake? How long will you be an undercover cop?"

He shrugged. "I don't think much about the future. The job's good, my life's good." He stroked his hand across her thigh, feeling her warmth through the denim. "I'll keep on as long as I can."

"It's a dangerous job," she said quietly. "What if . . ."

"I'm seriously injured or get too old for it?" He tried not to think about that. "I'll deal with that if it happens."

She rested her hand atop his. "I hope things work out the way you want. I know I'll think of you after you're gone, Jake. Very fondly. But"—her voice firmed—"I'll try to think only about our times together. I won't want to imagine you out on the streets doing your job. Putting yourself in danger."

"I get it. That's one of the reasons cops don't do very well in the marriage department. The spouses worry too much." He thought for a moment about Karen MacLean. That would be another handicap for her. How could a normal guy handle being married to a woman who put her life in danger every day? It would take a special man. She was probably right, that marriage and kids weren't in her future. Any more than they were in his. The difference was, she wanted them

"I'd go crazy," Brooke said. "You know, Dave's become overprotective since Anita died. And last year, we had a scare when Robin was hit by a car. Now, he's even more restrictive with her. And I see it, and my brain says it's wrong and he should loosen up, yet my heart agrees with him. Our instinct is to wrap her in cotton wool so she'll never get hurt."

"If you did, she'd never learn, she'd never toughen up, she'd never be able to handle the world on her own. Trust her; she's a smart, sensible kid."

"Easy for you to say. She's not your grandchild." She gave a soft chuckle. "Yes, you're right, I know. But it's hard for me. Since I cleaned myself up, I've become a cautious person."

"And yet you're helping me hunt down a murderer."

"That's different. It's not about my family's safety, for one thing. And it's not my ordinary life." She lifted her head from his shoulder and eased away a little, so she could turn and look at him. "This whole thing, including my relationship with you, is out of the ordinary. It's this little space in time, something special and exciting. Later, I can look back on it and revel in it. But it's not the way I want to live."

Her face and voice were so serious, he wanted to lighten the mood. "You don't want great sex every night?" he teased.

Her face lit and she gave him a flirtatious smile. "Gosh, I don't know. I haven't had enough experience to decide. I need at least another couple of nights before I make up my mind."

"Then let's start now."

He leaned toward her, she met him halfway, and their lips touched. Touched, firmed with passion, parted; tongues darted; heat flared. Jake had been feeling kind of relaxed and lazy, but now his blood surged and his cock thickened with need.

When he tugged open the snap buttons of her shirt, she broke away. "Not here. Someone might drive by."

He groaned, but she was right. Impatiently, he waited while she unlocked the front door and tugged off her cowboy boots before going inside. Once the door was closed, he thrust a hand inside her shirt and bra to find her firm breast and budded nipple. Too impatient to take her up to the bedroom, he said, "The living room couch."

"I've taken your clothes off there before," she agreed mischievously.

This time, it was a battle to see who could undress the other first, and in mere seconds they were both naked, flushed, and aroused, standing on the rug by the couch.

"I want you," she said.

He figured his erection was sending the same message, but women needed words. "I want you too, Brooke." He eased her down until she lay where he had a few days ago, when she'd nursed him. This time, it was his turn to take care of her, in the most sensual way he could.

Chapter Seventeen

An hour later, as Brooke lay draped on top of Jake, she murmured, "It keeps getting better."

"And we have the whole night ahead of us." He glanced across the room at the clock. "It's barely past nine o'clock."

She sat up slowly and ran her hands through her tangled hair. "It's been a full day."

"Tired?"

"Not really. I could use a cup of tea. Want one?"

Coffee was more his drink, but he didn't hate tea. "Sure."

He was sorry he'd agreed, though, when she pulled herself off him and onto her feet, then began to put on her clothes. "Hey," he protested.

She held her shirt across her breasts and shot him a seductive glance. "I'm modest."

"Sure you are."

But he let her go to the kitchen, then dragged himself upright and put on his jeans and golf shirt. Oh yeah, he was achy, but that was nothing new. What was new was the same feeling he'd experienced that afternoon: contentment.

From the kitchen, he heard the faint sound of music from that radio station she always had on. It was probably habit for her, because she was used to being alone, to flick on the radio for company. He did that with the TV himself.

He sat down again on the couch, lifted his feet to the coffee table, and noticed the cat peering cautiously around the door frame.

"It's okay, Sunny," Jake said. "The coast is clear now."

The cat stalked in, leaped up on a chair, circled a couple of times, then curled up, all the while not looking at Jake.

Brooke returned bearing a tray with mugs and a teapot. "It's Irish Breakfast. I figured you'd like it better than Earl Grey."

Like he'd know one tea from another? "It'll be fine."

"Milk, sugar, honey?"

He shook his head no.

"Cookies?"

He chuckled. She really did like looking after people. "I'm still full from dinner. Sit down and drink your tea."

She put the tray on the coffee table and shifted a pile of books aside. "Darn, that library book's due on Monday and I haven't finished it." She sat beside him and poked an elbow into his ribs on the uninjured side. "I haven't been doing any reading since you showed up."

He'd disrupted all her careful routines. The least he could give her was the chance to finish her book. "I can probably live another hour or two without having sex again. Go for it."

"How about you? Do you like to read?"

When would he have time to start and finish a book? "Why don't you pick one of those mysteries in your bookcase?" He'd rather flick on the tube and find a game to watch, but that might disturb her reading.

She popped to her feet again. "Okay." Then she came back and handed him a paperback by an author called Janet Evanovich. It figured she'd pick a woman writer. He'd bet the book would be heavy on romance and light—and inaccurate—when it came to action. Still, he didn't want to offend Brooke.

After pouring tea for both of them, she curled up against the opposite end of the couch with her mug and book, then stretched her legs out to tuck her bare feet under his thigh.

He smiled and stroked her calves through her jeans. Then he took a sip of the tea, which was tolerable, and opened the book. He'd barely turned two pages when Sunny leaped up on his lap, circling again and poking sensitive parts, then settled into a purring ball. Jake grinned, stroked the golden fur, and returned to the story.

A while later Brooke's voice broke in. "Enjoying the book?"

He realized he'd been laughing out loud. "It's not exactly a police procedural and it sure won't win any points for accuracy, but it's pretty funny. Great cast of characters."

She smiled, seeming pleased rather than smug, and went back to her own book.

He read on until he realized she was shifting position, putting her book on the coffee table, and yawning. "Finished. Ready to pack it in?"

The clock told him it was almost eleven. "Just a couple more pages. Got to find out what Stephanie's grandmother is up to."

Brooke leaned over and ran her tongue lightly around the outside of his ear. "I'll be the one in bed."

He glanced at her face, then at the book. Nope, no contest. He put the book facedown on the coffee table. "I'll be the one on top of you."

If Saturday had been unusual for Jake, Sunday was an eye-opener into life in Caribou Crossing. He put himself at Brooke's disposal, as Arnold in public and Jake in private.

First they took a brisk hour-long walk on country roads, pausing to stroke horses' necks, pat dogs, and chat with anyone who happened to be out and about. Then they went to church, which wasn't his thing at all, but it did give him an opportunity to meet a few other pillars of the community.

Seeing people interact with Brooke reinforced how far she'd come since she'd turned her life around. Now she was not only accepted as part of the community, she was genuinely liked.

Funny thing was, she didn't seem to realize the depth of people's feelings for her. She saw civility; he saw respect, affection, friendship.

After church they went grocery shopping and piled up a cartload of food that didn't include a single frozen dinner or tin of stew. Lots of vegetables and fruit. No cookies, because Brooke said she always baked her own.

Home-baked cookies. His mother had always bought packaged. Neither of his parents had spent much time in the kitchen, and on the infrequent occasions the family sat down for meals together, it was more of an ordeal than a pleasure. His upbringing was about as different from Robin's as could be imagined. Brooke's granddaughter sure wouldn't turn out to be a loner the way he had.

Brooke imagined Jake must have been bored to tears but he hid it as, after a lunch of Mexican omelets, they went to work in her yard. Robin had been after them to go riding again, but Brooke wasn't about to let her garden get out of control. So she put Jake, wearing Arnold's golf shirt and khakis, to work pushing the lawnmower back and forth as she weeded borders.

Several riders came along the road and stopped to say hi, and the occasional car passed. A small plane buzzing overhead had both of them looking up. "It's from the flight school," she said. "I can tell by the color."

Thinking what a picture of domesticity she and Jake made,

Brooke forced herself to remember who he really was. It was getting harder and harder to recall the man in black leather, the long hair and beard, the bike. The gun. She wondered where he'd hidden it.

She straightened and stretched as Jake dumped the last load of grass cuttings into the compost box. Could she see the real Jake Brannon mowing a lawn?

And why was she trying to? It wasn't like he was going to stay. It wasn't even like she wanted him to.

When he came to join her, she said, "Bet it's a while since you mowed a lawn."

"When I was a kid my parents made me do it."

His voice was flat, as it always was when he spoke of his parents. As if he'd schooled himself to not feel, much less express, emotion for them. They had hurt him. They hadn't wanted to know who he was, only to shape him into what they wanted him to be. Poor little boy.

She wrapped her arms around him and gave him a big hug.

He pulled back. "Hey, Brooke, not that I don't like this, but I'm Arnold."

"It was a cousinly hug. There's a difference. Come on inside and I'll show you."

Together in the shower, they fooled around as they showered off the sweat and garden dirt, then they made long, sweet love in her bed. After, they showered again and went downstairs to see about dinner.

Jake lit the barbecue while Brooke strung cubes of marinated pork on skewers. Then she started to make potato salad from potatoes and eggs she'd boiled earlier.

Handing him a bunch of green onions, fresh from the garden, to chop, she asked, "Can you handle this much domesticity?"

"It's sure different." He paused, then said almost reluctantly, "Kind of relaxing for a change."

"Tell me about where you live. You have an apartment in Vancouver?"

"Yeah, it's nothing special. A one-bedroom on the tenth floor of a midsize building. I rent it furnished. It's got everything I need and I'm hardly ever home anyhow. When I'm undercover I'm out of town a lot, usually living in a hovel somewhere, or on the streets."

She tried to picture his apartment. A microwave, tins of stew, beer in the fridge—those were about the only personal details he'd given her. No plants; they'd never survive his absences. Last night, she'd realized he wasn't much of a reader. "Television, music?"

"The place came with a TV. I watch sports when I'm home."

Was there a game of any kind on tonight? She'd been worrying about how to entertain him, thinking that another night of reading would have him climbing the walls.

Suddenly she had an idea. A mischievous one. Besides, it would provide him with another opportunity to meet more townspeople. She turned from stirring homemade mayonnaise into the salad. "How are your injuries doing after all the gardening?"

"I'm good as new." He tossed the chopped green onions into the bowl. "Just a little itchy, where everything's healing."

"Hmm. How do you feel about line dancing?"

"Line dancing?" He frowned. "You serious?"

"Sunday nights were pretty slow at the Wild Rose, so Dave had the idea of offering line-dancing classes. I go most weeks. It's fun, good exercise."

He raised his eyebrows. "I'm pretty sure Arnold doesn't line dance."

"Ah," she said mischievously, "but nor did he ride. If he's checking out Caribou Crossing, he should be open to our way of life."

He groaned. Then, "Would I get to dance with you?"

"Not, uh, clinch dancing. But of course as your hostess, I'd look after you."

"This is sounding better."

If he'd really intended to open a business in this town, Jake mused that evening, the best bet would be a Western clothing store. Before coming to Caribou Crossing, he'd never seen so many cowboy boots, cowboy hats, Western shirts, and bolo ties in his life.

The forty or so people at the Wild Rose, with the sole exception of himself, all wore some variation of that uniform.

There was some initial socializing, during which he talked to a number of people he'd already met plus a few new ones, but learned nothing of interest to his investigation.

Then the instructors, an elderly couple named Jimmy B and Bets, started the lessons.

They were damned sprightly for folks with white hair, Jake thought admiringly. This line-dancing business was like a cowboy version of an aerobics class, with feet going this way and that in crazy, hard-to-follow patterns. People were laughing, clearly having a great time.

Jake was always up for a physical challenge, but deliberately made Arnold a little stiff and awkward.

Line dancing. Just wait until he told Jamal.

Jake had had some pretty weird U/C assignments in his career, but this was one of the strangest.

When he found a chance to speak a private word with Brooke, he teased, "If I'd stuck with my first cover, the seedy biker, I wouldn't have to be doing this."

She flashed a brilliant smile. "But you wouldn't be going home with me either." Then she whirled away from him and back into the dance, her boots tapping a quick rhythm on the floor.

Finally, the music changed to something slower and Brooke

returned to him. "They took pity on you, Arnold. Care to dance to Patsy with your cousin?"

"I wouldn't say no." Patsy, he figured, must be Patsy Cline. As Brooke slipped into his arms, the singer was crooning about being crazy for loving someone. He had to agree; the whole love thing seemed like damned risky business to him.

Lusting after someone was another matter, though. It was tough to force himself to hold his partner at a respectable distance. To distract himself, he glanced around and noted that their teachers were still on their feet too, swaying together. "Jimmy B and Bets look more like teens than seniors."

"I know. Aren't they great? So much energy. They've been married almost fifty years, you know."

"Wow."

"Imagine finding someone whose company you enjoyed that much. It's about so much more than sex."

"Bet the sex would have to be pretty great too, for a couple to last that long together." Out of nowhere came the thought that with him and Brooke the sex was stupendous. And he really did enjoy her company, whether they were cooking a meal together, reading books in her living room, scheming how to catch a murderer, or discussing how to get a hooker off the streets. Damn it, he really did like the woman. As well as lust after her, respect her, and trust her.

He couldn't remember the last time he'd liked someone this much. The only person he'd ever felt this close to was Jamal, which was a whole different ball of wax.

Brooke was singing softly along with the music now, her voice low and pure.

When the song finished and another slow one came on, he noticed Tiffany, an assertive thirtyish redhead he'd met earlier, bearing down on them. Quickly he said under his breath, "Brooke? Want to head home before we have to dance with a bunch of other people?"

"Hmm?" She glanced up and saw Tiffany. "Yes, I am awfully

tired, Arnold. I do think it's time to go." She smiled at Tiffany. "Sorry."

Tiffany winked. "Just talk Arnold into moving here; then I'll have plenty of dances."

As Jake and Brooke moved toward the door, she muttered, "Right, like I'd do it for her."

"Don't like Tiffany, or you jealous?"

"Tiffany's fine. Just a little superficial."

"I see."

"Okay," she huffed, "so I'm jealous. You're mine for the duration, right? That's the agreement."

"That's the agreement." And he had not the slightest desire to modify it.

They stopped at the bar to say good-bye to Dave Cousins, who'd been bartending and not dancing. The man reached over the counter and tapped Jake on the shoulder. "I'd say you're going to fit in just fine around here, Arnold."

"Uh, thanks. But I haven't decided anything yet."

"That's what you say." Dave winked at Brooke. "Some of us know better."

As they walked to the car, Jake said, "What was Dave talking about?"

"I guess he thought you were enjoying Caribou Crossing."

"You don't figure he's on to us?"

"We were perfectly circumspect."

Well, they'd tried to be. But they had exchanged a few whispers and maybe a couple of personal glances. He opened the car door for Brooke. "Let's go home, where we can be perfectly uncircumspect. My fingers are itching to pop those snaps on your shirt."

The next morning, after spending an hour on the phone with Jamal getting an information update, Jake headed into town. When he walked into the small, plainly furnished

RCMP detachment, he was Arnold at his most circumspect in suit, tie, and glasses.

Karen MacLean was working at a computer and came to greet him. A corporal like Jake, she was one rank below Miller.

The detachment, according to the staff list Jamal had provided, was made up of Miller, MacLean and another corporal, and a half dozen constables.

After exchanging greetings with MacLean, Jake said, "Is Sergeant Miller in?"

She narrowed her eyes and tilted her head. "You don't trust what I had to say about the crime rate here?"

"It's not that. I'd like to meet the man who's in charge of the community's safety."

"Polite answer." She called over her shoulder, "Hey, Sarge, someone here to see you."

Jake had, of course, seen Miller before, from Brooke's bedroom window. Now he got a closer view. Brooke had called the man a redneck, and he could see why. He was as far overweight as a man could get without failing his physical, his face showed the broken veins of a drinker, and his handshake went past firm to trying to make a point. As Arnold conceded the contest, Jake took pleasure in knowing he could, in mere seconds, have the man writhing on the floor in agony.

"I met Mr. Pitt at the fund-raiser on Friday night," MacLean said. "He's thinking about moving to Caribou Crossing and opening an accounting practice."

She'd left out the most important bit of his cover story, so he added it. "My cousin, Brooke Kincaid, told me an accountant had just left town."

Miller smirked. "You're Brooke's cousin?"

Jake understood immediately that this man had condemned Brooke long ago and didn't believe in second chances. No such thing as an open mind here.

Jake wanted to punch him out. The reaction was instinctive and pure. He breathed in slowly, quelling it.

Karen MacLean made a small movement and he glanced at her, reading in her eyes that she understood exactly what was going on. Now he saw why she hadn't mentioned Brooke's name.

He liked MacLean.

Jake breathed out again, slowly. "I'm tired of gang wars, drug trafficking, hookers on the street. I hear Caribou Crossing doesn't have those kinds of problems?"

Miller gave a snort and turned to MacLean. "When's the last gang war we had?"

She gave a small, polite smile. "Only gang we've ever had trouble with was the bikers Death Row, a few years back. The sergeant discouraged them from visiting."

Death Row was almost as famous as Hell's Angels—and known to be heavily involved in the drug trade. Jake knew it was hard to discourage The Row. He figured either the bikers had decided the town had little to offer, or Miller was selling to them down in Vancouver.

"And what about violent crimes, drugs, prostitution?" Jake asked.

"Let me show you our stats," Miller said. He took Jake to his office, where he located a file on his computer and turned the monitor so Jake could see. "We compile statistics and present them at meetings of the town council and chamber of commerce."

Jake studied the graph and had to admit the statistics were impressive. Especially when it came to drug offenses. "You don't have a problem with drugs?"

"Oh, shoot!" Miller glanced at his watch. "Glad you reminded me. I have to head out. I'm giving a talk at the high school." He ushered Jake out of his office.

"Is that how you deter drug use among teenagers?"

"We have numerous initiatives. A zero-tolerance policy. I make that very clear to students, once or twice each year."

They were walking past MacLean's desk and Jake noticed her studying both of them, a frown on her face. After shaking Miller's hand again and leaving the detachment, Jake puzzled over just what that frown might have meant.

He was frowning himself, dissatisfied with the outcome of this visit. He had a lot of unanswered questions, and it would be difficult to find an excuse for another visit with Miller. So far, he'd learned nothing against the man. He might dislike the sergeant intensely, but the man's crime stats were good and it said a lot for him that he went to the schools to speak to students. Of course, it might just be part of his cover—discouraging drug use in public while in fact he was growing BC Bud out in the hills.

Jake popped into Beauty Is You to see if Brooke had time for lunch, and caught both her and Kate leafing through beauty magazines. "Mondays tend to be slow," Kate said. "How about letting Brooke give you a Caribou Crossing haircut?"

He thought of how good Brooke's hands had felt on his scalp the last time. She massaged when she shampooed. It was a real turn-on. He was tempted. But the slicker Vancouver style was part of his Arnold image so he said, "While I trust Brooke implicitly, my stylist in Vancouver would throw a fit if I let someone else touch my hair. Besides, I came by to see if anyone is interested in lunch."

They both took him up on his offer.

He liked the sandwich shop the women took him to. Named Big & Small, it offered a variety of sandwiches, wraps, and salads—everything available in full- and half-sized servings. The women chose half-sized salads and half-sized wraps, while he went for a full salad and the day's special, grilled chicken and mushrooms on focaccia bread. The meals cost half what they would in Vancouver, and his tasted great.

Though he'd have preferred to have Brooke to himself, he enjoyed Kate's company. She had the same commonsense approach as her niece Jessica, and a wicked sense of humor that provided him with some insights into various towns-people. It was also clear that she was very fond of Brooke. Fonder than Brooke let herself realize.

Couldn't the damned woman give herself some credit? Or was she nervous about letting herself have friends? About making commitments, taking responsibility.

When they walked outside after lunch, Brooke pointed across the street. "Arnold, I don't know if you've been in that store yet, but I think you'd find it interesting. Vijay Patel has a great collection of arts and crafts as well as tourist items. You might pick yourself up a Caribou Crossing T-shirt." Eyes twinkling, she said, "Or a bolo tie."

"Uh-huh," he said dryly. "I'm more interested in the arts and crafts." He'd already met Patel at the fund-raiser, but it wouldn't hurt to check out the store—plus he'd like to get something for Brooke, to thank her for . . . everything.

Inside, Patel was occupied with a couple of tourists doing souvenir shopping, so Jake browsed on his own. The place was too cluttered for his taste but it carried a good selection. As well as the to-be-expected cowboy- and gold-mining-themed souvenirs, tees with the Caribou Crossing logo, and miniature caribou, there was elegant silver and gold jewelry by local First Nations artists, corn-husk and dried-apple dolls, and patterned silk scarves that looked as if they'd come from India.

A few minutes later, Patel bustled toward him. "So sorry to keep you waiting, Mr. Pitt. I am honored to have you visit my shop."

"I'd like to buy a gift for my cousin, to thank her for her hospitality."

"Ah, yes. What do you think Ms. Kincaid would like? And,

if I may make a delicate inquiry, do you have a price range in mind?"

"I'm not so worried about price. I want something she'll really enjoy." He'd noticed she had a couple of paintings of flowers on her walls, so he headed to the display of watercolors. "She likes flowers."

"Here you see the work of two local painters, both women. One, as you can see, is more traditional in her representations, and the other more abstract. I do not know Ms. Kincaid well, so I am not in a good position to judge."

Jake was drawn to an abstract of a country garden overflowing with summer blooms in shades of peach and pink. The colors reminded him of Brooke's lingerie. "This one."

"An excellent choice."

Jake bit back a smile, guessing that Patel would have said the same thing no matter which item he chose.

While the man wrapped the painting and Jake paid the bill in cash—avoiding using a fake debit card, even though the transaction would have gone through—they chatted. Jake left the store feeling pretty confident Patel was no drug dealer.

He hid the painting in the trunk of his Lexus, then wandered the streets of Caribou Crossing, popping into the various businesses and chatting with salesclerks and proprietors. The more he saw of this town, the more he could see why Brooke stayed here.

And yet Anika's killer was from Caribou Crossing.

Chapter Eighteen

Deciding to do a little surveillance, Jake drove to the town's one high school. After cruising the neighborhood, he chose a parking spot on a quiet side street, with a view of the front door.

As kids flowed out he saw the usual stuff: girls in groups giggling; boys in groups horsing around; girls and boys holding hands; kids on their own trying to look like they didn't care they had no friends. Some of the kids could've been in Vancouver and others exhibited the more typical Caribou Crossing Western style.

Three boys came out, and Jake's attention focused on them. They were a little on the grungy side but not particularly different from many of the other kids, yet there was that indefinable something about them that to Jake said pothead.

They piled into a beat-up old Camaro and when they hit the main street Jake was behind them, a couple of cars back. He kept them in sight as they turned this way and that, and finally onto the highway.

He hung back as they drove several miles north. When they exited at a road marked by a Greenbrier Nursery sign, his pulse quickened. Maybe they lived out this way but his gut told him they were up to something. Like a drug buy.

Letting them get a good lead, he turned onto Greenbrier Road. It was narrow, twisty, and went into the woods. Another big sign, with landscaping around it, marked the nursery. He checked the parking lot. Six vehicles; no Camaro.

He continued down the road, creeping now with his eyes peeled and window down, glad for the Lexus's near-silent engine. When metal glinted through the trees ahead, he pulled over and slid out of the car, easing the door shut so it didn't make a sound. Using the trees along the road for cover, he snuck forward.

The road dead-ended and two vehicles were parked in the turnaround: the Camaro and a black truck with a tinted-window canopy and big tires. Bingo! It was the same truck that had been parked at the grow op.

He crept closer. The three boys were talking to a man: roughly midtwenties, nondescript, about five feet ten, 160 pounds, slim but not very fit. He wore jeans, a gray plaid shirt, and a green baseball cap. The kind of man you could see a dozen times and still not remember. Unless you were a cop, and trained to observe every detail.

It was a drug deal, no question. The three boys passed over some bills and the nondescript man handed over a couple of bags. Jake squinted. Pot in the large bag, and something else in a small baggie, but he couldn't identify it before one of the boys pocketed it. Crack? E? Crystal meth? Heroin? There were so many possibilities.

He snuck back to his car, quietly backed down the road, then turned and drove to the nursery parking lot. He turned his car to face the road, engine idling. When the black truck came past, he'd follow it. He had the plate number on the Camaro; he could always find the boys again. It was the dealer he was really after.

"What are you doing?" The female voice spoke through his open window and he jumped, hitting his head on the roof of the car.

It was Corporal MacLean. She stood back from the car, her hand resting on the Smith & Wesson at her hip. "Engine off and out of the car, Mr. Pitt. Hands in sight at all times. And no fast moves."

He obeyed her to the letter, wondering where the hell she'd come from. He glanced around the parking lot, noting that there was a new car, one that might well be an unmarked police vehicle.

"What's the problem?" he asked. "I was thinking about getting Brooke a plant for her garden and someone recommended this place."

"Someone at the high school?"

"Uh . . . What do you mean?"

She rolled her eyes. "Can it. I've been behind you all the way."

Shit. He'd picked up a tail and not realized because he'd never even considered the possibility. Hell of a cop he was.

A middle-aged couple came out of the nursery, accompanied by an attendant pushing a wheelbarrow full of plants and gardening supplies. The three of them glanced in Jake and MacLean's direction, then busied themselves loading up the back of a red truck.

Jake studied the corporal's face. She was definitely on guard but she looked excited and curious. God knew what she thought he was. Pedophile? Drug dealer?

It wasn't like he had a lot of options, so he made a quick judgment call. "My name is Jake Brannon. Corporal Brannon. RCMP U/C, from headquarters in Vancouver. I'm here investigating a murder committed by a drug dealer."

Her mouth fell open. Then she closed it again. "Go over to my car. Walk slowly, keep your hands in sight."

"Wait, there's a truck parked down that road. The guy's dealing drugs. I need to follow it."

"It's you I'm interested in right now. You do a pretty good

job of tailing, Mr. Pitt-Brannon, but you don't watch your own butt very well."

He scowled. "Where did you pick me up?"

"At the school. Saw you drive up and park. After all your talk about drugs and the schools, I got suspicious. When you peeled out I followed you."

"Look, can we climb into one of our cars? I don't want those guys coming down the road and seeing us, with you in uniform."

She studied him through narrowed eyes. "Go to my car. I'll check you out."

He strode toward her car. "Don't use your radio, and don't call Miller."

The couple in the red truck drove past, heads craned curiously.

"Notice you can identify an unmarked," MacLean commented. "Now let's see if you remember the position."

He leaned against the car and spread his legs.

She searched him thoroughly and went through his wallet. "Arnold Pitt."

"It's my cover. My sergeant at headquarters put it together for me."

"We'll see. Get in the passenger seat."

As he climbed in, the Camaro came back down the road. "Those are the kids who bought drugs," he said. "A black truck'll be coming. He's the seller."

MacLean got into the driver's seat, keeping one hand close to her firearm.

The two of them watched the road in silence, and sure enough the truck drove past. She nodded slowly. "Okay, I know who that is."

"Who?"

She ignored him and opened her cell phone with her free hand. She'd listened to him, wasn't using the police radio.

"Who are you calling?"

"HQ in Vancouver."

Not Miller. Did that mean she had her own suspicions about her boss? "My sergeant's name is Estevez."

She spoke into the phone. "Give me Inspector Morrissey."

He shrugged. Fine, let her do it her way. Points to her that she knew Kathleen Morrissey. He had a lot of respect for the inspector.

"You folks got a member called Brannon?" she asked. "Jake Brannon? Says he's a corporal."

She listened, then said, "Uh-huh. Describe him."

Listening, her mouth quirked into a grin. "Guess he's had a haircut recently. Traded the leather for a suit and tie." She handed the phone to Jake. "Say hello and see if she identifies you."

"Hey, inspector. You can check with Estevez. He'll tell you what I'm doing here."

"I'll do that. Hang on."

"Before you go, I take it you know MacLean?"

"You're checking me out?" Corporal MacLean hissed.

He nodded, then listened as Morrissey gave a strong recommendation. He handed the cell back to MacLean. "She's checking with my sergeant. She'll get back to you."

They waited in silence for several minutes; then MacLean said into the phone, "Okay." She laughed and closed the phone. "She wants a photo of you in a suit and tie." Then her expression went serious. "What's this about?"

"Drugs and murder." He watched her face. "Maybe a corrupt cop."

Her eyes didn't flicker.

"You were at the school this afternoon too," he pointed out. "You've been thinking about what Robin said. You went to see if you could pick up on any signs of drug dealing, even though that's stuff Miller handles personally. And you didn't phone him to check me out. You suspect him of being involved."

"He's my sergeant," she said slowly.

"You don't want to say anything against him because you don't have evidence. So I'll tell you a story, and then we'll see where we stand. But not here. People shouldn't see us together."

She gnawed on her lower lip. "Yeah, okay. We'll meet somewhere."

"Brooke's house."

"You shouldn't have brought Brooke Kincaid into this."

"It's a long story. When does your shift end?"

"I'm on my own time now. I signed out the unmarked overnight."

"Good, but we don't want anyone seeing it at Brooke's. I'll follow you to your place, you park it and grab some civvies, then sneak into my car. I'll bring you back later tonight."

She reflected. "Fair enough."

He nodded. "I can trust you on this, right, corporal? It's not just me, it's Brooke's life we're talking about."

"Yeah, I get that." An edge in her voice, she said, "And you were the one who brought her into this. It's not right, corporal, using an innocent civilian."

"You try saying no to Brooke Kincaid."

She gave a quick snort of laughter, then choked it off. "Later, Brannon."

Brooke was pleased to see Jake's Lexus in the driveway when she arrived home from work. She opened the front door calling, "I'm home."

"In here," he called from the living room.

She hurried in that direction, eager for a kiss, then stopped dead in the doorway when she saw he wasn't alone. Karen MacLean, in jeans and a white T-shirt, her dark hair pulled back in a neat ponytail, was curled up on the living room couch. Jake, in khakis and a long-sleeved shirt with the neck open and sleeves rolled, was on his feet, coming to greet her.

He did it with a quick hug and kiss. A kiss on her lips. And his smile was Jake's cocky grin. Over his shoulder, Brooke saw Karen's eyes widen but the other woman said nothing.

"Uh, Arnold? What's going on?" Brooke asked.

"It's okay, MacLean knows who I really am. I've told her the whole story."

"Oh, my gosh," was all she could think to say.

Jake put his arm around her waist and urged her into her own living room.

"Hello, Karen," she said warily.

"Cup of tea?" Jake asked her. Then, to Karen, "Want a beer? Cold drink? Tea?"

Brooke said, "Yes, tea," and Karen chimed in, "That's good for me too."

Jake went into the kitchen and Brooke hurried after him. "What's going on?"

"I hung out at the school this afternoon and tailed some kids to a drug buy. MacLean tailed me. Didn't have much choice but to tell her who I really was. We checked each other out with headquarters."

He lowered his voice. "She's got a good rep, and her story makes sense. On Friday night I told her what Robin said about drugs in the schools. Near the end of her shift today, she decided to hang out near the high school and see if anything was going on. She saw me." He shrugged. "I talked to Jamal and he says to work with her. You think she can be trusted?"

"I don't know her well. Normally I steer clear of police—" She broke off, chuckling. "Oh my, and now I'm working with you, not to mention sharing my bed." She shook her head. "Okay. Karen MacLean. From what I've seen she's a decent person. She's always treated me with respect. Unlike Sergeant Miller." The kettle was whistling and she poured water into the teapot and swirled it around. "So what are you and Karen going to do?" She dumped the water back out.

"Haven't got to that part yet. Figured you might want to sit in. You're part of the team."

She caught his arm, pulled him to her, and gave him a kiss. A real kiss.

His arms circled her and he made a growly, purry sound low in his throat.

"When you came in," she said, "you kissed me in front of her. And it wasn't cousinly."

"She knows who I am; she might as well know about us. She's going to be here for a few hours and I can't stay away from you for that long." He pushed her back and held her at a distance. "Would you rather no one knew? I don't want to ruin your reputation."

"Karen's not going to tell anyone. Besides . . ." She moved close again, aligning her body with his. "You'd only do good things for my reputation. Brooke Kincaid can catch herself a hot young guy."

"Am I hot?"

"You know you are. Especially when you're being Jake." She ran a finger down the open neck of his shirt and released another button before she finished making the tea.

Jake took the teapot into the living room.

She followed with mugs and a plate of raisin oatmeal cookies. "Milk, sugar, honey?" she asked Karen, who seemed quite at home, stroking Sunny.

"Nope. Just clear, thanks."

Brooke poured the tea, then looked around, deciding where to sit. Jake beckoned from the big chair he'd chosen, and she was tempted to settle on his lap but figured that would be pushing things. Besides, it would be awfully difficult to concentrate on work. She chose the opposite end of the couch from Karen.

He gave her a humorous scowl, then turned to Karen. "Tell Brooke about Miller."

She swallowed a bite of cookie. "Delicious, Brooke. But, Jake, I have to say, I'm strongly opposed to endangering a civilian."

"Would everyone stop trying to protect me?" Brooke protested. "I involved myself. Jake needed a cover and I could provide the safest one."

"I understand, but I still disagree," Karen said severely. "Still, since you're involved, you're entitled to information. As long as it helps keep you safe."

Brooke nodded.

"Okay," Karen said. "About Miller. As anyone including him will tell you, he's got a rep for being death on drugs. Very few people get arrested for trafficking or using. We have a few crimes where the kids are stoned and they're stealing to get money for drugs, but it's rare. Sergeant Miller personally handles any case that might be drug related and, according to him, many of these cases really aren't."

"What do you mean?" Brooke asked.

"He says we—the corporals and constables—see drug problems where they don't exist. When kids are just drunk or acting out. He says we keep getting ourselves confused with big-city cops. He points out that anytime we bring in the dogs to sniff out drugs we either come up empty or catch some really small-time stuff."

"Robin said the serious users get a tip-off ahead of time," Jake said, reaching for his second cookie. "I imagine that would also apply to dealers."

"If they do," Karen said, "it has to come from inside our detachment or Williams Lake's."

Jake nodded.

Karen went on. "Then there are the sergeant's little talks at the schools designed to discourage drug use."

"Why would he do that if he's dealing drugs?" Brooke asked.

Karen's fingers scritched under Sunny's neck and the cat purred, but Karen was frowning. "I know the high school principal. His wife is a friend of mine. Last year he had an off-the-record chat with me, asking if there was some way I could do the talk instead of Miller. He said Miller isn't effective. Apparently there's nothing in his words that's really objectionable; there's just a tone. He keeps saying Caribou Crossing isn't the big city, and our kids aren't like those worldly, sophisticated big-city kids. We've got more old-fashioned, traditional values."

Brooke groaned. "The last thing any teenager wants to be is old-fashioned."

"Yup," Jake said, "he's telling them that if they want to be cool they'll use drugs."

"That's what the principal is worried about. He said he's tried to talk to Miller about it but Miller says he's interpreting it all wrong, and underestimating the kids of Caribou Crossing. He says they've got good role models and know right from wrong."

"This is the Sergeant Miller who hangs out in the bar on Friday and Saturday nights," Brooke said. "Such a great role model."

Karen said, "For the most part, what the sarge said is right. Most of the kids are good, they do have good parental role models, they're active in the church, sports, or one of the teen social clubs. They do 4H and ride in Little Britches rodeo. They work on their families' ranches and farms. They're mature and responsible. Kids like Robin."

"But that's not all the kids," Jake said.

Karen shook her head. "There's another group, the borderline ones. Some come from dysfunctional families but some are just restless, exploring boundaries, maybe unhappy. Given the right guidance, most of them will straighten out and do just fine. But they're vulnerable."

"It's touch and go how kids like that'll turn out," Jake said. "I was one of them."

"Oh yeah?" Karen didn't look surprised.

"It's possible Miller is the brains behind the grow op," Jake said. "He's selling to someone—maybe Death Row—and probably buying small quantities of other drugs like heroin, crystal meth, crack, and Ecstasy from them. He's got his aging hippies out in the hills growing the stuff, and his local guys dealing to the kids. Like the man MacLean and I saw this afternoon. The guy was driving the same truck I saw out at the grow op. MacLean, you recognized him?"

"Pete Snyder. He's a loser, a small-time criminal, but somehow we never find evidence to convict him. Maybe that's Miller's doing. Pete Snyder does odd jobs here and there, mostly for his brother, who's got a construction/handyman business. Lives with his brother too. Oh, and the kids who were buying were grade twelve students: Rob Oppenheim, Adam Mark, and Jim Schultz. They're borderline kids. Could turn out like Snyder if no one intervenes."

"Snyder," Jake said thoughtfully. "Any relation to Richard Snyder?"

"Richie's his older brother, the guy he lives with," Karen said. "Why?"

"Richie got his pilot's license?"

"Yes. He was in the air force for a while but got kicked out. Why?"

"He was flying a small plane last Tuesday morning," Brooke said. "Right, Jake?"

"Yeah. He was in the air when Brooke saw a little plane circling around like it was looking for something. Looking for me, probably. If this guy's a handyman, he could be the one who rigged the water for the grow op, figured out how to steal the power. It looks like both Snyder brothers are connected to the grow op, but we still don't have a clear tie-in to Miller."

Brooke curled her hands around her tea mug. "What do you think, Karen? You know Miller pretty well. Is he capable of dealing drugs? Of . . . murder?"

Karen put her mug down abruptly, jarring Sunny. The cat shot her a look of displeasure. He removed himself from her lap and transferred to Brooke's.

Karen said, "I don't like him, okay? He's a male chauvinist pig, a racist, and a homophobe. But he's also a member, and I don't want to think he's gone bad. So, having stated my biases pro and con, I'll try to be objective."

"Please," Jake said.

"Yeah, I guess I could see him trafficking. He thinks people who use drugs are scum. He's got no pity, no sympathy. He wouldn't mind making a buck off them. He doesn't respect women. I could see him visiting prostitutes." She gave a quick laugh. "Hell, I could see that more than I could imagine him giving his wife a good time in bed. But murder . . . I hate to think it, yet he's got a cruel streak. I've seen him hit people when he arrests them. He looks for excuses to rough them up, and I swear he takes pleasure in it."

Brooke nodded. "He takes advantage of people who are weaker than him. Back in my drinking days he was both suggestive and rough. When he arrested me for DUI, he implied he'd drop the charges if I, uh, gave him a blow job. When I refused he slapped me around a little."

"Damn!" Jake spat the word out.

She shook her head. "It was a long time ago. Let it go."

"I want him," Jake said, his voice icy. "But we need a lot more than we've got."

"I could arrest Pete Snyder for dealing drugs to those kids," Karen said, "but I'm afraid that will tip our man off— whether it's Miller or someone else. We don't want to catch the small fry and let the shark get away."

"Damn right," Jake said. "Well, we could dig and dig and see if we can unearth tiny scraps of evidence that might build a case against Miller. Of course, if we're seriously suspicious of him we really should report it to Internal. Right?" He glanced at Karen.

She nodded. "But that's horrible, to report another member when we're not sure."

"He's got another alternative," Brooke said. "Right, Jake?"

"You know me too well. Yeah, I'm thinking we can use Snyder to trap his boss."

"What?" Brooke said, just as Karen said, "How?"

"Let's work on that. I'll have to run it by Jamal too. But first, before I demolish all these cookies, how about dinner?"

"Let's order a pizza," Karen said.

"I have chili in the freezer," Brooke said. "It won't take long to heat it in the microwave."

A couple of hours later, Jake drove Karen home. Alone in the house, Brooke loaded the dishwasher, then ran a bath. She tossed in a homemade lavender and rose bath bomb, then climbed in with a sigh. It had been an interesting and challenging evening.

Jake and Karen had a lot in common. She'd witnessed the way their minds worked, how they communicated with a minimum of words. Several times one of them had paused to catch her up. They'd done it nicely, so she didn't feel insulted. They'd even listened to her opinion. But she knew perfectly well she was, at best, a temporary and probationary member of the team.

Fine by her.

Over the weekend she'd gotten used to a Jake who read, gardened, and line danced. She'd almost lost track of the bearded cop who'd pulled a gun on her rather than risk his mission. But that was the real Jake, and tonight she'd seen

him again. He was coolly efficient, and the language he spoke
came out of mystery novels. And yet, from time to time, he'd
given her a special smile or reached across to touch her arm.
He'd never let more than ten or fifteen minutes go by without
reinforcing the bond between them—even as he and Karen
plotted to trap the criminal the Snyder brothers worked for.

Brooke stirred restlessly, the silky warm water rippling
around her. The summer-garden scent of lavender and roses
wasn't having its usual soothing effect.

Her life was getting far too complicated. Yet she couldn't
regret having taken Jake in. Tomorrow morning, she would have
known him for a week. Just a week. And, if the trap worked,
he'd be gone in a couple of days. Out of her life. Forever. It
had to be that way. There was no other option for either of
them. The thought shouldn't make her feel depressed.

Besides, Jakes leaving wasn't what most worried her. He
was going up against a killer. He was capable, so was Karen,
but the criminals they were chasing didn't mess around.
They'd killed a teenager and put a bullet in Jake.

Downstairs, the front door opened and closed. Jake called,
"Brooke?"

"In the bath."

In a few seconds he was standing in the doorway. "Now
there's a fine picture."

"You could join me." She tried for a flirtatious smile but it
didn't feel genuine.

He sniffed the air. "And stink of that girly stuff? I don't
think so. But I'll wash your back. And other fun places."

She pulled the plug and rose. "I'm done." She reached for
a towel but he beat her to it.

He held out a fluffy peach-colored one and enfolded her in
it. "What's wrong, Brooke?"

"Tonight I saw you at work. I got an idea of what your job
is really like. I'm worried. What if something goes wrong
with your plan? These men have already shot you once."

He grimaced. "Won't happen again. MacLean and I are each other's backup." Then he turned on his sexy, cocky Jake grin. "Trust me, babe."

Easy to say, but so many aspects of the plan were out of his and Karen's control. Still, as she'd said about Robin, she couldn't wrap up everyone she cared about in a security blanket and protect them from the world.

She took a deep breath, forced herself to appreciate the steamy, flower-scented air, then let it out. If she only had a couple more nights with this incredible man, she should make the most of them. Deliberately she dropped the towel. "Coming to bed?"

And yet, when they made love, she found herself gripping him tighter than before. She was fine with knowing he'd go back to Vancouver—really, she was—but right now he was on her turf. She couldn't bear the thought that tomorrow he might get injured. Or worse.

Chapter Nineteen

Jake recognized the adrenaline high and welcomed it, but tried to act normally with Brooke as they ate breakfast in her kitchen. She was subdued and he knew that she, too, was keeping her feelings in careful check. His excitement, her concern—they weren't a comfortable match.

MacLean arrived in her RCMP cruiser, wearing her uniform and Kevlar vest. Her stride was steady as she walked up the steps and into the house, but she radiated an energy that told him she, too, was buzzed. She handed him a uniform and a vest. "These should fit."

Brooke's eyes widened at the sight of their vests.

Jake said quickly, "They're part of the uniform. Doesn't mean we're expecting trouble."

"You weren't expecting trouble the night you got shot," she retorted.

"Well, if anyone shoots at me today, the vest'll prevent me from getting hurt."

"If they're stupid enough to shoot you in the chest," she muttered. "And those things don't stop knives, right?"

"You read too much."

"But I'm right."

"Okay, yeah, you're right." He grabbed the uniform and hurried upstairs before she could ask any more questions.

A few minutes later he stared at himself in the mirror. Since he'd started working U/C he hardly ever wore a uniform, so it was a shock to see himself, short hair and all, looking the way he had years go.

When he returned to the kitchen Brooke studied him, her expression strained. "I'm going to work. Good luck, you two." Her lips trembled and he wondered what else she wanted to say. A bunch of warnings, he guessed.

"We'll be careful," he told her.

She pressed her lips together. "Good." Her eyes stared into his for a long moment; then she turned and hurried away. No good-bye hug or kiss.

Despite—or perhaps because of—the way he felt about Brooke, he was glad to have her gone. He gestured MacLean to a chair. "Let's go over it one more time."

An hour later, MacLean at the wheel, they pulled into the Snyder yard. The house was dilapidated, the yard unkempt and decorated with rusting appliances, but Jake had seen worse. The black truck sat on a patch of scrubby grass near the house. Two scrawny mixed-breed dogs ran over, barking and snarling as MacLean parked the cruiser.

"Looks like Richie's out," she said. There was no sign of the van she'd told him Richie Snyder drove: dingy white, lettered to advertise his business. That was a relief. It was Pete they had the evidence against, plus MacLean figured him for the weaker, and dumber, of the two brothers.

"Don't count on it," he warned her. They couldn't afford to make assumptions. The van might be parked around back, or in the shop for repairs.

Cautiously they exited the cruiser, hands on their firearms.

The dogs backed away, still snarling. Jake glanced at MacLean. "Here we go."

She gave a quick nod and he saw the blaze of excitement and trepidation in her eyes. This was hardly a normal day for a small-town cop.

A man appeared on the sagging front porch, dressed in ragged jeans and a dingy undershirt. Jake recognized Pete Snyder. Didn't look like he was carrying, but the jeans were baggy enough there might be a weapon in the pocket, or tucked in the waist at the back.

"What the fuck's going on?" the man demanded as the two uniformed officers mounted the steps.

"Hey, Pete," MacLean said. "Where's your brother?"

"Richie's repairing a roof over at the Youngs' house. Fuck, man, what you want him for? He ain't done nothin'."

While they spoke, Jake sized the guy up. Snyder was MacLean's height, three or four inches shorter than Jake, slim but out of shape, with eyes that said he was stoned. He didn't look like much of a threat, but there was always the possibility he had a weapon. He struck Jake as telling the truth, not because he was a naturally honest guy but because he had no reason to lie. That didn't mean the house was empty, though.

"Mind if we come inside?" MacLean asked.

"Fuck, yeah, I mind." The man propped fisted hands on his hips and glared at them. "You got a fucking warrant? What's your beef with Richie?"

Jake would've liked a chance to search the house, verify that Pete was alone. He stood a few paces back from the other two, keeping an eye on them, the house, and the dogs, alert for any movement that might indicate someone else's presence.

Snyder squinted at him. "Who the fuck're you?" The guy sounded confused, like he really couldn't believe there were two cops on his doorstep.

"Corporal Brannon." In a level tone, he added, "Drug squad." The man blanched. "Where's Miller?"

MacLean's shoulders hunched as her muscles tensed.

Jake's heart beat a little faster. It was circumstantial—it wasn't even evidence—but it was the first thing they'd heard that linked Sergeant Miller to drug crimes.

"We'll get around to that," he told the man. "Let's talk about you first." He nodded to MacLean.

She began the spiel. "Peter Snyder, you are under arrest. . . ."

That was their plan. Arrest Snyder for trafficking, then offer him a deal if he set up his boss.

Jake let MacLean handle the arrest. Snyder didn't ask for a lawyer. Instead he said, "You got it wrong. Talk to Miller, he'll tell you."

Jake exchanged a signal with MacLean and she stepped back to cover him as he moved into Snyder's space. "Miller can't help you this time," Jake said. "We saw you selling drugs to three high school boys yesterday, out on Greenbrier Road. And we know about the grow op, and Jango and Herb. How many kilos of Bud come out of those trailers in a year?"

Pete's jaw was hanging. "Shit, it was you that night."

The guy really was an idiot. "At the grow op? Yeah, it was me. And I've got a bone to pick with the guy who shot me. Guy who drives a black truck, looks just like the one parked over there." He crowded Pete, getting up close and personal in his face. "Figure you're that guy."

"No!" The smaller man backed away. "Richie, it was Richie. We were both out there but he was the guy who shot you."

Jake could barely stifle a grin. Looked like this loser was going to make their case for them. "Guess you and your brother'll be going to prison together then. Nice to have company. It's not a friendly place."

"Jesus, I don't wanna go to prison."

MacLean spoke up, playing her prearranged good-guy role. "Pete, you've screwed up this time. It's gonna be hard avoiding doing time. But I know you're not a bad guy. Richie either. I mean, it's just a few drugs, right? Everybody does drugs."

"Trafficking's illegal," Jake snapped. "They should get the max."

"Oh come on, Brannon," she said. "Don't be such a tough big-city cop. Don't you think it's unfair how it's always the little guys like Pete and Richie who end up in jail? While their boss is sitting in the bar, merrily belting back Caribou Crossing whisky?"

Jake took a deep breath and played his next card, praying he was on the right track. "I'll lock up Miller if you get me the evidence."

"Miller!" Snyder's eyes widened. "You mean you know about—" He broke off abruptly.

Triumph sent adrenaline flooding through Jake's veins but he didn't let on. Just said, "Yeah, we're on to him but we don't have the evidence. So we'll have to lock up the small fry like you and your brother. We'll be asking for the max, to discourage anyone else from working with Miller."

"Hell, Miller's the one who got us into this! He should do the time."

Jake saw MacLean glance his way and knew she wanted to flash a victorious grin. But she hardened her expression and focused on Snyder. "Then let's make sure he does. Help us take him down, Pete. Things'll go easier for you if you do."

"A deal? You'll cut me a deal? I can get off without going to jail?"

"Depends on what you give us," she said. "The more you help, the better the deal."

Two hours later, Jake and MacLean were out at the grow op. The RCMP cruiser and Jake's car were parked back in the trees with the hippies Herb and Jango cuffed in the backseat of the cruiser. A few migrant workers were cuffed together in the locked bunkhouse.

After scouting the site, Jake had decided he and MacLean would hide in one of the trailers and have Pete Snyder, out on the steps, lure Miller into a conversation.

Jake wrinkled his nose against the pungent scent of cannabis plants in flower and drummed his fingers nervously on a workbench. Under his breath, he said to MacLean, "Snyder's stupidity worked for us in the beginning, but I don't know if he's got the wits to carry this off."

She glanced toward the open door, where Snyder sat on the step, one leg jiggling at high speed. "Know what you mean. And if he fails, then Miller's been alerted. He might even try to kill Pete."

"That's not so bad. Then we've got Miller for attempted murder. Of course we'd intervene and stop him."

She held up a hand. "I hear a car!"

Snyder heard it too. He stood up. "It's him."

"Okay," Jake said from behind him. "You know what to do. Get him into the trailer and get him talking."

"Let's hope he doesn't search the trailer," MacLean whispered to Jake.

"He's confident. He's never had any reason to be otherwise. He won't suspect it's a setup." Jake hoped he was right. He gave MacLean's shoulder a reassuring pat; then they each faded into the hiding spots they'd picked, her squeezing into a cupboard and Jake cramming himself under a workbench in a dark corner. He pulled his Beretta.

"Pete? What the hell did you bring me out here for?" Miller said, his voice coming through loud and clear as he shouted at Snyder.

"Come into the trailer. I don' want Jango and Herb to hear."

"Where are they?"

"Workin' in the other trailer." So far Snyder was sticking to the script.

The trailer shook as the hefty Miller negotiated the steps. "I'm losing patience, Snyder."

Footsteps sounded inside the trailer, and the door closed.

"Okay, here's the thing. I want out. It's gettin' too fucking dangerous." Snyder's voice sounded high and shaky, but Miller would see that as natural under the circumstances. "You know someone broke into the grow op. They're on to us."

Jake's position was such that he couldn't see either man, and, hopefully, they couldn't see him. Footsteps paced, and from their heaviness Jake identified them as Miller's.

"You and your brother must have been imagining things," Miller said. "You say you shot some intruder, but no one's seen hide nor hair of the guy."

"Someone opened that squeaky door on the other trailer."

"It was the wind."

"No fucking way. It was some guy, some dude who escaped on a bike. He might've been a fucking cop."

"I'm the cops around here."

"W-word is, you've been doin' too much talking."

"What the hell?" Miller sounded astonished. "Talking to who? About what?"

Jake tightened his grip on the Beretta. Could Snyder pull this off? He'd already given them enough to connect Miller to the grow op, but Jake really wanted the man for Anika's murder.

"Got a call from a Death Row d-dude in Vancouver. Asked what the hell was goin' on with our operation. Said you were a . . . uh, what was that fucking word?"

Jake held his breath, then let it out again when Snyder continued. "Weak link, that's what he said. You'd been talkin' to some fucking whore, givin' stuff away about our operation." Snyder was talking faster now, too fast, hurrying to get through his lines.

Miller laughed. "Hell, is that all? I took care of that little problem."

"Huh? How'd you do that?"

There was a pause and then Miller said, "Like this."

"Christ, Henry, that's a knife!"

Snyder sounded scared out of his wits and every muscle in Jake's body tensed. He made a "stay back" gesture in Mac-Lean's direction, hoping she could see his hand and would hold on for just another few seconds.

"Damn right it's a knife. It's got that girl's blood on it and it'll have yours too if you don't pull yourself together. Weak link? Hell, you're the weak link."

Go! With his hand Jake telegraphed the message.

Before he'd finished, the cupboard door slammed open and Karen sprang out, Smith & Wesson drawn. "Henry Miller!" she called.

Jake eased out from under the bench, prepared to provide cover and backup, to deal with anything unexpected.

Now, for the first time, he could see what was going on. Snyder was backing his way toward the closed door, one hand behind him as he fumbled for the knob. Even if he escaped, Jake knew the idiot wouldn't get far on foot. He focused his attention on Miller. The fat man had frozen, knife raised, gaping at Corporal MacLean.

"Drop the weapon!" she ordered.

"MacLean? What the hell are you thinking?" the man blustered.

"You're under arrest for the murder of Anika Janssen."

Miller's mouth fell open. He dropped the knife and fumbled for the firearm at his belt, clearly not believing his corporal would shoot him.

"Hands in the air!" Jake bellowed at exactly the same time MacLean shouted the words.

Miller swung toward Jake, his hand still at his belt, his

eyes wide with shock. He made no move to draw his weapon, but nor did he put his hands in the air.

While MacLean trained her firearm on the sergeant, Jake approached the man and relieved him of his gun, baton, and pepper spray. He pocketed the knife and searched Miller, wishing like hell he could rough the guy up a little. Prison was too good for this asshole.

After retrieving a .22 from Miller's pants pocket, he faced the man.

Miller still looked utterly stunned. "Pitt?" he croaked.

"Corporal Jake Brannon, out of Vancouver." With a feeling of deep satisfaction, he went on, "Corporal MacLean's going to finish reading the charges and give you the proper warning. We want to do everything by the book, don't we?"

He turned to MacLean and saw her triumphant smile as she stepped forward.

Brooke had been useless all day. She'd even put burgundy highlights rather than sienna in Kim Tam's black hair. Kim had been great about it, saying she loved the new look, but Brooke was annoyed at herself.

She was furious with Jake too. How dare he invade her Caribou Crossing life, make her care for him, then go out there and risk his scarred hide.

She kept imagining what might be going on. A shoot-out? Sergeant Miller was a murderer, and a highly trained cop. He wouldn't surrender easily.

In a break between clients, she called Dr. Allenby and made an appointment for later in the day so she could ask about getting her meds adjusted.

Each time a phone rang, each time the door opened, her heart leaped in fear.

When, finally, her cell rang, she croaked, "Hello?"

"It's me. It went fine."

The voice was Jake's and it was not only healthy, it was victorious.

"F-fine?" Her lips could barely form the word and she realized tears were pouring down her face.

"Pete Snyder came through. MacLean and I both heard Miller admit not only to the grow op but also to Anika's murder. He, both the Snyders, and the workers at the grow op are in custody."

"And you're okay?"

"Okay? Oh sure, MacLean and I are both fine. It ended up being really tame."

Tame. He sounded almost disappointed. And she'd been in agony all day. Fury boiled in her chest.

"Brooke? I could be quite late tonight."

"I'll see you when I see you," she said, trying to hold her voice steady. Then she slammed down the phone and hurried toward the ladies' room, ignoring Kate's worried call. If she'd been a guy—a guy like Jake—she'd have slammed her fist through the wall. How could he do this to her?

She turned to the mirror and saw her drawn, tear-stained face. Automatically she ran cold water.

Jake hadn't done it to her. He'd done his job, that was all. She'd done this to herself, by letting herself care about him.

Care? Damn him. She *loved* the rotten jerk.

Thank God he was leaving. She couldn't go through another day like this. She knew she wasn't ready for love and she knew she and Jake were all wrong for each other, so how could she have been such a fool?

"Brooke?" Kate tapped on the closed door. "Are you all right? What happened?"

"I'm okay. Out in a minute."

She would never cry for Jake Brannon again. Well, she might cry when he left, because she'd miss him, but she would never again imagine him on the job and cry out of worry for him.

Brooke splashed cold water on her face, then blotted her skin on a soft, disposable towel. She smoothed on a soothing, cooling aloe vera lotion, then opened the door and went over to Kate, who was nearby, fussing with the coffee machine.

"I'm all right," she told her. "As for what happened . . . I can't tell you yet because it's, uh, a police matter, actually. I'm sure it will be made public soon." She thought about the town learning the truth about nasty Sergeant Miller, and found a smile. "I can promise you, the next couple of days are going to be very interesting."

Then she headed for the phone and cancelled her appointment with Dr. Allenby. It wasn't her bipolar causing her highs and lows; it was Jake. Once he left town and she got her life back on an even keel, she'd be just fine.

Brooke had no appetite for dinner but forced herself to eat a cheese sandwich, some celery sticks, and an apple. Then she went to her regular Tuesday A.A. meeting. Last week when she'd gone, a bandaged Jake had lain on her couch. She couldn't believe how much had happened in a week—and she really couldn't say anything to the folks at A.A. until the arrests became public knowledge. Still, the routine and the familiar faces calmed her. A little.

Home again, she tried to read but had trouble concentrating. She wanted to see Jake more than anything on earth, but she also wished he had already left town and she could get on with life without him.

When she heard a car drive up around eleven, she closed her book but remained in her chair.

Jake opened the front door and walked in.

"Congratulations," she said. Then the reserve she'd been cultivating shattered and she sprang out of the chair and rushed to embrace him. "I'm so glad you're okay. And Karen too. It's so great you got Miller's confession."

He hugged her tight. Very tight, almost as if he'd never let go. But she knew it was a celebratory hug more than anything else. In her small way, she'd been part of his team.

She pulled back. "Are you hungry? Do you want a beer?"

"We got pizza at the station. But a beer would be good. I'll get it."

When he returned, she led him to the couch. "Tell me all about it." She'd thought long and hard about whether she wanted to know the details but had decided she had to. The truth could never be as bad as the things she'd imagined.

Jake told the story methodically, almost like an officer filing a report, and her anxiety level eased.

When he finished, she said, "You must be so pleased. I bet you can't wait to tell the Janssens." She touched his arm, not knowing what to wish for. "When are you going back to Vancouver?"

"Day after tomorrow." He took a long swallow of beer. "There's going to be a huge investigation. Of the grow op, the Caribou Crossing RCMP detachment, Death Row. Can't have the local cops run it, except for MacLean, who's undoubtedly clean. A team's already on its way. Including Jamal. He and MacLean and I will meet with the inspector who's coordinating the investigation; then Jamal and I are done with it and back to our regular jobs."

So they had the rest of tonight, plus one more night. Would he be working late tomorrow as well?

Did she want to spend more time alone with him? The more intimate they were, the more she'd care and the more it would hurt when he left. An idea came to her. "We should have a celebration. Especially if Jamal's in town."

Jake grinned. "That's a great idea. You and me, Jamal, Karen."

"Will you be finished work by dinnertime tomorrow?"

"We'll make sure of it. What's the best restaurant in town?"

"The Wild Rose. But let's eat here. It's more friendly. I'd love to cook for all of you. It'll be a small good-bye present."

His face sobered as if he'd only just realized that their time together was almost over. "Oh hell, Brooke," he said, as he reached for her.

She slid into his arms. *Keep it light*, she told herself. That had been the deal from the beginning, and it was the only way she could handle this relationship. She nipped his ear. "Ready for bed?"

Chapter Twenty

News of Sergeant Miller's arrest had been released, so Jake said Brooke was free to tell Kate all about it. That took up their entire Friday lunch hour, at the Big & Small. The only part Brooke left out was her personal relationship with Jake. She didn't want to seem like a middle-aged fool.

And she wasn't. She cared about him and she knew that, in his fashion, he cared about her.

Tomorrow he'd be gone. Out of her life, forever.

Intellectually, Brooke knew it was better this way. She and Jake had no long-term place in each other's lives. She could count the reasons on the fingers of both hands, and still need more fingers. But the short term had been so special, it was hard to imagine her life without him.

"Just the same as before," she muttered to Sunny as she assembled the ingredients to make lasagna. Except, before she'd been happy with her life. It had seemed perfect. Now she knew there would be something missing. No, someone. It wasn't just a man's touch, great sex that she'd miss. It was Jake. Scratching her cat, reading on the couch, helping her make salad. Talking across the kitchen table. Slowly, bit by bit, revealing himself to her.

Jake, the man who had brought Anika's killer to justice, the man who wanted to get a teenager called Sapphire off the street. The man she'd fallen in love with.

For the second time in her life she'd foolishly given her heart, but at least this man deserved it. So, where did that leave her come morning? Bereft?

Brooke squared her shoulders. Hardly. Lonely, missing him, but not bereft. She knew she could live a full, happy life without a man.

She dropped lasagna noodles in a large pot of boiling water, put a container of homemade tomato sauce in the microwave to thaw, and began to sauté ground beef.

Thanks to Jake, she had wonderful memories to call to mind. Best of all, she'd know that the two of them had shared something special. That he respected her and truly cared for her. They might never see each other again but in a certain way he'd be her friend for life.

For her, it was the best outcome. She'd learned that she had healed enough to be a woman who could love, a woman who could win the affection of a wonderful man. That was a huge step. Maybe, some years down the road, she'd meet another great guy—a different kind of guy, one far more compatible with her. Perhaps then she'd be ready to take another step forward and feel confident that, despite her illnesses and her track record, she was ready and able to handle the pressures and responsibilities of marriage.

She poured the tomato sauce in with the beef, and stirred.

As for Jake, she hoped he'd learned something too. He didn't believe his parents loved him. He wouldn't let himself admit that Jamal was his dear friend, not just his colleague. He had apparently never—until now—let a woman get close to him.

This man who thought nothing of risking his hide was terrified of putting his heart in jeopardy, because his parents had taught him he didn't deserve love.

But then . . . Wasn't she the same?

As the thought flashed into Brooke's mind she caught it, to examine as she went automatically through the steps of making béchamel sauce.

She knew she didn't deserve Evan's love; that was a fact. And yet over the past year he'd given it. Even with Jessica and Robin, she couldn't quite believe—accept—the affection they showered on her. Then there was Kate. Her boss.

Her friend, too, she realized now. That's what Kate wanted, and she'd been patiently trying to draw Brooke in that direction, but Brooke had held back. Undeserving, untrusting of herself.

Was it time to take another step forward? To open her heart to the friends who were just waiting for her to hold out her arms?

Yes. Jake had helped her realize she did deserve other people's love. Just as he did.

Should she tell him she loved him? The idea was scary, but why should it be? It wasn't like she wanted anything from him in return.

She smiled to herself. Honesty was her policy, so, yes, she'd tell him. Maybe the knowledge that he was lovable would help him to one day find a woman to love. Someone his own age, maybe someone like Karen who understood his work. A woman who could live with him putting himself in danger, who could share his excitement over the challenges of his life. A woman far different from herself.

All the components now prepared, she assembled the layers of lasagna and put the large pan in the preheated oven, then went upstairs to change. She chose a short denim skirt because she knew he liked her legs, and a blue-green blouse he'd once said matched her eyes.

Her reflection in the mirror showed the same old Brooke, and yet not. Same hair, same face, same body—but a new sparkle in her eyes. Jake's gift to her. She now knew herself to be a desirable, sexy woman.

Another step in her healing. There'd been lithium and A.A. Plants to care for, then Sunny. Evan's return, and his marriage. Jess's pregnancy, and then, just when Brooke had thought her life couldn't get any better, Jake.

Steps to becoming whole. A grandmother, and a sexy babe. She was grinning at her reflection when she heard a car drive up. A quick glance out the window told her it was Karen MacLean, and she hurried downstairs.

Karen came up the steps wearing jeans, a pretty gold-colored tee, and a huge smile. Her dark brown hair was loose on her shoulders.

To Brooke's surprise, Karen caught her in a big hug. "We did it!"

"You and Jake did."

"Nope. Couldn't have done it without you. We should make you an honorary member of the force."

Brooke shuddered. "No thanks. I'm too risk-averse. A little bit of excitement every now and then is all I can handle."

Karen winked. "You can handle Brannon, and I'm guessing that's more than a little excitement."

"Karen, you haven't told anyone? I don't mind you knowing, but . . ." She shrugged, embarrassed. Others would think her a fool, not a sexy babe.

"Your private life is your private life. I'm not telling. But you mean you're not going to keep seeing each other? You're perfect for each other."

Brooke chuckled. "Far from it. But it was fun while it lasted. No, we have no plans to see each other again." The truth was, they'd never really discussed it. But in her mind their time together was perfect just as it was. She couldn't imagine trying to prolong it, or to force it into a different shape. She was positive Jake felt the same.

Karen shot her a skeptical glance but all she said was, "Something smells great." She held up a bag. "I brought champagne."

"What fun. I'll put it in the fridge." Too bad she wouldn't be able to drink it. Nor, she realized, would Jamal. She wondered what excuse he, a closeted alcoholic, would find.

The two women went into the kitchen. Karen took two bottles out of the bag and handed them to Brooke. The champagne was nonalcoholic. Brooke raised her eyebrows and Karen said, "You've got to drink the toasts too."

Touched, Brooke smiled at her. "Thanks."

She heard a car and headed for the door again, arriving just as it opened. Jake stepped through and caught her in his arms, "Hey, babe."

She hugged him back. "Hey, yourself." Then she turned to Jamal, who had followed him in. "Nice to see you again, Jamal."

He was grinning like his face would split. "You too, Brooke. Or babe, as some may call you."

Was Jake actually blushing? Was such a thing possible?

Jamal glanced over her shoulder and grinned again. "Hey, Karen."

"Jamal."

There was something in Jamal's eyes, and something in Karen's voice. Brooke glanced between them, then toward Jake, who winked. He wrapped his arm around Brooke's waist and she leaned into him. She'd take every last opportunity to touch him.

"Karen brought champagne," she said, then added, "nonalcoholic, so I can drink it." She avoided looking at Jamal.

"Sounds good," Jamal said easily. "Karen, why don't you pop that cork, and let's start celebrating?"

As Brooke had learned, it didn't take alcohol to have a good time. Soon the four of them were clustered around the kitchen table, eating with gusto and laughing and talking as they rehashed the case and celebrated their victory.

"I always liked my job," Karen said, "but the detachment will be so much nicer without that ass Miller."

"Who'll be taking over for him?" Jamal asked.

She shook her head. "Don't know yet." Her eyes gleamed. "But I'm going to be the acting commander."

"Congratulations!" everyone yelled.

She shrugged. "It's not that big a compliment. I'm the only one they're relatively sure is a straight arrow, who knows the community."

"It's still a compliment," Jamal assured her, serving himself a second helping of lasagna. "It'll look great on your record. Though I s'pose in the long run they'll want a sergeant."

"Yup. Replace a sergeant with a sergeant."

"How long've you been a corporal? Enough to write your sergeant's exam?"

"Not yet. But I'm studying. I want that promotion."

"Unlike some folk," Jamal said, shooting a pointed glance at Jake.

"Hmm?" Brooke said.

"I wrote the damned exam," Jake growled. "Got tired of you hounding me."

"And you passed with top marks, God knows how. But now you won't apply for a sergeant's job."

"I like what I'm doing. Not everyone wants to be a desk jockey." He scowled at Jamal. "Old man."

"You've lost me," Brooke said.

"Generally, as you rise through the ranks, you do less active duty," Karen explained. "You coordinate others rather than doing the street work yourself."

"And you're in less danger?" Brooke asked.

The other woman nodded. "That's usually true."

"Then I can see why Jake wouldn't want a promotion," Brooke said. She glanced at Jamal. "Though I'd hardly call you an old man myself."

"Nor I," Karen chimed in.

Brooke noticed how her and Jamal's gazes caught and held. It didn't surprise her one bit when Karen and Jamal both decided to make it an early evening, and the corporal offered to drive him back to his motel.

After they'd gone, Brooke said, "That's an interesting development. Karen found a guy who isn't intimidated by her."

"Not much intimidates Jamal."

"So I figured." She clicked off the outside light and went back to the kitchen. "I'll just load the dishwasher."

"I'll help."

Working smoothly together, they tidied the kitchen. Brooke said, "Is Jamal like you? No plans for settling down?"

"Dunno. We've never talked about it."

She tried to imagine what it would be like working year after year with someone, going undercover for weeks on end, trusting that person with your life, yet never talking about whether you believed in things like marriage, children, love. "I hope Karen knows what she's doing."

"I'd bet on it. And Jamal'll be straight with her."

"I'm sure he will. Just like we've been with each other."

"Right." He sounded slightly uncertain as he caught her hand and pulled her toward him. "You're still okay with that, right, Brooke? About this being temporary?"

"Well, sure. I mean, we don't exactly fit into each other's lives, do we?"

He gave a lopsided smile. "Not exactly. But it's been a fun week."

"Yes, it has." She broke away from him and set the dishwasher to run. When she ran a practiced eye over the kitchen, it met her high standards.

She leaned against the counter and gazed up at him. Bright lights, cheery yellow walls, the dishwasher rumbling, and the scent of lasagna in the air. Not one bit romantic. This was perfect. She didn't want to terrify the poor guy, but she did want to tell him tonight. Before they made love. Before they said good-bye.

"Jake, there's something I want to tell you. Just so you'll know." She swallowed, then rushed it out. "I love you."

He looked like she'd socked him in the belly. "Wh-what?"

"I love you. You're a wonderful man. A fantastic lover, but also a fine man. And I love you. I'll always remember you with love and be grateful for our time together. I'm a better, stronger person for having known you."

"You . . . love me?" He looked like he wanted to turn and dash out the kitchen door.

She had to laugh. "Aha, I managed to scare the tough undercover cop. No, seriously, Jake, don't get upset. It's just that I don't think many people in your life have told you they love you, unconditionally love you, and I do. So I thought you should know."

Frown lines creased his forehead, and she guessed he was thinking of his parents.

She took his hands and held them lightly. "Do you believe me?"

He stared down at their hands and then he squeezed hers. "Yes." Then he squeezed harder. "Thank you." He pulled her to him and held her body as tightly as he'd gripped her hands.

She hugged him back. "Ready for bed?"

He hadn't said the words back to her and she hadn't expected him to.

What she did know, as they made love through that last long night, was that with each movement he was telling her, in the only way he could, that she was as special to him as he was to her. It was the perfect ending to a perfect week. She was almost sorry they'd have to deal with the morning, and saying good-bye.

Brooke woke to find Jake sitting on the bed.

Dressed in jeans and a casual shirt, his hair damp from the

shower, he gazed at her. "I think I'll go now. No breakfast, okay?"

She nodded and forced words past the lump in her throat. "I'll get up and see you off."

"Don't. I want to remember you this way. I can't . . ." He shook his head. "I don't do well at good-byes, Brooke. I just wanted to say, you're amazing. One of the strongest people I've ever known. I'm so glad I met you."

"Me too."

He handed her a piece of paper. "Here's my contact information. If you ever need anything . . ."

"Just try to stay safe. That's the one thing you can do for me."

"I'll do my best."

He was going. The moment she'd known had to come was now here. Soon, very soon, she'd get back to her normal life.

Except, the prospect didn't seem very appealing.

He leaned over her and touched his lips to her forehead, and then, soft as a feather, to her mouth.

Fighting tears, she caressed his cheek, then nodded, giving him permission to go. Then she lay back and closed her eyes, refusing to watch as he left. When she heard his footsteps on the stairs, she let the tears escape.

Then there was the click of the front door as it closed. The car starting up, then driving away. Driving away in such civilized fashion, compared to the way he'd arrived.

The tears fell harder. This was the right thing- -the only thing—for both of them.

A soft thud, and the bed shifted.

She opened her eyes to see Sunny perched on Jake's pillow. "It's just you and me again, pal," she murmured, reaching out to stroke him.

She could lie there and cry all day. Call in sick. She could go down and open one of the beer bottles she'd bought for Jake. But she wouldn't. Resolutely, she threw back the covers.

"I haven't been to fitness class in two weeks," she told the cat. "I need to get back to my routine."

She was halfway to the bathroom when she saw the painting. It sat on the floor, resting against the wall across from her bed. She stood back and studied it, enchanted by the romantic garden scene. Delighted by the idea that Jake had bought her such a wonderful gift.

He hadn't given her the opportunity to thank him. He hadn't hung it, perhaps because he didn't want to wake her or maybe because he wasn't sure she'd want this memory of him in her bedroom.

But yes, this was the perfect place for memories of Jake.

Chapter Twenty-One

A month later

In shock, Brooke gaped at her GP. "No, it's not possible."

Carlene Young, petite and thirtysomething, tucked her black braid behind her shoulder. "Are you saying you haven't had intercourse in the past month?"

"Yes, I mean no, I'm not saying that. But we used condoms."

"Every time?"

"Yes!"

"Your partner always put the condom on before any semen could have entered your body?" she asked matter-of-factly.

Brooke thought of all the times, and all the ways, she and Jake had made love. "I, uh, think so."

"Even when you use condoms properly, they're not one hundred percent reliable."

Brooke groaned. "This can't be happening."

Dr. Young gave a sympathetic smile. "I'm sorry, Brooke. You're only a few weeks along but you're very definitely pregnant. You'll want to discuss this with the father." A hint of curiosity lit her dark eyes. She knew Brooke had been sexually inactive for a very long time.

"The father isn't in the picture," Brooke said quickly. "Good Lord, I can't be pregnant. I'm forty-three!"

"Many women in their forties have safe pregnancies and healthy babies," the doctor said quietly. "But with your bipolar disorder, you'll definitely want to consider all your options."

"Abortion," Brooke whispered. She believed in a woman's right to choose, but she'd never once believed she would face that choice herself, in her forties.

"Yes, that's one alternative. Along with, of course, having the baby and keeping it, or having the baby and putting it up for adoption. But Brooke"—the doctor leaned forward to clasp Brooke's hands in hers—"if you continue with the pregnancy, you might need to go off lithium. You'd have to talk to Dr. Allenby about that."

"Off lithium?" Brooke pulled her hands free and shook her head frantically. "I need lithium to control the bipolar."

"Medication during pregnancy can have a negative impact on the fetus."

"I'd be scared to stop taking lithium." It had been her salvation, and just the thought of doing without it made her heart race.

"You need to talk to Dr. Allenby and think about this. If you decide to terminate, you can of course continue taking lithium and we'll schedule the procedure."

A racing heart, a pounding head, she was on the verge of a panic attack. Surely an abortion was the only realistic choice. "I guess we should do that."

"No, Brooke," she said sympathetically but firmly, "don't give me your answer today. You must get all the information and think this through very carefully. I strongly recommend that you discuss it with the father and also your family."

Brooke tried to imagine phoning Jake with this news, or telling Evan and Jessica. Good Lord, her daughter-in-law was pregnant. How could Brooke be pregnant too?

Dr. Young touched Brooke's hand. "Talk to Dr. Allenby today. I'm sure he'll make time to see you."

Brooke nodded, still unable to believe this was happening. When she'd missed her period, she'd put it down to the recent excitement and stress in her life. She wouldn't even have mentioned it except she'd been in for her regular physical and the doctor asked about her period.

Thank heavens she was finished for the day at Beauty Is You. Feeling dazed, she walked a couple of blocks from the small office building where Dr. Young worked to the renovated old house where Dr. Allenby lived and ran his practice.

His wife, who also worked as his office manager, greeted her. "Brooke, we weren't expecting you." Penetrating gray eyes studied her face from behind red-framed glasses. "You look pale, dear."

"Can you squeeze me in?" she begged. "Something's happened."

"He'll be free in half an hour. In the meantime, come into the kitchen and have a cup of coffee with me."

Brooke followed her into the cozy room. Caffeine was a no-no during pregnancy. Besides, it certainly wouldn't soothe her jangled nerves. "Could I have herbal tea instead?"

"Of course, dear. That's a much better idea. I'll have the same myself."

Mrs. Allenby seemed to sense that Brooke didn't want to talk. She simply made and poured the tea, then puttered around the kitchen making meatloaf while Brooke sat, sipping tea and trying not to think. Finally, Dr. Allenby came into the room.

"Well, Brooke, this is a surprise. Did you want to see me?"

"Oh yes, please."

She followed his broad-beamed back into his office and perched nervously on the edge of her usual chair. "I'm pregnant."

When his eyes widened and his mouth dropped open, she realized she'd never seen him lose his composure before. For some reason, it lifted her spirits. "I'm middle-aged and bipolar, but I'm not dead," she pointed out. "And I happen to like sex."

"Well . . . of course." He stroked his graying beard. "But you never said you were seeing anyone. I thought you'd decided against having a relationship."

"I did. I have. This isn't a relationship. Oh, damn!"

"Brooke? I haven't heard you swear in years."

"I haven't been pregnant in years." She remembered the slogan "God never dumps more on us than we can handle" and didn't know whether to cry or laugh.

When she began to chuckle, Dr. Allenby joined her. He was a bit of a Santa Clausy kind of man, and when he laughed his rounded belly really did shake. And that made her laugh harder.

After they both calmed down, he said, "Good for you. That's a healthy reaction. So, you're pregnant. I take it this wasn't a deliberate choice?"

She sat back in her chair and told him the whole story, omitting not a detail. He was the only person in the world she'd ever been so frank with. Besides Jake.

When she finished, he said, "So you're thinking seriously about having an abortion, but you'd like more information before you make up your mind."

"Dr. Young wouldn't let me decide today. She said I needed to think about it, and to talk to you." And to everyone else in her life, she thought wryly, but that was advice she wouldn't obey.

"There are several issues," he said, his expression serious now. "One is health, yours and the fetus's. You know you're a little old to be having a child, even though you're in excellent shape. And then there's your medication. Lithium is one of the safer bipolar medications to take during pregnancy, but there's some risk of it causing congenital problems in the fetus, such as defects."

She shuddered. "I'm five weeks pregnant and I've been taking lithium all that time."

"If a problem had already occurred, chances are you'd have miscarried. We'd certainly do an ultrasound around sixteen to eighteen weeks, to assess heart and vertebral body development. And of course, given your age, an amniocentesis is indicated."

She nodded.

"If you did decide to proceed with the pregnancy, we'd have three choices."

She leaned forward, listening intently.

"One is to continue the lithium but try reducing the dose and monitor you and the fetus closely. Another is to get you off the lithium and monitor even more closely. You know there are bipolar patients who manage the illness with no medication."

"We tried that," she said nervously. "It didn't work for me."

"Things change. You're healthier, more confident, more self-aware now."

Because of the lithium. "What's the third option?"

"To try alternative treatments." He stroked his beard again, reflecting. "Though lithium is one of the safest medications, and pregnancy isn't the best time to experiment with new treatments."

"So, that leaves lithium or no lithium. Taking it could hurt the fetus. If I don't take it . . ." She swallowed hard, thinking of her manias and the black depressions that had made her feel suicidal. Of drinking, to escape the depression. "What's likely to happen?"

"Possibly nothing. Or possibly a recurrence of symptoms. I'd want to see you every week. You'd need to be particularly diligent about your diet, regular exercise, lots of rest, avoiding stress. You know the symptoms to look for. And if you ran into the slightest problem, we could put you back on lithium. The first trimester is the most critical time for the fetus. But if you did well, we'd try to go the whole pregnancy without medication."

Brooke lifted her chin and stared him straight in the eyes. "I'm terrified at the idea of going off lithium."

He gave a sympathetic smile. "It's done a great job for you. But bear in mind, you're a different person, Brooke. You're far healthier and stronger than when you were diagnosed."

"But I'm bipolar. It's like being an alcoholic. It doesn't just go away."

"And I wouldn't suggest we take you off lithium indefinitely. We'd put you back on it when the baby is born, because there's a high rate of symptom recurrence during the postpartum period. No breast feeding, because the lithium gets into your milk."

He studied her face intently. "There are no guarantees, but I think we could get you and the fetus through the pregnancy without any serious problems. But that's only the beginning."

She swallowed hard. "I know. The child could have bipolar disorder. We talked about that risk when Jessica and Evan were deciding whether to have a baby. And the risk would be higher for me than for him, because I definitely have it and he probably doesn't."

"Is there any sign of bipolar disorder on the fetus's father's side?"

"I'm sure there isn't." Jake would have mentioned it.

"That helps. And remember, we don't have many solid facts about this condition. A child may inherit the gene but never develop the illness. Environmental factors like loss and abandonment can have a huge influence. And that's something you can control, to a large degree. Plus, you—or adoptive parents—would be on the lookout for symptoms, and if the child was bipolar, he or she would be diagnosed very early. As you know, medication and therapy can be very effective."

Adoptive parents, definitely. She couldn't raise a baby herself; that was far too scary. Yet who'd adopt a baby knowing there was a risk it had bipolar disorder? "Treatment isn't effective for everyone. You said yourself that I've been lucky."

He nodded.

"I can't go off lithium. I can't risk bringing a . . . damaged baby into the world." And expecting someone to adopt it, to love and care for it no matter what happened.

"You're saying you want an abortion?"

No! What woman ever *wanted* an abortion? She just wanted somehow, magically, to not be pregnant. Slowly she said, "You told Evan and Jessica that no child comes with a guarantee."

He smiled. "That's the truth. And lots of parents who have hereditary conditions—physical or mental problems—make the conscious decision to have children."

"I wouldn't. If it had been a decision, I wouldn't have done it."

"But now it's done. And now it is a decision."

"If I have the baby and put it up for adoption, what are the chances it would find a good home?"

"I think they're good. People adopt babies and children with fetal alcohol syndrome, drug addiction." He leaned over and patted her hand. "This is a lot to take in. Why don't you come in again tomorrow, after you've had some time to think?"

From Dr. Allenby's, Brooke went home to change, then drove to Boots, knowing Jess and her students would be finished for the day. Usually, she rode with Robin, but sometimes when she was stressed, she took Beanie out on her own. Riding in the country soothed her and helped her sort out problems.

She brought the pinto mare in from pasture, saddled and bridled her, then headed out on a favorite trail.

"What am I going to do?" she said, bending forward to stroke the horse's warm coat.

She couldn't have the baby. There was no possible way.

Tomorrow she'd call Dr. Young and ask her to schedule the procedure. No one but she and her doctors would ever know she'd been pregnant.

She felt so alone.

Beanie tossed her head, letting Brooke know she'd like to speed up the pace, and Brooke eased up on the reins and let the horse fall into an easy, ground-eating lope.

No, Brooke wasn't alone. Being out here on Beanie was a reminder of that. She had family, including the wonderful granddaughter who'd taught her to ride. There was just this one decision she had to make on her own.

For a moment she regretted having met Jake, but then, when she remembered the way he'd touched her, the passion and tenderness in his eyes when they'd made love, she changed her mind. Meeting Jake had been a blessing.

It was only the baby—no, she wouldn't think of it as a baby, just an unwanted pregnancy—that was a problem. But she'd solve it.

Riding alone in the country made her feel strong, competent, self-sufficient. She might not know the answer right now, but she'd figure it out. Without telling her family, or Jake.

Of course she wouldn't tell Jake. It was the last news he'd want to hear.

She finished her ride, tended to Beanie, and returned home to make a healthy supper.

After eating, Brooke sat down in the living room, with the country station she'd come to love playing and Sunny beside her, and picked up a book. She remembered sitting this way with Jake.

He'd asked to borrow her Stephanie Plum book so he could finish it. She'd told him to keep it. It was silly to have him mail back a used paperback. It was kind of like pretending they'd stay in touch.

That was one of the things she liked about their relationship. Once they'd decided to trust each other, there had been no pretense or deception between them.

It wasn't being dishonest if you didn't tell a lie, just remained silent.

And that, Brooke knew, was a cop-out. At least in her terms. Had playing the Arnold Pitt game got her back into the habit of living her life dishonestly?

Jake might not want to know about her pregnancy, but she had to tell him. For her own peace of mind, her self-respect.

She went into the kitchen to find the paper on which he'd scrawled his contact information. Staring at his bold handwriting, she tried to decide what to say. To imagine how he'd respond.

No, she couldn't do it by phone. There he'd be, utterly shocked, trying to find words as the silence between them grew. She should give him a chance to digest the news before responding. A chance to not respond at all. After all, she wasn't asking for his participation or his opinion; she only wanted to be honest with him.

E-mail then. Except it was so informal. It didn't seem . . . substantial enough for such weighty news. For this, she'd use the good old-fashioned method.

Brooke went to her desk and found a notepad. *Dear Jake*, she wrote, and then she paused. Everything she could think to say sounded trite, superficial, downright stupid. Finally, she continued:

I really hope all is well with you, and with Jamal as well. I'm healthy and happy, except that today I got some surprising news. You might rather I didn't tell you, but I don't think it's fair to keep secrets from someone I care about. Anyhow, the news is that I'm pregnant.

As the pregnancy was unplanned—and unwanted by both of us—the logical step seems to be to terminate it.

Brooke looked at her words, written neatly in blue ink: *the pregnancy; terminate it.*

When Jessica had announced her own pregnancy, they'd immediately started talking about the fetus as a baby. But

Brooke couldn't afford to think of her own pregnancy in the same terms.

She bit the end of her pen, then wrote:

This all sounds so cold and matter-of-fact. If you were here, in the living room with me and Sunny, I'd be able to talk to you. We never had any trouble talking. But we had a relationship that we both knew was time-limited, and now that time is past and here I am, writing you with news I know will shock you. Part of me wants to rip up this letter but another part wants to write on and on, to tell you about the garden and how well Jessica is looking and how I've seen Karen MacLean a few times and she mentions Jamal with astonishing frequency. But you probably don't want to know those things, any more than you want to know about my pregnancy.

Anyhow, I will understand completely if you choose not to answer this letter. The past belongs in the past. But please, Jake, because you know me so well, understand that I wrote because I had to, because honesty is so important to me. Not because I wanted to hurt or upset you, nor because I want anything more from you than the wonderful gifts you've already given me.

She reread her words. Some phrases sounded like the real her, and others were so formal and stuffy. She could try again but doubted she'd do any better.

The only part about the letter that was easy was how to sign it. She wrote, *Love, Brooke.* Then she folded the paper and addressed the envelope.

As Brooke prepared for bed, she automatically reached for the bottle of lithium and unscrewed the cap. She shook a pill out into her hand and gazed at it for a long time. Eventually, she put it back in the bottle. Missing one wouldn't do any harm. She should at least sleep on her decision overnight.

* * *

Jamal and Jake, in street disguises, entered the seedy bar in a run-down area of Winnipeg. Since Jamal had become a sergeant he didn't do much street-level U/C work, but this assignment needed a black male and he'd said he'd do it if he could work with Jake.

They sauntered up to the bar. Jake ordered a beer and Jamal got tomato juice with bitters. They chose a table midway across the room, where they could keep an eye on all the action.

The Black Devils were a new gang, and Winnipeg wanted to bust them before they got a foothold. Rumor had it that the gang was using this bar as a headquarters for dealing drugs to kids from the local high school and college.

"Don't recognize any members of the gang," Jamal said quietly.

Jake shook his head. "Those kids playing pool in the back corner look kinda squirrelly, like they're maybe hoping to make a buy."

"We'll hang out a while," Jamal said. He took a swallow of his drink. "One hell of a job for an alcoholic."

"You need any motivation to stay sober, just take a look over there." Jake cocked his head toward a scruffy old guy who could barely get his glass to his mouth, even though he'd wrapped both shaking hands around it.

Jamal looked, and shuddered. "Hard to believe that's the route I was headed on."

"Harder to believe Brooke was doing it too," Jake murmured.

"Amen. That's one hell of a lady."

"Yeah." Jake thought for the millionth time of what she had said. She loved him. At first her declaration had scared the shit out of him, but now it made him feel warm inside. No matter how rotten the world might treat him, there was one special woman who loved him. Hell, not that he knew anything about love, but maybe he loved her too.

"There you go, all mushy faced again," Jamal teased.

"Don't tell me you haven't been thinking about Karen MacLean. The two of you seemed to be getting on pretty well that night you left Brooke's so early. Almost makes a guy think . . ." He deliberately let his voice trail off.

Jamal waggled a finger at him. "Don't go there." Then he laughed. "Believe it or not, we sat up all night talking."

"Talking? What did you find to talk about all night?" Jamal wasn't known for being wordy.

"You know. Her job, my job. Parents, schooling. What she wants out of life. What I want out of life."

Jake stared at the other man. "Hell, I've known you ten years and we've never talked about that shit."

Jamal shrugged. "That's a woman for you."

"Yeah, I guess." He'd had those same conversations with Brooke. After a few seconds, curiosity made him ask, "So, what the hell do you want out of life?"

"The usual, I guess. Good woman, couple of kids. Job I enjoy. House, maybe a dog. Did you know Karen has a German shepherd?"

"Well, hell." Brooke had a cat, and her family had horses. There was something to be said for animals.

A few minutes went by in silence, and then Jamal asked, "You thinking I'm crazy? You can't see me teaching some little boy or girl how to play basketball?"

"Huh. Yeah, I can." It surprised Jake, but the picture was clear in his mind. "You'd go for staff sergeant, and it'd really be a desk job?"

"Likely. Figure priorities gotta change when you hook up with someone special."

Damn, this might be the last assignment he and Jamal worked on together.

"Action," Jamal said under his breath.

Two Black Devils had entered the bar and were drifting over to the pool tables.

Jake took a couple swallows of beer. "So you're going to see Karen again?"

One of the pool players made eye contact with one of the gang members.

"Thought I might head up that way when we get back. How about you and Brooke?"

It seemed like all Jake had done since he left Caribou Crossing was think about Brooke. He remembered the sex, sure, and her dynamite body, but also some weird things like both of them reading in her living room. Riding and line dancing together. Helping her prepare meals in her cozy kitchen. Sitting down with her family.

Reluctantly he shook his head. "Don't see it happening. She's got a good life going for her. Doesn't need me."

"Yeah, but do you need her?"

"Don't need anyone."

The college kid headed for the men's room, down a corridor at the back of the bar. After a few seconds the gang member went after him. Jake said, "Here we go."

"Got it." Jamal had already lifted his smartphone like he was going to make a call, but instead surreptitiously snapped photos before putting the phone to his ear. Into the phone, he said, "You two got pretty strong chemistry."

"Yeah, that's for sure." He swallowed, confessed. "And I care about her. But it wouldn't be fair to her. I can't come and go in her life. She's not that kind of woman. She wants stability, peace. She doesn't want some guy who spends his life like this." He gestured around the smoky bar.

"You plan on doing this for the rest of your life?"

"Don't know what else I'd do."

"Don't see the basketball thing working for you?"

Jake gave a snort. "Guess I don't see myself as a parent. Most parents fuck up their kids' lives. Don't want any part of that."

"You think I'd fuck up my kid's life?"

Jake thought about the question. "You'd try not to. Besides, seems to me Karen's got her head on pretty straight."

Jamal gave a private little grin. "So you're seeing me and Karen?"

"Aren't you?"

"White gal."

"Didn't seem to bother her. Does it bother you?"

"Nah. Poor mongrel kids, though. White, black, and Hispanic."

"Could be pretty." Jake grinned. "If they take after Karen, not you."

Jamal lowered his phone and pretended to dial another number, but really he was taking more photos as the college kid came back down the hall. From the way he was sniffing, it looked like he'd gotten himself a sample of the merchandise. The kid said something to his friends and they abandoned the game of pool before it was finished.

As the group left the bar, Jamal closed his phone and put it away. "Free table. Shoot some pool?"

"Why not?" The two gang members were still there, maybe looking to make another connection.

Jake kicked back his chair and stood up. Then he leaned over and muttered, "When you go to Caribou Crossing, get Karen to take you line dancing."

"Line dancing?" Jamal rose to join him. "Brooke do that?"

"She's good."

"Bet she's good at most anything she chooses to do."

"That's the truth." Jake picked up his beer glass and drained it.

"Never saw you like that with anyone before."

"Like what?"

"Relaxed. Happy."

Happy. What kind of word was that?

"Get us some more drinks, will ya?" he told Jamal. "I'll grab the table before someone else gets it."

Chapter Twenty-Two

In the morning, Brooke didn't take her pill. She did mail the letter on the way to work, and arrived at Beauty Is You with a bag of donuts and a racing pulse. By the end of the morning she felt panicky and had trouble holding herself together until the end of the day.

What a relief to sit in Dr. Allenby's office in her usual chair. This man had, quite probably, saved her life. She could always count on him to help her. She told him about the skipped pills and her symptoms.

He shook his head, smiling sympathetically. "I didn't tell you to stop taking lithium. We wouldn't do it that way, cold turkey, we'd taper it off gradually. But in any case I doubt your anxiety is the result of skipping two pills. You're doing it to yourself, Brooke."

"You think so?"

"You're scared what will happen without lithium, and now you're making it happen. You're also, quite understandably, anxious about the decision you have to make. Once you make up your mind, whichever choice you make, you'll feel more settled—as long as you don't rush the decision. You need to be sure. Especially if the decision is to terminate. Once it's done, there's no changing your mind. And, given your age and personal situation, this is likely your last chance to have a baby."

She shook her head vigorously. "No, I wouldn't keep the baby. I'd make a terrible mother. Look what I did to Evan."

"Brooke, Brooke. We've been over this so many times before, but clearly we need to do it again. You are not the same person now. You were a child when you had Evan. A selfish, immature teen. You were in a dysfunctional marriage with a man who was a terrible husband and father. At some point, precipitated by losing your family and by the stresses of marriage to Mo, your illnesses came into play. You're a different person and you know it."

She listened to every word, and yes, he'd said them before. She'd said them over and over in her mind as well, these past five years. Now, she took a deep breath, then let it out slowly. "You're right. And I know I'm a good grandmother to Robin and I plan to be wonderful with Jess's baby. But that's different from having a child of my own."

"You're planning on baby-sitting the new baby? Maybe keeping the baby and Robin at your place overnight so Evan and Jessica can have a little time alone?"

"Yes, but—"

"You're right, Brooke, that's not the same as being a mom twenty-four/seven. But don't underestimate yourself. Don't make decisions based on who you were, not who you are now."

"Who I am now is a forty-three-year-old bipolar woman. I don't want to raise a child. As for the pregnancy, it's possible something horrible could happen—to me or to the, uh, fetus." She couldn't call the thing inside her a baby.

"I'd do my best to make sure that didn't happen. The goal, in treatment during a pregnancy, is to minimize fetal exposure to toxins while maintaining the mother's mental health. But yes, there are risks."

"It could inherit my bipolar."

"True. But as I said yesterday, you know the kind of environmental influences that can trigger a problem, you know the kind of symptoms to look out for, you know a fair bit about treatment. You're well equipped to deal with a child who has a problem."

"I wouldn't keep it, and adoptive parents wouldn't know all of that."

"They might, especially if one of them has bipolar, or they already have a child who does. If not, they'd learn."

She leaned forward and studied his face. "Are you saying I shouldn't terminate?"

A smile flashed. "Are you still trying that old trick? You know I'm not going to tell you what to do. Except to say that you need to think about it seriously in light of the woman you are now. Consider your strengths and, yes, your weaknesses too. Be honest. Think about what you want, how you feel."

She watched his face intently as he went on.

"Imagine terminating, and how you'd feel after. Imagine going through eight more months of pregnancy, feeling that fetus grow inside you, laboring to bring your baby into the world, then handing that little girl or boy over to adoptive parents, in hopes they'd take good care of it."

Her baby. Hers and Jake's. How could she be sure it found good parents?

"Then," the psychiatrist said, "imagine what your life would be like with a baby in it. A toddler, a teenager. You'd be—let's see—over sixty when the child graduated from high school. That's not old these days, but it's not young either. And then there's college, university, whatever else the child decides to do with his or her life. When you have a kid you're in it for the long haul. And if the father really is out of the picture, you're in it alone. Your family and friends will help, but the responsibility will be yours alone. It's not easy being a parent, and it's less easy when you're a single one."

She nodded slowly. "Last night, I pretty much decided to terminate. I just wanted to get all the facts and give it a bit more time before I made up my mind."

"Let's taper you off the lithium for the next few days, and monitor you closely. I've photocopied a few articles for you, and I'd suggest you discuss this with your family."

"I can't. I'm too embarrassed."

"They love you, Brooke. They'd understand."

Maybe. But she'd caused Evan so many problems in the past. She wanted to help him now, not be a burden.

Dr. Allenby stroked his beard. "I still encourage you to talk to the father."

"I wrote to him," she confessed.

"Excellent. So, let's give him a chance to get your letter and respond, before you decide."

It wouldn't change anything. Still, she didn't mind waiting a few more days before she made a decision that was so . . . irrevocable.

Dr. Allenby turned the discussion back to the anxiety she was experiencing, and how best to cope with it as well as how to monitor her condition.

By the time she left his office, Brooke was feeling calmer, though she had no idea what she'd say to Jake if he called.

But Jake didn't call, not in the next week, and no letter came.

During that week, Brooke read the articles Dr. Allenby had given her and took a reduced dosage of lithium. She saw the psychiatrist three times and worked at staying healthy and calm as she followed his instructions, trying to envision what her life would be like depending on which of the three options she chose.

If she terminated, could she view that decision practically, as the best thing for all concerned, or would she feel horrible? If she carried the baby to term, could she hand it over to someone else and trust her own judgment in finding parents who'd give it everything it deserved?

If she had the baby and kept it . . . The idea was terrifying. The idea was exciting and heartwarming.

She was a new woman. Perhaps she really could do it, and do it well. If she wanted to.

The day Brooke caught herself picking out girl names and boy names, she realized she'd made her decision. She had stopped thinking of the life inside her as a fetus, as an *it*. To her, it was a growing boy or girl. Her child. That child might not turn out perfect, but she loved him or her already.

Sunny was curled on her knee as she lounged in the cushioned loveseat on the front porch, catching the last rays of sun. She picked him up under his shoulders and looked into his eyes. "Guess what? We're having a baby."

Then she laughed, and tears of joy slid down her cheeks. "I'm having a baby."

She went inside and phoned Evan's house. Jessica answered and Brooke said, "How are you feeling?"

"Healthy as a horse," Jess said cheerfully. "I may be able to get through this pregnancy without morning sickness."

"I sure hope so. Say, I was wondering if the three of you would like to come over for dinner tomorrow night?"

Brooke spent Saturday fussing nervously, and was relieved when she heard the sound of horses in her driveway. She went out to say hi and saw not only Evan on Rusty, Jessica on Conti, and Robin on Concha, but also Beanie on a lead rein held by Robin.

Evan dismounted and handed Rusty's reins to his wife, then came to hug Brooke. "We thought it'd be fun to go for an evening ride after dinner."

"That does sound fun." If they were still speaking to her.

Jessica and Robin deftly took off saddles and bridles, and turned the horses into the small paddock beside Brooke's rental property, a paddock Jessica's father, Wade Bly, had built specifically for that purpose after Brooke moved in.

Brooke had made chicken and herbed dumplings, one of her and Robin's favorites, for dinner, but was so nervous she had to force herself to eat. She only picked at the strawberry cheesecake she'd baked, and as soon as Robin finished, she said, "Rob, there's something I need to talk to your mom and dad about. Why don't you go get the horses ready for our ride?"

Her granddaughter looked only mildly curious. "Sure."

When the girl left the kitchen, Evan said, "What's up, Mom? You're not yourself tonight. Are you okay?"

She should suggest they all go into the living room and sit somewhere more comfortable, but her body was trembling so badly her legs might not hold her up.

Brooke wrapped her arms around her still-flat belly. There'd be no hiding the fact of her pregnancy once she was a few months along. She lifted her chin. "Yes, I'm healthy. But I'm pregnant and I'm keeping the baby."

They looked so stunned that she found herself laughing. "It's okay, I'm happy."

Evan's brow was furrowed. "But how did this happen?"

She laughed again, suddenly in high spirits. "Much the same way as you and Jess got pregnant, I expect."

"But . . . but . . ." Evan stammered.

Jessica put a hand over her husband's. "I think Ev wants to ask who the father is."

"You know my cousin Arnold—" she began.

"Oh, Jesus, you and your cousin!" Evan said. Then he shook his head. "Right, he wasn't your cousin, he was a cop. So, you . . ." He couldn't seem to finish the sentence.

"Had sex," Brooke said crisply.

"You're my mother!"

"I'm a woman. I enjoy sex. Get over it."

Jessica prodded Evan's arm. "Yeah, get over it. Way to go, Brooke. But did you intend to get pregnant?"

Brooke shook her head. "We thought we were being careful, but I guess we weren't careful enough."

"Oh, Christ!" Evan snapped.

Jessica poked him again, then focused on Brooke. "You say you intend to have the baby. What about the father? What's his name again? Is he going to—"

"Marry you," Evan broke in. "He's damn well going to marry you."

Brooke scowled at him. "Stop acting like you're my father. My parents and Mo's forced us to get married, and look how that turned out. No, we're not getting married. Jake and I—his name's Jake Brannon—had a wonderful time together and I'm extremely fond of him but all we wanted was a temporary fling."

"What kind of example are you setting for Robin?" Evan asked.

"Evan!" This time Jessica glared at him.

He buried his head in his hands and dug his fingers into his scalp. When he lifted his head he looked apologetic. "I'm sorry, Mom. But this is a shock."

"It was for me too."

Now he reached across the table and gripped both of her hands. "How are you? You really are happy about this?"

She nodded. "It took me a while. I did a lot of thinking. Then I realized I . . . I already loved my child. I know it'll be hard and there are risks. But this is a second chance for me. I can be a mother again, and this time do it right. Tell me you don't think I'm completely foolish."

"I think you'll be a wonderful mother to this child," he said stiffly.

She bit her lip, wishing she could remake the past. "Oh, Evan. I wish I'd been that kind of mother to you."

"Yeah." His eyes were sad. "Me too. But if this is what you want, I'm happy for you."

Jessica leaned over to put her arm around Brooke. "We'll be pregnant together. We can shop for maternity clothes. And gosh, Brooke, our kids will grow up together."

Brooke's eyes filled with tears. "My child and my grand-child, growing up together. It's strange, isn't it? But wonder-ful too."

Evan rose and came over to bend down between Brooke and Jessica and put his arms around both of them. "Yes, I guess it is pretty wonderful."

She guessed how difficult the words, the acceptance, were for him. What had she done to deserve such an amazing, gen-erous son?

Then he straightened. "Uh, not to be rude, but you're a little old to be having a kid, aren't you? Is it safe?"

No way was she going to worry them by revealing that she was going off lithium. "Safe enough. I'll take good care of myself and my doctors will look after me."

"Good." He ducked his head, then said softly, "Are you worried about the baby having bipolar?"

"I thought about it a lot. All we can do is pray both babies are all right."

Jessica gripped her hand. "And if there's a problem, we'll support each other and do our best. Whatever happens, our two babies are going to be loved."

Evan hugged them both once more. "They sure are."

Through the window they heard the sound of footsteps on the back steps, and he stood up. "When do you want to tell Robin?"

"Now, if it's all right with you."

"Why not?" He was smiling and shaking his head. "Oh boy, this whole thing could be a lot of fun. Starting with Robin."

The girl, who'd opened the kitchen door in time to overhear

his last words, said, "What's starting with me? Are you done with the grown-up talk? The horses are ready."

"Over to you," Evan said to Brooke.

"I have some wonderful news," she said. "Come here, you."

When Robin came over, Brooke hugged her. "I hope you'll be happy for me. You know the undercover policeman who was pretending to be my cousin? Corporal Jake Brannon? Well, he and I got to be good friends and, uh, the result is I'm having a baby."

"A baby!" Robin stared at her grandmother with wide eyes. "That's seriously cool. You and Mom, at the same time."

"Yes, I think it's seriously cool too."

"So, where's Cousin Arn—I mean, Corporal Brannon?"

"He's gone back to Vancouver. That's where he works. He's not going to be around, even though he's the baby's father. You know that lots of women raise children on their own?"

"Yeah, and so do some men." Robin reflected for a moment, then squinted up her face and turned to Jessica. "Mom, what's my relationship to Gramma's baby?"

"Oh!" The three adults stared at each other.

Evan blurted out, "Mom's baby will be your aunt or uncle!" and began to laugh.

Jessica and Brooke joined in the laughter but Robin frowned. "No way. It'll be a baby and I'm almost a teenager."

Jessica wiped a hand across her streaming eyes. "Ev, it'll be your sister or brother."

Brooke straightened her mouth. "I'm glad I'm causing you all such amusement." Bless her family for taking her announcement so well.

"I'm not amused," Robin announced.

"Well," Evan said, "no one ever said we were a conventional family."

"We're a special family," Jess said warmly. "And very lucky to have each other, and the two little ones who are coming along." She patted her own stomach, then reached over to pat Brooke's.

"Just as long as I don't have to call it Aunt or Uncle." Robin tipped her head to one side. "Mom should have a boy and you should have a girl. Then we'll have one of each."

"Sounds like a plan to me," Evan said. "But it seems to me that whatever we end up with we'll be lucky."

"Uh-huh," Robin said. "Now can we go riding? Gramma, go put on your jeans and boots."

"You bet."

Jake stepped inside his apartment and glanced around. It seemed even smaller and dingier than he remembered, and smelled musty and neglected.

He thought of Brooke's house. Warm colors, plants all over the place, good smells coming from the kitchen, the golden cat purring. Brooke waiting, with a hug and kiss.

All that awaited him here was a small stack of mail the building manager had collected for him. Because Jake worked undercover so often, and for long stretches of time, he handled most things online and didn't get much actual mail. He tossed the dozen or so envelopes on the coffee table, flung open the windows, and strode through to the bathroom. There, he stripped, and took rubbing alcohol to the temporary tats that had been part of his disguise. Then he stepped into the shower.

He and Jamal had succeeded in their mission. Based on their evidence a couple dozen arrests had been made, and they'd shut down another pipeline that supplied drugs to young people. Of course another would already be opening in its stead. The war was never-ending.

When he stepped out of the shower, Jake felt drained. He and Jamal had worked damned hard, finished up the paperwork in the small hours of morning, and then, rather than get

a few hours' sleep at a hotel, they'd caught an early morning
flight home. Jamal had booked off a few days and was heading up to Caribou Crossing to see Karen MacLean.

Jake wondered whether if he showed up on Brooke's
doorstep she'd take him in. But no, that wouldn't be good for
her. He knew his job scared her, and she deserved better than
a guy who came seeking her company in between assignments. She deserved the man who belonged behind that
picket fence with her and Sunny.

Jake toweled his hair halfheartedly, staring at his reflection
in the mirror. It was good to be rid of the grungy hair and the
fake tattoos. He wouldn't bother shaving, though. Who knew,
he could easily be sent out on assignment again in the next
few days and need to look scruffy.

Although he was exhausted, he was also wired. The adrenaline was still pumping and he knew it'd take a while to
unwind. Later tonight maybe he'd cruise the streets, take a
look for Sapphire, see how she was doing.

When he'd returned from Caribou Crossing he had reported to her, just like he had to Anika Janssen's parents.
Unlike them, she hadn't cried, but he'd seen moisture glitter
in her eyes. Damn kid, so determined to be tough. He'd
bought her a mochaccino and given her some information
about a work-study program for the hospitality industry. He'd
almost thought he was getting through to her, but then he
had to go to Winnipeg and couldn't follow up.

Later tonight, he'd find Sapphire. For now, he was hungry.

The fridge contained a six-pack of beer and half-full jars
of peanut butter and pickles, and he found a box of stale
crackers in the cupboard. He took a bottle of beer and everything else—an odd breakfast, but he'd had worse—into the
living room and glanced through the mail as he snacked.
Nothing looked worth opening until he saw his name and
address handwritten in curvy feminine writing, and checked
the return address sticker, one of those little ones charities

gave you when you make a contribution. *B. Kincaid* in Caribou Crossing.

Brooke.

Slowly he slid his finger under the flap. What could she want to say to him?

He hoped it was a friendly, gossipy letter, telling him things were going well with her and passing along news of her garden, cat, family. He really hoped it didn't contain guilt and recriminations.

He took a deep breath and began to read. When he finished, he read it again. Well, shit. Just fucking shit!

He put the letter down on the coffee table and picked up his beer. He drained the bottle and went to the fridge for another.

Pregnant.

He'd had sex with his share of women but they'd always been careful and, as far as he knew, he'd never gotten anyone pregnant. Until now.

Brooke was pregnant with his child.

Brooke, the strongest yet most fragile woman he'd ever known. The only one he'd ever truly cared for.

He picked up the letter and glanced at the date. She had written three weeks ago. She'd been planning to have an abortion.

Hell. That quickly, he'd had a baby and lost it.

Unable to stay still, he paced, chugging the beer as he went. Why had she told him?

That was easy. She was Brooke. Honesty was important to her. But what had she expected him to do?

God yes, what had she expected? He drained the bottle. She'd written three weeks ago and he hadn't responded. She'd given him an out, said she'd understand if she didn't hear from him, but what must she think? That he didn't give a damn about her?

It wasn't true. She'd been on his mind all the time. For the first time in his career, he'd had trouble concentrating on his assignment. Missing her had been a constant ache.

His cell phone rang and he wondered irrationally if it was Brooke. But no, it was Inspector Dawson from headquarters.

"I know you just got back, Brannon," the inspector said, "but something's come up. I was going to send Estevez down to Seattle for a week or two to work with an IBET. We've got some intelligence about a new ocean-based operation for smuggling drugs. But Estevez has booked off for a few days so now I'm looking at you."

He'd worked with Integrated Border Enforcement Teams before. The concept was a good one, combining Canadian and American resources to battle cross-border smuggling of drugs, illegal aliens, and terrorists. "Yeah, I'm good for it. But, uh, can you give me a day? Got some personal business I have to take care of first."

"Can you drive down tomorrow night, be at work the next morning?"

"Sure." He just needed a day to get turned around and figure out what to do about Brooke.

He flopped down on the bed with his hands behind his head. How hard it must have been for her. Perhaps even harder because the family was so happy about Jessica's baby.

Hell, how could he have gotten Brooke pregnant? They'd used condoms.

Not exactly the most foolproof means of birth control. Other women he'd known had been on birth control, so he'd never had to rely totally on condoms before.

The fact was, it was fucking irresponsible of him. Brooke had slowly and painfully made herself into a respected member of the community—and now she was an unwed pregnant woman. In her early forties.

A pregnant woman with bipolar disorder. A condition that could have a genetic component. When they'd talked about

Jessica's pregnancy, he'd seen how fearful Brooke was, underneath her genuine joy.

Didn't he remember reading in one of her books that a pregnant woman wasn't supposed to take lithium? But Brooke needed it to control the bipolar.

He sat up suddenly. What was he thinking? She'd had an abortion. These issues weren't relevant anymore.

But they had been. When she'd written to him, she must've hoped he'd call.

He sprang to his feet. It might be three weeks too late, but he had to let her know he hadn't abandoned her.

Let her know he cared.

Chapter Twenty-Three

Brooke finished washing her dinner dishes and made herself a cup of chamomile tea. She should do some work in the garden but she tired easily these days. It didn't help that her job kept her on her feet all day. Perhaps she ought to look into buying a stool, and she should definitely invest in a heating pad.

"Hey, Sunny, come on outside with me. It's such a beautiful evening."

She collected her knitting. She'd never knit before, but now she wanted to. Janey at the Wool Bin had started her with a simple pattern for a knitted hat for the baby. She planned to progress to booties and little sweaters. The wool she'd chosen for her first project was the purple-blue of the lavender in her garden, and soft as a cloud.

"Funny," she said to the cat as he tagged along at her heels, "I don't think of blue as being a boy's color. If the baby's a girl I'm sure she'll be happy with blue. But I wouldn't put a boy in pink. Isn't that odd?"

Sunny meowed plaintively, registering his annoyance that she'd taken up knitting. He used to spend a lot of time in her lap but now the poor puss had to contend with flailing needles.

At this time of day, just before the sun went down, Brooke

always chose the front porch because the house faced west. She put her tea on a little white table and settled on one of the green-and-white-striped cushions that adorned the pine loveseat. Sunny hopped up and curled in a ball on the other cushion.

Brooke got the needles working and after a while Sunny forgave her and began to purr. Patsy Cline crooned in the background, a reminder of dancing with Jake. The end-of-the-day scent of warm flowers drifted up from the garden.

Next year she'd be sitting out here rocking her baby. When she'd told Dr. Allenby she was pregnant, he'd asked her to imagine different futures. Now, she had no trouble seeing herself with a child, and the picture made her smile.

Engine noise told her a car was approaching and she wondered who was out and about. When she glanced up, she dropped her knitting.

A motorbike whipped around the curve and into her driveway. Jake stepped off, removing his helmet.

Brooke rose and stared. Was it really him? What was he doing here?

He strode toward her.

She wanted to go to him but her feet were locked in place. Her eyes drank him in: hair longer and messier than Arnold's but not as long as when she'd first seen him; no beard but one of those sexy bad-boy unshaven scruffs; a beat-up brown leather jacket and worn jeans. He looked amazing, and she still couldn't believe he was there.

Why had he come?

He took the front steps in a single leap, and then he was standing in front of her.

"Jake," she whispered.

"Brooke." He reached for her hands and she let him take them.

She gazed into his eyes and read confusion. It seemed he wasn't sure why he'd come either.

She knew one thing, and so she told him. "It's so good to see you." She freed her hands from his and wrapped her arms around him. Oh, he felt good. So solid and warm and male and Jake.

He stood rigid in her arms for a second, and then his own arms swept around her and pulled her tight. "You too. So good."

They held each other for a long time, not saying a word. Not kissing, not even looking at each other, just clinging together. Dimly she was aware of Sunny twining around their ankles, purring his own greeting. Finally, Brooke stepped back. "What a surprise."

"I was out of town and got back today. I only just got your letter."

"Oh! I hadn't realized." Hadn't realized he'd be sent out of town on assignment again, so quickly. And of course, if he was undercover, mail addressed to Jake Brannon wouldn't be forwarded to him.

"I didn't want you thinking I didn't care."

"I know you care. But I figured we'd said our good-byes and you thought it was best to leave it that way."

"But, Brooke, you were pregnant. You shouldn't have had to go through that alone. Finding out, making the decision, going to get"—he swallowed—"the abortion."

Oh my. Of course he thought she'd had an abortion. That was what she'd been planning when she wrote the letter. And she was only nine weeks along now, not showing yet.

She had to tell him, but she stalled for a moment, searching for the right words. Then she bent to pick up the scrap of knitting that had tumbled to the floor when she first saw him, and she held it up. "Jake, I decided to have the baby."

"You—" He gaped at her.

She placed the knitting beside her tea mug, sat on the loveseat, and tugged him down beside her. "I want the baby. I decided I wouldn't be the worst mother in the world and—"

He gripped her hands in his, his touch warm, firm, and reassuring. "Damn, I admit I'm stunned. But I know one thing. You'll be a fantastic mother. The best."

She gave a shaky laugh. "Thanks for your confidence."

"I know you messed up the first time. You won't this time."

"Thank you. That's what I realized. And the more I thought about what to do, the more I knew I already loved the baby."

He ran his hands through his hair, messing it further. "I can't get my head around it." Sunny jumped up and settled in his lap. Automatically, Jake stroked the cat.

Brooke picked up her knitting again, running the soft wool through her fingers. "It took me a while too. But Jake, this was my decision. It doesn't change anything between us. It doesn't need to affect you in any way."

"It's my child too," he said slowly. "It's got to affect me."

"That's something only you can decide. I'm sorry if I've made things harder for you. That's not what I intended."

His lips curved up. "Yeah, well, I'm sorry I got you pregnant. That's not what I intended. And that sure as hell made things harder for you."

"Yes, in some ways. But it's also made my life so much richer." She rested a hand on his thigh, beside the purring cat. After a moment he linked his fingers through hers.

Jake was here, his hand interlocked with hers. He cared about her. He thought she'd make a good mother.

She thought about knitting. How you linked stitches and strands to create something new, something both practical and lovely. Smiling with contentment, she said, "It's the next step in my rebirth. And it's the most important one, my ultimate test. I'm not going to fail."

"I know you're not."

The quiet certainty in his voice brought moisture to her eyes.

"Have you told people about the baby?"

"So far only Evan, Jessica, Robin, and Kate."

"How did they take it?"

"They've been wonderful." Remembering her son's initial reaction, she shook her head ruefully. "Once Jessica and I talked Evan out of coming after you with a shotgun and forcing you to marry me. I convinced him that wasn't what I wanted."

"You're sure?"

Why was he asking? His tone and his face were expressionless.

"Of course. We were never about the long term. Were we?" She knew the answer—the only possible answer for both of them—but for a moment her heart stood still, waiting to see if he'd deny it.

"It'll be hard, though, being a single mom."

Her heart beat again, a slow, sad beat. Pregnancy had messed with her hormones, making her sentimental rather than practical. "At my age. That's what you're thinking."

"At any age. If you're older, you have more wisdom but maybe less energy. And, well, some people will talk. You haven't told the rest of the town. Is that because you're scared of how they'll react?"

"Partly." She summoned a small grin. "People have barely recovered from Sergeant Miller's arrest, and learning about my involvement in the investigation. I don't know which shocked them more. They've had to revise their image of me a number of times and now I'll be asking them to do it again."

"You think it'll be easier if you put it off?"

She shook her head. "No, but I want to wait until after the first trimester, until I've had an ultrasound and an amnio and know things are on the right track."

"Makes sense."

"I just hope," she said softly, "that if people think badly of me they won't take it out on the baby."

"Me too."

She squeezed his hand. "Hey, can I get you a drink? Have you had dinner?"

"It's okay."

"Have you had dinner, Jake?"

"I drove up without stopping." A sudden yawn wracked him. "Come to think of it, I haven't slept in a couple of days either."

Brooke took her knitting and mug inside. In the kitchen she braced her hands against the table and leaned there for a moment. Jake was here. He wasn't trying to argue her out of having the baby; he supported what she was doing.

She went to the fridge and pulled out a container that held leftover lasagna. She popped it in the microwave and was ripping up lettuce when he came into the kitchen.

"We could get married," he said.

She turned, her hands dripping, unable to believe she'd heard him correctly. "Married?" Her voice came out in a squeak.

"To make the baby legitimate."

"Oh." Of course that was all he'd meant. Yes, she knew he cared for her, but he wasn't a white-picket-fence-and-baby kind of man. And it wasn't like she wanted marriage anyhow. Well, maybe she wouldn't mind. After all, if she could take on the responsibility for a child, a man should be easy. But not an undercover cop who risked his life every day.

"If we got married, people wouldn't judge you as harshly," he said. "We could later split up, and they'd feel sorry for you and the kid. And you wouldn't have to take my name or call the baby Brannon. Not unless you wanted to."

She hadn't thought about the baby's surname, but now that he'd raised the subject she knew one thing. "The baby shouldn't have Mo's name."

"How about Brannon, then?"

"I had a really nice grandfather named Nicholas," she said tentatively. "I was thinking of Nicholas for a boy or Nicola for a girl. Nick or Nicki for short." She swallowed and tried them out. "Nick Brannon. Nicki Brannon. They sound good."

He nodded. "They do."

She smiled and turned back to the lettuce. "Then maybe I'll do that. But I'm not marrying you, Jake. That'd be crazy. You know I don't believe in lies, and a marriage in name only is a pretty serious lie. Besides, Mo and I married for the wrong reasons and it was a disaster."

He touched her shoulder, making her jump. "We'd do it for the right reason. For our baby, Brooke."

Our baby. Oh Lord, there went those hormones again.

She turned away, blinking rapidly to hold back the tears, and finished assembling the salad. The microwave beeped and she took out the lasagna and served it onto a plate. "I'm afraid I don't have any beer."

"Milk's good." He took the container from the fridge and poured a glass, then took his old place at her kitchen table.

She slid into her place across from him. Was this real, or was she dreaming? She'd come to terms with the idea that she'd never see Jake again, and now here they were in her kitchen, talking about baby names. About marriage.

He ate hungrily for a few minutes, then said, "Did you have to go off the lithium?"

"Good Lord. Do you remember everything you've ever read?"

"If it's important."

Remembering details about her illness was important to him? "Yes, I've stopped taking it, but I'm doing fine."

"Honest?"

"Really. I was nervous for a while. But my psychiatrist helped me work through it. Most of the weird symptoms I was experiencing were due to anxiety. And normal hormones associated with pregnancy."

"I'm glad. How about morning sickness?"

"Not yet. Touch wood." She rapped on the table. "Nor has Jessica, and she's more than a month ahead of me."

"She and Evan and Robin are all okay?"

"Sure. Busy as ever."

He rested his elbows on the table and propped his unshaven jaw on his fists. "You're really okay with this? You want the baby?"

She nodded firmly. "Yes. It's a miracle, having a baby, and I've been given a second chance to experience it. You've given me that second chance."

He gave her a slow, warm smile. "You're a generous woman, Brooke Kincaid. But I already knew that."

Jake watched Brooke as she moved around the kitchen, putting his few dinner dishes in the dishwasher, wiping the counter, hanging up a dish towel. Amazing to believe that inside her lovely body their baby was growing. Even more amazing to find he wanted her more than ever before.

As he'd told her, it had been days since he'd slept. Then he'd ridden his Harley, repaired and repainted in his absence, for more than five hours. On top of all that, he'd just weathered what was probably the biggest shock of his life. After all that, it wasn't logical that the thing he most wanted was to take Brooke to bed.

She stretched and pressed a hand to her lower back.

"Sore?"

"Standing all day didn't used to bother me, but now I get a little achy. Kate suggested I buy a heating pad, but I keep forgetting. Usually I take a bath before bed and that fixes it."

She stood at the sink with her back to him even though she'd stopped tidying. He guessed she was feeling awkward, just like he was.

He went to stand behind her, resting his hands on her shoulders. "I'd like to talk to you some more about the baby, but you're tired. I don't want to keep you from that bath. Unless you'd settle for an alternative."

She tensed. "An alternative?"

"How about a massage?"

She stood still, her muscles taut under his hands. Then she turned to him. "A massage sounds good." She gazed up at him and her eyes were asking a question.

He answered it. "I want you, Brooke. I'd like to spend the night. Give you a massage, make slow, gentle love, sleep with you in my arms. But only if you want that."

She nodded quickly, as if she'd already considered the possibility. "Yes."

And then she was in his arms again, but this time it was very different from when they'd greeted each other on the porch. This time it was hungry.

They kissed greedily and their hands were all over each other, wrenching at clothing, trying to find bare skin. "Maybe we won't start with the massage," he said, his voice coming out rough and shaky, and he figured the lovemaking wouldn't be all that slow and gentle. At least not the first time.

"Let's go to the bedroom." She freed herself from his grasp and reached for his hand.

Upstairs, he clicked on the bedside lamp. The room hadn't changed, except that she'd hung the watercolor he'd given her. He smiled at that, then forgot all about it when Brooke pulled her T-shirt over her head, revealing one of her pretty, lacy bras.

When he pulled his own tee off, she ran a hand over his side where the bullet had torn his flesh. "It healed well," she commented.

"A scar to remind me of you. Did I tell you when I first came to and saw you leaning over me I thought I'd died and you were an angel?"

"An angel?" Her face lit with laughter.

"And I was right," he mused, smoothing his hand over her

chest and down to touch a breast through the lace of her bra. Then he reached behind her back and undid the clasp. Slowly he pulled her bra away from her body, let it drop to the floor, and cupped the soft weight of her breasts in both hands.

"When you first opened your mouth you let out such a string of curses, I thought you were the devil," she said. "Then you pulled a gun on me and confirmed it."

"What do you think now?"

"You're just a man, Jake, and I'm just a woman. But together we're something special. And our baby will be someone special."

He undid the fly-front zipper of her khaki skirt and slipped his hand inside to curve around her belly. Just inches from his fingers, their baby was growing. Their child might have bipolar disorder. It might be dark like him or fair like her, a boy or a girl. Whatever, it definitely would be someone special. Now that he was with Brooke again, he knew her decision to have the baby had been inevitable.

She wriggled her hips and her skirt began to slide down. She reached over to place a firm hand across the front of his jeans, where his hard-on strained the fabric. "I want you, Jake. I want to make love to you while I'm pregnant with our child."

He did too. At first he'd just thought it was his normal lust for Brooke, but now he realized there was an added appeal in knowing she was carrying their child.

It was a bizarre, scary thought and he wasn't about to analyze it. Instead he helped her undo the zipper of his jeans.

She put her hands in each side, at the waist, and eased the jeans down his hips, then hooked her fingers into the band of his briefs so they would go along for the ride. Pausing there, she teased, "Not going to stop me this time?"

"What would you have done if I hadn't stopped you that first day?"

"Died of embarrassment. And lust."

"So you were lusting after my body even then," he joked, flattered and aroused at the thought.

"From the moment I saw you. Even though I figured you were the devil incarnate." Finally, she took up where she'd left off, inching his jeans and underwear down so that his erection sprang free.

"A churchgoing lady like you isn't supposed to be turned on by the devil."

"Mmm." She ran her tongue around her lips. "I guess I must be very wicked." She continued to tug his jeans and briefs down until they hit the floor.

He bent to pull off his boots and socks, the tangled clothing, then straightened to stand naked in front of her. "Then have your wicked way with me, woman."

"I fully intend to."

Her fingers wrapped around him and he groaned with pleasure. Too much pleasure. He pushed her away. "Slow down or I'll come."

"Then we'd just have to do it again." Suddenly she gave a little frown. "Condoms? I mean, not for pregnancy but . . ."

He felt a moment's hurt. Irrational hurt. "I'm clean, Brooke. And I haven't been with anyone since you."

Her eyes sparkled. "This'll be something new!"

His hurt vanished in a flash. The idea of really coming inside her was mind-blowing. No barriers, just his body and hers. He scooped her up and placed her gently on the bed. "The second time will be slow and gentle. Right now, I just need to be inside you."

She lifted her arms to him. "Then stop talking and come on in."

He did exactly as she said.

It was over in about two minutes flat. But her body convulsed around him, and she cried out his name on a high, joyous note.

Afterward he stayed inside her—what luxury, not having

to pull out and deal with a condom—and shifted their bodies so they were on their sides and his weight was off her. He ran a hand down her side, wondering how her skin could possibly be so soft. "You're so beautiful."

"You're not bad yourself." She tangled her fingers in his chest hair and tugged gently.

He leaned closer and touched his lips to hers. The kiss started out lazy but grew like wildfire and he hardened again inside her. He moved a little and she whimpered and pushed back against him, taking him deeper. He encircled her with his arms and shifted position again, so he was lying on his back and she was astride him.

"Take me, babe," he murmured. "Take whatever you want. Show me how to please you."

"You always please me." But she accepted his invitation and began to rise and fall slowly, sliding up so just the tip of him remained inside her, then pushing down again so she encompassed him fully. Grinding her body into his for that extra bit of friction.

He tried to keep his hips on the bed, tried not to thrust into her, tried to let her control their rhythm.

She leaned over him, hands gripping his waist, breasts bouncing.

He captured those breasts in his hands and lifted himself until he could suckle one of her nipples.

She moaned and moved faster until her body tightened and clenched around him. Then she cried out and her internal muscles contracted in spasms around him as she climaxed.

He fought for control, waited until her eyes opened and focused on his.

"Mmm," she sighed. "So good."

Then he took her up again, plunging into her, lifting both their bodies off the bed as he reached into her very center, and, finally, when she cried his name and spasmed again, he let himself come.

Chapter Twenty-Four

The morning light woke Brooke, as it always did. And, as she always did, she gazed across at the watercolor Jake had given her and smiled. Then she remembered.

Yes, he was still there. Curled on his side facing her, his body covered to the waist with a sheet.

His hair had grown and she was glad. That gypsy look suited him. So did the dark stubble on his face. She touched her own chin, remembering how surprisingly soft that hair was.

What a precious gift this had been, another night with Jake.

What would happen now? Would he go back to Vancouver and out of her life? Again? Was that what she wanted?

It would be easier. Seeing him again confirmed how much she loved him.

This marriage idea of his was crazy. He didn't really mean it, did he?

They needed to talk. Later. Right now, she wanted to seduce him. She lifted the sheet that covered his lower body.

* * *

Brooke made a breakfast of omelets and toast, and Jake dove into it with relish. He sure did work up an appetite when he was with her.

She took a small bite and asked, "Are you going back to Vancouver today?"

"Have to. They're sending me out on another assignment."

"But you just got home from the last one."

"That's my life, Brooke."

After a moment, she said, "I know. You and Jamal. At least you take care of each other."

"This one isn't dangerous; it's just a task force. And Jamal's not involved. He's taking a few days off. Visiting Karen."

"Oh, really. That's very interesting. Good for them. I suppose." She frowned. "I guess Karen knows what she's getting into, what kind of work Jamal does."

"Yeah, and it's not like her work is exactly safe either."

He thought about Jamal's basketball dreams. Maybe his colleague would move up here, take up with Karen and her dog. It'd take half the fun out of his own job, not working with Jamal. "Your letter said that Karen's been talking about him?"

She smiled. "You know, I barely knew Karen, and I've always been wary of the police. But now we go for coffee all the time. I think we're . . . becoming friends." Her voice softened on that last word.

Jake smiled too. Oh yeah, Brooke was changing, if she could let herself trust in friendship.

Her smile became a grin. "To answer your question, yes, she's been known to mention Jamal."

Looked like his partner really might be heading for a driveway with a basketball hoop.

And Brooke was heading for . . . what? He doubted she'd be teaching their child how to play basketball. She deserved to find a good husband—though for some reason that thought didn't please Jake. Finding one would be harder, though, with a baby.

Evan would be there. The kid would have a man in his—or her—life.

Strange, not knowing what sex the baby was. Made it harder to envision the kid. Not that he really wanted to be doing that.

He polished off the delicious omelet and asked the question that needed to be asked. "So what do you say about getting married?"

Brooke gave a little jerk when he asked the question, and he guessed he had kind of tossed it out of the blue again. But then she gazed steadily into his eyes across the table and said, "I appreciate the offer. But I can't imagine swearing those vows knowing that they were a lie. That we were only marrying to make the baby legitimate, and we'd divorce afterward."

Divorce. Such a harsh word. People divorced when they no longer cared for each other, and he couldn't imagine not caring for Brooke. So . . . maybe they could marry and not divorce? See each other when he was between assignments? It'd be nice to come home to her and her house rather than his lonely, dingy apartment.

But no, she'd hate that kind of life. Hate worrying about him when he was off on a U/C job. He couldn't do it to her.

"Don't have to decide right now," he muttered. "But you'll start showing. If we're going to do it, we might want to do it before then."

"Not until I've passed the first trimester and we know everything's okay. Otherwise it would be pointless."

He didn't want to get married. Not one bit. Yet words like *divorce* and *pointless* were painful little stabs in his heart, even though he knew she didn't mean them that way. He got up to pour himself a refill of coffee, and leaned his hip against the kitchen counter. There was another question he had to ask. "You're not seriously worried about the kid having bipolar?"

She'd been toying with her food. Now she put down her fork and gazed across at him. "Yes, I'm seriously worried."

"Oh. Uh . . ."

"We'd be on the lookout for symptoms so, if the child had it, the illness would be diagnosed early. But not everyone responds to treatment as well as I do. The bottom line is, this baby could suffer a severe form of the illness that isn't amenable to treatment."

Crap. He wished he hadn't asked, hated to see the worry on her face. But she should be able to talk to someone about these things. Besides, as the kid's father, he had a responsibility too. "If it's any help," he told her, "I don't know of any genetic problems on my side."

"That's good. We'll hope the baby gets your healthy genes rather than my unhealthy ones."

He couldn't argue with that. He hoped the kid looked like her, though. Especially if it was a girl. If it was a boy—well, he had to admit it was kind of a kick to think of his own features replicated on a little-kid face. But looks were secondary; health was what mattered. "You're positive you want to have this baby?"

Brooke picked up her tea mug, then put it down without drinking. "I wouldn't have made a decision to get pregnant. But this pregnancy happened, so it was a different decision. I started out thinking about terminating a pregnancy, then suddenly I was picking baby names."

She touched her abdomen. "This little guy or gal had become a child to me. My, our, child. I loved it and had to give this child its chance."

He knew what she meant. He thought of it as a child too.

A child he might never know. He cleared his throat. "You're brave, facing the risks."

"Says the man who risks his life every day. Jake, there are all kinds of risks. We each decide which ones we're prepared to take. I couldn't do what you do. I couldn't even be married— I mean really married, not just in name—to someone who does what you do. But nor could I deny our child his or her chance to have a life. Not a perfect life, I'm sure, but a life with more joy than sorrow." Her eyes narrowed in a challenge. "Do you disagree?"

"Nope. I just think you're one hell of a gutsy lady. And our kid is damned lucky to have you as a mother."

She ducked her head. "As long as I stay sober. And keep responding to the lithium."

He reached across the table and lifted her chin so he could gaze into her eyes. "You'll stay sober. And if the lithium stops working, you and your doctor will find something else that does. I know you, Brooke Kincaid. If I could pick any woman in the world to be the mother of my child, you'd be that woman."

Her eyes flooded and he said, "Oh, hell, don't cry."

She brushed a hand across her eyes. "Sorry. Crazy hormones. But honestly, Jake, that's the nicest thing anyone's ever said to me."

He shrugged. All he'd said was the truth.

"Eat your breakfast," he ordered. He picked up her empty mug. "Want some coffee?"

"No, I'm sticking to herbal tea for the duration."

He leaned down to kiss the top of her head. "See? A good mom already."

Her teapot sat on the counter, draped in one of those knitted things to keep it warm. He poured tea into her mug, brought it back to her, and took his seat across the table. "Brooke? Whether or not we get married, I want to help support the kid."

She pressed her lips together, then released them. "You don't have to. I have it under control. Kate will let me bring the baby in to work, so I won't even have to take much time off. And I make decent money. Not a lot, but life isn't that expensive in Caribou Crossing."

Yeah, he figured she'd have thought it through, and he knew she had Evan, Jess, and Kate to fall back on if she ran into problems. But that wasn't the point. "Look, this is my kid too. We made him—her—together. I want to do my bit."

She'd been watching his face carefully as he spoke. "Think about it some more, Jake. If you still want to, of course you can help." She glanced at her watch. "I need to get to work."

"And I have to hit the road. Brooke, I'm not going to change my mind. I'll write you a check when I get home. I'll send one every month." He'd buy life insurance too, and name Brooke as the beneficiary. But he wouldn't tell her, or she'd worry even more about him.

They both stood slowly, and walked outside without speaking. He put on his old leather jacket and shuffled his helmet from hand to hand. "It was good seeing you."

"You too, Jake. Such a nice surprise." She was smiling but he saw a shadow in her eyes. He'd come because he cared for her, yet he'd given her more stress.

"Let me know about getting married. Call. I'll have my cell with me this time. This assignment should only be a couple weeks; then I'm due some time off. You could invite your family and friends, we could do it up properly. Make people think it was for real."

In her garden, with all those flowers, and one of those flower-woven arches set up. Brooke in a dress that matched those tropical ocean eyes. Flowers in her hair. Jess as matron of honor, Robin as bridesmaid, Evan to give the bride away.

In less time than it took to blink, the whole picture formed in his head.

"Oh, Jake," she said.

He did blink, and the wedding scene disappeared.

"I don't think I'm going to change my mind, but you're

so sweet to offer." She leaned forward and touched her lips to his.

Sweet. He wasn't sweet. He was crazy about her and he'd knocked her up. He was doing his best to cope, like any decent guy would.

"Drive safely," she said. Then she winked. "Stay out of the path of speeding bullets."

Surprised, he gave a quick laugh, then sobered. "You take care too, Brooke. Let me know if you need anything."

She smiled but didn't nod or say yes. Then she turned and walked toward her house.

He watched her as he put on his helmet and kicked the bike to life.

When she reached the porch she turned, her face shaded by the overhang so he couldn't see her expression, and gave a brief wave.

He waved back and drove away, suspecting he wouldn't be hearing from her. She was independent. And wary of letting herself get too involved with someone like him.

Clever woman.

Brooke let the tears run down her face unchecked as she tidied up the kitchen. No, she couldn't marry Jake Brannon. If she didn't love him she might consider it, but loving him would make it far too tough.

She didn't like highs and lows. They reminded her of her manias and her depressions. Last night she'd been on such a high, seeing Jake again, touching him, making love. And now he was gone and the bottom had fallen out of her world.

In the bathroom she pressed a cold, damp cloth to her swollen eyes until she could face the reflection that looked back at her from the mirror. Normally she didn't wear much make-up, but today was definitely a day for it.

Her best efforts weren't good enough, because Kate gave her an extralong hug and said, "You okay, hon?"

"Hormones. I'm fine." She debated telling her friend about Jake's visit but knew she'd start to cry again.

Her second customer of the morning was Dave Cousins. She had a soft spot for Dave. He'd been her first customer back when Jessica had introduced her to Kate and Kate had given her the job.

Since his fiancée, Anita, had died of cancer, he'd been quiet and subdued. Typically Brooke tried to draw him out, talking about Robin, the Heritage Committee, and Riders Boot Camp, since he was on the board of directors too. Today she had no energy for chat, so she clipped away in silence.

When she was finished Dave said, "Got any plans for lunch?"

"Lunch?" She wouldn't feel like eating but she had to, for the sake of her own health as well as the baby's. "Not really."

"Come on over to the hotel and I'll treat you."

His undemanding company was exactly what she needed. "Thanks. I'll see you in a couple of hours."

When Brooke walked over to the Wild Rose Inn at noon, the summer sun was hiding behind clouds, a counterpoint to her gloomy mood. It was all she could do to force a smile and exchange a few words with Madisun Joe, a local girl Evan had sponsored to go to business school in Vancouver— removing her from an abusive family situation in the process. Madisun was back for the summer, working in Evan's office part-time and also helping out at Boots. She'd turned into a confident young woman who wasn't about to take any guff from her dad.

Evan had been abused by his dad. Physically. Brooke knew that her own parenting had constituted emotional abuse. Yet

Evan had turned into a man who, rather than replicating that dysfunctional pattern, would help someone else combat it.

He was a son to be proud of, and she did have lots to smile about.

When she stepped into the lobby of the Wild Rose and saw Dave behind the desk, she gave him a genuine smile.

He smiled back, made a quick phone call, and one of his staff came to replace him.

"I reserved us a window booth." He led Brooke to the dining room.

"Dining in style," she commented. This room was quieter than the pub where she'd gone line dancing with Jake, and had a touch of old-fashioned elegance in the dark wood, brass, and leather. In the pub, the staff wore informal Western wear; here, they wore costumes modeled on clothing worn at gold rush hotels in the 1860s.

As she and Dave walked through the room, they said hello to a number of people. The air was filled with delicious aromas and now she did have an appetite. "Something smells great."

"Mitch's specials today are chicken pot pie and quiche with smoked salmon and chives. They both look terrific."

She'd had scrambled eggs for breakfast, forcing herself to eat. "I'll go for the pot pie."

"Me too." Dave raised a finger and Karin, the waitress, came over to take their order. When she was gone Dave said, "How are you feeling?"

"Good." In fact, better by the moment. Now that she was getting over the depression caused by Jake's departure, she realized a couple of truths. He hadn't ignored her letter about the baby; in fact, he cared enough about her that he'd hopped on his bike and come to her the moment he got it. And he cared enough about her and the baby to offer something he knew she valued highly: respectability. In the past, she'd won respectability all by herself. She could do it again, and it would be easier than a fake marriage to a man who didn't love her. But she had to do what Jake had done, and consider her baby's best interests.

"You don't look so good," Dave said bluntly.

"You sure know how to flatter a girl," she teased. Without lying, she could tell him she'd had a rough night. But Dave was almost part of the family. He and Jess had remained good friends and, even more surprisingly, he and Evan had become pals. Besides, the whole town would know once she was in her second trimester and starting to show.

She glanced around to make sure no one was near them, then leaned across the table. "I'm not sick, I'm pregnant."

His jaw dropped and his eyes went round. "Preg—"

His voice was too loud and she cut him off. "Dave! I'm not ready to tell the world."

"Sorry." He lowered his voice to a whisper. "Really? Are you sure?"

"I've known for a few weeks, and I'm really happy about having a baby. I've told Jess, Evan, and Robin, Kate as well, and sworn them to secrecy."

An expression of hurt crossed his handsome face. In that instant she realized something. Here was another person who considered himself her friend.

She reached across to touch his hand. "I didn't mean to shut you out, but there are so many risks in the first trimester. I didn't want everyone to know, and to worry, if I ended up"—she gulped—"losing the baby." But, each day, she felt more confident that this baby was going to be just fine.

He squeezed her hand, then released it. "I understand, Brooke. And thanks for telling me now. But wow, that's a surprise, to put it mildly." Then he scowled. "So, where's the Arnold Pitt cop? Did the jerk run out on you?"

"How did you know it was him?"

Chapter Twenty-Five

Dave shrugged. "There was something between the two of you."

"Oh, come on. You thought he was my cousin."

"Several times removed, I figured. Your feelings for each other weren't cousinly."

Brooke couldn't help grinning. "No one else picked up on anything."

He studied her affectionately. "I know love when I see it, Brooke."

Love. It warmed her immeasurably to think that this perceptive man had interpreted Jake's feelings for her as love.

"So," Dave demanded, "where is he?"

Before Brooke could respond, Karin arrived with their lunch: chicken pies in individual ceramic casseroles, and a colorful salad in a big bowl so they could serve themselves. Brooke poked a knife into the golden crust of the pie and inhaled the aroma of chicken, onions, carrots, herbs. Oh yes, she was ravenous. She took up the salad servers and dished a sizable helping of salad onto Dave's side plate, then her own.

Between bites she filled him in—up until last night. She gave him even more details than she'd felt comfortable sharing with her son and Jessica. There was something about Dave;

he was such an easy person to talk to. And she appreciated having a male perspective.

When they had both polished off their pies, Brooke succumbed to Karin's recommendation of Miner's Mud Pie—a delicious concoction with a chocolate wafer crumb crust and an ice cream filling topped with chocolate sauce and whipped cream. When the waitress went to get it, Brooke patted her stomach. "Sometimes this little creature robs me of my appetite but mostly I really do feel like I'm eating for two."

"You're going to be a great mom, Brooke."

She gazed at him affectionately, and made a decision. "Can I tell you something, and ask you to keep it a secret?"

One corner of his mouth tipped upward. "You're feeling guilty for keeping secrets from me before?"

"Maybe. But I'd value your opinion. I don't want to tell Evan and Jessica, at least not yet. I already know what Evan would say and I don't want to be pressured."

"I'm intrigued. And of course I won't tell anyone if you don't want me to."

"Jake asked me to marry him."

Dave didn't seem surprised. "Well then . . ." He paused as Karin placed the pie in front of Brooke and gave him the cappuccino he'd ordered.

"He was here last night," Brooke said. "I'd written him about the baby but he'd been out of town and only got the letter yesterday. Anyhow, we talked about it and he said maybe we should get married."

He raised an eyebrow. "Should?"

"For the sake of the baby. And my reputation. He'd marry me, make the baby legitimate, give both of us his name if I wanted. Later, we'd get divorced."

"A marriage of convenience?" He sounded offended. "Gimme a break, those went out with the Dark Ages."

She forked up a piece of pie, then put the bite down again,

untasted. "You were wrong about the love," she said softly, sadly. "Jake doesn't love me."

"You love him?"

"Yes, but it takes two."

"Oh, Brooke." He poked a spoon into the foam on top of his cappuccino, stirred the coffee, then gazed up at her. "Wait a minute. I saw the way the man looked at you when he thought no one was watching. It looked like love to me. Maybe he doesn't realize it yet."

"I know he cares. Maybe it's what you and I would call love. But he's not ready to believe in love." She finally ate that first bite of pie, but it didn't taste as sweet as she'd expected.

"If you build it, they will come."

"What are you talking about?"

"You know that movie *Field of Dreams*? A voice spoke to this guy, telling him that if he built a ball field, the players would come. And they did."

"You're saying, if we build a marriage, the love will come?"

"Yup."

What a tantalizing notion. But that was all it was. A fairy tale. "I don't think so. Jake isn't talking about living here; he'd just marry me, then go back to work. He's always undercover, risking his life. A real marriage doesn't fit with his life. And he loves his work; he loves danger." She bit her lip and told Dave the rest of it. "I do love him, but even if he loved me back, I couldn't handle being married to him. I wouldn't ask him to give up his job, but I couldn't live with the constant worry. I'm strong, but not that strong."

He nodded slowly. "I can relate to that."

Brooke knew he could. Since he'd lost Anita he was Mr. Cautious with the people he cared about.

"What's your alternative?" he asked. "Never see him again?"

"I guess so," she said sadly. "That's probably easiest— best—for both of us. He says he wants to provide financial support, so I guess he'd just send checks, or set up a trust fund or something."

"How could a man not want to see his own child?" Dave looked utterly baffled.

"Maybe because his parents never taught him about love. They made unreasonable demands; they didn't ever show that they loved him. He couldn't wait to escape from them."

Dave stirred his coffee some more and didn't look at her.

She winced. "You're thinking about Evan. Mo and I didn't teach him about love."

He shrugged. "Sorry, I didn't want to say it."

"It's true." She nodded fiercely. "We were horrible parents, probably worse than Jake's. And Evan figured out about love all by himself when he met Jessica again. She taught him how to love; then he opened his heart to Robin, and to me as well."

"So, if the right woman comes along, even a diehard like Jake can learn. And I think you're the right woman."

"Maybe I do too. But Jake doesn't." Then she squared her shoulders. "And it's just as well. His work would drive me crazy. I like my peaceful routine. I need it."

"I understand how you'd worry about his work. But as for the routine . . . You needed that when you were first recovering, but you're better now. That's why you can handle having a baby. You can bet having a child isn't going to be peaceful and routine. I'd also point out, your routine went out the window when Jake was in town, and you did okay."

"Except for getting pregnant." She grinned. "Yes, I did okay. And I'll do fine with the baby. But there's no way I could move to Vancouver and be married to Jake when he'd always be off on dangerous assignments. I'm a lot stronger than I used to be, but I'm not that strong." She took another bite of pie, this time being sure to get lots of chocolate sauce and whipped cream. Mmm, that was better.

"No chance he'd move up here?"

"He's talking about divorce in the same breath as marriage."

She put down her fork. "But he's also offering legitimacy for the baby. I have to think of what's best for my baby. What am I going to do?"

Dave frowned. "Wouldn't it tear you apart? Loving him, being married to him, yet knowing it would end?" His voice was soft and caring.

A hormonal surge brought moisture to her eyes. "Yes. But if it helped the baby . . ."

"Legitimacy isn't such a big deal these days. This town knows you, Brooke. The new and improved you. Most folks aren't going to judge. If some do, ignore them."

"That's how I was planning to do it, before Jake showed up last night."

"You're the mom. If something's bad for you, how can it be good for your baby?"

"Hmm." She glanced past him, musing on that. Her gaze hit on the antique pendulum clock. "Oh gosh, I need to get back." She shoved the unfinished pie away. "Thanks, Dave. I really appreciate being able to talk to you."

"Any time." He caught her hand as she stood up. "I mean that, Brooke."

"I know. And the same goes for you." She squeezed his hand. "Thanks for being my friend. You can't imagine how much it means to me."

Jake came out of an IBET meeting in Seattle headquarters to find that he'd missed a call from Brooke.

On voice mail, she said, "Thanks for the check, Jake."

He'd mailed one from Vancouver last week, before driving down to his latest assignment.

"And," she went on, sounding awkward and formal, "for the, uh, proposal. But I really can't marry you. The baby and I will do fine on our own."

He felt a pang. He was glad she was strong—it was one of

the things that drew him to her—but for some reason it hurt that she didn't need him.

"If it's all right with you," she said briskly, "I'll show you as father on the birth certificate and give the baby your last name. I'd like our child to have something of yours. Beyond, you know, your genes."

He would too.

There was a long pause and then she said, very softly, and not businesslike at all, "Bye, Jake."

She was moving on with her life. Without him. "Bye, Brooke," he murmured as he put the phone down.

He'd continue to send checks. For the child he'd never see. The child who might look like him, or like Brooke. The child who might ride horses, play basketball, love gardening. Want a motorbike rather than a car. Surely, when the baby was born, Brooke would at least tell him if it was Nick or Nicki.

He slammed his fist down on his borrowed desk. Everyone in the room looked up, then quickly away. Yeah, he hadn't been the easiest guy to work with these last few days.

Maybe things would level out now that he knew Brooke's decision. Except he was convinced she'd made the wrong one. She was making things harder on herself and the baby. Why did she have to be so damned independent!

It was one thing to make decisions for herself, but now she was making decisions for their baby. Brooke might think she and the baby would do just fine, but what if the kid had a different idea? What if the kid wanted a dad, not just a surrogate like Evan or that Dave Cousins, whom Brooke thought was the nicest man in town? He was damned sure Brooke wasn't going to drink again, but what if the lithium stopped working and her bipolar disorder came back? What if their child turned out to have bipolar?

He slumped back in his chair. What-ifs. There were so many of them. Life had become so complicated.

But Brooke was trying to uncomplicate it for him. She'd

given him every opportunity to opt out of her life, and the baby's. He should take her up on it.

Hell, he couldn't stop mixing into Sapphire's life. What were the chances he could leave Brooke and the baby alone? She'd been his woman when he was in Caribou Crossing, and damned if he didn't still think of her that way. He wanted to make everything right, easy, happy for her. And for their child.

But what did he have to offer them? He knew his job scared Brooke. She valued and needed stability.

He closed his eyes. What would be best for Brooke would be to marry a man like Dave Cousins. A stable, decent, nice man who would make her a perfect husband and be a perfect father to her child.

The best thing for Jake's child would be to have another man as its father. And the best thing for his woman would be to marry someone else.

His gut clenched and twisted. He barely made it to the men's room before he threw up. As he hovered over the toilet he swore he'd never again eat greasy fish and chips from a sidewalk vendor. Food poisoning. It had to be food poisoning.

Or was it the thought of Brooke making love with another man? Looking up at him out of those dazzley blue-green eyes and telling him she loved him?

On his way back to his desk he grabbed a tin of soda from the fridge and then, needing to hear a friendly voice, dialed Jamal in Vancouver.

"Had coffee with your CI, Sapphire," Jamal said.

"Oh yeah? She pass along anything good?"

"No tips this time. She'd been looking for you but settled for me. Wanted to talk about a program you mentioned to her, that work-study for people who want to get into the hospitality industry."

"You're kidding. She's actually thinking of getting off the street?"

"Says what happened to Anika Janssen got her thinking."

"Good for her. I'll see her as soon as I get back."

"Yeah, I told her that. Oh, and other news that'll interest you. Miller got roughed up in jail. He fired his first lawyer and is shopping around for another. Won't do him any good, though. We're putting together a real strong case."

Henry Miller had been sent down to Vancouver, where the judge had denied him bail, figuring there was a strong probability he'd use his connections to skip the country and never show up for trial. The man would be sitting in prison for months until his case came to trial.

When they finished talking about work, Jake said, "How was your visit with Karen?"

"Great." Jamal sounded self-satisfied.

"Did more than talk your way through the nights?"

"Ain't saying."

"Don't have to." He was happy for Jamal. Really he was. "You see Brooke?"

"Went line dancing."

"Hell, you did go line dancing! Wait a minute. You saying Brooke was there?" He scowled at the phone. Should she be shaking the baby up like that?

"She looked like a pro."

"Who was she dancing with?"

"I hear jealousy. Hmm, let me see. Just about every guy in the room. Couple of teenagers, the geezer who teaches the class, the guy who owns the hotel. Danced a couple with me too."

Damn. Everyone but Jake had been holding Brooke in their arms. "She's okay?"

"Not pining away since you're gone? Nah, she looked just fine. Kind of glowing, actually."

"She ask about me?"

"Not so's you'd notice. You're gonna lose her, man, if you don't do something quick."

Jake hadn't told Jamal about Brooke's pregnancy nor about his trip the previous week, much less his proposal. They'd never talked about that kind of stuff—not that there had ever been that kind of stuff to talk about before—but now he wouldn't mind his partner's take on the situation. He sure as hell didn't want to do it over the phone, though.

"Goin' back this weekend," Jamal said. "Any message?"

"You're going back so soon?"

"There're advantages to a desk job with regular hours. Yeah, I'll fly up late Friday."

"Have fun."

"Could ya sound like you mean it? Hey, if you want to see Brooke, just go do it."

"I don't want to see her." It was an out-and-out lie and he knew Jamal knew it.

"How long you gonna be stuck with the IBET?"

Jake glanced around the room. A man and a woman were clicking away on computers, two men stood gesturing at a chart on the wall, an undercover gal with dreadlocks and piercings was slumped in a chair drinking coffee. "I could leave now and they'd never miss me. I could be as much help in Vancouver, working by phone and Internet."

"So come back. And come up to Caribou Crossing this weekend." When Jake didn't answer, Jamal changed the topic. "Say, man, you seriously bummed about me giving up U/C work?"

"Hell, no. You can be replaced."

Jamal laughed. "Don't I know it." Then his voice sobered. "Life doesn't stand still. We've been doing it a long time. Lucky we're still alive."

That was true. But it was more than luck; it was how they watched each other's backs. It wouldn't be the same without Jamal.

Hell, it hadn't been the same for a while, not since Jamal took the promotion. And in Winnipeg, even though they'd been together on the street again, Jamal was talking about Karen half the time and his own thoughts were with Brooke.

Hadn't stopped thinking about her since then, either. The damned woman had taken up permanent residence in his mind. Or was it his heart?

Chapter Twenty-Six

Brooke woke on Saturday smiling. This was it. Five years of being sober.

She hadn't told Evan and Jessica. They'd make a fuss, and she didn't want them doing that in front of Robin. Yes, the girl knew her grandmother used to have a problem with alcohol but she didn't need to be reminded of it. Brooke wanted Robin to view sobriety as something normal, not an achievement to be celebrated.

But it was. For her, it was a huge achievement.

Sunny rose from where he'd been sleeping on the pillow beside her, stretched, and came to plunk his heavy weight on her chest. She scratched him around his ears and under his chin, then let her hand drift to rest on her belly. "Good morning, Nick-Nicki," she murmured.

Sunlight filtered through the curtains and touched the watercolor Jake had given her. She loved the joyous abandon of the garden in the painting. It inspired her to experiment with her own garden, rather than be as neat and formal as in the past.

After breakfast she'd head off to Greenbrier Nursery. She might pick up some sweet pea seeds. Sweet peas were about as messy as you could get, but their colors and fragrance were lovely.

There was something miraculous about planting seeds or bulbs, seeing the little green shoots come up, eventually watching buds open.

Having a baby was even more miraculous.

Humming, she rose and pulled on her robe.

As she was having breakfast, the phone rang. It was her A.A. sponsor, calling to congratulate her. Later, as she was returning from the nursery, Tonia, the girl she sponsored, phoned for the same reason. These people knew what she'd gone through, which made their congratulations particularly meaningful.

After lunch Brooke gardened, then took a nap. When she rose she began dinner preparations, humming along to the radio as she worked. She'd recently learned how to make homemade pizza, and today was trying out a vegetarian one with feta cheese and olives. If it worked, she'd make it for Robin next time the girl came over.

On the radio, Glen Campbell was singing "Gentle on My Mind." The song always reminded her of Jake. Yes, so often he was there on the back roads and rivers of her memory. Just there, keeping her and their baby company. Keeping her heart warm.

In the beginning with Jake, she'd thought she was creating sexy memories, and yes, she certainly had those, but she had other ones too: Jake in her kitchen, riding and laughing with Robin, helping in the garden, reading together. Ironic that the big tough undercover cop, the sexy guy on the Harley, had created memories that rested so gently on her mind.

She was slipping the pizza in the oven when the door-bell rang.

When she opened the door, she gaped in amazement at the huge bouquet of flowers. "Oh, my gosh!" The creamy blooms and green leaves filled the doorway and she couldn't even see who was holding them. Below, there were Western boots that looked new, and well-worn jeans hugging fine legs. Above, the top of a black cowboy hat.

"Happy five years."

She'd know that voice anywhere. "Jake!"

"Can I bring these in?"

"Of course." She stepped back and let him come into the house. He'd remembered her five-year anniversary.

As he moved past her, she took him in. This was another version of Jake, looking far more at home in Western wear than Arnold ever had. Under the sexy cowboy hat, his hair was longer, tousled, and her fingers itched to thread their way through it.

She concentrated instead on the flowers. Beautiful, but she didn't recognize them. The exotic, lightly spiced scent was familiar, yet she couldn't identify it. "What are they?"

"Plumeria. Found a florist in Vancouver who could get them."

Plumeria, like her shampoo. "You . . . you got me plumeria and came all the way up here to congratulate me on making five years?"

"Not exactly." He was walking toward the kitchen and said the words over his shoulder.

Oh. So he hadn't come just to see her. He'd probably had to come up on police business. Still, it was incredible he'd remembered her anniversary. Once, he'd asked her how long she'd been sober, and she'd told him to the day. Once.

She followed him into the kitchen, found a large vase, and arranged the exotic blossoms. "How on earth did you manage to carry these on your bike?"

"No bike this trip. Rented a little plane and flew up."

She'd forgotten he was a pilot.

"Gonna give me a proper welcome now?" he asked, and opened his arms.

She went into them, happy but confused. When she'd left

the message on his voice mail, she really hadn't expected to see him again.

He hugged her tight but she sensed something was on his mind. His embrace wasn't the usual passionate one, but almost perfunctory. Her heart sank. It seemed their days of being lovers had passed. She told herself it was better this way; look how she'd cried the last time he'd left. Now perhaps they could start to establish a casual, friendly relationship.

And then another thought struck her. Maybe he was going to challenge her for custody of the baby. Perhaps he'd decided she wouldn't make a fit mother.

He released her and moved restlessly around the kitchen.

She studied him anxiously and then took a deep breath, a slow one, then let it out. No, this was Jake. He would never take her child away from her.

"Are you hungry? I've got pizza in the oven. It'll be ready in twenty minutes."

That stopped him. "Pizza? Homemade? I didn't know you made pizza."

"I've just learned."

He gave a quick laugh. "That's great. I love pizza." He paced away then back toward her, then away again.

Brooke pressed her hands to her lower back. "I've been standing cooking for a while. I need to sit down. Come into the living room."

When they got there, she sat in her reading chair. He tossed his black hat on the coffee table, strode across the room, and examined the bookcase. "Should've brought your book back. I finished it."

"Jake! I told you to keep the stupid book. Why are you here?"

"Oh. Well." He fished in his jeans pocket, took something out, and gripped it in his hand. Tightly. Then he strode over to her and thrust his fisted hand toward her. "I want to marry you." He unclenched his fingers and a small velvet box dropped into her lap.

She gaped at it. "But I said no."

He squatted in front of her. "That was a different question. Before, I said we could get married, and maybe we should. Now I'm saying I want to."

"For the baby."

"Yeah, but mostly for me, and I hope for you. Brooke, you once said you loved me. Is it still true?" His smoky eyes were a deep, intense mauve as they stared into hers.

She could never lie to Jake. "I still love you."

His lips formed a nervous smile. "Well, I love you too."

"You . . . love me?" she said cautiously. He'd spoken the words but she couldn't tell if he really meant them.

"You, and the baby too. I want us to be . . ." He gulped and forced out the words. "A family."

Her heart lurched. "It would be a huge step. For both of us."

"Man, do I know that!" The words exploded out of him as he rose to his feet. He pulled the other chair over so he could sit facing her, their knees almost touching. "But it drives me crazy thinking about not being with you and the baby."

The baby. Although he said he loved her, it was really the baby he was thinking of.

"What if we got married and"—she gulped, because she hated to think of the possibility—"there was no baby? If I miscarried, or the amniocentesis showed up some awful problem?"

"Then we'd have each other. I love you, Brooke." It was the second time he'd said the words, and he sounded more convincing. "It's the baby that got me thinking seriously, but then I realized I do love you. I've never felt anything like this before, so it took me a while to figure it out."

He took her hands gently in his. "If I never have kids, that'd be okay by me. But it wouldn't be okay to live my life without you. And if you and I have a child, then that's great.

I don't know much about being a good father, but I figure you'll help me learn."

Her heart fluttered as if a butterfly were trapped in her chest. Good heavens, she was actually starting to take him seriously. And oh, the idea of a loving marriage with Jake was so enticing.

But no, it could never work.

"I'm sorry, Jake," she said softly. She squeezed his hands, then released them. "I do love you but I'm not strong enough to handle worrying about you. You go away for days, weeks at a time, and your life's in danger." She remembered what that one day had been like, when he and Karen had set the trap for Sergeant Miller, and she imagined every day being like that. "I'd go crazy. And I'd be all alone in Vancouver, with my family and friends up here in Caribou Crossing." She'd just discovered family and friends. How could she be separated from them now?

"I'll move here."

Her eyes widened, staring at his familiar face. She couldn't believe she'd heard correctly. "Here? You, in Caribou Crossing?"

"Don't you see the boots and Resistol?"

A Resistol, not a Stetson. Again, he'd listened. "I see them. I'm not sure what they mean."

"Caribou Crossing's a nice town. You showed me that. I won't do undercover work anymore." He scraped his hands through his hair. "I'll be honest. I don't know if I can give up police work completely. There's Miller's job; I might be able to get that. I've passed the sergeant's exam so I could apply. Or security consulting, private investigation. Jamal and I might even—but that depends on him and Karen."

No, this had to be a dream. Brooke squeezed her eyes shut, then opened them again.

Jake was still there, looking confused and concerned and sincere.

"Jamal's going to be moving on," Jake said. "We did some

talking, on our last job. He's got dreams of a family. He's going to be a staff sergeant, take a desk job. When you left that message on my machine saying you wouldn't marry me, it got me thinking. You're planning to move on with your life. So's Jamal. Guess it's time for me too."

Was this for real? Could she let herself hope? "Jake, you need to be sure. Right now you're feeling . . . left out, left behind, but—"

"Yeah, but that's not really it. I haven't done much thinking about the future. Jamal has. You have. You have an idea what it's going to look like. When I thought about mine, I couldn't form a picture. A guy of forty-five, fifty-five doing U/C? A loner whose only home is a dingy apartment, who has no one to share his life with? I want more than that."

"Oh yes, and you deserve it. But don't you want a woman your own age? The opportunity to get to know her, then start a family?"

"I want you." He grabbed her hands again, more firmly this time, like he was determined not to let her pull away. "I do know you, Brooke Kincaid, better than I've ever known anyone else. And you're the one I want to be with." He leaned forward and peered into her eyes. "You're like your name, you know. When I'm with you, it's like I'm sitting beside a gently flowing brook. You bring me peace, deep inside."

"You'd get bored. Gardening, reading by the fire, riding with Robin . . ."

"Not once she lets me gallop. Or we could always go for a ride on my Harley, or a spin in a little plane."

The side of her that craved excitement burst out with, "Oh! I'd love that."

"I know you would. Besides, I bet it's hard to be bored when there's a kid around. And when little Nicki or Nick is sleeping, we could find new places to make love." A quick grin flashed. "There's one thing I know for sure. I'll never get bored making love with you, sexy lady."

His hands gripped hers so hard she could almost feel the bones grinding together. He was nervous. Jake Brannon was afraid she would turn him down.

"I love you, Brooke," he said softly.

She stared into his eyes long and hard, and knew he meant it.

Her breath coming in quick, shallow pants, she dragged her hands from his and pressed them to her face. She loved this man, and he loved her and wanted to marry her. He'd answered all the objections she'd raised in her mind. And yet she was terrified.

She sucked in a deep breath and let it out slowly, and as her breathing settled she realized her real fear had less to do with Jake than with herself. She forced herself to lower her hands and look at him. "I've been married before. I was really bad at it."

"You were a different person then. And you weren't married to me." He flashed her the Jake grin that always made her heart do somersaults. "We make a good team."

"We make good lovers. We worked well on your case. But marriage is a whole different thing. I was rotten at it."

"With him. With Mo. With me, you'll be great." He gripped her hands again. "Okay, I know we both have some learning to do. You had bad experiences and I had bad role models. But we love each other, we're smart, and we'll figure the rest out as we go. Together."

He smiled and repeated, "Together," as if he liked the taste of the word on his tongue.

"Together," she murmured. It really did taste sweet. And exciting.

"Think you can handle it if I'm a cop or a PI? Whatever I do, it's not going to be completely risk free."

No, she'd never been able to imagine Jake in a job like accounting. That would be like clipping a wild bird's wings. "Risk," she murmured. "Life's full of risks, isn't it?"

He nodded. "No avoiding them. Having a baby's a risk. Getting married's a risk. Riding a horse is a risk."

She imagined a lifetime of worrying about Jake, and about their baby. Then she imagined a lifetime without them. "Promise you'll be careful?"

"Always am. Honest."

"Mmm. And you've got the scars to prove it."

"I'll try not to add any more."

She couldn't be like Dave, who wanted to wrap his loved ones in cotton wool.

He poked the box that rested on her lap. "You gonna open this? See if you like it?"

She shook her head.

His face went expressionless. "Oh."

She realized he thought she was turning him down. Quickly she reached up to catch his hand in hers. "Not yet. First there's something I want to say. I love you, Jake Brannon. I'd be pleased and proud to marry you."

Slowly his face relaxed, as he took in what she'd said. Then his eyes sparkled, his lips curved. "Well, hell. You're saying yes."

"Well, hell, I guess I am." She grinned at him.

"No swearing around the kid." He grinned back.

She hated to look away from him but she did, for just a second, to pick up the jeweler's box. She held it out. "I want you to open it. To put the ring on my finger."

He flicked the box open and she saw a beautiful multicolored stone surrounded by small diamonds.

"An opal," she murmured, touching it gently. The stone was greenish blue, with sparks and swirls of other colors: pearly white, fiery red, sparkly gold. Her breath caught. The ring was exquisite.

"It reminded me of you. Of your eyes, kind of, but mostly of what you're like. Fire and passion, depth and complexity. The saleswoman told me opal is supposed to bring you love, joy, and emotional balance. If you believe in that sort of stuff at all."

"Love, joy, and emotional balance," she echoed. "Wow. I can't think of anything more to wish for."

She held out her left hand and watched as Jake carefully slid the ring onto her finger. Then she looked up into eyes that held a wealth of emotion. "Oh, Jake. We are going to be good together."

He nodded. "I know it."

He stood and tugged her to her feet. She slipped into his arms almost shyly but met his lips eagerly.

She was so engrossed in the kiss that she jumped when a buzzer went off. "Pizza's ready," she said.

"Then take it out—and take me to bed."

Epilogue

Six years later

Jake winced as pain stabbed his side. He reached down and carefully detached his daughter's fingers. How could a five-year-old girl have such a powerful grip? "Okay, Nicki, we'll take the Harley. But you're going to have to fight your mom over who rides pillion."

It was only since her last birthday that they'd let her ride behind Jake. They'd had to acknowledge that if Nicki could ride a horse on her own, she could probably manage to hang on to her dad on the bike.

"I get pillion," the girl announced. "Mommy has to carry the brownies, so she gets the sidecar."

"All right," Brooke said, coming onto the front porch to join them. "I'll take the sidecar on the way there, but I get to ride pillion on the way home. You'll be asleep then anyhow, honey."

Jake grinned, thinking about riding home under a starry sky, with Brooke curved against his back, her arms snug around his waist. "Sounds like a fair deal to me." His eyes met his wife's and her wink told him she knew exactly what he was thinking.

He stretched, feeling the summer sun soaking through his T-shirt, smelling the sweet peas in the garden, enjoying the sight of Brooke in shorts and a tank top that matched her eyes. His beautiful, sexy, strong wife. He could hardly remember what his life had been like before he met her. Didn't even want to remember, because things were so great now.

He reached down to stroke Sunny, who was sitting on the top step. When the cat yawned up at him, he said, "Guard the house. We'll be late."

When he and Brooke got married—in her garden, just the way he'd once imagined—they hadn't wanted to leave the cottage with all its wonderful memories. The Blys had been kind enough to sell them this small piece of the family ranch. Jake had built an addition, so now both Robin and Nicki had their own rooms, he had a home office, and Brooke had a greenhouse. He'd also built a barn to house his and Brooke's horses and Nicki's pony. It was home, behind that white picket fence. For the first time in his life, he truly had a home. Like Sunny, the stray cat, when Brooke had taken him in, he'd discovered his domestic side.

He smiled at his wife. "Have we got everything? Bathing suits, long pants, sunscreen, bug dope?" He glanced down at the bundles that littered the porch.

She nodded. "Potato salad, brownies, fruit juice."

"Water pistols," Nicki contributed firmly. This summer she and Alex, Evan and Jess's son, had discovered the joy of squirting water at each other, and at the grown-ups.

"I've got them," Brooke said, "but you have to promise to be careful around Karen and Jamal's baby."

When Jake had taken the sergeant position in Caribou Crossing, Jamal had gone to Williams Lake as staff sergeant. Karen had remained at the Caribou Crossing detachment, working with Jake. She and Jamal had married five years ago and bought a house midway between their two places of work.

"Babies are no fun," Nicki said. "They don't do anything."

"You were a baby once," Jake said. "You did lots. Pooped and peed and spat food all over the place."

"Daddy! Yuck!" His daughter scowled.

Jake laughed and tousled her hair. "Okay, I admit, you're more fun now that you can walk and talk, ride a horse, catch a ball, read a book."

"Robin'll look after the baby. She likes babies," Nicki said. "And she's the best baby-sitter in the world, even for kids who aren't babies anymore."

"That she is," Brooke agreed. "And at the rate she's growing up, it won't be all that long before she has a baby of her own."

"And we'll be great-grandparents?" Jake gaped at her.

She gaped back. "Oh, my gosh! I hadn't thought of that."

"So what would that make me?" Nicki asked. "The baby's grandmother?"

"Um . . ." Jake said.

"Great-aunt?" Brooke said doubtfully, and then they both began to laugh.

"We do have the strangest family," she said.

"We have the best family," he said.

As they strolled down the front walk, their arms laden with bundles, Nicki said, "Mommy, it's too bad your family isn't here for the first picnic of the year."

"We'll have another picnic when they visit in August," Brooke assured her.

Jake smiled at her, happy that she and her parents and sister had grown closer, after all the years of separation.

His old Harley, with the sidecar attached, sat polished and gleaming just outside the front gate. Horses were great, but he still loved his bike. He opened the gate and ushered his females through. "Strap on your helmets, ladies," he ordered, "and let's get this show on the road."

Brooke handed him her packages so she could climb into the

sidecar, and then he handed them back, taking the opportunity to give her a hug and a kiss.

He got Nicki seated on the back of the bike.

Before climbing on himself, he glanced around and then carefully shut the gate his daughter had left open.

Six years ago, he'd crashed his bike through that white picket fence. Now, each spring, he gave it a fresh coat of paint, and with each stroke counted his blessings.

Author's Note

I grew up in a city (Victoria, British Columbia) and have lived in both Victoria and Vancouver, so maybe it's natural that I've mostly written about urban settings. However, I've also spent a lot of time in the country and I love it, and I was one of the many girls who fell in love with horses as a child and never lost that feeling. So now I figure it's high time to indulge my adult self with a little country-style romance.

Rather than set the story in a real town, I made up Caribou Crossing. It's a composite of a number of small towns in the interior of British Columbia. Set along the old Cariboo Wagon Road, it has a gold-mining history and now its economy is based on ranching and tourism. (And if you're wondering if there's a typo in the last sentence, no, it's just one of our weird BC things. The animal is a caribou and the region was named after it, but it's spelled Cariboo.)

Gentle on My Mind is dear to my heart because the heroine, Brooke Kincaid, is the oldest and the strongest heroine I've ever written about—though she doesn't realize exactly how strong she is until undercover cop Jake Brannon crashes his Harley through her white picket fence. At the age of forty-three, Brooke has survived abuse, bipolar disorder, and alcoholism to transform herself into an upstanding citizen. She has reunited with her son Evan and become part of a loving family, yet she lives a cautious, controlled life. Jake shakes things up, and together they learn that life can be fuller, richer, and more exciting than they'd ever imagined possible.

The previous title in the Caribou Crossing series, *Home on the Range*, tells the love story of Brooke's son, Evan, and Jessica, the girl he never managed to forget. I hope you'll also look for Jessica's parents' love story, in the novella *Caribou Crossing*.

I'd like to thank all the people who helped bring this book to life: Audrey LaFehr and Martin Biro at Kensington; Emily Sylvan Kim at Prospect Agency; and my critique group, Michelle Hancock, Betty Allan, and Nazima Ali.

I love sharing my stories with my readers and I love hearing from you. I write under the pen names Susan Fox, Savanna Fox, and Susan Lyons. You can e-mail me at susan@susanlyons.ca or contact me through my Website at www.susanfox.ca, where you'll also find excerpts, behind-the-scenes notes, recipes, a monthly contest, my newsletter, and other goodies. You can also find me on Facebook at facebook.com/SusanLyonsFox.

If you enjoyed *Gentle on My Mind*,
don't miss Susan Fox's

HOME ON THE RANGE
A Caribou Crossing Romance

Also includes the full-length prequel novella
Caribou Crossing.

A Zebra mass-market paperback and eBook
on sale now.

Turn the page to begin!

Chapter One

"You're out of your frigging mind! You want me to go to a dude ranch?" Evan Kincaid glared across the table at the man who had, until two minutes earlier, been his favorite client.

"Calm down, you're making a scene." Gianni Vitale, a stocky, middle-aged man, flung out a hand in an extravagant gesture that encompassed the restaurant. Evan's gaze followed the hand. At one o'clock on a Thursday, Gramercy Tavern was filled with well-dressed people: businessmen like themselves, shoppers pausing for a break, and tourists gawking at the Robert Kushner murals and elegant décor.

The atmosphere was laden with garlic and gossip, and not a single person was staring at them. Why would they? Two typical Manhattan businessmen in suits and ties?

Evan turned back to Gianni and glared again. "I am not making a scene. And no way in hell am I going to a dude ranch."

"You're not listening. The Crazy Horse isn't a working ranch, it's a resort ranch. You won't have to play cowboy."

A ranch was a ranch. "I won't have to play anything because I'm not going."

Gianni blew out air. "You're worse than I was when Elena

told me where she'd booked our holiday. But trust me, it's great. You ride every day and you learn a lot about horses."

"Ride? No way." As a boy, growing up in Hicksville, he'd sworn no power in the world would get him up on a horse, and he'd stuck to that vow.

"There's also a wonderful spa. The facilities and staff are first rate." Gianni lowered his voice. "The food's even better than here. You'll have the time of your life. It's quite upscale. Upscale rustic." He took a sip of his dry martini.

"Upscale rustic?" Evan echoed disbelievingly. "Gianni, you don't have a hope in hell of persuading me." His client didn't know Evan had grown up in ranch country and hated it.

Gianni leaned forward, both elbows on the table, and did some glaring of his own. "Evan, you've been my investment counselor for five years. When Addison & Carruthers first assigned you to me, I protested—"

Evan's brows rose. "I didn't know that."

"It's true. But Winston Addison told me you were a rising star, and said your style would suit me. It did. Three years ago, when you left A&C to set up your own business, I was your first client."

It was true. When Evan's style had diverged too far from A&C's traditional one, he'd come to an amicable agreement with the partners. An agreement that allowed him to take a few clients with him in exchange for referring appropriate clients to A&C in the future. "I haven't lost my memory."

"You need reminding. I brought you millions of dollars of my own business and added more than a dozen clients to your list."

"And I've done very well for you and your colleagues, despite the recession. You've gotten your money's worth, and then some." Still, a sense of obligation niggled at Evan's conscience. There weren't many billionaires who would have left the security of an established firm like A&C to risk their fortune with an upstart, especially in a shaky economy.

Gianni leaned even closer. "I like to think we have become more than client and counselor. Are we not friends?"

Trust Gianni to play that card. "You're breaking my heart." Evan knew his words lacked conviction. Gianni wasn't exactly a buddy, but their relationship was more than a strictly business one. And that was rare for Evan. Although he'd outgrown his childhood awkwardness, sociability still didn't come easily. Besides, there was little time for developing friendships when you were on a fast track to the peak of the business world. But who needed friends? He'd had one once, and look how that had ended up.

"And you will break my heart, Evan, if you don't give this opportunity a fair appraisal."

"I didn't say I wouldn't appraise it. Just not on-site. Have this wrangler person e-mail me her financial analysis, her business plan, her projections, and I'll give them full consideration. Though I have to say, I'm surprised. This is hardly your normal type of investment. What did you call it again? No-frills riding? What does that mean?"

"There are dude ranches where guests play cowboy, and resort ranches like the Crazy Horse, where Elena and I went. TJ Cousins wants to open a riding camp that focuses completely on horses and Western riding, with no distractions. Riding lessons every day, trail rides, horse care, communication with horses, and—"

"Yeah, yeah," Evan broke in as an image sprang into his mind. A girl with chestnut hair pulled back in a ponytail sitting across from him in the high school cafeteria. Jess Bly. Animated, lunch forgotten, telling him her latest horse-crazy dream.

As always when he thought of Jess, he felt a flood of conflicting emotions. Predominant was a sense of loss. He felt that poignant emotion every time something major happened in his life and his first instinct—bizarrely—was to tell a girl he hadn't seen in ten years.

Annoyance with himself and his client put an edge in his voice. "God, Gianni, this reminds me of a girl I knew when I was growing up. She and your TJ Cousins sound like two peas from the same pod. And let me tell you, the pod might well have come from outer space."

It wasn't fair to tar the unknown TJ with a Jess Bly brush, but this no-frills horse stuff sounded like just the kind of kooky scheme his old pal would have dreamed up. Jess had been the sweetest, kindest girl—any happiness he'd experienced in his childhood was due to her—but she'd definitely not been the most practical person.

When she was eight, she'd wanted to breed racehorses, ride them herself, and win the Triple Crown. She'd just read *National Velvet*. When she was ten, it was a riding school that would make its students learn both English and Western style. When she was twelve—

Oh, what did it matter? Jess Bly was a part of his past. A part he tried not to think about. He had messed up badly, in so many ways. And paid the price, all these years. He'd lost his best friend. True, he hadn't deserved forgiveness after acting like such a shit, but all the same he'd have thought those years of childhood friendship would count for more than a cool e-mail dismissal from seventeen-year-old Jess. She'd said they should make a clean break, forget the past.

Forget? He wondered if Jess had managed to do that. For him, though he rarely thought of Caribou Crossing or his parents, it had proved impossible to forget Jess.

Gianni reached across the table and snapped his fingers, demanding Evan's attention. "I didn't write out a check; I came to you. The ideas are exciting, the woman is impressive, and I need you to tell me if it's a realistic investment. I don't need a huge return, but I want a reasonable prospect of success."

Putting aside his guilt trip down memory lane, Evan focused on his client. "How much money are you talking?"

"Investing between three and four million, I'd guess. She already has the property. We'd want to get things started with a few cabins, a lodge, a training ring, and of course great horses. It would expand from there. Also, TJ's idea is to have a sliding scale on the pricing, basically so guests pay what they can afford."

Evan snorted. Oh yeah, that was as businesslike as one of Jess's old schemes. Had Gianni left his brain back at the Crazy Horse? "As I said, have Ms. Cousins forward me the information."

Gianni shook his head emphatically. "You have to go there."

"That's absurd." Evan shoved away his unfinished black bass entrée. Delicious though it was, he'd lost his appetite.

Gianni pointed an accusing finger. "You don't get it. And you won't get it, not here in Manhattan. I wouldn't have gotten it myself if Elena hadn't dragged me to the Crazy Horse. You must talk to TJ in person and see her work with the horses. Her method draws strongly on Monty Roberts's techniques and—"

"Spare me the details." It was too much like talking to Jess, back when they were kids with big dreams. He remembered the hundreds of hours they'd spent together while she enthused over her horsy dreams and he expounded on how he was going to become king of the hill in the Big Apple. They had loved and supported each other. She'd been the only good thing about Hicksville. She'd been his first—*Damn!* Evan put the brakes on that train of thought.

"Let me get this straight," he said. "Ms. Cousins works for the Crazy Horse and she's soliciting guests to invest in a competing business?"

"No, no." Gianni shook his head vigorously. "Not competing. The two operations will be complementary, like your firm and A&C. Her concept would appeal to the more serious riders. And no, she's not soliciting guests, we just happened to get talking one day."

Yeah, sure. After this Cousins person had Googled Gianni and figured out how rich he was.

"I've never asked you for a personal favor," his client said.

Damn again. Gianni was pulling out all the stops.

"You're overworked, Evan. You need a holiday. I'll give you a paid one."

Now that was complete bull. "Cynthia and I were in Paris last month and Tokyo the month before."

"Those were work trips. Your estimable girlfriend doesn't take real holidays. Nor do you."

Evan shrugged. He hadn't thought of it that way, but what Gianni said was true. Every trip was business for at least one of them and often both. Her work as a corporate finance lawyer and his as an investment counselor often took them in the same direction. In fact, they'd met at a conference in Geneva.

Yes, they usually did plan their trips with an extra day or two to shop and visit museums and galleries, but they'd never taken a true holiday.

A holiday. For a moment, the idea was tempting. Oh, not to go to some idiotic dude ranch that reminded him of his crappy childhood, but perhaps to lie on a beach in the south of France. No, what was he thinking? He'd be bored out of his mind. He thrived on work. Sure, maybe he did get the occasional stress headache, but a good workout at the fitness club dealt with that. His personal trainer had even given him a set of stretches to do at the office, to ease out the kinks.

Hell, Gianni ought to be the first person to understand that holidays had no place on the fast track to success.

"When's the last time you had a vacation in the country?" his client asked.

"Never." When he'd lived in Caribou Crossing, it had been

anything but a vacation. "It sounds like sheer hell. Where is this Crazy Horse? Texas?"

"Canada. The interior of British Columbia. They call it the Cariboo. You fly into Williams Lake, then it's an hour or two drive."

Evan's heart jerked to a stop. Caribou Crossing—Hicksville, as he'd called it—was an hour or so from Williams Lake.

Dimly he was aware of Gianni waving at their waiter, and in a moment two martinis arrived. The waiter removed Gianni's empty glass. Evan didn't drink alcohol in the middle of the day, but his hand reached out automatically. Caribou Crossing, damn it. Miles and miles of open countryside, horses, Jess Bly. His mother.

His hand jerked back from the martini glass. His mother—and his abusive, runaway dad—were the reason he was so careful with alcohol.

Hell! He didn't need these memories.

And he sure as *hell* didn't need a holiday. He worked hard, yes, but he wasn't overworked or stressed out. He'd achieved his childhood dream and he relished it, building his business bigger and better—and not just making his clients more money but helping many support worthwhile charities. He and Cynthia led a jet-setting life. They had acquaintances to dine with in Paris and Rome, Hong Kong and Tokyo, London and Sydney. He lived in New York, the best city in the world, the boldest and bravest, the one place that had always drawn him, that still enthralled and impressed him on a daily basis. He was living his dream. No way was he going back to the hellhole where sheer misery had spawned that dream.

"Afraid you'll fall off a horse?" Gianni asked with pseudo-innocence.

"Don't be ridiculous."

"Elena's strongly in favor of the investment. She says I'm a new man since our holiday. Part of the deal with TJ is that we'd have a free cabin for a month a year, a place to unwind and to ride. To smell the roses, as they say at the Crazy Horse."

Evan recognized a threat when he heard one. "You're saying that if I don't go and meet this wrangler woman and analyze her proposal, you'll let Elena convince you to throw away several million dollars?"

Gianni grinned hugely and stretched his diamond-ringed hand across the table. "Good, you will go. Thank you, Evan, I knew you would protect my money."

"Wait a minute."

Gianni withdrew the hand and scowled.

"Where *exactly* is this place?" There'd been no Crazy Horse resort ranch anywhere near Caribou Crossing when he'd lived there.

A shrug. "I never looked at a map. What's the difference?"

Having transformed himself into the consummate New Yorker, Evan wasn't about to claim the Cariboo as his boyhood home. He shrugged. "Just curious." He drew in a breath and let it out. TJ Cousins . . . there'd been a bunch of Cousinses in the Caribou Crossing area—he'd gone to school with three of them, including Dave, the basketball star and class president—but there hadn't been a TJ. Chances were, this Crazy Horse was nowhere near Caribou Crossing. Even if it was, he'd never have to track down Jess. Or visit his mother.

Gianni really was his best client, and the closest thing he had—other than Cynthia—to a friend. He couldn't let the man throw away millions on some crazy scheme just because his wife, a normally sane woman, had developed a temporary passion for riding horses and smelling roses. "Okay," he said grudgingly, "you're on." This time he stretched his hand across the table. Gianni grasped it and pumped enthusiastically as Evan wondered what he'd gotten himself into.

"Free up your calendar for two weeks," Gianni ordered.

Evan snorted. "Two days."

"No, you'll need the full time to learn all you need to know. I don't want you going in as my investment counselor and grilling TJ. You'll go undercover, yes? As a regular guest. Take it slowly, get a feel for her and her methods. You can't understand the no-frills riding camp idea without understanding the context, the ambiance, the person behind it."

Evan frowned. Much as he hated to admit it, Gianni had a valid point. The success or failure of a new venture hinged not only on the business plan, but on the person behind it. His own company was a prime example. But a few days, a week max, should be sufficient.

"Have Angelica call me for the details," Gianni said. "Go as soon as possible, because Elena and I are anxious to get started on this, provided you approve it. The riding package starts on a Sunday, runs two weeks, and you return on a Saturday. The day after, you'll come to our apartment for Sunday brunch, thank me for the holiday, and tell us what you think of TJ and her plans."

Evan clenched his jaw. He wasn't used to surrendering control.

"Oh, by the way." His client's dark eyes sparkled.

He studied Gianni suspiciously.

"Take Cynthia if you want."

Chic Cynthia, at the Crazy Horse ranch. Evan's jaw unclenched and his laughter joined Gianni's rich chuckle.

The two of them left the restaurant together, then parted. After a short, brisk walk, Evan arrived at his sleek, modern office. He asked his assistant, Angelica, to phone Gianni and then call the Crazy Horse to see if it was possible to make reservations for a week. With any luck, the damned place would be booked up for the rest of the summer.

Toward the end of the afternoon, Angelica clicked across his marble-tiled floor. "You're in luck. There was a cancellation for next week at the . . . Crazy Horse."

Evan's lips twitched as the efficient Angelica's own lips—

colored a bizarre purple that he assumed must be the height of fashion—hesitated over the name. It was clear his assistant thought "crazy" was a fitting term to apply to him. He couldn't wait to see Cynthia's reaction when he told her at dinner tonight. Maybe he'd even pass along Gianni's suggestion that she join him, just to see her horrified expression.

"I booked you for two weeks."

"I said one."

Angelica held up a hand. "The Crazy Horse only books in two-week blocks. You can always find an excuse for leaving early. Like fall off a horse and break a leg?" She said it straight-faced, but he thought he saw a twinkle in her eye.

"You're a big help," he grumbled.

"Mr. Vitale told me to bill everything to your card and he'll reimburse you. He didn't want anything put in his name, since you're going undercover, as he termed it."

She handed over a file folder. "Here's your e-ticket and your confirmation number at the Crazy Horse. The price there is all-inclusive. At six thousand US dollars for a week, one would certainly hope so. I gather it's a world-famous, exclusive spot. I got you a few hundred dollars in Canadian money in case you want to do some shopping, though I can't imagine there's much to spend money on there." Her eyes were wide, and it wasn't with envy.

"Nor can I."

"The Crazy Horse e-mailed me their brochure and I printed it out for you. You should know . . ." She gave a little cough and he thought she might be stifling a giggle. It was a startling thought, because he'd never heard the all-business Angelica giggle. "Uh, with regard to clothing, you have to have . . ." She choked and this time he knew it was a giggle.

"Spit it out. This can't get any worse, can it?"

She let the giggle go and it soared buoyantly between them. "It can," she choked out. "Cowboy . . . boots. You . . . have to have Western . . . riding boots." She spluttered for a few moments, then managed to say, "I've put together a list of stores in Manhattan that sell them."

"Thanks, I think." He studied her, so sleek and chic. "Have you ever been on a horse?"

"I had a boyfriend who rode in Central Park and I went along once. I broke a fingernail and came back with my clothes smelling of horse. Disgusting. How about you?"

"Not once in my life." Yes, he'd lived ten years in horse country, and his best friend was the horse lover to end all horse lovers, but he'd refused to ever mount a horse. Partly, it was knowing that he, such an unathletic boy, would embarrass himself in front of Jess, but he'd also had a gut-level instinct that to ride would be to surrender. To accept that his life—his utterly miserable life in Hicksville—was all he'd ever know.

Riding. Damn it, this time he'd have to do it. But he was a big boy, and he could deal with it. He sure as hell wasn't going to turn into a country boy, and even if he didn't prove to be a skilled rider, there'd be no Jess to taunt him. Besides, he was no longer a klutz, and he would do his homework.

He was about to send Angelica to the bookstore when his brain flashed back to Jess teasing the shit out of him for trying to learn how to skate from a book.

"All right," he said. "I guess I'm really going." He glanced at his watch. Almost five o'clock. "First priority for tomorrow is to clear the calendar for next Monday and Tuesday. Maybe Wednesday. That should give me enough time to learn what I need to about Gianni's proposed investment." He rose and pulled on his suit jacket.

"You're leaving now?" She looked stunned.

No wonder. He rarely left the office before seven, after putting in at least a thirteen-hour day. "Going shopping. Have to find those cowboy boots," he said wryly.

She gave a hoot and departed in giggles.

Evan shook his head. Would wonders never cease? First,

Gianni had persuaded him to do something that, had he been asked this morning, he would have said was inconceivable. Then, the ultrapoised Angelica had been reduced to giggles. And finally, Evan Kincaid, the quintessential New Yorker, was heading out to buy cowboy boots and a how-to book on riding horses.

On the way past Angelica's desk, he asked, "Did anyone mention the nearest town?"

"Let me think. Something to do with deer. Or maybe moose. No, it was caribou. Caribou Crossing. Quaint, isn't it?"

"Caribou Crossing." The name had been on his mind ever since Gianni had started talking about horses, yet now it hit him like a sucker punch.

"Is something wrong?"

"No," he muttered, thinking things couldn't possibly go any more wrong. Then he squared his shoulders. So the Crazy Horse was near Caribou Crossing. As he'd resolved earlier, there was no reason in the world for him to lay eyes on his mother. Or Jess Bly.

Not unless he wanted to. Which he most certainly did not.

Chapter Two

It was his butt Jess Cousins noticed first.

Monday morning, and the latest group of resort virgins bustled and chattered in her barnyard like a flock of nervous magpies. Amid them this one guy stood still, his back toward her as he studied the row of horses tethered to one of the hitching rails. She took in pleasant impressions of height, ranginess, breadth of shoulder, length of leg, and a truly outstanding butt. Many of the Crazy Horse's guests were pudgy and a few were scrawny. It was rare to see an admirable physique and even rarer to see a world-class—

Jess snorted under her breath. What the heck was she doing, ogling a guest's backside? Was it just because she hadn't had sex in so long she'd almost forgotten what it was like, or was the backside in question really so outstanding? She was dragging her gaze away from the denim-clad object of her admiration just as the man turned around.

"Ev!" His name caught in her throat, emerging as a squeak. He'd changed a lot in ten years, but she recognized him instantly. Despite his pole-axed expression.

He strode toward her as his mouth formed her own name.

Her muscles locked her in place as he approached, and all her brain could do was repeat, *Evan, my God, it's Evan.*

She pulled herself together to demand, "What are you doing here?" just as he spoke the identical words.

He grasped her by one shoulder and herded her away from the group. Dimly she was aware of the milling guests, but it was hard to care about anything other than the fact that this man stood in front of her, his hand burning through the cotton of her embroidered Western shirt. Her heart thudded so fast she could barely breathe and her mind was a jumble of thoughts. For the life of her she couldn't pull a single one free and form a coherent sentence.

He gazed down at his hand as if only just realizing where it rested. Then he yanked it back as quickly as if he'd reached out to stroke a bull in a bucking chute.

Evan was at the Crazy Horse. Had he discovered her long-held secret? Was he here because he'd found out about Robin? The possibility stole what breath she had left. Finally, she managed to draw air and force out a few cautious words. "I work here."

"Oh." He seemed to be weighing the concept more carefully than it deserved. "They said the head wrangler would meet us here. TJ Cousins. That's . . . not you?"

Her breathing settled a little. He really did seem surprised to see her. No, he couldn't have known about Robin. And she mustn't say anything to give away her secret.

She nodded. "I don't use Jessica for my work. People kept making *Man from Snowy River* comments and it drove me nuts."

He shrugged, clearly baffled. "Huh?"

Hadn't she made him watch the movie, way back then? No, she must've had the sense to know Mr. City-bound wouldn't be interested in a film about horses and cowboys in the Australian Outback. He wouldn't know that the free-spirited, horse-loving heroine was called Jessica.

Now that she thought about it, they hadn't watched many movies. When he wasn't studying and she wasn't outside with

the horses, the two of them spent most of their time talking.
Sharing dreams. The dreams they'd always known would take
them in opposite directions.

And now he was back on her turf. Looking like a man
rather than a boy. A striking man rather than a cute but nerdy
kid. A kid she'd believed to be the love of her life, yet known
she had to give up.

Robin's father.

Jess had broken her heart over Evan Kincaid. How dare he
come back?

He'd run away, and then—*finally*—e-mailed a couple of
times from Cornell to apologize. *E-mailed,* didn't even have
the decency to phone! She didn't remember the exact words
she'd typed with such pain and deliberation, but she knew the
essence of the message she'd sent: Get lost and stay lost.

"Cousins," he said on a note of revelation. "Dave? You
married Dave?"

She lifted her chin. "Yup." No need to tell him they'd since
divorced.

"You were friends in high school, hanging around with
that *in crowd*"—he said it as disparagingly now as he had
back then—"but I didn't think the two of you— " He broke off
suddenly and she knew what he was thinking. She and Dave
had been friends, but not romantically, or sexually, inclined.

Evan was remembering the night at Zephyr Lake—when
she'd had sex with him, not Dave. Even after all these years,
she could still read his mind.

No, of course she couldn't, nor did she want to. But the
lake was so obvious. A pink elephant in her barnyard. Would
they both tiptoe around it, pretending it didn't exist?

He cleared his throat. "I never connected TJ with Jessica."

Yup, Evan was going to tiptoe. Well, that was fine by her
because her tongue was hog-tied, bound up good and tight by
strands of conflicting emotions. Her bruised heart urged her
to rail at him for rejecting her all those years ago, yet if she

was going to be fair about it, she had rejected him, too. She'd refused his overture of continued, long-distance friendship. How could she write chatty letters to him while nursing a broken heart and holding back the huge secret of Robin's existence?

She'd done the right thing, and yet she'd missed him so badly. Even now, a part of her mushy heart yearned to envelope him in a gigantic hug.

But the strongest emotion, by far, was maternal instinct. She had to protect Robin, the product of that night at Zephyr Lake. *Jesus, this is Robin's biological father*. She'd thought she'd never see him again, but here he stood, strong and solid and very male.

Again, fear caught her breath. Why was he here? Evan, who had his own investment counseling firm in New York City—and yes, she'd Googled him. Evan, who'd sworn to never set foot in Hicksville again. Had he somehow found out? Come to claim his daughter?

But why on earth would he do that? He'd never wanted children.

She couldn't stand the uncertainty. "What in holy blue blazes are you doing here?" she demanded, her voice one notch south of a holler.

He shot a glance toward the dudes who chattered nervously as they eyed the horses tied to the hitching rails. She lowered her voice. "You're not a guest?"

He shrugged uncomfortably. "Actually, yes."

"Ac-tu-al-ly," Jess parroted the word, exaggerating the cultivated accent he'd acquired since she last saw him, "you're the last person I'd have expected. Back in school you couldn't wait to shake the country dust from—" She paused, snagged on another memory. This one triggered a surge of affection, a response as unexpected as it was undeniable. "From those beautifully polished leather loafers you hitchhiked into Williams Lake to buy, back in grade twelve."

Suddenly, the mess of unresolved issues flew out of her mind. All she could think of, in that moment, was that this was Ev, the guy who'd for years been her best buddy.

She smiled freely and, after his mouth fell open in surprise, he smiled back. "Good Lord, Jess, it's actually you. You look"—he eyed her up and down—"just great."

She read sincerity in his blue-green eyes. And something else, something that made her blood fizz.

Now came the scary memories. The memory of feelings she'd never experienced in the same way with any other man. Not even her ex-husband, Dave. She moistened lips that had gone dry. "You look good, too."

The package-creased tan denim shirt and well-worn designer jeans hugged a fine body. She'd always found him appealing— a scrawny kid with beautiful eyes and ears too big for his head—but now he was a total hottie. His face was craggy and his eyes were devastating. To her chagrin she remembered those eyes perfectly, the mingled blues and greens of brook water flowing over gray stones, flecked by sparkles of golden sun.

She closed her own eyes briefly, then looked again. He was beyond handsome; he was compelling. And sexy.

An image flashed into her mind. Evan's gangly young body rising above hers, the moon on his shoulder, as they made love on the lakeshore. She sucked in her breath and, afraid he could read her face, dropped her gaze.

Happily, the new image brought her down to earth. Literally. She saw exquisitely tooled chestnut leather Tony Lama boots. She cleared her throat. "They're not loafers, but I see you haven't lost your touch with the shoe polish. Hate to tell you, but the dust is going to stick. And we have far worse than dust to dish up at the Crazy Horse." She tilted her head and dared to look at his face again.

He glanced down to where his feet were planted in a

mixture of dirt and manure. His grimace of distaste was so typically Ev that she gave a snort of laughter.

"Okay, city slicker, enough of the chitchat. I have work to do." Jess strode toward the other guests, trusting that habit would carry her through.

Evan Kincaid. At the Crazy Horse. This couldn't really be happening, could it?

He hadn't mentioned Robin. If he'd come about her, surely he'd have said something by now.

Jess had made the decision not to tell him when she found out that those few rushed minutes at the lake, combined with her too old condom, had resulted in pregnancy. A baby would ruin all his long-held dreams. It wasn't fair to do that to him, and besides, it wasn't like things could have worked out for her and Ev. He'd have spent his life resenting her and their child for tying him to the place he'd scornfully called Hicksville.

Her own dreams were more flexible, and could easily, joyfully, bend to incorporate a child. Her and Evan's child.

No, not Evan's. Robin's father—the man who'd raised and loved her—was Dave Cousins.

Evan had never wanted kids. He wouldn't have wanted to know about Robin all those years ago, and he didn't deserve her. Not then, and not now. Nor could Jess have her daughter learn that her mom and dad had been lying to her ever since she was born.

About the Author

Award-winning author **Susan Fox** (who also writes as Susan Lyons and Savanna Fox) writes "emotionally compelling, sexy contemporary romance" (*Publishers Weekly*). Susan is a Pacific Northwester with homes in Vancouver and Victoria, British Columbia. She has degrees in law and psychology and has had a variety of careers, including perennial student, computer consultant, and legal editor. Fiction writer is by far her favorite, giving her an outlet to demonstrate her belief in the power of love, friendship, and a sense of humor. She was thrilled when *Cosmopolitan* excerpted her book *Sex Drive* as a Red-Hot Read, and even more excited when *Publishers Weekly* selected *His, Unexpectedly* as one of its Top 10 Romances for spring 2011.

Visit her on the web at www.susanfox.ca

GREAT BOOKS, GREAT SAVINGS!

When You Visit Our Website:
www.kensingtonbooks.com
You Can Save Money Off The Retail Price
Of Any Book You Purchase!

- All Your Favorite Kensington Authors
- New Releases & Timeless Classics
- Overnight Shipping Available
- eBooks Available For Many Titles
- All Major Credit Cards Accepted

Visit Us Today To Start Saving!
www.kensingtonbooks.com

31192020447270